Praise for *Tuscan Soup*

A Tuscan Comedy of Manners and Errors, beautifully observed and painfully funny.'

Meera Syal

'Treat yourself. Buy this book and savour the delicious ingredients in Tuscan Soup.'

Sue Townsend.

'A cure for the blues. Lou Wakefield knows how to make us happy.'

Dr Dorothy Rowe

'I loved the novel: I saw myself in it and all of Tuscany. It's tightly written, it's very funny and once started, couldn't be put down.'

Miriam Margolyes

'All the right ingredients; given a good stir; delicious outcome!'

Jenni Murray

Tuscan Soup

Lou Wakefield

CORONET BOOKS
Hodder & Stoughton

Copyright © 2001 by Lou Wakefield

First published in Great Britain in 2001 by Hodder & Stoughton
A division of Hodder Headline
First published in paperback in 2002 by Hodder & Stoughton
A Coronet paperback

10 9 8 7 6 5 4 3 2 1

A CIP catalogue record for this title
is available from the British Library

ISBN 0 340 73390 2

Printed and bound in Great Britain by
Mackays of Chatham plc, Chatham, Kent

Hodder & Stoughton
A division of Hodder Headline
338 Euston Road
London NW1 3BH

To Avril

Acknowledgements

I leaned heavily on several guidebooks during the writing of *Tuscan Soup*, especially the excellent *Frommer's Tuscany and Umbria* by Reid Bramblett.

My thanks to Jean Ramsay, who checked my art references and corrected me accordingly, and to Paola Sardo for correcting my Italian, by e-mail, from Verona. Any mistakes still remaining are entirely my own. Last but not least, thanks to Kate Shaw for thinking up the title.

Chapter One

Marion had already started to regret her hasty decision the day before Tom Cowlishaw stopped her in the corridor with a cheery: 'Hasta la vista! The tickets have come!'

'That's Spanish,' she'd said, and 'Oh.'

'No regrets I hope? Don't tell me, Edith Piaf — she was French.'

'No, no, it's just . . .'

'That's all right then,' Tom said, rubbing his hands together self-consciously. 'That's a relief. Only I've doled out for them already on my credit card, and it says on the tickets it's non-refundable. Have you got your cheque book on you?'

What could she have said? She had to go now.

Four weeks later she was looking with loathing at a pile of summer clothes lying next to her empty suitcase on the bed. None of them were right for her, everything was awful, nothing suited her as she was *now*. How could it, when even she didn't know what that was? She hated shopping for clothes almost as much as she hated looking in mirrors these days, so there were only a couple of skirts, a pair of jeans and a few T-shirts that she wore for slopping about the house. She refused point blank to take anything that she wore for school.

Her hand went to the telephone. She couldn't go. She'd just have to tell them.

'Hello it's Marion. I'm terribly sorry, I can't possibly go to Italy with you tomorrow after all. I haven't got a thing to wear.'

She knew it was pathetic. Anyway they were out.

Two and a half hours later, struggling home on an overcrowded bus, she tried to remember without peeking in the carrier bags what she had bought and to feel positive about it. She gave up and looked. How had she come to buy so much beige? She hated everything. None of it would do. It would all have to go back.

At a quarter past midnight – the flight was at ten thirty the next morning – she had, in sudden desperation, rushed to the attic and salvaged two bursting bin bags, and brought them downstairs. Marion was a hoarder. By dawn her new image was washed and pressed and packed in her old tote bag. She felt lighter and happier than she had in ages.

These clothes were her, now.

Coincidentally, they had also been her at Liverpool Art College in 1977.

At some point around seven, when Tom Cowlishaw's wife Janice had resorted to signalling SOS in Morse code on the front doorbell, and Tom was engaged in the more manly pursuit of yelling through the letterbox, Marion sat bolt upright in bed looking like a startled baby starling. Her swollen eyes were huge and heavy lidded, and her hair was in a dry point on the top of her head. Irreparable, irreparable. She hadn't meant to fall asleep. She couldn't possibly go now.

She opened the bedroom window to call out to them below, and was struck hard in the face by a fistful of small pebbles.

'Sorry,' Tom called up, abashed, after a surprised silence.

'Only we were beginning to wonder if something had happened to you.'

Whilst Janice 'used the facilities' (unnecessarily noisily, Marion thought, who always aimed for the porcelain herself, and who now realised that there might be *other* noises she might have to get used to from this couple she hardly knew over the next seven days), Marion looked balefully inside the tote bag and started to unpack her art materials. In her euphoria of the small hours, after she had rediscovered her former self in the attic and found that it had fitted, she had been stupid enough to believe that she might also paint again. Now she set about removing the tubes of oils and watercolours, the sketch pads and the pencils, the pastels and the palette. None of it could go. It would just sit there and accuse her. It would all have to come out.

'Where have you hidden him — in the cupboard?'

Marion swung round. 'I'm sorry?'

'You look like you've had a hell of a night!' cackled Janice. 'Go on, you go downstairs, I've made a cup of coffee. I'll finish this.'

'No, no, I . . .'

'Go on lazybones, Tom's wearing out your carpet. My God, you're still in your nightie — don't you think you'd better change?'

'I have. This is my dress.'

'Oh. Oh yes, so it is. Isn't it lovely? Hippie, isn't it? It's all coming back — did you pick it up at Oxfam? I love old clothes, don't you?'

And Janice chatted and chivvied jovially as she repacked Marion's thwarted ambitions back into the tote and called out: 'Tom, have you found her stopcock yet and checked her doors and windows?' Then she swept them both out of the door and into the car, singing 'Volare' all the way down the motorway and 'We're All Going on a Summer Holiday' all the way into the check-in, where they were told by a smiling air hostess that, due to a computer error, their flight had been over-subscribed, but

3

that with these five-pound vouchers they may have a nice day at Heathrow until the next plane would fly them to Pisa at five o'clock that afternoon.

Janice's resolve evaporated, Marion was interested to see, before this smiling face of ruthless corporate efficiency, and she even went so far as to thank them for the vouchers.

'Let's go and have some breakfast then,' she said daringly, waving the three pieces of flimsy paper which were worth fifteen pounds on day of issue only at Heathrow Airport, but nothing at all at any time in the rest of the world.

If Marion had not already decided that her best defence against Janice's steamrolling energy was to go with the flow, she would have been very angry indeed and created a scene. As it was she settled for glaring poisonously at the First Class and Club Class queues, who seemed to be swapping their luggage for boarding cards without any problem at all.

'Bit of a bloody cheek though,' ventured Tom doubtfully as he watched a small woman in an outsize overall go fishing for his fried egg in a tin tray of oil.

'Never mind, it doesn't matter,' said his wife. 'Two sausages on each please and — what's a hash brown?'

'Dunno — 'tato I think, innit Corinne?' screeched the small woman, whose staff badge proclaimed her as 'Hi! I'm . . . MRS BLOCK . . . How may I help you?'

'Come on, cheer up, you're on your holiday,' said Janice to Tom, guiding her husband towards the Beverage Bar. 'Tea or coffee? Loosen up, enjoy yourself. Not every day of the week you get a fry-up like this at half past nine in the morning.'

And Tom, looking down at his tray, was forced to agree.

Marion had been sent on ahead to 'bag a table in smoking', and had asked for a black tea and a croissant, so she was appalled when Janice slapped a full portion of The Great British Breakfast Experience on the table in front of her and invited her to 'get herself outside that'. She tried to protest, but Janice pointed at her sternly with her knife, flicking Tom's new lightweight windcheater with brown sauce on the way. 'None of your flim-flam,' she said. 'I'm a nurse and I say you want feeding.'

'It's no use arguing with her,' Tom opined affectionately, sucking his windcheater. 'She's been dying to get her hands on you all term. Thinks you look stringy.'

'Not stringy, peaky,' Janice remonstrated, digging him jovially but painfully in the ribs.

'Well, stringy, peaky – her new mission in life is to fatten you up.'

'Just one cornetto, give it to her,' sang Janice as she negotiated a whole hash brown from plate to oesophagus in one.

Marion excused herself and went to the Ladies, where she peed silently and cursed loudly. Why oh *why* had she come?

'Actually, it's not feeding she wants,' diagnosed Janice after she and Tom had watched her leave and exchanged a marital look. 'It's a man. Or more to the point a f—'

'How do you know?' Tom cut in quickly, aware of Corinne's interest as she tried to reclaim Marion's untouched plate. 'No, she's not finished, she'll be coming back.'

'Well it's obvious isn't it? She's never got over Colin Menseley going off.'

'But that's been nearly two years.'

'Long time for a woman to go without,' said Janice, spearing a sausage on the end of her fork and finding it would fit in her mouth sideways. 'And speaking as a woman who's been on nights for a fortnight, I know how she feels.'

Looking smoulderingly at Tom, she wiped her mouth with the back of one hand while she palpated his thigh with the other. Tom felt his trousers growing uncomfortably tight and decided to leave the rest of his egg.

'I . . . I was just saying,' he said hastily, as he registered Marion's return, 'bit of a bloody liberty isn't it, them being able to change your flight whenever they like, and us not even allowed refundable tickets?'

Marion had noticed the smouldering and palpating from afar, and now wondered with dread about the sleeping arrangements in their rented apartment. 'I noticed the upper classes weren't inconvenienced in any way,' she said, and dunked a piece of bread in her baked beans in the way her mother had always told her not to. She crammed it into her mouth defiantly and glared about her, daring anyone to tell her she was being common. They could go and stuff themselves as far as she was concerned.

In fact, moulded into leather armchairs in the air-conditioned VIP lounge, Frederick Mayer and Christopher Bassett were doing exactly that.

'I've never flown First Class before,' said Frederick, licking his salty fingers after a particularly delicious canapé of salmon caviare in millefeuille pastry, and taking another swig of champagne, 'so I thought we'd push the boat out.'

'I know, you're being really sweet.'

Frederick felt himself blushing with modest pleasure and suppressed a boyish grin, lowering his eyes in a gesture that had been endearing when he'd been a gay young thing, but now in his mid-fifties looked a little sad. Christopher smiled and raised his glass. 'Here's to a fun time,' he proposed, and Frederick seconded him with enthusiasm.

'Why don't you fly First? On your business trips I mean.'

'Well, it would mean Beryl booking it and she'd absolutely refuse. She's very against classes of any sort, I gather. I've only recently persuaded her to allow me to fly Club.'

'Sack her and hire a secretary who has a sense of style,' said Christopher airily.

'Oh no, I could never do that. She'd never agree to type her letter of dismissal.'

Christopher laughed, partly because he always enjoyed hearing the ongoing saga of Frederick's brushes with Beryl, and partly because he had just seen a woman in a fur coat – evidently newly initiated into the glamour of the VIP lounge – trying surreptitiously to photograph him. He liked being recognised. It made him feel warm and expansive, particularly now, when he hadn't even done a telly in months, let alone a film. Good old Frederick, shelling out for his ticket. He was by no means poor after his period between engagements, but there was no need for Freddie to know that, and it was always nice to be treated.

'I wonder where Terence and Beatrice have got to,' said Frederick, glancing anxiously towards the door.

'Knowing them they'll roll in just before take-off,' said Christopher.

'I didn't know you did know them?'

'Oh yes. Well, I know Bea of course — we worked together on *The Man of Steel* . . .'

'And *weren't* you steely?' gushed Frederick, unable to stop himself. 'Goodness, those naughty, cruel eyes! I particularly remember the scene in the sauna . . .'

The champagne was evidently going to Frederick's head and all points south, and Christopher began to be bored. God, the things one had to do for one's career! He didn't mind flirting mildly with Freddie in order to further his ends, but he'd be buggered if he'd be drooled over.

'Yes, as a matter of fact Bea and I had a wonderful steamy affair on location in Tangiers, which all started in that sauna. They could hardly prise us apart to do the takes.'

'All over now I hope?' said Frederick suddenly sobering. 'I wouldn't want anything to upset Terence. This is by way of being a business trip just as much as pleasure, and Pamela would be very cross if . . .'

'I have no intention of causing our gracious hostess one moment of displeasure, nor indeed of pleasuring Queen Bea for another moment more.' Was that true? Chris wondered. His affair with Beatrice had been lovely, and he had meant it to continue after filming was completed. But then he'd had to go to LA on another job, and when he'd finally returned to London, Bea had taken up with Terence Armstrong. In fact, the reason he'd accepted Freddie's offer of the holiday had been because of the chance of seeing her again. Still, better not to worry him now.

'Hardly seen her since anyway, and that was ages ago. You are a silly old thing, Freddie. As if I'd do that to *you*.'

He smiled his best and prettiest smile at Frederick, since even Christopher thought it was too early in the holiday to bite the hand that was feeding him, and just for good measure and for the fun of seeing him blush again, he gave Freddie's knee an affectionate squeeze.

'Oh Christ, it looks like I've peed myself now!' said Frederick, who had jumped violently at the gesture, upsetting his champagne. Nobody had touched him below the waist in more than fifteen years, and he sometimes wondered if he'd ever want them to again. Romance was what he pined for. Passion left him cold.

'Sorry darling, didn't realise I was so electric,' murmured Christopher thickly, who had now begun to notice that the fur-coated woman was crossing and recrossing her legs at him. 'Better hop along to the little boys' room and powder your crotch. Sorry, silly joke, bad taste . . . need any help?'

But Frederick was already sidling over to the VIP washrooms with his attaché case strategically placed. Thank goodness he maintained a lifelong habit of carrying his toiletries in his hand luggage. It had saved him on countless occasions, but never from anything as embarrassing as this. If only he hadn't worn his pale grey suit, now darkly wet in his most private of places.

Terence Armstrong and Beatrice Miller-Mander (daughter of Sir Roland Miller-Mander the actor knight) caused quite a stir in the airport shop in search of their cigarettes, so recognisably famous were they. Beatrice located her Pierre Cardin Menthols without difficulty, but Terence could not find his Park Drive UnTipped. It amused him to remind the world of his working-class origins with little gestures such as this. 'The saddest day for the working man was when they changed the design of the Woodbine packet,' he would tell international press conferences. This, when it was printed, had half a dozen American students of Contemporary Drama reaching for their Oxford English Dictionaries, and a seventh, less assiduous, to report with assurance in his thesis 'Terence Armstrong – The Work and The Man' that his guru had grown up smoking Virginia Creeper.

'Ay look,' said Janice Cowlishaw excitedly, 'isn't that Whatsisface and Thingummybob – the one that you like Tom?'

'Beatrice Thingummy, blimey!' Tom whispered, his mouth hanging open in astonishment, for here was the subject of some of his best fantasies, standing not five yards away. She was even more beautiful than she looked on the screen. 'She's not as tall in the flesh, is she?' he said, clearing his throat and trying to sound offhand.

Marion flicked a disdainful look towards the famous couple. All she saw was a middle-aged man with a paunch and a girlfriend practically young enough to be his daughter. Big deal. And besides, one thing she couldn't stand, even more than the privileged classes, was the gawping under classes being impressed. She paid for her duty-free gin and ignoring 'Not to be consumed until outside country of purchase' on the receipt, she broke the seal on the bottle and drank it neat out of the bag. God, it must be these clothes, she thought, wiping her dribbling chin. I'll be shouting 'Down with the Establishment' in a minute and organising a sit-in. She tugged self-consciously at her tie-dye kaftan, feeling the magic wearing off. Far from making her feel lighter and freer now, she felt an absolute prat.

'I'll be in the boutique next door,' she called to Janice and Tom. They were arguing over how numerate the Italian Customs men would be and battling over a bottle. Tom nodded and wrenched a litre of sweet martini from Janice's wire basket.

'I don't think she'll find anything in there to her taste,' said Beatrice Miller-Mander watching Marion's multi-coloured retreat. 'Thank goodness *you* don't cling to the culture of your misspent youth, darling.'

But Terence Armstrong didn't hear her. Seeing Marion reminded him of his Oxford days, and he stroked his upper lip thoughtfully, wondering what he would look like now with his old hippie moustache.

Frederick had joked nervously to the first five visitors to the VIP men's room as to why he was aiming a hair dryer at the fly of his trousers, but finding them for the most part to be incurious or foreign ('Les anglais – ooph!'), he now had his head down to the job in hand.

'Hello Freddie, giving yourself a blow job?' asked Terence Armstrong, coming up behind him and slapping him heartily on the back.

'Terence! Terence! You're here! Ha ha! Spilled some champagne. All right now I think. Dried out nicely, ha ha! Jolly useful little implement!' laughed Frederick wild-eyed, waving his hair dryer.

'The jolliest and the most useful,' agreed Terence amicably, unzipping his fly. 'A boy's best friend.'

'No no, I meant . . .' began Frederick, averting his eyes.

'Just a joke Frederico, ha ha.' Terence vigorously shook what he was pleased to call his Leading Man, but which was known to ambitious young actresses as Terence Armstrong's Casting Assistant. He looked at it fondly for a moment, then put it away. 'Called our flight yet?'

'Not yet, no, but any minute I think. You cut it a bit fine.'

'Cock-up over the tickets is why. My bloody stupid PA forgot to book them.'

'Oh my goodness – is the flight crowded? Have you managed to get on?'

'I should bloody well hope so after all the air miles I've clocked up with them. No, Fiona rang first thing this morning and they're supposed to be sorting it out.'

They were now walking past the VIP reception and Terence was called over to the desk. 'Get me a coffee Freddie, be with you in a minute.'

'Yes of course, if there's time.'

The duty manager twitched his tie and smiled self-deprecat-ingly: 'I'm most terribly sorry, Mr Armstrong . . .'

'I'm not flying Club.'

'We've done everything we can to help you. We've vacated three Tourist seats . . .'

'Don't know why you did that, there's only two of me.'

'They were a party travelling together, the only passengers not to have collected their boarding cards when your Personal Assistant rang and alerted us to . . .'

Terence cut him off tetchily. 'I don't know *what* this has got to do with me.'

'. . . And two of our Club Class passengers have kindly agreed to be downgraded to Tourist, so . . .'

'So get two of your First Class passengers to be kindly downgraded to Club.'

'I really don't think that I could . . .'

'I have every confidence that you can,' smiled Terence.

And so it came to pass that, when the ten-thirty flight to Pisa was announced, Terence Armstrong and Beatrice Miller-Mander were shown graciously to their First Class seats; Frederick Mayer and Christopher Bassett were presented with (another) bottle of champagne and offered a generous discount if they would kindly consent to go Club; two furious Italian women who had no known VIP connections were each made two hundred pounds richer and crammed into Tourist (Smoking); and Tom and Janice Cowlishaw exchanged wistful looks with their travelling companion Marion Hardcastle, and wondered how they would fill the next seven hours.

Chapter Two

Marion was going through a rough patch. This is what she told herself on her good days to try to cheer herself up. Life was a series of peaks and troughs, and currently she was in a trough. Life being cyclical, she reassured herself, another peak was bound to appear soon. On her bleaker days — and it has to be said there had been more of these in a proportion of, let's say, thirteen to one (she had started going to a sauna once a fortnight) — she reminded herself that this trough had lasted twenty-five months. In her really desolate periods she often wondered if it hadn't actually been going on for as many years.

Twenty-five years ago, having taken her A-levels and attained three rather good passes, she had decided to take a year off before committing herself to her higher education. At that time, with History, Art and English at her disposal, she had no idea what her career might be, nor indeed what degree to go for. Careers advice had been in its infancy, as had the notion of what women might do, and the Careers Teacher was in fact the upwardly mobile Latin Mistress doing extra-curricular duties in the hope of becoming Head of Department. For the boys she recommended the Army, banking or accountancy, and for the girls, teaching or personnel management. Marion knew instinctively that these were not for her.

So having earned some money from a vacation job in the

Vehicle Taxation Department at County Hall (and through this Marion was able to strike Local Government off her list of possible careers as well), she set sail from Dover for the Continent, as the rest of the EC used to be known.

Arriving in Paris she had managed to get herself a job as a chambermaid (hotel management, if it had ever appeared on her list, was now ruled out), and she had met Frank and fallen in love. Frank was a Californian 'doing Europe', and he was the nearest thing to perfection that Marion had ever seen. He was tall – six foot two – he was blond, and he had immaculately white straight teeth such as British dentistry, in those days, had yet to achieve. Marion couldn't believe her luck. She felt small and mousy and in urgent need of orthodontia beside him, and she could never quite see what he saw in her.

But something about her obviously appealed to him. He said astonishing things like 'I never believed in Fate before but, I was meant to leave Paris the week before you arrived and – something stopped me', 'I have never had this kind of mind-trip with anyone ever before', and 'You are the grooviest chick I have ever balled'. Of all these declarations, the last one thrilled her most. She was eighteen, he was twenty, and together they travelled as the mood took them, sometimes with friends made along the way, at other times alone.

These were halcyon days. If they needed money they worked, the rest of the time they played. On sunny terraces and golden beaches they drank Ricard or ouzo or sangria or grappa, savouring the fruits of whatever country they found themselves in. They ate pasta and poulet, paella and psari. They learnt a little of each language to be polite to the natives. And everywhere they went they visited the galleries and museums. Frank was Into Art and he felt that he had been born on the wrong continent and out of his time. He wanted to be Michelangelo. He liked to paint, but then he thought that he might sculpt. Perhaps he would become an architect and right what he saw as the wrongs of modern America. The world was his oyster and Marion, for reasons beyond her ken, was his pearl.

When she fell pregnant in Italy, Frank was delighted. They would go to England to tell her parents, and he would ask for their daughter's hand. Then they would fly to California to introduce his bride to his parents, he would enrol as a student of architecture (architects could afford to have families, he decided, artists could not), and she would bring up baby and paint in her spare time. If she were a girl she would be called Jonquil, if a boy then Jake would be his name.

Little J was a three-month foetus when Mummy and Daddy flew from Rome, full of hope. They were to spend three days in London before travelling north to Marion's parents. Frank hadn't done England, and the great galleries had to be seen. They took a bus to Earl's Court, found a cheap hotel, and so as not to waste a minute, set off again immediately to see London by night.

And that, as far as Marion was concerned, thinking back, was the last time she had been truly happy. They had walked up The Mall from Buckingham Palace to Trafalgar Square and Frank had been enthralled. So much history – the Duke of York Monument, Admiralty Arch, Nelson's Column and all that – and looking across the Square, the National Gallery and the Portrait Gallery which they would visit the next day. But of course, they never did. They were about to cross Whitehall to go down to the river via Northumberland Avenue when Frank stepped off the pavement a pace or two ahead of Marion, looking the wrong way from a lifetime's habit, and was mown down by a taxi. By the time they had arrived at the hospital, Frank and J were dead; her husband-to-be from a fatal head wound, and her son (it was a boy, the hospital told her) miscarried from shock.

'Penny for them,' said Janice Cowlisham SRN, dispensing sweets like medicine.

'No thanks.'

'Go on, have this one – toffee brazil.'

'No thank you.'

'Tom, did you take the caramel whirl? Give it back here — don't put it in your mouth! Here you are Marion — who can resist?'

'Me, I'm afraid — no thanks.'

'You could do with the sugar to perk you up.'

'I could do with a drink.'

Janice and Tom shared a look of concern. They had originally invited Chalky and Elizabeth White (German and Home Economics) to share their holiday, but the rising mortgage rate had crippled them financially, and apologetically they had had to withdraw. Janice tried to drum up a replacement from the Hospital, but everybody had had their holidays booked since Christmas or else couldn't afford to go. The rent for the apartment (which had been paid for in advance) being an unbelievable £500, they *had* to find someone to share. And then Tom had suddenly remembered hearing that in Tuscany there was a lot of Art — who better than the Art teacher? — and without even checking with Janice, he persuaded Marion to join them.

'Actually, she didn't take much persuading,' he'd said, waving her cheque triumphantly aloft. 'She practically jumped at the chance.'

'Why?' his wife had asked.

'I dunno — maybe she was wondering what she was going to do with herself this year.'

'It's not as if she knows us very well. At least, *I* don't know her very well,' she'd said, with narrowed eyes.

'*I* don't know her very well either, apart from mending her wardrobe last term,' said Tom. He was Woodwork.

'Then why did she rush to come on holiday with us?'

'She didn't *rush*, she sort of — looked at me, very alert, you know — the most alert I've seen her actually — and she laughed and she said, "Why not? Maybe it's time for Catharsis."'

'Is that near to where we're going?'

'Dunno. Thought it was in Greece. Anyway, point is, she's paid her whack, coughed up on the spot.'

Janice had reluctantly given in. After all, you couldn't argue with money. But she felt uneasy. Three was a bad number, especially if two of them were a married couple and the third a single women. What would they do with her? Would she tag on to them all the time? What did she look like in a bikini? Did she fancy Tom? He was, after all, the most attractive bloke at School – his bum was even nicer than Greg Jones's (Games). The nurse in her had diagnosed in Marion borderline manic depression. The working class in her had scented out a snotty middle-class cow. But the woman (and that, as Tom said, was Janice all over) had settled for making the best of a bad job. She was now engaged full-out in bringing Marion round.

'What's the time?' she asked, and Tom said, 'Half past twelve.'

'Soon be time for dinner,' she said enticingly to Marion, 'and then we'll have a glass of wine.'

Marion didn't answer, save for a sardonic smile.

'Or a beer,' ventured Tom. 'How much have we got left on the vouchers, Jan?'

'Nothing I'm afraid. The breakfasts came to twelve pounds odd and they said they didn't give change on vouchers.'

'This is ridiculous,' said Marion, rising. 'This is absolutely bloody well out-bloody-rageous.'

And before either of them could stop her, she strode through the crowds in the Departure Lounge, and had disappeared from their sight.

'Where's she gone now?' asked Tom.

'How should I know? She's your friend, not mine.'

Tom suppressed a small sigh.

'I shan't be sorry if she's gone home,' continued Janice darkly. 'She's a right bloody wet blanket.'

'I suppose you know what you're letting yourself in for?' demanded Marion coldly of Mr Froggatt, Customer Relations. 'You do know who I am?'

'Er, yes Mrs — *Miss* Hardcastle,' said Froggatt nervously, consulting his handwritten note.

'Ms.'

'I do beg your pardon.'

'The Editor told you in his letter, I imagine, that I was doing this article?'

'Article, yes, I do seem to remember,' said Froggatt, wishing to God that the mists would clear from his mind. 'For whom, did you say?'

'For *Which?*.'

'I beg your pardon, for which? For *Which?!?*'

' "Which Airline? — Marion Hardcastle Contrasts and Compares". Surely it was mentioned when the booking was made? It is our usual policy.'

'I'm *sure* it was — Theresa! Find me the letter from *Which?*.'

'Which what?' asked Theresa crossly. She was in the middle of tricky negotiations on the telephone with her new boyfriend Troy, and had just come to the part that began, 'It's not that I don't fancy you . . .'

'I'm sorry, we've had nothing but temps all summer, Ms Hardcastle, and I've been away on leave.'

Marion smiled, willing to be friends.

'Anywhere nice?'

'Nowhere special,' said Mr Froggatt evasively, who had in fact been in a clinic, drying out.

'Theresa, forget it . . .' It was patently clear that she already had, '. . . and fetch Ms Hardcastle a glass of — wine?'

'That's very kind.'

'And, just to be sociable, you'd better bring one for me.'

Theresa scowled across the office. 'Sorry Troy, I'll have to ring you back. He's gone on the booze again.'

Mr Froggatt smiled desperately at Marion, and reached for the phone and dialled. 'Hello, Trevor? Nigel Froggatt here, Customer Relations. What on *earth* has been going on . . .?'

Marion sipped her wine and listened and smiled. She was glad now that she hadn't found anything suitable in the airport boutique. These clothes gave her strength. It was like wearing a disguise. Maybe her holiday might do her good after all.

Tom and Janice sat open-mouthed in the Departure Lounge as Mr Froggatt apologised profusely on his airline's behalf. There was unfortunately no way of getting them to Pisa now before the five o'clock flight, but the least he could do would be to offer them lunch in the first class restaurant of the Ambassador Hotel.

Tom was less impressed when he'd listened to Marion's story of deception. He'd been enjoying his steak, but now it turned into stolen goods, right there in his mouth. He swallowed the evidence guiltily, and laid down his knife and fork.

'What if they find out?' he hissed, looking furtive, glancing round.

'Tough. They should have given us all this as a matter of course. We've paid for a service that they've failed to provide.'

'Anyway,' chortled Nurse Cowlishaw, who was enjoying the joke, 'what could they do – give us a stomach pump?' Her estimation of Marion had risen immeasurably. Her eye roved to the sweets trolley and then to the cheese board. 'I wonder if I could manage both?'

'They could give us a bill,' said Tom stiffly, 'and that wouldn't be funny. Besides, Marion and I are teachers – what if it ever came out at school?'

'What you don't get given, you sometimes have to take,' his wife instructed him. 'People of privilege get this kind of behaviour all the time. Profiteroles please.'

Marion made that two, and raised her glass in a toast.

'The nurses and teachers strike back!' she proposed.

'Up the workers!' agreed Janice, clinking her glass.

'Well I'm not having pudding,' said Tom.

By the time the two women had drunk coffee and brandy and Marion had smoked a cigar ('Good grief,' thought Tom, 'don't tell me she's Women's Lib!') it was almost time to board. Janice had kept up the party spirit with her tales from Men's Surgical, all of which Tom had heard before, and most of which he would have preferred never to have heard again. When she got to the one about the Superglue, he stood up in what he hoped would seem an assertive manner, and knocked over his untouched coffee.

'I . . . we ought to go and stand by the Departures Board,' he said lamely. 'We don't want to miss this one.'

'Hang about a bit,' said Janice, 'I've just come to the punch line,' and ignoring him, duly delivered it.

Marion rewarded her with a burst of raucous laughter, while Tom pushed his napkin under the spoilt table cloth to protect the wood from damage.

Walking back to the Departure Lounge unsteadily arm in arm, Janice asked Marion if she was afraid of flying.

'I'm terrified myself,' she said, digging in her pocket, 'so I've got some Betablockers if you want one.'

'No thanks,' said her new friend, 'I'll stick with the Prozac.'

'I wondered if you were depressed. What's up? Do you want to tell me about it?'

'How long have you got?'

'Seven days,' riposted Janice, cackling, the wit of which nearly floored them both.

There was no error this time over their seats, and the hostesses had obviously been instructed to smile at them extra hard. The girls gave Tom the window seat as he'd brought his Instamatic, and it was no secret he was cross. Janice, in the middle, rubbed his thigh with hers and snuggled against his arm. 'Can't wait for my bed,' she whispered smoulderingly, with promises of things to come.

It was not long before her travelling companions had fallen asleep, Janice from a Betablocker and too much wine, and Tom from nervous exhaustion. Marion declined her in-flight meal but accepted a large whisky in lieu. Froggatt had done his stuff. She didn't usually drink this much – well not often anyway – and she felt that she deserved it. Following the orders of Captain Lambert, his cabin staff and crew, she settled down to a pleasant flight, drifting towards Tuscany and back in time. Why had life been so cruel to her? Where now was the promise of her youth?

After Frank had died and she'd had the miscarriage, her parents had come to the hospital and taken her home. Having her immediate plans curtailed, and by so cruel a blow, Marion's will deserted her. The days came and went, and she rarely left her room. Most of her friends were by now away at college, and there was no one of her own age to talk to. She was nearly nineteen and her life had stopped. Seeing her daughter making no recovery, Marion's Mum tried a different tack. She'd allowed her a generous period for grief and mourning, had talked sympathetically when invited to do so, had planned small outings and made tempting food, all to no avail. Now she tried direct manipulation.

'He was a very handsome boy,' she said to Marion, looking through the photos yet again. 'And talented, you say?'

'He was going to be an architect,' keened Marion, nodding. 'He loved art and beautiful buildings. He was going to revolutionise LA.'

'Did you talk of a career for you?' asked Mrs Hardcastle, knowing full well that they had.

'I was going to bring up Jake and paint.'

'And *paint*, I see. Was that Frank's idea, or yours?'

'Frank's mainly. He didn't want me to sacrifice myself for the children. We were going to have three.' Another bout of wailing, another of Daddy's handkerchiefs.

'He must have thought you had talent, then.'

'He seemed to think so. I don't know why.'

'Well he must have known if he was so clever himself.'

'He was brilliant Mummy.'

'I wonder what he'd want you to do now?'

'He'd want us to be together,' sniffed Marion.

'I don't think so darling, under the circumstances,' responded Mrs Hardcastle crisply. 'I think he'd want you to let him live through you.'

'How can I? He's dead, I can't bring him back. Jake's dead. I've got nothing.'

'You've got your talent to paint. The talent that Frank, brilliant as he was, spotted. Don't you think that's what he'd have wanted you to do? To take that talent, to nurture it, to show it to the world? For Frank? He chose you, of all the girls he must have known, not just because you're pretty . . .'

'I'm not.'

'. . . Not just because you're clever . . .'

'Oh yeah!'

'But because you and he together shared this great love of Truth and Beauty, of Art and Understanding. Frank's gone now, it's true, but his dream needn't be. Marion, you could help his vision live through you. Paint, Marion, paint as you have never painted before. Study Art, and let Frank's light shine on!'

Going back downstairs, Marion's mother wasn't proud of herself, but she'd had to do something. And even Mr Churchill had had to say some pretty silly things to boost morale during the War.

'Any headway?' asked her husband, looking up from his newspaper.

'I've left some prospectuses with her. I'm going to phone round to see who still has places free.'

So Marion had taken Frank's light to Liverpool, and kept it shining there for three years.

'Are we there yet?' asked Janice, peering through her proverbials in the snow. Her face was certainly white and Marion hoped fervently that she wouldn't need to use the facilities provided in the pocket of the seat in front of her.

'Another half hour.'

'Oh.'

She settled down to snooze again, but Marion had had enough of reviewing her earlier life and wanted conversation.

'What's this place we're going to like?'

'Don't know really. We did it through an advert in the paper. Can't remember which. One of them big ones I don't normally read – a patient had left it behind, and I was just flicking through. Was it the *Guardian*, Tom?'

'Think so.'

'But haven't you seen a photograph, or some particulars?' asked Marion incredulously.

'Not really,' said Janice. 'She said it'd got two big double bedrooms, bathrooms en suite, kitchen, living-room, and good views.'

'Who's "she"?'

'The woman who owns it. It's an apartment in her house. Sounded quite nice.'

'How do we get there from the airport?' Marion demanded, thinking ahead.

'Dunno. I think we take a train and bus. Tom worked it out. Tom?'

'But we're seven hours later now. Have you checked the timetables to see if we can still do it?'

'Tom?'

'Oh shit.'

'So you didn't then?'

'I haven't got any timetables. Anyway, why is it always down to me?' retorted Tom sulkily.

'It isn't. Marion sorted out our dinner.'

'I can always try that again, at the airport in Pisa. Get them to pay for a taxi.'

'No,' said Tom hastily. 'If necessary we'll hire a car.'

'I thought you said it would be prohibitive,' challenged his wife. 'You said we'd have to see how the money went, and perhaps get one for a couple of days later on.'

'Yes, well, when I said that I didn't know *this* was going to happen, did I?' snapped Tom, by now fractious and travel-worn.

'I don't know what all the fuss is about. There'll probably be no bother with the train. If there is we could hire a car for a couple of days, do our trip out tomorrow, and spend the rest of the time lounging round the pool.'

Marion saw the holiday turning into a nightmare. No transport, unable to get to the museums and galleries, forced to lounge around a pool with two brain dead companions who didn't normally read 'big papers'.

'Is it *very* remote?' she asked now, desperately.

'She said it was off the beaten track.'

Her heart sank.

'We can always hire bicycles if we get bored hanging round the villa,' said Tom cheerfully, he of the athletic bum. 'This is more of an exploring holiday anyway than a package. Travel and adventure.'

'Mm,' said Marion through tightening lips. She had had enough travel adventures in her youth to last her a lifetime and she didn't ride a bike. 'Do you normally take a package then?'

'Well normally, yes.'

'Except when we did the Lake District,' said Janice helpfully.

'Oh yes, except when we did the Lakes,' agreed Tom. 'We had a great time, didn't we Jan? No bother at all.'

Having ascertained at Informazione that there were indeed no train or bus connections that night, the trio trooped across to the car-hire desk. It *was* prohibitive. Even a tiny Fiat was more than they had planned. They withdrew from the desk for a conference.

'We could have it for three days,' said Tom, fingering the traveller's cheques in his pocket, 'but then it'd definitely have to go back.'

'Couldn't we pay by credit card?' said Marion.

'Not after last month, with the air fares,' he replied.

'On mine then.'

'We haven't really budgeted for it.'

24

'Pay me back later, over a period of time,' she said shortly. Really, if they were going to have these lengthy discussions over every decision, the holiday was doomed. But Tom would neither a borrower nor a lender be. 'I prefer to settle up as I go along,' he said firmly. Marion exploded.

'For God's sake Tom, don't be so po-faced!'

'I'm not being po-faced, Marion, I'm being realistic. So much money comes in, so much money goes out. It has to balance.'

'What *have* you budgeted for then?' she asked, not trying to keep the sarcasm from her voice.

'Hundred and fifty pounds.'

'Each?'

'You must be joking!' laughed Tom uneasily. He couldn't bear arguments.

'My God, are you mad?!' demanded Marion, who didn't mind them at all. 'Italy's notoriously expensive. Even a cup of coffee's—'

'The rest of abroad isn't,' said Janice, rising to Tom's defence. 'We've been to Spain and Greece and come back with money in our pockets.'

'Anyway, that's why we chose self-catering. We'll be eating in at the villa, except for the odd Occasion.'

'And we've brought most of the staples with us,' Janice added, 'including jars of coffee.'

Oh Italy! Home of espresso and chocolate covered cappuccino! Maker of pizzas, grower of porcini, presser of extra-virgin olive oil! To return to her arms after so long a parting, only to eat baked beans on toast with Tom and Janice Cowlishaw. It was like a sentence of doom.

Night fell at a stroke as they kangarooed cautiously out of Pisa Airport in the world's smallest rental car, Tom Cowlishaw, travelling adventurer, at the helm.

'Drive on the right, Tom, drive on the right!' screamed Janice, clutching the dashboard and leaning as far back in her seat as she could.

25

'I know, I know!' said Tom crossly as he crashed the gears. 'What's he hooting at? I'm in the inside lane. Bloody Italian drivers!' He hooted back.

'He's telling you about your lights – put them on!' screamed Janice, the while waving ingratiatingly through the windscreen at the apoplectic driver. Tom switched on the wipers, the emergency indicators and the de-mister before finding full beam. 'Where's the flipping dipswitch?' he shouted, cars honking all around. 'Shut your blithering row, you stupid blasted Wops!' He found the switch, which seemed to satisfy the honkers in front, but behind them and around them others still hooted angrily.

'Actually you *are* in the fast lane,' Marion said faintly from the back seat. 'It's like a mirror – you have to imagine everything backwards here.'

'You're not kidding,' snapped Tom viciously, wrenching the wheel. 'Who's got the directions? Janice? Where are we aiming for?'

'I don't know. Wherever the train would have taken us I suppose. I haven't got a map.'

Another Prozac would not be the answer, Marion decided reluctantly, she would have to take control. 'Follow the signs to Arezzo,' she said firmly, 'and we'll stop at a petrol station and ask.' She couldn't wait to get to the villa, to shut her bedroom door on this dreadful day, to be alone.

'How far is it do you think?' asked Janice, 'Cos I'm bursting for a pee.'

Italy unfolded slowly and frighteningly before them, mile after mile of darkness swallowing them up. They were relieved to see a petrol station – Janice perhaps even more than the others. Before the car had come to a complete stop she leapt out and followed the international sign of mercy, the one-legged woman in the triangular skirt.

A forecourt attendant walked over to Tom's window and asked how much petrol he'd like and Tom, blushing foolishly in

the harsh lights said, 'English, English, no comprendo Italian.'
Marion struggled out of the back seat and, explaining that they
merely wanted to buy a map, was directed to the shop. When she
returned with map and chocolate, she smiled awkwardly at Tom.

'Not far now. We're doing quite well I think.' She opened the
map for him to see and pointed with her finger. 'We're here.
We'll turn off past Arezzo and take this small road here, to the
village where the bus would have gone. And then we'll ask.
Shouldn't be more than an hour.'

Janice skipped back towards them, lighter of body and freer
of spirit. 'Hello you two, you look like boy scouts,' she said. 'It's
really nice in there. Scrupulously clean and fully plumbed. You
never know Abroad.'

The atmosphere amongst them lightened. They knew where
they were and almost where they were going. They munched
chocolate, and Tom and Marion tried to harmonise when Janice
sang her songs. Everything was going to be all right.

They had been on this small road for half an hour, twisting and
turning up and down hills, their eyes straining through the
darkness, when simultaneously the storm broke and the car
lurched violently to the left.

'Shit a brick!' Tom exclaimed, struggling with the wheel.
'We've only gone and got a puncture!'

They sat miserably in the car, waiting for the rain to stop
looking so like stair rods, smoking cigarettes in stony silence.

'It's me,' said Marion finally. 'You shouldn't have brought
me, I'm a jinx.'

Janice turned round and smiled encouragingly. 'It's not. It's
us. We always break down on holiday.'

Marion smiled back at her. She didn't know whether to feel
grateful or forewarned of worse to come.

The rain abated and Tom changed the wheel skilfully and
efficiently. He was almost jaunty when he told them they could
get back in, feeling for the first time that he had earned his

passage. He was no good at lying for his lunch, he couldn't speak Italian, but he knew exactly what was what when it came to anything practical. He pulled out from the verge, feeling at one with the machine.

'Any more chocolate?' he asked, settling himself more comfortably in his seat.

'Only two pieces,' said Janice next to him. 'But they're both for our Golden Boy.'

She popped them in his mouth and started to say that at least nothing else could go wrong, but the others shushed her. It was tempting fate.

When they got to the village not a soul was in sight. It was one a.m. and the houses were in darkness. Even the village shop, which Marion had rightly deduced would have a bar, was dark and sombre and waiting for the morning. What energy they had left now drained from their inert bodies, forlornness taking over.

'Didn't she give any directions at all?' Marion asked Janice. She was dog tired and her stomach felt empty and full at the same time. She wanted a wash, she wanted some coffee, she wanted to sleep. Instead she opened her bottle of gin and they solemnly passed it round.

'Not really,' Janice answered after drinking deeply. 'We were to ask at the shop for Claudio, and he'd have taken us in his car. I don't think it's far, but she said it was too complicated to explain.'

Marion squashed a disloyal thought. It was no use apportioning blame. They were all in this together, damn and blast it.

'Hang about a bit,' said Tom unnecessarily, since he was at the wheel and the car wasn't going anywhere. 'Didn't she say it was near a college?'

'Ooh yes,' said Janice, 'There might be a sign.'

Tom started the car and drove out of the village, the faint stirrings of hope beating against their tired breasts. They travelled for two miles in breathless expectation, peering through the windscreen, seeing nothing but dark trees and little twisting lanes branching off the road, all unsigned. Tom wearily announced his intention of turning round and going back out of the village the way they had come, when Janice grabbed his arm excitedly.

'Look!' she commanded, pointing ahead. 'Is that Italian for college, Marion?'

'It is indeed,' said Marion warmly, and they all cheered like mad.

They followed the sign which directed them to the left, up a narrow track with woodland either side of them, and stopped abruptly at a pair of wrought-iron gates, towering above them hugely in the headlights.

'Now what?' said Tom, defeated.

'See if they're open,' answered Janice, springing out.

She struggled with the fastening and pushed with all her might, the gates giving way before her firm resolve.

'Ought we to go in?' protested Tom, every inch a British serf. 'It might be private and they'll all be asleep.'

But the women vetoed niceties and pressed him to drive on, Janice clanging the gates shut behind them with an air of finality. The car crunched across a gravelled drive, and there before them rose a huge and ancient building. It was larger and grander and more beautiful than any building they had ever visited without first paying admission.

'It's a palazzo,' said Marion, 'or it was.'

Feeling rather uncertain and overawed they all got out of the car, trying to crunch the gravel quietly underfoot. Signs told students in several languages to keep off the grass and not to play ball games anywhere. They walked around the imposing building trying to find a door, and found far too many for a simple choice. They were coming back around one of the twin towers that flanked the main body of the college when Marion, looking up, saw a light shining from a window four storeys above.

'Then it's this door,' decided Janice, and searching for a bell, pulled an ancient iron handle in the arch. Instinctively they drew together, looking up and listening, three wet and tired trespassers, waiting on their fate. The storm had followed them, and was flinging gobbets of rain the size of florins on their heads.

'Please God, let us in,' thought Marion.

'Please God, give us a bed,' thought Janice.

'Please God, speak English,' thought Tom.

All their prayers were answered when the lighted window was flung open, and a woman's head thrust out.

'Who are you?' she cried imperiously in the cut-glass tones of the English upper classes. 'And what on earth do you want at this time of night?'

Janice ran a little way into the gravelled drive to show herself, and looked up at the dark figure above, shielding her eyes from the rain.

'I'm Janice Cowlishaw from England,' she yelled, 'looking for Mrs Fratorelli's house. Can you tell us where to go?'

'Hell!' said the woman, banging the window shut and turning to her guests within. 'They're here.'

Chapter Three

Frederick's laughter died on his lips. He was not a cruel man, and
though Pamela had been very amusing doing her impressions of
her expected paying guests, now they had arrived he was
ashamed. He had had a pleasant flight in spite of his and
Christopher's puzzling demotion to Club, and they had picked
up the pre-booked cars from Pisa Airport without a hitch: a
Lancia for him, a Mercedes for Terence. Having time in hand
they made a short detour to lunch in Lucca, the beautiful
medieval walled city, and the others had been suitably impressed.
Not least, Frederick felt sure, by his ability to order their meal in
Italian, and even to make a joke with the waiter, who had roared
with laughter in what had genuinely seemed to be an appreciative
and not a derisive way. Really the Italians were jolly good fun.

The drive had been exciting and beautiful, watching the
gentle Tuscan landscape unfold, delighting in Christopher's
wide-eyed appreciation of colour and form and his admiration
of the Italian road planners, who had tunnelled discreetly
through the hills rather than ripping chunks off them as their
British brothers would have done in their place. The Lancia had
been comfortable and easy to get the hang of, the efficient air-
conditioning keeping them deliciously cool in the heat of the
afternoon.

This was Frederick's fourth trip to stay with the Contessa at the Palazzo Fratorelli, and he looked forward immensely to the reaction of the others when they swept through the imposing gates and saw where he had brought them. He knew they could not fail to be as overwhelmed as he had been on his first visit to the ancient palace, built of honey-coloured stone. With its imposing towers, its gracious archways and its lovely courtyards, it was like something from a dream. He knew too, from past experience that Pamela would greet them with iced champagne laced with crème de framboise, home-grown olives and crostini spread thickly with chicken livers, and that they would be received in the Green Room in this palace of paintings.

The family Fratorelli had been substantial landowners, clever at making money (and until recently, at keeping it), and successively men of artistic bent. The first Count, Paolo, had started to build in 1374 and his sons and grandsons had improved on his vision. In 1639 with the building completed, the then younger son, Giovanni, had earned his keep from his brother the heir by painting the famous Fratorelli frescoes in all the major rooms. Of all of these — and there were many — the Green Room was by far the most spectacular (and, as it happened, the least pornographic).

Pamela had not disappointed him, nor indeed had his fellow guests who were visibly and audibly impressed. Frederick had basked delightedly in reflected glory, and had been grateful to Pamela when she had asked for his opinion as to where they should eat. They had decided on the Serata Splendida, and it was. Luigi himself had come to their table and embraced Frederick warmly, chiding him for staying away for so long.

'Frederick makes friends wherever he goes,' Pamela had said to his smiling friends, as his nose was being crushed against Luigi's broad chest. 'One wouldn't dream he'd be such an ogre around the negotiating table.' This was for Terence's benefit, warning him that her father's work would not come cheap.

'Yes, he's a lion,' agreed Terence as the smiling, blushing Frederico was returned to an upright position by his amico Luigi, and he reached across to straighten Freddie's glasses which were now set at a jaunty angle across his nose.

If it had been his birthday, Frederick could not have been more pleased. Christopher solicitously poured him some wine, and the beautiful Beatrice lifted her glass. 'To Frederick, for bringing us to such a wonderful place, and to Pamela, for being such a marvellous hostess,' she proposed.

They all agreed and drank. Pamela inclined her head gracefully in recognition of the compliment, and smiled to herself secretly when Christopher added, 'Yes, Pamela, thanks so much for having us.' Oh yes, she thought, looking him over and liking what she saw, I'll have you all right, not half my pretty lad. She had been rather cross that they were coming, having plagued poor Freddie for almost a year to arrange it. She needed money certainly, that was in no doubt, but just recently she had started a charming affair with one of the students on the summer course at the college, and she was reluctant to have it interrupted.

La Contessa Fratorelli had been born plain Pamela Fox, only (legitimate) offspring of the late Benjamin Fox, Bloomsbury poet, painter, and writer of short stories. If only he had managed a novel, his place in literary history would have been assured, as would his surviving daughter's financial security. But Benjamin had been too much the dilettante to concentrate his efforts for so long, and his private life had taken precedence. He had also rowed with Leonard and Virginia (who hadn't?), and they had turned their friends against him. As a consequence he'd hardly been mentioned in any of their books save for the odd diary entry, unflattering in the extreme.

As a young woman, Pamela had been beautiful – was beautiful still – and several artists had painted her in all kinds of positions. At twenty she had persuaded her current boyfriend Peter, a royal correspondent for the *Daily Express*, to take her to Italy following the young Princess Margaret's first tour abroad. The Italian glitterati had taken her to their hearts. Some had gone further and taken her to their beds. She said a tearless farewell to Peter, thanked him nicely for her passage, and settled down to find her fortune in Rome.

Like her father before her, Pamela had difficulty in making a commitment. She had been brought up by any amount of his girlfriends, her mother having found peace in an early grave when Pamela had been only four years old. The princes had come and gone, the counts and dukes, the opera singers, the actors and the pugilist. At twenty-five she had conceived (with whom remained her secret) and none of her well-connected boyfriends had been eager to give the child his name. Nor, it may be added, was she keen to settle down. Eventually at forty-five, with long-term security at last her objective, she had gritted her teeth and seduced the ageing Conte Vincenzo Paolo di Fratorelli, and had returned a blushing bride to his Palazzo and his land. She had easily outlived him. However, he who laughs last has by tradition the biggest giggle of all, and the old Conte had enjoyed the joke hugely as he read to her his will shortly before his demise. The money had all gone, most of the land had been sold, and most of the Palazzo had been made over to the people of Italy. The Fratorelli fortune had been frittered away, all except Pamela's tower.

Being British and patrician, if not by birth then by inclination and by marriage, she had weathered the shock pragmatically, and had turned her hand and mind to making money. Her late husband had left her with some olive groves, so she supplied the English market with their oil – bottled and shipped exclusively to Harrod's. Through some wonderful Italian law she found this made her a farmer and eligible therefore in the future for an agricultural pension when she finally threw in the trowel. She found that the four floors of the tower were more than sufficient to her needs, and converted one floor into a spacious apartment, another into a two-roomed flat, both of which she rented out to English paying guests. There was a slight problem with this arrangement at the moment, but she'd soon put that to rights.

Her latest scheme for her pecuniary progress was under discussion now, and Frederick, an entertainment lawyer and therefore her agent in these affairs, nudged her gently under the table as Terence began to speak.

'I've read your father's short story, and I'm must say I'm impressed. There are one or two things we'll have to discuss — minor details' — he waved them away with a flick of his hand — 'that shouldn't stand in our way if we're sensible. All things being equal, and if we agree to terms with your leonine and litigious lawyer' (all eyes now smiled at Frederick, squirming with pleasure at this inaccurate but flattering description of himself), 'we can option the book and get going on adapting it into a musical straight away.'

'Who had you thought to do the music?' asked Frederick, anxious to know how seriously they were being taken.

'Oh Johnny I think, don't you?' answered Terence airily. 'No point in getting less.'

Pound signs now spun happily in their millions in front of Pamela's eyes.

'Shall we settle up?' she suggested. 'And have liqueurs at home?'

She excused herself to go to the powder room, and on her return was pleased to note that somebody had kindly taken care of the bill.

Showing them to their quarters earlier had been the only fly in her ointment, but she had rallied quickly, and as quickly rearranged. Frederick, as a personal friend, was to have his usual room in her own apartment, and Christopher, as his personal friend, was to have the room next door. Pamela had been incurious as to the exact nature of their relationship when Freddie had asked to bring a friend, but judging others as she judged herself, she'd assumed that he would want access to Christopher at night. Now that she had seen this young Adonis in the flesh, as it were, she rather thought that Freddie would have to beat her to it. But that could wait. It would be icing on her cake.

However, the problem had arisen when she had shown Terence and Beatrice to their self-contained accommodation on the first floor. There was a large and stately sitting room with wonderful views across the plain, where she had thoughtfully provided a bowl of fruit and some bottles of water. With this they were delighted, and said so. She also had her work room on this floor which they duly admired (the frescoes here were particularly salacious and it amused her to sit at her word processor beneath the frolicking forms). She demonstrated the double locks between their room and hers, showed them the secret passage she could use to gain entry to her study from above, and assured them they would never be disturbed. She whisked them through the kitchenette and bathroom since they were small and meanly built, but then turned with triumph in the bedroom to see their reaction to the vast outrageous bed. Scores of fat cherubs were carved into the wood, conjoined in frantic pleasures and positions unknown to most mere mortals, fucking in a frenzied frieze.

She was about to go into her usual patter about which Fratorelli had commissioned it for which bride, but was arrested by Beatrice wringing her hands and by Terence who asked, 'And where's the other bedroom?' Pamela was nonplussed. She was quite used to couples of all kinds asking shyly if they might sleep together, but never before a couple who asked if they might be apart.

'Other?' she now enquired. 'I'm afraid there isn't one. I'd rather assumed . . .'

'Of course,' said Terence quickly, in defence of his manhood. 'And you were absolutely right. But you see I'm an insomniac, and I have to *sleep* alone.'

'I see,' said Pamela thoughtfully, and concluded, 'Va bene, you'll have to sleep upstairs.'

Frederick and Christopher had followed them for the tour, and Freddie now asked anxiously if she hadn't told him it had already been let.

'Oh yes,' she replied dismissively, 'but only to some dreadful woman from the Midlands. There are three of them, which is why I'd given them the larger flat, but I'm sure they'll manage quite nicely here. They're probably a ménage.'

Now she left her distinguished guests drinking their post-prandial liqueurs and descended the stone stairs to the cavernous hall which extravagantly took up the entire ground floor. Flinging open the door she decided to open negotiations on the attack.

'You're very late,' she said to the three white startled faces standing in the rain. 'I was about to go to bed.'

'I'm very sorry,' said the dreadful woman from the Midlands, known to her friends as Jan, 'but the flight was over-booked and we had to wait till five. Then the car broke down and my husband – this is my husband, Tom . . .' Tom bowed stiffly in embarrassment and mumbled how d'you do, 'had to change the tyre. And then we didn't know how to find you, what with Claudio being closed.'

'But you managed,' Pamela concluded curtly. 'Would you care to bring in your things?' While Marion and Tom ferried cases from the car, Janice burbled happily on.

'We'd only stopped on the off-chance, to see if anybody knew the way. When you said it was near the college I hadn't expected it to be *in* it.'

'My late husband the Count graciously left the larger part of the Palazzo to the people of Italy,' lied the Countess. There had been nothing gracious in his gift, owing as he had thousands of millions of lire in unpaid taxes. 'It is now the home of the illustrious and celebrated Tuscan International College of Art and Architecture, whose students and staff are currently renovating it to its former beauty.' And she'd made pretty damn sure that they'd restored her part of it first. 'Follow me please,' she commanded, helping them with not so much as a toothbrush as they struggled with their things. 'Bolt the door behind you and switch off the lights as we go. You can't imagine how frightful the bills are, particularly after summer guests.'

'I suppose that makes you a Countess,' said Janice in her wake. 'Should we call you anything special?' (Hm, thought Marion darkly, I can think of plenty of names.)

'Contessa will do. Perhaps Pamela if we get to know each other better.'

'Oh, I'm all for informality, Pam,' said Janice, oblivious of her tone. 'I call the senior heart consultant Reggie to his face. I'm a nurse by the way, and Marion and Tom are teachers.'

Pamela couldn't have cared less what they did for a living, but stopped herself from saying so. They had arrived at the first floor apartment and she had yet to tell them of the change of plan. She suddenly decided on the coward's way out: she'd let them find out for themselves. She opened the door to the sitting room and flicked on the light. 'I'm frightfully tired and I have left my guests alone. If you will excuse me I will leave you now. I'm sure you'd like to sleep after your trying journey. If you have any questions you may ask me in the morning. Good night.' The travelling trio were delighted to let her go, and called their goodnights and thanks to her briskly retreating form.

Stepping inside their quarters they were overwhelmed by its splendour. The room was furnished simply but expensively to throw all focus on to the paintings. The theme of the frescoes, which marched around the walls and ended on the ceiling, was well-worn but incongruous in this setting. Rich men, it warned, hadn't an earthly of getting past St Peter, whereas the poor and pure of heart could go directly to Heaven. The poor and pure of heart were very picturesque however, by way of compensation, having colour co-ordinated their clothes and being surprisingly well fed. Marion, who knew a thing or two about Art, suspected that the family at the front of the heavenly queue who were positively shining with goodness, was the famiglia Fratorelli. Further back down the road their opulent enemies were having all kinds of bother with plague and pestilence, and the flames of hell flickered out from behind the skirting board, singeing a few toes. Above them on the ceiling, God was the usual white-haired old buffer with a beard, and at his right hand sat Jesus, shining his light on the world quite literally, since he was holding the ceiling rose from which hung a huge chandelier.

'Blimey Charlie,' said Tom, looking rather gormless with his head thrown back and his mouth hanging open, 'it's like a mausoleum.'

'Who's a clever girl then?' demanded Janice, wanting praise. 'Who'd have thought you could get *this* out of an advert in a paper?'

'Bizarre,' said Marion. 'And what about Cruella de Vil?'

'Pam? She's all right. She was probably worried about us, that's all,' said Janice, charitably but inaccurately. 'I wonder what's behind that door?'

'A hundred and one dead Dalmatians?' offered Marion, who was a tougher nut to crack, and she went to look.

What she found, of course, were a hundred and one lewd cherubs, dancing round the bed. She pushed open two more doors within the bedroom ('Conversion job,' assessed Tom the carpenter) and found the kitchen and bathroom.

'Will you look at this bed!' squealed Janice, throwing herself upon it. 'Ooh Tom, I reckon we might learn a few tricks in here.' On the most cursory examination, embarrassed to look too closely, Tom rather hoped not. Though he loved Janice for her earthiness he was a missionary man himself, having injured his back early in their courting days. 'Marion might like this room,' is all he said. 'Let's have a look at the rest.'

'There is no rest,' said Marion bleakly, returning to their side. 'Only a locked door in the sitting-room. What you see is what we've got.'

It was three o'clock in the morning and Nurse Cowlishaw prescribed more gin. Seeing it was an emergency she laced it with vermouth and doled it out in tumblers. Tom had tried the locked door but hadn't managed to budge it, and they all assumed it was a mistake and that they'd get the key in the morning. Nobody wanted to face Pamela again that night. Tom volunteered to sleep on a sofa in the sitting-room, but was overruled by Janice on medical grounds for his back, to Marion's huge relief. She was so tired she could sleep anywhere, she insisted, but really what she wanted was solitude. Since Colin Menseley had moved out of her house she had grown accustomed to living on her own. She was tired of talking and taking group responsibility.

Janice and she reorganised the bedding, liberating a pillow and a blanket from the 'interesting bit of old wood carving' as Tom had now chosen to call the bed. They said their goodnights and took turns in the bathroom, and Marion tucked herself in with the blanket around her ears on the overstuffed couch. She prayed silently to the old man on the ceiling that His creation Janice Cowlishaw would be too tired for rampant experiment that night, but she wasn't overly surprised when she heard Tom wail. Quick work, she thought drowsily, now go to sleep like a good boy. But the connecting door was flung open and Janice thundered through.

'You'll never guess what's happened now!' she challenged, holding aloft an outsize pair of men's pyjamas. 'Tom's only gone and picked up the wrong case at Baggage Reclaim!'

Above their heads, and over the heads of God the Father and God the Son, Terence Armstrong played patience on his bed while Beatrice Miller-Mander slept soundly in her own. Over them in Pamela's flat, Frederick Mayer whistled softly in the land of Nod, dreaming of tapping chorus boys in Benjamin Fox's smash hit musical. Next door, Christopher Bassett laid down his sleepy head, listening to Pamela's footsteps creak lightly across the hallway, back from whence she'd come. He had been surprised but not astounded, and had been polite enough to oblige. 'Droit de seigneura', as she wittily explained an hour ago when she had slipped into his bed, and he had given himself over to the laws of this new land.

Soon the tower held them all, soundly and safely asleep within its ancient walls. God was on his ceiling, all was right with the world.

Chapter Four

Marion was lying on a huge bed, naked but for a pair of pendulous earrings which beamed spangled light on to the sweating face of Colin Menseley. 'I'm going to shaft you,' he was grunting. 'I'm going to come into you like a waterfall.' She heard a voice which must have been her own, shouting its assent. Looking up past his shoulder she saw their reflection thrown back at them from the mirror on the ceiling, and now noticed that they were not alone. She was surrounded by erect and throbbing penises, penises she recognised, penises she had known and loved — or at least passed the time of day with. There was Sean McCarthy from Liverpool Art College — how had he tracked her down here? — Steve Harter from teacher's training, Mick Doyle, Keith Simmons with his interesting twist on the top like Chesterfield spire, Dennis Wearing, and some bloke she'd met at a party in nineteen eighty-something whose name she couldn't quite remember . . . This was outrageous, this was an orgy, how could it be happening, God it was wonderful. The door opened, and a shaft of golden light fell across their writhing bodies. 'Marion,' said Frank. 'Marion, I've come back.'

She awoke crying, snivelling in shame and disgust. How could she ever have been unfaithful to him? She would never do it again. He was so pure, so clean, so loving, his teeth had been so white, his hair so golden. He was everything she'd ever want, everything a man should be. But dead.

As she came slowly to her senses she heard Tom and Janice Cowlishaw at it like knives on the other side of the door, and looking up, came face to face with God the Son holding on to his chandelier with a long-suffering air. Her body was bruised and stiff from the over-stuffed couch, her head ached, and her mouth tasted disgusting. Yesterday's traumas flooded into her mind and she sat up, furious, ready for a fight. She needed coffee, but the kitchenette was built inside the Cowlishaw's room. She needed to pee, but ditto the bathroom. She looked around for a serviceable receptacle, and saw instead the view.

At the end of the room, a square stone bay housed a velvet seat beneath dramatically long and beautifully proportioned windows. Her body rose of its own accord and her spirits soared over the pink and green Tuscan plain. It was beautiful, breathtaking, timeless. The window, divided by stone pillars into three arches, looked exactly like the thirteenth-century triptychs she had seen when she'd been here with Frank — they could have been painted here, from this perspective. And nothing marred it: no national grid pylons, no by-passes or motorways, no factories, no satellite dishes, no housing estates, no high rise.

A perfectly pitched top C sounded behind her, gathering in volume until it rose to its crescendo and hung quivering in the air, molto vibrato. Janice Cowlishaw had got her oats. Marion smiled despite herself, cheered by the view and pleased for Janice. Why shouldn't she enjoy a good lusty congress with her husband? She was a nice woman, salt of the earth. Marion regretted her unfriendly thoughts of yesterday, and vowed to be more charitable today.

Noiselessly, she hoped, she went through the door of their bedroom and let herself into the bathroom immediately inside. Aiming for the porcelain as was her wont, she peed silently and with huge relief.

'Bring us a cup of coffee, Marion,' called Janice Cowlishaw's voice loud and clear through the partition wall, 'I'm parched and

Tom's knackered.' Shocked by her close proximity – the loo must be situated immediately behind the bedhead she now realised – she splashed her face with water and crossed the small hallway to the kitchen. 'There's some Nescaff on the side and some powdered milk. Tom takes two sugars and I have one,' Janice yelled. 'Make yourself one and bring it in here.' Marion did as she was told and carried three cups of coffee through to the bed.

'Just what I needed,' pronounced Janice as she drank it in one quaff. 'Shove up Tom, make room.' Tom, damp and tousle-headed, couldn't look Marion in the eyes. He hoped in vain that she hadn't heard the wild noises of the last hour or so. He was dying to go to the loo but realised in horror that beneath the bedclothes he was, to borrow one of his wife's phrases, stark bollock naked. He wriggled around to keep the pressure off his bladder.

'Must pay a call,' said Janice, springing pink and buxom from the bed and dancing through the room. Tom rescued the bedclothes just in time to preserve his modesty, spilling his coffee painfully down his chest.

'I'll get out of your way,' Marion started to say, as Janice's impression of Niagara Falls in full flood cascaded through the hardboard wall.

Tom thought that he might die. 'They should have used a bit of rock wool if they were going to partition with thin wood,' he said gruffly. 'Or even egg boxes would do the trick.'

'Well mind you don't let it get you constipated,' grunted Janice, inches from their ears. 'You know what you're like. He didn't go for two weeks in Greece, Marion, when we had to share a loo. I don't know where he put it all!' Her peal of merry laughter was joined by the sounds of flushing. No problem in that department with her, evidently.

'Now then,' she said, reappearing at the door, 'who fancies luncheon meat and Ryvita for breakfast? It's all we've got till we do a shop.'

Marion declined, and amid their protestations said that she

was going to beard Pamela in her den about the sleeping arrangements. 'Well if you're really sure you don't want me to come with you,' said Janice, 'can you ask if you can use her phone to sort out about the suitcase mix-up? The other chap's bound to have phoned the airport by now – he won't get anywhere near fitting into Tom's clothes, will he, my little sparrow?'

'I'll try,' said Marion, 'but I expect she'll direct me to the nearest telephone box.'

In fact, directions of any kind would have been helpful at this moment, thought Marion grimly, as she found herself outside the flat in the long stone corridor, with not even a trail of breadcrumbs to guide her on the outward journey to the wicked witch. Eventually, pulling aside a hung tapestry, she discovered the stairs which led up to Pamela's quarters, and followed the sounds of merriment into the room where La Contessa was entertaining her guests. The room fell silent as she entered. Pamela held her in an unblinking glare.

'Good morning,' said Marion briskly, not about to be intimidated. If she could walk into the nest of vipers that was Form 5C on a Monday morning, she told herself, she could handle anything, even this. 'I think there's been some misunderstanding about our accommodation.'

'Really?' drawled Pamela. 'How tedious. And what is it, may one ask, that you have failed to understand?'

'We have paid for accommodation for three people and been given accommodation for two,' countered Marion crisply. 'So I think perhaps the failure of comprehension, if any, is yours. Can we have the key to the locked door of what I assume is the spare bedroom, please?'

Beatrice Miller-Mander played nervously with her napkin, guilt creeping out from under her exquisite maquillage and crawling across her face. This was all their fault. If only Terence could relax in her company at night, how much happier her life with him would be. What was it about her that prevented him from sleeping, she wondered for the hundredth time, for how could she fail to take it personally? Why couldn't he take comfort from her, as she took from him? Terence, unabashed, was gazing in admiration at Marion once more, remembering her from the airport. Indeed, such an effect had her old clothes had on him yesterday, that this morning he had shaved around the shape of his old moustache, and was willing it to grow.

'The door to which you allude is private,' said Pamela. 'There is a perfectly adequate couch in the living-room. I thought I'd made that plain. And now if you'll excuse me, I must attend to the needs of my guests.'

'We are your guests too,' said Marion, raising her voice to Pamela's insouciant back, 'and if you think I'm going to spend another night on that goddamned sofa you've got another think coming. We're paying a fortune for this bloody place and we're being ripped off. Now either you do something about it or—'

'Or?' drawled Pamela complacently. 'I'm sorry, are you threatening me? Frederick, how does the law stand on personal threats in one's own home?'

Frederick, blushing crimson, hated a fuss and was now compromised. 'I know nothing of Italian law,' he blustered. 'But I wonder, must it come to that? Perhaps some other equitable plan could be thought up, to everyone's satisfaction?'

'Good,' said Pamela, rising, 'then I'll leave it in your capable hands. You'll excuse me if I leave you. I have matters of importance to pursue. Christopher, would you help me please? I need a man's strength for what I have in mind.'

Christopher had no doubt about the kind of strength she was after and hoped this wasn't going to become a daily habit. For now, though, there was nothing for it but to follow dutifully at her heels. Anxious to make her escape from this embarrassing scene too, Beatrice in her innocence asked, 'Can I come with you? Is there anything that I can do to help?'

'What a sweet thought,' laughed Pamela, stroking the child-like downy cheek with one bony talon. 'But I really don't think so. Of course, if you have finished your breakfast . . .'

'Yes, yes,' cried Beatrice. 'Honestly, I'd like to help in any way I can!'

'Dear child. Then perhaps you would clear up and wash the plates. Come, Christopher.' And going before, Pamela's heels tapped him to his tasks.

'What a bitch!' said Marion. 'Sorry if she's a friend of yours, but really — Jesus!'

'Sit down and catch your breath,' invited Terence warmly. 'Bea darling, don't take the coffee, and bring us another cup for — sorry, I don't think I caught your name?'

'Marion Hardcastle,' said Marion shortly.

'Terence Armstrong,' said Terence, shaking her by the hand, 'and Frederick Mayer. Don't worry, he's in entertainment, doesn't know a damn thing about domestic litigation, do you old son?'

'I wonder how this can best be resolved?' mused Freddie. 'Is the sofa so very uncomfortable?'

'Put it this way, I'd be comfier on the floor.'

'And I suppose that solution is out of the question?' asked Freddie, half-hopefully.

'What, at five hundred quid for the week? Would *you*? I've got a good mind to sue her when we get back, and bugger the expense.'

'I don't think we should be over hasty,' said Freddie nervously. 'I'm sure we'll arrive at a solution if we're prepared to be calm and think this through.'

'I wonder, darling,' ventured Beatrice, returning with the cup, 'would it be possible do you think for us to do a swap?'

'No, love,' said Terence tetchily, unwilling to have their nocturnal life discussed. 'But what about Pamela giving up her workroom for the duration, Fred? Marion's right, it's only logical that that should be the other bedroom to the flat, it being right next door. I mean, what work is it that she does in there?'

'She has been working for a number of years on her father's biography,' Frederick replied.

'On commission?' asked Terence.

'No, on spec.'

'Oh well in *that* case,' said Terence, 'she can easily take a few weeks off.'

'I rather think she has been wanting to get it ready to coincide with the opening of your show,' protested her agent in these affairs. 'So I am not sure she will be persuaded.'

'Are you kidding, Freddie?' laughed Terence. 'She could write three biographies and a bodice ripper by the time this baby hits the West End stage. Let her have a holiday. And let Marion enjoy hers.' He smiled broadly at Marion and winked. 'Otherwise, tell her, Marion'll drag her through the English courts for being a Rackman-style landlady, and that won't endear her to potential investors. No investors, no show, and certainly no biography of dear Papa. Her future depends on this.'

Frederick got wearily to his feet. When he had dreamed as an undergraduate of being an agent and nurturing great talent, he had never suspected that it would mean quite so much nannying of great egos. 'I'll go and find her,' he said, 'and put your case as strongly as I can.'

'Bravo, Frederico!' cheered Terence, turning to Marion triumphant. 'You see, babe – stick with me and I'll give you jelly beans the size of diamonds. Us working class have got to stick together.' His old regional accent was getting thicker as he spoke.

Beatrice shifted uneasily in her seat. She had witnessed Terence's enthusiasms for women before, and it always ended in tears. She wouldn't mind, but the tears were always her own. She couldn't understand it. She was reckoned to be beautiful. She was certainly young. This woman was ancient – almost as old as Terence – and her neck was starting to go. It simply wasn't fair. And all this class stuff, it was so wearisome, so passé.

Marion had started to thaw a bit with the taste of the excellent coffee. She quite warmed to Terence – he was a lot like some of the lads she'd grown up with, and didn't seem to be too stuck up considering he must be a millionaire a few times over.

Beatrice seemed very different from her on-screen persona — much more nervous, and strangely lacking in self-confidence despite the fact that she was even more beautiful in the flesh. He probably led her quite a dance. Marion could see that her presence made Beatrice nervous and was sorry for her, but not too sorry to enjoy Terence's obvious admiration. It had been a long time since she had caused a frisson and she found herself feeling better by the minute.

'Do you think you can use your influence to get her to let me use the phone?' she asked him now. 'My friends have had a mix-up over their luggage and we need to sort it out.'

'Bloody hell, you are having a time of it aren't you?' chuckled Terence. 'Yeah sure, there's a phone over there, go right ahead.'

While Marion made her phone call, Terence watched her with admiration and Beatrice watched him. Her hand strayed to tickle the hairs on the back of his neck, to which he tried to respond without getting irritable.

'Have you shaved this morning?' she asked, peering proprie-torially close. 'Your upper lip's all stubbly.'

'Yes, thank you,' her lover retorted. 'Have you?'

Tears pricked behind her eyes. 'I'd better do the washing-up,' she said, gracefully withdrawing.

'Right,' said Terence, and turned his attention back to Marion. He couldn't stand it when Bea got insecure — she always moved in on him and made him feel claustrophobic. He closed his mind conveniently as to *why* she felt insecure in the first place, and luxuriated in blaming her entirely. Youth was all very well when it came to the figure and skin department, he thought, but there wasn't much depth to her in the personality and brain areas. Marion was speaking in Italian, which really turned him on. He bet she was a real goer, like some of the girls of his youth. In some ways she reminded him of his Aunty Ivy, for whom he'd always had a soft spot ever since she'd come to stay for a weekend when he was eight, and he'd seen her in her pink rayon petticoat when he'd taken in her tea. So vivid and erotic had it been, it had stayed in his fantasies for years, and even now could be a help when he was flagging. She'd pulled him to her to kiss his cheek and then given him a hug, his flushed face pressed between her ample breasts, perfumed with Devon Violets. He could almost smell them now.

'You parliamo very well,' he complimented Marion as she put down the phone. 'All sorted?'

'Not really. Apparently the guy did phone the airline, but he didn't leave a contact number so we can't call him. We've got his name and address — it was on the suitcase label — he's about an hour's drive away. I'd better go and tell Janice and Tom that we'll just have to chance it.'

'Let them go — it's their problem after all and you've done your bit,' suggested Terence. 'Spend the day with us. We're driving over to Perugia, aren't we Freddie, to see the Art?'

Frederick, who had just entered, was white faced and green about the gills. 'What? Oh, yes, by all means,' he said, and sat down heavily, looking for all the world as if he were about to cry.

'What's up, old chum?' asked Terence, always alert to the drama of a scene. 'Was Pamela tricky?'

'She-er, yes. Or rather — no,' Frederick replied enigmatically, his voice wavering. 'I didn't quite get the chance to put the case to her, she was — otherwise engaged.'

'She isn't shagging Chris already is she?' enquired Terence accurately. He was one of those people who always knew the plot of films and plays before it was five minutes in. 'Did you catch them in flagrante? Come on, give us the dirt — who was on top?'

'If you'll excuse me,' said Freddie, rising again unsteadily to his full height, 'I think I will spend the day resting. I appear to be feeling a little nauseous. Perhaps it was something that I ate. I will try to talk to Pamela later, Miss Er . . . and um . . .' His voice trailed off as he shuffled out of the room.

Terence turned back to Marion. 'Whoops! Didn't even think of that. Poor old Fred obviously had thoughts in that direction himself. Chris is such a tart, he's probably been leading him on. Sorry, am I shocking you? We're a bit laissez faire in the biz.'

'Not at all,' lied Marion, feeling very provincial indeed. 'I *do* come from the town that spawned Joe Orton, you know.'

'Leicester!' exclaimed Terence. 'I knew I knew the accent. Derby me. We're neighbours! So then, fellow Midlander, where shall we spend the day now there's just thee and me?'

'Not forgetting Beatrice,' corrected Marion.

'Oh Bea'll have a headache,' said Terence, 'I could see all the signs of one coming on at breakfast. She's a martyr to her migraines. Tell you what, you go and tell your chums where they've got to go for their suitcase, and I'll meet you out the front in half an hour. You'll be useful to me speaking the language – I don't know a word myself.'

'I'm afraid that that's the case with Janice and Tom too,' said Marion reluctantly. His energy was irresistible. She found to her annoyance that she was playing girlishly with a strand of her hair, and swept it behind her ear brusquely. 'They're pretty hopeless. I'll have to go with them to navigate and translate.' In a way she was glad of this excuse, needing to get some distance. Having been single for so long she was out of practice for so determined an advance, and she wanted to catch her breath and collect her thoughts, wanted to get back in control. She also needed to banish completely the images of her dream which kept inconveniently coming into her head, the powerful eroticism of which still hung about her in some way – visible, she felt sure, to the predatory Terence.

'Fine,' said Terence amicably, his fine neat teeth showing in a seductive grin, 'if you won't come with me on my adventure, I'll go with you on yours. That is if your friends won't mind?'

Chapter Five

Janice, predictably, was cock-a-hoop. 'Terry Armstrong, Marion? Blimey, you don't waste much time!'

'Don't be silly,' said Marion, caught out hurriedly applying her mascara in the tiny bathroom mirror. 'He's just bored and coming for the ride.'

'Oh yes, nudge nudge, wink wink – and what kind of ride is that?' Janice cackled coarsely, digging her in the ribs. 'I say Tom, you wouldn't be bored with Beatrice Thingy-Whatsit would you – *you* think she's gorgeous.'

Tom grunted self-consciously, not at his best. He had spilt his second cup of Nescafé down his only pair of trousers, and so the top half of his torso now rose out of the folds of Signor Sonelli's outsize corduroys, cinched at the waist by one of Janice's patent leather belts. He did not, needless to say, feel at his most sartorially elegant, and was as embarrassed as an adolescent that this had to be witnessed by such a cool dude as T. Armstrong, millionaire playboy and international jetsetter. Or indeed anybody, if truth be told. Catching sight of himself in the mirror, he was reminded of the knitted crinoline lady whose skirts hid the spare toilet roll in their bathroom at home. 'Have you seen what he's wearing, Marion?' Janice giggled unhelpfully. 'It was a toss up between Giant Haystack's trousers or my sarong.'

Marion was already getting used to squashing disloyal thoughts where the Cowlishaws were concerned and hated snobbishness of any kind, but at this moment, surveying her two companions — one drowning in a sea of corduroy and the other overflowing out of floral polyester — she could have wished them, if not dead, then poorly on the sofa and unable to come out to play.

'Right then,' ventured Tom, already anxious about tackling foreign roads again, 'we'd best be off.'

Terence found them fighting to get into the tiny hired Fiat in the drive. For some reason the front passenger seat would not fold down, and Tom was trying to persuade Marion to crawl over it to sit down in the back. Refusing point blank, Marion was now tussling with him for possession of the keys.

'If it's so bloody easy you do it,' she shouted. 'Give me the sodding keys, I'll drive!'

'No, I have to drive it, it's only insured for me,' Tom countered, infuriatingly holding the keys too high for her to reach.

'That's outrageous, I paid half!'

They froze mid-scuffle as the red convertible Mercedes purred softly to their side.

'Ready for the off?' asked Terence. 'Shall we all go in mine?'

Janice needed no persuading, vaulting straight over the rear wing and bouncing up and down on the leather upholstery, demanding the stereo and joking about the drinks cabinet. But Tom sulked and stood his ground.

'It's a waste of the hire charge, not using the Fiat,' he said stiffly, 'and anyway, it'll be cramped in there with two of you in the back.'

'I'll be fine, thank you,' replied Marion, getting in the front passenger seat and fastening her belt.

'Come on, Tommy,' said Janice coquettishly, 'there's plenty of room for your little bum — even in those daft trousers.'

Outnumbered, Tom transferred Signor Sonelli's suitcase to the boot of the Merc, and fearing for his back for the second time that morning, reluctantly attempted to fold himself in three to join his wife in the back seat.

'Actually, you're right you know,' said Terence, turning round and viewing them just when Tom was at his most embarrassingly contorted. 'It's ridiculously small back there – I don't know why they pretend it's a four seater and put a seat in at all. Do you want to drive yours, and we'll go in convoy?'

'Oh he'll be all right, Terry, he's in now.' Janice was determined not to miss out on this part of the adventure. She smiled cheerily at the glowering Tom as she wedged bits of his flesh painfully in around hers. Looking up at the Palazzo she saw Beatrice, white-faced, struggling to open an upper window. 'Is that your friend Beattie, Tez? Do you think she wants to come?'

'No, no,' replied Terence without looking, and his foot pressed hard on the accelerator, spraying gravel far and wide.

Beatrice, left behind, was filled with doom. She felt like a fairy-tale princess locked up in her tower, with no one to let down her hair for.

As the car cleaved through the countryside and she started to relax, Marion felt young again. The wind was cool against her face, and music surrounded them from the swanky stereo. It felt exciting, like being in a road movie. She hadn't been in an open-topped car since the Spitfires and Midgets of the boys from her youth. She navigated as seamlessly as Terence drove, an unspoken frisson between them, his hand – accidentally? – brushing once against her thigh as he changed to high gear. It was as close as perfection came without an ejector button for the back seat. Janice, singing along lustily, now heaved herself forward and jammed the upper part of her body between their seats.

'This is from one of your shows, isn't it Tel?' she screamed into the wind.

'Yes,' replied Terence, his eyes crinkling a smile at her in his rearview mirror. 'Have you seen it?'

'Not live,' shouted Janice. 'We've seen clips on the telly on the *Royal Variety Show*, haven't we Tom? We're waiting till they bring it to the Haymarket at Leicester. They sometimes give us nurses tickets. Too dear to see it in London. Thirty quid!'

'Not if you know the director,' quipped Terence. 'You must come as my guests. Do *you* get down to London much, Marion?'

'From time to time,' Marion responded. Naturally enough, since London had been the scene of the crime that had destroyed her life, she avoided it as much as possible. To keep herself in the present she consulted the map, and not a moment too soon. 'We need to turn right here.' Braking, Terence turned as he was told, tyres squealing.

'Ooh, we'd love that, wouldn't we Tom?' asked Janice. She had disappeared momentarily into the back as the car took the bend, and now clawed her way forward again. 'You're from the Midlands, aren't you Terry? I read it in *Hello!*'

'Belper. My old Mum's still there.'

'Belper! You'll have to drop in on us when you visit her next! It's not that far! You could stay over and make a night of it – Marion's got plenty of room in her house now she's on her own, haven't you, Maz?' Oblivious to eyes narrowed dangerously, Janice thundered on, 'You probably get bored with hotels, Terry, travelling round all the time. A bit impersonal aren't they, and having to be in the breakfast room by a certain time? That's why we prefer the freedom of apartment living when we go away. Do you miss Belper, Terry? But I bet your Mum must be proud. I saw the pictures of your place – in Hampshire, isn't it? Fantastic. Palatial. That swimming pool! But it's not as good as Derby, is it, the Home Counties? There's nothing to match the grandeur of the Peaks.'

'That's right,' said Terence easily. He seemed genuinely charmed and gently amused by her.

Marion, however, was having fantasies about killing her, and was mentally selecting a garotte. She saw in her mind's eye her hands pulling cheese wire tight and Janice's head rolling neatly off. Still talking, of course. She must remember to punch her in the teeth first . . . Good God, she thought suddenly, is it hormones? My interior life is getting dangerously vivid.

'As a matter of fact, I'm going to be spending more time up there this year, directing a film,' Terence continued, sneaking a look at Marion for her reaction and hoping he was not mistaken by the fire in her eyes. Unnecessarily he changed gear again, the hairs on the back of his hand grazing her knee. A trickle of desire ran up the inside of her thigh, pulling her thoughts from homicide to puzzlement. What did he want with her when he had the lovely Beatrice Miller-Mander to warm his bed, she wondered?

She pulled down the sun visor to protect her eyes from the glare, and caught sight of herself in the vanity mirror. Too cruel, too cruel, her face creased up against the bright sun, the wind making her hair stand on end like a lunatic or a clown. Who was she kidding? He was playing with her. It wasn't personal – it was a reflex he had to any available woman. He was a knee-jerk Lothario. Over-privileged git, she thought, angrily. It's not as if he's an oil painting himself. If he wasn't Terence Armstrong he'd be just another middle-aged man with thinning hair and a paunch. Thinks he can have anything. Well not me. She jerked her own knee away from him crossly, under cover of rustling the map and examining it minutely.

'Nearly there,' she said, shortly.

'No, we're not,' thought Terence, and censured himself inwardly for his boorishness. He'd become too used to the quick and eager responses of sycophantic actresses. This one was going to take more subtle manoeuvring. Marion is a lady, he heard himself thinking, with some surprise.

'Do you hear that, Tom Tom?' asked Janice, falling back to join her husband. 'Nearly there, and then we can have you out of this big baggy corduroy nappy and into your cute little shorts!'

Tom shifted uneasily inside the folds of hot fabric, not least because his wife's hand was currently engaged in assessing exactly how full said nappy was. 'Stop it!' he hissed from the corner of his mouth, his eyes not moving from the road ahead.

Janice chuckled and snuggled against him, chubbing his arm. 'You wouldn't like it if I did,' she said happily. Sometimes Tom wondered if that were true.

For a while they motored on in silence, listening to the maudlin lyrics of a song about unrequited love and thwarted passion. The shame of Marion's dream floated back to her, her infidelity to the memory of her deceased beloved filling her with misery. Terence, sensing that the party was now no longer going with a swing, suddenly and unexpectedly stopped the car outside a taverna.

'I need to buy some cigarettes,' he announced, turning in his seat to Janice for support. 'Shall we stretch our legs and have a drink?'

Before Tom could warm to his subject of not wanting to be late, Marion shook off the dark mantle of her incipient despond, and threw open her door.

'Great idea,' she said, and strode with purpose to the pretty outside tables, where she sat down. Tom, muttering about alcoholism this early in the morning, disentangled his long limbs from his wife's plump curves and followed reluctantly, rearranging Signor Sonelli's short wide trousers as best he could.

Terence decided on Campari sodas all round, which Marion ordered while he admired.

'This is nice,' approved Janice, taking in the houses of the small village, the terracotta pots of flowers, the vines trailing over their heads. 'Pity you didn't bring your painting things, Marion, you could have done a picture while we're here!'

Terence was interested, and leaned forward to enquire, 'You're an artist, then?'

Marion demurred. 'No no, not for years. I dabble, nothing much. Now I teach.'

'Italian?'

'No, Art.'

'So how come your Italian is so good?'

56

A slight hesitation, a mental sifting-through of versions of the truth. 'I lived here once, for a short time, travelling, studying – you know.' The waiter brought the drinks just then, and spared her further enquiry for a while.

'Ah,' said Terence appreciatively, 'Italy in a bottle. You're right about the Peaks, Janice, but sipping a pale ale just wouldn't be the same. A toast! To Italy and sunny days, and to the tastes and colours thereof.'

Tom, sipping his Campari suspiciously, wrinkling his nose, was reminded of nothing more or less than the tastes and colours of childhood medicine, but the others – his wife included, he noted, with a sense of resentful betrayal – quaffed theirs to the last lip-licking drop, their mood improving visibly as they drank. Tom, as it happened, was a pale ale man. For him, quite simply, the phrase 'When in Rome . . .' was completed with '. . . do as you would in Leicester.' After all, hadn't the Romans bequeathed to them the wise city motto 'Semper Eadem' – Always the Same? Why torment your digestion with change?

Terence, adept as he was at sniffing out what his audiences wanted so that their prejudices might be kept intact (how else had he become so successful?) was now regaling them with theatre stories, duly tailored to disparage the jumped-up upstarts who pranced about on stage and thought the world owed them a living. At other tables he would tell these same tales with quite a different spin, but here, in the company of Middle England, and with Marion to impress, he talked with accent ever thickening of 'wankers' and 'toss pots', of posturing artistic egos spoilt and vain.

'They can't all be like that though,' protested Janice, star struck reader of *Hello!*, 'otherwise you wouldn't be with Bea.'

'I'm not *with* Bea, exactly,' said Terence, unruffled, aware of Marion's intent gaze. 'And you're right, she is a very sweet girl.'

'Don't tell me – you're just good friends!' roared Janice, walloping the table amid lusty guffaws. 'Isn't that what they say?'

'In a nutshell,' grinned Terence. He hadn't spent time with his fellows from his native land for what seemed like a lifetime, and a sentimental affection for this kind of coarse ribaldry (which in reality, he had hated and wished to escape) was stealing over him deluding him that he was presently in his rightful camp.

Marion, for her part, had given herself a good talking to as they had waited for the drinks. She was determined not to let the dream unsettle her and sweep her back to the tragedy of the past. She had finally, painfully, decided to put herself back on the road to recovery, and here was adventure staring her in the face. What did it matter that Terence was more than likely exactly like the toss pots and wankers he was affecting to disparage? Or that he had a beautiful and famous girlfriend practically half her age. Enjoy the moment! Live in the present! The future, as she knew, was dangerously unreliable, and the past was a carnage-strewn minefield. There was only this, and this was beyond imagining. A red convertible Mercedes, the warm Italian sun, a Campari, and Terence Superstar Armstrong smiling at her and — surely she wasn't mistaken? — caressing her ankle with his own. She should bloody cocoa! She relaxed into her seat and felt her skin breathe for the first time in years.

Back at Palazzo Fratorelli, Terence's Good Friend had finally succumbed to the migraine of which he had presciently foretold. She lay in the darkness of her room, the shutters pulled against the bright sunlight, a damp washcloth growing warmer on her brow. Unable to find anybody to talk to after Terence's departure, there had seemed nothing else to do other than to give in to the tightening band of pressure round her head. She had wept for a while, then stopped, reminding herself how ugly she looked with puffy eyes and bloated nose. Such was her lack of self-confidence that, without her beauty (in which she didn't personally believe but which seemed to fool most of the critics most of the time) she knew that there was no good reason why she should be loved. These gloomy thoughts were presently interrupted by a small knock at her door, which Christopher swiftly followed with his presence.

'My God!' he said, dramatically leaning back against the door, then locking it. 'I'm shagged. I've been picked to entertain the Queen. Command performances at every turn. Fancy a line?'

'I've got a migraine.'

'Taken some Nurofen?'

'Yes.'

'They'll kick in soon then. Have a line while you wait. Mind if I open the shutters a bit? Can't see a thing. Got a mirror?'

Beatrice struggled up on to her elbows, her eyes crinkling painfully against the glare. 'In my make-up bag, in the bathroom.' When Christopher wanted attention there was no resisting him, and perhaps he would cheer her up. They had between them the camaraderie of fellow actors, and, of course, their old affair.

'Where's Terence?' he called from the bathroom, clattering and scattering things in his search. 'Where did you say the bloody thing was? Ah, here!' he smiled as he emerged.

'He's gone out with the other guests,' said Beatrice, watching her ex-lover chop cocaine with his American Express card. She was starting to feel better already.

'What other guests? Oh, the Normals? My God! What on earth for?' He hoovered up his line efficiently, pinching his nostrils one after the other, the deeper to inhale.

'I'm not sure. Something about a missing suitcase. We were going to go to Perugia, but—'

'Here you are darling, get that up your nose,' Christopher interrupted, passing her a rolled up fifty-thousand lire note and the mirror. 'It's really nice stuff. Wonder if the old bag's got some champagne kicking about. Mind you, I don't know if I dare to and look. She's a fucking nympho.'

'Poor you,' said Beatrice ironically, but not without affection. Pausing between snorts she waved towards the kitchen. 'We've got some champagne in the fridge, I think. Can you get me some more Nurofen while you're there — they're somewhere on the side. Mm, this *is* nice. My teeth have gone all dead.'

'Yes, and without the inconvenience of root canal surgery.'

They giggled, eyes bright, feeling at the peak of their powers.

'Oh, this is better,' sighed Beatrice. 'You are clever, Chris. Weren't you worried, going through Customs?'

'No,' said Christopher returning and popping the champagne. 'To tell you the truth I palmed it into Freddie's pocket at Heathrow, and then hoicked it out again when we got here.'

'You didn't!'

'Why not? He was none the wiser. And nobody would frisk Freddie — let's face it, he doesn't look interesting enough to harbour vice.'

Beatrice laughed and clapped her hands. 'You're *outrageous!*'

'And you love it,' smiled Christopher, idly stroking the smooth skin of her leg. Mm, happy memories. She really was lovely. A curse on Terence Armstrong for taking her away. Still — nothing ventured, nothing gained . . . 'Shall I give you a massage? Would that help the head?'

'Oh heaven,' sighed Beatrice. She took off her top unselfconsciously and lay on her front. 'But can you be bothered? You aren't too tired out?'

'Too tired for you, darling? Never.' Christopher ran his hands over the soft underdeveloped muscles of her back and neck. 'Is that nice?'

'Wonderful.'

'Good. You're so wise not to go in for all this body-building gym stuff that seems to be de rigueur for you girls these days. So lovely and soft. I think a little bit of massage, another little toot, and then . . . Do you think Terence will be gone for long?'

At around that same moment in the trattoria, Terence noticed with satisfaction that he seemed to be winning back lost ground with Marion, and interrupting himself in the middle of another crowd pleasing story, he pointed to the empty glasses (all but Tom's) and said, 'Another? How do you say "same again" in Italian, Marion?' But as 'Ancora, per favore,' came rolling off her tongue, Tom huffed and puffed and stood up, tugging at the swell of trousers around his hips. 'You can have mine if you like,' he said ungraciously, 'I think we'd best be getting on.'

Seamlessly Terence rose himself and went inside to pay, amicably waving aside their offers to contribute. Marion frowned horribly at Tom and said, 'Yes, best not enjoy ourselves. Good God, anybody would think we're on holiday!' Never taking her eyes from his averted face, she knocked back his drink in one and stood. 'Okay with you if I buy some fags?' she asked aggressively, and stomped off indoors, after Terence.

'Did you go this morning?' Janice asked, after they had gone.

'What?'

'You know how you get if you miss a day.'

'There is nothing wrong with my bowels, Janice,' Tom growled, red-faced, sphincter clenched. 'Just leave it alone, will you? We decided we'd be somewhere at a certain time, so we've got no place to be lolling about round here.'

Janice decided not to pursue it, but made a mental note to cook the baked beans for their tea. He probably just needed roughage. 'I hope they won't both be smoking in the car,' he said grumpily as he heaved himself unhappily back in. 'The wind'll be flicking ash all over us. We could catch on fire.'

Conflagration was the least that Marion was wishing them as, still standing by the vending machine, she tore the cellophane from her new packet and accepted Terence's light. 'Jesus,' she exhaled, on smoking breath, 'a week of this!'

Terence chuckled. 'He'll be all right when he's wearing his own keks,' he said, relishing the vernacular of his youth. 'How do you know them?'

'Tom and I teach at the same school,' said Marion, 'but I don't know them really. I said yes on a whim, and regretted it straight after. It's been a nightmare ever since we left.'

'Yes, it's funny how just sharing the same profession doesn't necessarily mean one has much in common with one's peers,' said Terence, and let the thought hang there, pregnant with possibility. 'Well,' he continued lightly, breaking the spell, 'we shall have to find some ways of making it better for you.' He smiled. 'I shall kidnap you regularly and take you away.'

Marion smiled back at him. The Campari had had a softening effect. 'I don't know what your friends'll think of that,' she said, thinking more of Pamela than of Beatrice.

'Then we'll have to kidnap each other,' he rejoined, conspiratorially. The air crackled between them, their look lasting just a little too long. Don't milk it, he told himself firmly, in much the same manner as he gave his actors notes after opening night. He took her arm companionably. 'Come on, we'll sort out his suitcase, dump them back at Pamela's, and whizz over to Perugia. It shouldn't take long.'

Oh famous last words.

Chapter Six

Standing on the doorstep of Casa Sonelli, Tom felt anxious about coming face to face with the owner of the trousers he was wearing, and whose prior consent he had been unable to obtain. He made little throat-clearing noises as he waited for the doorbell to be answered, practising a speech which he would get Marion to translate, about how he insisted on paying for them to be dry cleaned, even though he had only been wearing them for a couple of hours and hadn't been anywhere dirty at all. Or, if Mr Sonelli preferred, and if he would allow him to change into a pair of his own trousers now, he would take them himself immediately to the dry cleaners, if Mr Sonelli could tell them where the nearest one might be. Then again, if there wasn't one in the immediate vicinity, would it be possible for Tom to take them away now and return them later? Or tomorrow? Or if there was no same-day service in Italy would it be all right if he brought them back in a couple of days? Damn, no, that would mean keeping the Fiat a day longer to drive them back. Okay then, would it be all right if he returned them by post? Or would they handwash perhaps? Because if they were guaranteed shrink-proof, he could . . . no, no, his wife Janice, Signora Cowlishaw, who was a state registered nurse, could have them hand laundered in a jiff, either here, now, or . . .

'Well, they're obviously not in,' said Marion at his side,

stepping back from the house and gazing up at the windows. 'We'd better leave a note.'

'Or maybe the doorbell doesn't work,' said Tom desperately, unable to conceive of leaving his suitcase behind, so near and yet so far. But Marion was already walking back towards the car in search of pen and paper. The thought of using Janice's tiny Ladyshave again on the coarse stubble on his chin, or not having clean socks, suddenly emboldened him to rain a tumult of blows against the solid front door. Nursing his fist, he let out a soft groan of pain, and was surprised to hear it in stereo. Surely . . .? He cocked his head to listen, and pressed his ear against the door. There it was again!

'Somebody's inside! I think they're hurt!' Tom called back to the car. He banged loudly on the door again and shouted, 'Hello! Hello? Can you hear me?'

This time, his enquiry was met unequivocally by a woman's full-throated scream from upstairs. The others were at his side in an instant as Tom started to shoulder-ram the door. Inside, the groans and the screams swelled in volume.

'Try round the back!' shouted Nurse Cowlishaw, running off in that direction.

'Break a window!' shouted Terence, looking round impractically for a stage manager to oblige.

'Try the bloody door!' said Marion sensibly, elbowing Tom aside. She turned the handle and it opened, and the four of them swarmed inside.

At the bottom of the stairs the living template for Tom's temporary trousers was lying like a beached whale, a piece of broken banister at his side. Blood ran from a wound on his forehead and words streamed from his mouth, competing with the urgent female screams coming from upstairs.

'Pretty superficial I think, but he'll need a couple of stitches,' Janice diagnosed, dodging Signor Sonelli's waving arms as she knelt to examine him. 'There there, calm down, we're here now. Ask him if he's been unconscious, Marion. Is he talking any sense?'

'Plenty,' said Marion. 'You'd better get upstairs. His wife's giving birth – he was on his way to phone when he tripped.'

'Bloody Nora,' grinned Janice, in her element, 'it never rains but it pours. Here Tom, get your clean hanky and press it on his wound, it'll stop the bleeding.' She started up the stairs, calling back orders, 'Tell him to stay still and then call an ambulance, Marion – don't let him move, I haven't had time to check him for breaks. Then follow me. Terence, find the kitchen and boil water, buckets of it. And Tom,' she turned at the top of the stairs and looked down at her ashen-faced husband, 'don't look at the blood. If you feel faint put your head between your knees like I showed you.' Filled with purpose, she pursued the screams, calling, 'All right, love, I'm coming, Janice is here!'

By the time Terence was taking the first two saucepans of water to the delivery room, Tom had not only regained his colour but was puce, trying to restrain the huge bulk of Signor Sonelli from struggling to his feet. 'No, no, you lie here,' he was shouting. 'No go wife, your head caput, maybe neck broke!'

'Or maybe he'll break yours,' warned Terence, juggling his cargo of boiling hot water as he shimmied round them. 'Mind your heads boys!' He was enjoying himself hugely, and making mental notes for future productions. And he'd always wanted to know what exactly was done with all the boiled water and torn sheets that were shouted for in old movies.

Seconds later, he knew why they always cut from the shouted request to some time later, when the baby was clean and dry and at its mother's breast. God, it was like Peckinpah in there. He scurried back down to the safety of the kitchen to get more supplies, now as ashen faced as Tom had been earlier.

Marion, having roused herself from her immediate shock, had completed her duties as instructed and was now taking the head end in the complicated procedure of birth. Her student Italian was sorely pressed when it came to gynaecological terms, but Signora Sonelli had evidently been through this before, and was pushing and panting obediently to Janice's English commands. Watching her brave struggle, Marion was filled with envy. Why couldn't this have been her? How old would her son have been now if he had lived? Old enough to be taking drugs, stealing cars, still living at home, and expecting her to do his laundry, she told herself firmly. She mopped the Signora's brow with something now approaching pity.

'Here it comes!' Janice announced gleefully, and Signora Sonelli nodded and grunted and tightened her hold of Marion's hand. 'One more big push, and yes! and another one! Good, and pant pant pant pant and one more push and yes – good girl! Here we are! Here it is! All over! All done!'

Signor Sonelli, finally shaking Tom off, thundered through the door at the same moment as his daughter hurtled from his wife's womb into Janice's capable hands. 'It's a girl!' she said. 'Hang about a bit, let me get her cleaned up and breathing before you go giving her a hug!'

Already unsteady on his pins, the proud father now sank to his knees in a hail of Mary's and a canon of saints, clasping his wife's head to his massive chest.

'Terence!' bawled Janice, 'More water! Where've you got to?!'

Tom, who had finally and reluctantly helped Signor Sonelli up the stairs, had hung back behind the safety of the door, and now called through, 'I'll go and help him, won't be a tick,' relieved to have something else to do.

'Here you are, Mum, here's your baby,' said Janice, handing the small bundle to Signora Sonelli's hungry arms. 'Now we're not all done yet, Dad, so give Mum some space, let her have some air.'

Marion had relinquished her position to Signor Sonelli, and watched through misted eyes as the middle-aged couple embraced each other and the tiny miracle between them. And it was a miracle. Surely these new parents were fifty if they were a day? Eyes shining, unable to stop grinning, she watched as Janice busied herself at the centre of the universe, tidying up, assessing the damage. 'That's good. Well done, Mum – who's been using her olive oil, then? Your perineum's perfect! You won't need a single stitch!' She seemed so capable, so strong, the giver of life.

Whatever this infuriating woman ever did in the future, however annoying, Marion vowed, she would always remember her now, doing this. And she would forgive her anything. At this moment, in something almost akin to religious awe, she loved her beyond words. She felt her heart swell in her breast. Not normally a demonstrative woman, she was unable to resist her impulse to go to Janice and take her in her arms and hug the breath out of her. Janice grinned broadly, hugging her back. 'Isn't it great? There's nothing like it in all the world, is there?' Marion nodded back dumbly, unable to laugh or cry.

Outside, there was a flurry of footsteps on the stairs, and Tom and Terence bounced in, triumphant heroes, carrying between them fresh supplies of boiling water and plenty of it. And at that same moment, with one last cry and another small push, Signora Sonelli delivered her placenta onto the bed, fresh and quivering, like a jellyfish washed to shore on an ebb tide of blood.

Which is why, when the ambulance finally arrived, and Marion translated Nurse Cowlishaw's debrief to the puzzled paramedics, they had one senile gravida, mother and baby doing well; one possible concussion, X-ray recommended; and two cases of very nasty scalded legs.

So much for the mutual kidnapping malarkey, thought Marion wryly, as she waited later in Casualty. Perugia and passion, it seemed, would have to go on hold.

There had been no holding passion at Palazzo Fratorelli, however, except perhaps Frederick's, and even he was currently holding his own, in the privacy of his darkened room, to comfort himself. He felt utterly betrayed by Christopher, although his reason knew that to be ridiculous. Ever since prep school he had always fallen for boys who were way out of his league. And if he really thought about it, would he want what Christopher had to offer? When he conjured up his idyll, the two of them together in a punt dressed in cream flannels and striped blazers and straw boaters, dreamily floating down the Cam, Freddie reclining on cushions, looking up at Chris's sensitive hands as he dipped the great pole in and out of the gentle waters, listening attentively, reflectively, a little sadly perhaps, to Freddie reciting Keats . . . No, absurd. Out of the question. Even if he were interested in Freddie (which Freddie doubted) Chris just wasn't the type to go in for the exquisite agony of passion restrained – it would be full-blooded consummation or nothing. Better the fantasy by far.

Pamela, less romantic than her agent, revivified by her second sampling of Christopher, had gone straight from her bed to her office – the first time in weeks, months, possibly – and had had a satisfactory few hours sifting through papers for her father's biography. Restless after so much sitting, but feeling virtuous for having worked, she was now striding around her sylvan empire, a spring in her step, a gleam in her eye, pressing small olives between finger and thumb and complimenting them on their growth. For surely they were larger, plumper, altogether more full of themselves, than they had been yesterday? Or perhaps that was just her.

She allowed herself a smile. The strange thing about having more was that it made one feel like having . . . well, more. She would call on Christopher again tonight. She suddenly remembered Patrick, the American summer student with whom she had been having an affair. Oh well, she'd told him she was having house guests, had warned him she'd be busy. He was sweet and very pretty, and she didn't want to lose him altogether, but he'd still be there when Christopher had gone back to England, and after all, Christopher was a film star and the very devil in bed.

Beatrice, the while, was musing on the miracle of his healing powers, since her migraine had now disappeared as completely as if it had never been. At this very moment he was sleeping naked as a baby, his head in her lap. She felt relaxed and grateful and contented at last, but underneath this was a deep layer of sadness that it had not been Terence who had brought about this restoration of her spirits, this lancing of her boil. What could she do to make him want her? Make him jealous? Tell him about Chris? Start wearing 60s retro like that bitch he had gone off with?

Chapter Seven

The bitch in question had cheered up considerably since her two-hour wait in Casualty. Terence and Tom had been more shocked than damaged and had been allowed to go home, but changing gear chafed Terence's scalded legs, and so Marion was driving the Merc. She loved it. She threw it around corners, marvelling at its power compared to her elderly Fiesta back home. She could definitely get used to this. In the passenger seat at her side, Terence looked at her and grinned. She was utterly magnificent, in charge — almost, he might say, ecstatic, her hair blowing in the wind. Reminded of the phrase, he burst spontaneously into Dylan's old protest song, and was joined with enthusiasm by Janice, who was cuddling Tom carefully in the back.

'They don't write songs like that any more, Tez,' shouted Janice, making Tom wince. He was still not over his shock.

'Life seemed so much simpler then,' agreed Terence. He looked again at Marion's determined profile. Yes'n how many times *could* a man turn his head, and pretend he just couldn't see? What had he ever seen in Beatrice, or her predecessor, or her predecessor's predecessor come to that? For here was Woman, double U, O, M A N, he'd say it again . . . Instead he sang it aloud, at full volume, and to his joy, Marion joined in lustily, a strange deep dry sound as if she had only just discovered her voice. He hoped that this discovery was in some small way attributable to him.

They were nearing the Palazzo and all of them (except Tom, who was looking forward to getting into the interesting piece of old wood-carving with some milky coffee and an aspirin, and was wondering if he could fashion a cage out of wire coathangers to keep the covers off his sore legs) felt regretful that the adventurous day was coming to an end. The sun was gliding closer to the earth by the minute, turning trees and buildings to pink and gold, and Marion, to her surprise, suddenly longed to paint it. In her mind's eye she was squeezing oils on to her palette, and eagerly mixing them with her knife.

'Let's all go out tonight,' Terence suggested suddenly, appealing directly to her. 'We'll go to a restaurant, al fresco, and wine and dine in style. My treat.'

'Great,' said Marion, and just for the hell of it, pushed her foot down as they drove through the great gates of the Palazzo, spraying gravel as she turned the car and brought it to a halt outside the door with a satisfying hoick of the handbrake.

Beatrice had been caught napping – or almost, she thought frantically, as the sounds below pulled her from her doze.

'Quickly!' she admonished Christopher, who was still sleeping, naked, in her lap. 'Get dressed. Get out of here. He's back!'

Christopher dressed laconically, impervious to her sense of urgency as she flung herself into clothes and bed-making at one and the same time, and was still buttoning his shirt as she pushed him in front of her and out of her door. She stole a quick glance out of the window to look down on to the drive, and saw Marion getting out of the driving seat of the Merc. The bitch! she thought, furiously. Terence never let *her* drive. This was getting serious. She debated for a moment whether to get back petulantly into bed, and to revive her illness to punish him, but then she saw with what difficulty Terence was negotiating himself out of the passenger seat and heard him grunt with pain as he made a low progress to the front door. He was hurt! On wings of guilt, he flew down the stone stairs to greet him.

Turning the last corner and coming down the last flight, she saw that he was smiling and leaning on Marion's arm, a smile that quickly faded at the noise of her approach. 'Darling!' she cried. 'Whatever's happened?' And in her eagerness to claim him, she jumped down the last three steps landing clumsily on the foot which had received the worst of the scalding and, pressing herself proprietorially into his unwilling embrace, crushed his throbbing thighs to hers.

'For Christ's sake, Bea, don't touch me!!' he growled through gritted teeth, and pushed her roughly away, ascending the stairs gingerly while she hung back, pink with embarrassment, her mouth flapping open and shut like a drowning fish.

Marion was embarrassed for her, and much as they appeared to be becoming rivals, counted this hurtful rudeness as a black mark against Terence. 'He's scalded his legs,' she said to Beatrice by way of explanation. 'We've had a bit of an eventful day,' she added, as Tom shuffled past them, similarly incapacitated, followed by Janice, gamely hulking their newly rescued suitcase in his wake.

'Gin all round!' prescribed Nurse Cowlishaw cheerfully as she struggled to drag the case up the stairs. 'We deserve it. Your place or ours, Tel?'

'Pamela's drawing-room and champagne!' he called back down the stairs. 'We're celebrating birth and death and nothing less will do. We've got a bottle in our room, I'll fetch it on the way.'

'Death?' asked Beatrice tremulously, her pink cheeks turning pale, for how would she explain that she had drained the last drop of the fizz while she herself was supposed to have been lying at death's door?

'He's exaggerating. Near death, I suppose he means. Potential death if we hadn't arrived in time?' offered Marion.

'From a bump on the head?' said Janice, laughing. 'Dramatical licence, Bea. He wouldn't last a day on my ward – he'd

73

be having the vapours every five minutes if he thinks that was a close call.'

They had reached the door to their flat where Janice followed Tom in, and as Beatrice and Marion carried on up the stairs they could hear her saying, 'Don't get into bed yet, Tommy, come and have some champagne!'

The next flight brought them to the open door of Terence and Beatrice's accommodation, where Beatrice paused for a moment and looked fearfully in at Terence, who was now staring into the empty fridge.

'No champagne, Bea?' he asked, in an icy voice.

'I . . . no,' Beatrice faltered, blushing, her lips forming the words clumsily. 'Christopher dropped by. He wanted some, so . . .'

'So,' said Terence, smiling strangely. 'Good for Christopher.'

'I thought we wouldn't mind?' Bea stammered, and looked, mused Marion, for all the world like a guilty child.

'Of course we don't. I hope that he enjoyed it as much as I might have done myself,' rejoined Terence, looking more amused and enlivened than he had since their return. 'You two go on up to Pamela's and see if you can scrounge another bottle from her. I'll just change out of these awful damp trousers and join you in a moment.'

Beatrice hovered in the doorway, reluctant to leave. 'Don't you want help?' she asked. 'I could find your trousers for you, and help you off with these.'

'I should imagine you've had more than enough of that for one day,' Terence smiled. 'Helping, I mean,' he added, to her tremulous, frightened look. 'Hasn't Pamela run you ragged with her chores?' Beatrice blushed again, uncertain what to say. 'No, no,' he continued, 'you take Marion up and get her a drink. She has been a heroine, up to the elbows in blood and guts, and is at least as deserving as Christopher, of our' — an almost imperceptible but nevertheless theatrical pause — 'open-handed hospitality.'

There was nothing for Beatrice to do but to drag herself away, and Marion, going with her, tried to puzzle out the secret code implicit in the irony of Terence's tone. Was she to assume that Beatrice had slept with Christopher in their absence, or was she reading too much into it? Perhaps jealousy fuelled Terence's rude and offhand treatment of this beautiful young woman, and would explain his flirtatiousness with middle-aged Marion herself? Or did they have an arrangement, an open relationship where liaisons were allowed? Certainly he had seemed more amused than enraged.

Each lost in her own thoughts, they proceeded in silence to Pamela's empty room, where Beatrice at last turned and smiled, collecting herself and rearranging her features into those of gracious hostess – or rather, thought Marion, eldest daughter, trying to amuse the guest until Mama returned, and said, 'Do sit down. I'll have a peep in the kitchen and see what I can find, and then you must tell me of your adventures.'

Left to himself, Terence pulled back the covers of Beatrice's hastily made bed, and bent to smell fresh sex on the sheets. He smiled grimly as he observed the empty champagne bottle by his foot, which had been kicked under the counterpane. His cup ranneth over on entering the bathroom, where he saw the small packet of cocaine spilling out on to the vanity unit next to Christopher's credit card and the fifty-thousand lire note. He helped himself to a noseful, sniffing deeply and with pleasure, and pocketed the rest. Beatrice had given him the perfect excuse for his intended pursuit of Marion, and Christopher had thoughtfully provided the icing on his cake. It would amuse him to return the credit card and money, but he would keep the cocaine in lieu. You had to admire the guy, shagging Pamela and Beatrice both in one day while dangling Freddie on a string, and not even bothering to cover his tracks.

Marion, examining the paintings in Pamela's drawing-room, heard Janice halloo-ing down the corridor as she tried to find her way, and called back to her so that she could follow her voice. As Janice entered one end of the room, exclaiming at its grandeur, Beatrice emerged from the kitchen with empty hands.

'I can't find Pamela,' she said, by way of explanation. 'There are some bottles, but I shouldn't like to take anything too special, and I'm afraid I'm hopeless at wines. Perhaps you'd like some coffee while we wait for her return?'

'No bother, Bea,' said Janice, 'I'll go and get our gin. Tom's gone mardy,' she added, to explain his absence to Marion. 'He's hopeless when he's in pain. I doubt we'll be able to come out with you to eat – he's curled up like a grumpy little foetus on the bed. Ay,' she said, turning to Beatrice again, 'did you manage to sort out with Pam about Marion's bedroom?'

'I think Freddie was going to speak to her, but I'm afraid I don't know if he did. I haven't been well myself today, so I stayed pretty much in my room.'

'But better now?' asked Terence, as he bounded through the door.

'Yes, thank you,' Bea replied uncertainly. Why this sudden change of mood, and no apparent trace of his former pain?

'You seem a lot better in yourself,' said Janice.

'Yes, a miracle,' he proclaimed, and looking directly at Beatrice, he sniffed loudly and smiled. 'I found something to take in Bea's bathroom, and now feel no pain.' Marion saw a startled look cross Beatrice's face, and looked back at Terence for a clue, but was none the wiser. Whatever their agenda, it was too hidden for the likes of her.

'What, no drinks?' he exclaimed, seeing empty hands where glasses should have been.

'I'm just off to get our gin,' said Janice. 'Bea didn't like to mess in Pam's cupboards without her.'

'Nonsense!' Terence strode through to the kitchen. 'I'm sure we're more than welcome. Where is she anyway? Not still shacked up in Christopher's bed since this morning, I hope?' he called through wickedly. 'The poor old girl'll be exhausted.'

He returned with bottle and glasses, studiously avoiding

Beatrice and sitting at Marion's side on a red velvet sofa. I'm in the middle of a domestic, she thought to herself, and I think I'm being used to make a point. She took the glass he offered her, and went over to Beatrice, who accepted it gratefully.

'Are you sure you should, darling?' asked Terence. 'Wouldn't alcohol exacerbate a migraine in your medical opinion, Janice?'

'To each her own medicine,' pronounced Janice, wiping her dribbling chin, mid-quaff. 'The patient knows best. And personally, I always feel better for a drink! Cheers!'

'To you,' toasted Terence, 'the bringer of life.'

'What's happened?' Beatrice wanted to know, trying desperately to bring social grace back into the room. 'You must tell me, I'm intrigued.'

'Well,' said Janice, who settled herself down with a great 'ooph' of relief next to Terence on the sofa. 'Tom, that's my husband who's downstairs in bed, got mixed up with the suitcases at the airport, so we had to go to the feller's place who had ours. He's a great fan of yours, you know, Bea, is my Tom. Thinks you're bleddy gorgeous. Which you are – isn't she, Terry? We saw you at the airport, and I said to Tom then, she's even more gorgeous in the flesh than on the screen – didn't I, Marion? I did. You are. You're lovely.'

'Thank you.' Beatrice started to relax. She was on more familiar ground now. She was never less than gracious with her fans.

'I'm just stating the truth. Anyway, we got to the house, and at first we thought that there wasn't anybody in . . .'

Janice continued with their story, warming to her theme, appealing in turn to Marion for verification of her words, and to Terence, who was jiggling his foot in an excess of energy which surprised Marion. Well, at least he isn't a baby like some men are with pain, she thought, and he's certainly looking happier than he was on the way back. Perhaps they'd given him some painkillers at the hospital that had just kicked in, with the help of whatever he'd found in Bea's bathroom.

Janice, embroidering what had now become a comic monologue, had just got to the bit about the placenta, the two men, and the boiling water, complete with actions, when Frederick wandered blearily in from his bedroom and was forced to hear more about a woman's reproductive system than he had ever, ever, *ever*, wished to know.

'Hi, Freddie,' said Terence, wiping his eyes. 'You really ought to try your hand as a stand-up, Janice, you've a natural gift for timing, hasn't she Bea?'

'Oh definitely,' agreed Beatrice, cut to the quick, since it was Terence's constant complaint when he was directing her that she didn't know comedy from a custard pie. 'Very funny. But they're all right, the Sonellis, and the new baby?'

'As right as ninepence,' affirmed Nurse Cowlishaw. 'Better than him and Tom,' she guffawed, elbowing Terence matily. 'Ay Tez? At least they got a baby for their pains!' But Terence had suddenly started to look misty around the eyes, as if, thought Marion, he were staring down a bottleneck of history. Of what? Of whom? Had he lost a baby at birth? And if so, who with? She racked her brains for showbiz gossip of him gleaned from papers, but found none. She'd never been interested in that kind of thing. Janice would know. She read *Hello!* She'd ask her later.

'Are you the Freddie that was going to sort out Marion's room with Pam?' Janice was asking now, and Freddie looked startled and passed a weary hand across his forehead at the memory, which he had been avoiding all day, of what he had seen when he had tried to do that very thing.

'Where is Pamela?' asked Terence, rousing himself from his reverie. 'Did you ever get it sorted, Fred? We really can't let her get away with forcing poor Marion to sleep on a settee.'

Beatrice didn't know which she minded most. The gentleness in his voice when he said 'poor Marion', or the jolting lapse back into his native vernacular when he uttered the word 'settee'. None of it boded well.

'No, no, I'm afraid I've been resting and reading in my room. I really have felt rather under the weather since this morning,' Freddie replied, in as offhanded a manner as he could muster.

'Blimey, has there been an epidemic?' asked Janice. 'A mystery bug? Bea's been poorly as well, haven't you Bea? Now don't all go sick on me, just because you've got a nurse staying with you. I've got enough on with Tom and his constipation and his scalds.'

'Well, all we need from her is the key to her office isn't it?' Marion said militantly. 'Isn't that where the two of you decided I'd stay, this morning?'

'Terence had that idea,' corrected Freddie hurriedly. 'I don't think we have any authority to announce it to Pamela as a fait accompli. It is really up to her.'

'Where is she, anyway? Do you think she might also be resting in her room?' asked Terence mischievously. 'And Christopher too? All victims of this mystery bug?'

'I think not,' responded Frederick testily. 'I saw her from my window half an hour ago, wandering through her olive grove. She looked perfectly well to me.' More like a satisfied bitch on heat, he had noted to himself bitterly at the time.

'Beatrice my love, why don't you pop along to their rooms and see what they're up to?' Terence prompted her, like a father to a child, thought Marion. 'We're going out to dinner tonight, I've decided. I do hope some of you will be well enough to accompany us.'

'Us?' asked Beatrice, blinking her long lashes.

'Us,' replied Terence, grabbing an affectionate armful of Janice in lieu of Marion, who, being the object of his desire (and also on the other side of the room), he could not with propriety embrace at this time. 'The conquering heroes. The adventure party. The deliverers of babies . . .'

'The scalders of knees,' added Marion, tartly enough to give Terence hope that he really was in with a chance, and he squeezed Janice's shoulders again just to check the reaction. Sure enough, both Bea and Marion were smiling tightly across at him with territorial eyes. Oblivious of this, Janice leant into his embrace. 'Ay, we should have a picture of this. Me and Terence Armstrong cuddling up. They'll never get over it at work. You'll have to do it again, Tez, when Tom's here with the camera.'

'An interesting request,' quipped Terence, 'and one that I have never hitherto received from a married woman.' Janice cackled obligingly, screeching that he was awful, and slapped him on the thigh, which almost put paid to his bonhomie, but not quite. (Chris's coke was excellent.)

'Well, I'm going downstairs to have a shower and see if I can persuade poor Tommo to come out to play,' announced Janice, rising, and draining her glass. 'What time shall we leave, Tel?'

Marion rose too. She didn't want to be left here in this strange atmosphere of strained relations. 'Which way is this olive grove?' she demanded of Frederick. 'I'll find her myself. I'm not sleeping another night on that couch.'

'Bravo, Marion,' Terence applauded, leaping to his feet, 'if a thing's worth doing . . . Just a minute,' he paused mid-stride, on his way, apparently, to double the size of her petitioning party. 'There's a secret passage to the office – Pamela showed us last night. If I can remember the way we can go and recce it now, move your things in, save Pamela the trouble.'

'I hardly think—!' exclaimed Freddie.

'We're here as her guests!' expostulated Beatrice.

'And some of us are paying for that privilege,' snapped Marion. 'If it's left to her she'll do nothing about it. I'm not going to be ripped off by some hard-faced rich bitch, and that's that.'

'Anyway I'm a nurse,' said Janice, lightening the mood. 'Her secret passage is safe with me! Lead on, Macduff!'

Frederick and Beatrice exchanged worried looks as Terence led the search party out of the room. Pamela was going to be furious.

'I think I might just go and lie down again for a while,' said Frederick. 'I really don't feel one hundred per cent.'

'Me too,' agreed Beatrice, 'my migraine is threatening to return.'

Chapter Eight

They had gone a short way down the corridor when Terence halted the small expeditionary party and started exploring the wooden panelling with his fingertips. Marion hadn't noticed his hands before. They were square and workmanlike, and had a great sensuousness to them. The word capable came into her mind. (Of what? Be still, oh trembling thighs!)

'You're like my Tom,' said Janice, interrupting her musings. 'He's always touching up wood.'

'Can't remember where it is,' Terence muttered. 'If you press one of these panels a door appears in the wall.'

'Blimey, it's like the Famous Five,' whooped Janice, her hands exploring the walls. 'Bags I be George — Anne's so wet. Come on Marion — start pressing. Many hands make light . . . woooh!!' She'd found it. With the faintest of clicks a door opened in front of her and she fell through it.

'Seems it's rather more like Alice in Wonderland,' said Marion drily. 'Bags you be the Mad Hatter. Are you okay?' But Janice was already on her feet and bounding along the corridor that had revealed itself to them.

'No probs,' she called back gaily. 'Where to now, Tez?'

'Straight along here till we find the staircase down, I think,' Terence replied.

At the foot of the first flight of stairs was another door, and when Marion and Terence joined her, Janice was already trying the handle.

'No, not that door. That's our floor. Yours is the next flight down.'

'Ooh, so you'll be able to visit us any time you like, Tel.'

'And vice versa,' he agreed warmly, smiling at Marion and the possibilities this new arrangement might open.

'Where does it come out?' asked Marion. 'I wouldn't want to barge straight into the Red Queen's boudoir. I could live very happily never having to see her again.'

'Don't worry. It opens on to the bedroom corridor, but there's a little spy hole — see? So you can see who's coming before you commit.'

Janice pushed the brass cover back and pressed her eye to the spy hole.

'Oh! Oh yes,' she said, suddenly brisk. 'Well, let's get on to our floor. We won't half give Tom a surprise.' She ushered them in front of her down the next flight of stairs, where they came to a similar door.

'This is it,' said Terence. 'This leads directly into Pamela's office — or your new bedroom, as it will henceforth be known, Marion.' He turned the key and pushed the door open with a flourish.

'Voilà. Not for the prudish,' he added, noting their jaws dropping at the sight of the frescoes. He had paid them scant attention when he'd been here earlier with Pamela and Bea, but now he examined the room more closely.

Janice and Tom's carved bed, erotic as it was, had in no way prepared them for these walls.

'But it's pure pornography!' exclaimed Marion the art lover, who had taken in the whole and was now poring over the detail.

'You've got a funny notion of pure,' said Janice. 'And this artist had a funny notion of sex. Seems like the men are having all the fun,' she sniffed, crossly.

'Yes, the women and animals aren't exactly taking a proactive role in the proceedings,' conceded Terence.

'Neither are the kids!' protested Janice, affronted. 'Look at that one – she can't be more than ten. It's bloody disgusting. It should be whitewashed over.'

'As it often is in life,' said Marion. 'How strange that of all the beautiful rooms at her disposal, Cruella chose this one for her study. She obviously has a high tolerance for the perverted.'

'And look at the size of their knobs!' proclaimed Janice, making a thorough examination. 'In their dreams!'

Terence was beginning to feel uncomfortable, being the only male member of the party and afraid that he might be tarred with the same brush as the artist. 'Look, I'm sorry about this,' he said to Marion, 'I really didn't take much notice when I came here before. Obviously this room won't do at all. We'll think of a Plan B.'

'It's fascinating academically,' Marion reassured him. 'Don't worry, I'm not offended. I'm not saying I like what I see, and it certainly might make for strange dreams . . .' She paused, her head filling, unasked, with images from her last strange dream, experienced that very morning in the room adjacent to this one. It too had been filled with wild cavortings. Was she psychic? Had her dream presaged her viewing this room? Or were the paintings themselves possessed of magic powers, entering the psyche of whoever was near? Remembering her dream she became gloomy, filled again with the guilt of her many betrayals of Frank's memory.

'Do you think you'll be okay here then?' asked Terence doubtfully. 'That day-bed looks quite comfortable I suppose. Providing you can ignore the decor.' He wondered if he'd be able to ignore it himself if he visited her here. For there was no doubt in his mind now that he would pursue her. Everything about her fascinated him. Everything about her was so different to Bea.

Her heart full of Frank, Marion turned to her would-be suitor with a new coldness. 'I'll be fine. Thank you for your help. Will you square it with Lady Muck or shall I? I won't have her using this room if I stay in here. She can do her typing elsewhere.'

'Oh I'll sort Pamela out, don't you worry,' Terence reassured her, puzzled by the sudden froideur. 'I doubt if she uses the study very much. She's playing at being her father's biographer, but I shouldn't imagine she'd be very serious about it. Not enough money in books for the likes of her.' As he talked, his mind scanned the conversation since entering the room. Had Marion been the victim of incest, perhaps, with her talk of whitewashing events? Or had a previous lover been into S and M? Was *she* into S and M? Now that might be a problem. He'd never seen the fun in flogging or being flogged, personally, although he'd tried half-heartedly a couple of times for those who had. He reckoned he could just about go a bit of light bondage if push came to shove.

'Who was her father?' asked Marion. 'Is she a descendant of whichever Fratorelli commissioned these frescoes, or did she marry in?'

'Oh no, she married in. Her father was Benjamin Fox.'

'Good God, really?' Marion's academic interest was aroused again. 'As in the Bloomsbury dilettante?'

'Yes, have you read his work?' Really, she was full of surprises. Beatrice wouldn't know an obscure dead scribbler if one smacked her round the head. Anyway, whatever – this new subject seemed to have altered Marion's mood.

'Read, no. But I've seen some of his sketches and illustrations. He showed great promise, actually, but no staying power. Too busy having fun, probably. One of my tutors at art college always used to cite him as an example of lack of perseverance and grit. "Beware, you will become like Benjamin Fox, for ever a dabbler," was his favourite admonition. So, she's Benjamin Fox's daughter. Well, that goes some way towards explaining why she's such a cow. She must have had to put up with a lot as a kid.'

'Why? What sort of thing?'

'He dabbled in relationships much the same as he dabbled in art and literature. Rarely finished one work before he started another. Sprogged a lot of bastards, allegedly. And there were some aspersions cast about how his wife actually died. That would be Pamela's mother I imagine – she is legit?'

'Oh yes, daughter and heir to the family fortunes. Which of course is why I'm here. Did they think he killed his wife?'

'Just speculation. She defenestrated – or was she pushed? But then again, with Lilith as a daughter, who wouldn't take the quickest route out? How do you mean, that's why you're here?'

'Fox managed to complete a short story or two, despite your art teacher's damning assessment, one of which we're thinking of making into a musical.'

'What's it about?'

'I've got a copy with me actually. I'll let you have it later and you can tell me what you think. I'd value your opinion.'

Janice had grown bored, and was now trying to gain access to their flat by using her shoulder as a battering ram. 'This door's stuck,' she announced, ignoring their conversation. 'I've turned the key but nothing's happening.'

'Oh yes,' Terence now remembered, 'Pamela demonstrated the double lock arrangement when she showed us round. It has to be unlocked from both sides. Do you have the other key?'

'Yes, but it's on the other side of the door,' said Marion, 'which means going all the way upstairs again and going round the other way.'

'But Tom's in next door,' Janice reminded them. 'All we have to do is attract his attention.'

'If you haven't already attracted his attention by attempting to bash the door down, I can't think what else we might try,' said Marion, 'apart from us all screaming blue murder, or setting off a bomb.' She had shrugged off her thoughts of gloom and guilt during the course of her conversation with Terence, and she had mentally booked herself for a good talking to later on when she was alone. She had done some thinking during her wait in Casualty, and she had suddenly realised with a shock that she was now twice the age that Frank had been when he'd died. She couldn't let a dead man – a dead boy, she corrected herself, still astonished at this new line of thought – stop her having a life. A middle-aged woman, pining for a dead youth. It was absurd. Or was she pining for her own dead youth? Was it that banal? It was the first time she'd entertained such disloyal thoughts in two decades, and as disconcerting as it was, she felt giddy with something that felt like optimism. So perhaps she was starting to believe in the future? It was certainly food for thought.

In the meantime, Janice had taken up her first suggestion and was screaming blue murder through the keyhole.

Tom had been enjoying this brief interval of being alone to nurse his wounds, recover his equanimity, and try to get up to date with his bowel movements. Janice had been right about that. Actually, she was nearly always right about what was ailing him, emotionally or physically, which was a bit annoying sometimes. It made having an unaccountable, irrational, irritable strop, to which he had been prone before he'd met her, an impossibility. Sulking had been a popular defence in his parental home, and he missed the solitude of it sometimes when his wife poked and prodded his unconscious motives with her clinical zeal. He also missed the luxury of being able to blame something or somebody else for his troubles which is what a good sulk afforded. However, as his sphincter snapped shut in shocked affront at the racket coming from somewhere close by when he had thought himself quite alone, an A1, full-blooded, constipated sulk seemed the only response.

Pulling his dressing-gown around him (at least he had the dignity of that now) he padded into the living-room and crossed to the connecting door, which was trembling at his wife's assault. She was still screaming his name when he quietly, and with exaggerated calm, turned the key in the lock. For the second time in half an hour, Janice fell through an open door. She laughed.

'There you are! Were you on the pot? Did you manage anything? We've just come through a secret passage from upstairs! This is going to be Marion's room now – look at the wallpaper! Isn't it gross? We're going out for dinner with Terry later. How's your legs? Ay – watch your dressing-gown – you're showing the family jewels!'

Tom's superior mien left his face as he scrabbled to readjust his clothing. Terence, though no slouch himself at displaying the family jewels at the drop of a robe, saw his discomfort and felt for him. 'I'll let you get settled in then. See you later. Call for you around eight.' He touched Marion lightly on her arm. 'Don't worry about Lilith. I can be the very Devil myself, you know.'

Hardly had the sound of his retreating footsteps died in the secret passage outside the room, when Janice elbowed her matily in the ribs and said, 'You're on there, you know, Maz.'

'I don't think so,' Marion replied, trying to look cool and not grin. 'He's spoken for. I don't mess with other women's blokes.'

'What — not even when the bloke's woman is messing with someone else?'

'What? Who? How do you know?'

'I saw Bea through the spy hole, in the bedroom corridor, as large as life. Snogging Christopher Bassett!'

Chapter Nine

Pamela was in a towering rage.

'It is out of the question. Quite out of the question. I need constant access to my study. I thought I had made that perfectly plain. And it is private. There are things I keep in there which are of a personal nature.'

'Deeply personal,' said Terence, enjoying himself. He was no stranger to the prima donna's tantrum. 'I'm surprised you can keep your mind on your work with all that activity going on on the walls.'

'Giovanni's frescoes? An artist's joke. A rather poor one actually.'

'Really? I don't get it. Refresh my sense of humour.'

'Giovanni was the younger son,' explained Pamela irritably, 'and so, having no money of his own he was forced to accept the patronage of his brother the Count. He spent his entire life painting the walls of the Palazzo, which is why of course he isn't known. The frescoes in that room are the last he did before he died. I suppose he thought he had nothing to lose. They were supposed to depict the Count's — shall we say "eclectic" — sexual appetite and expose the hypocrisy depicted in the other works — the recurrent homage to God, the selfless acts of charity and so forth. He was biting the hand that fed him.'

'Which is a bad thing.'

'Naturally.'

'Not unlike fleecing paying guests.'

'What a vulgar expression.'

'What? Fleecing, or paying guests? You're going to have to go with the flow, Pamela, if you need their cash. Talking of which, spoke to Johnny just now, in New York.'

This stopped her in her tracks. Jonathan Jarmain, multi-millionaire writer of musical scores, whose very name assured success, whose shows ran for years on Broadway and in the West End.

'He's read Benjamin's story and thinks it has great potential. He's very excited'

'Really? That's marvellous.'

'Not half. If we get it right, your days as a landlady will be over.'

Pamela smiled tightly, willing herself to be polite. 'You're blackmailing me.'

'Counselling you. You don't want a whole lot of fuss and bother over this, letters to the *Guardian*, complaints to the tourist board. It's the kind of publicity we can do without just now. You're bigger than that, Pamela. You can rise above it.'

'But my work . . .'

'Take a holiday from it. It's only for a week. Actually, Marion could be quite helpful. What she doesn't know about Art hasn't been written. She's a big fan of your Dad's. She's dying to get off to a better start with you, ask you all about him. Join us tonight for dinner. Let's build bridges, let's party. And speaking of which – do you ever indulge in cocaine?'

It happened that she did, provided it was someone else's, and within minutes she was as gay as could be.

Freddie was having an agonising tussle with himself in the privacy of his bedroom. It wasn't just that he fancied Christopher. He had fallen hopelessly in love. Why? Why did it always have to be somebody like Chris, somebody wildly unattainable, a flirt, a tart? There was some satisfaction in calling him names. A gigolo. A flibbertigibbet. A cock on legs. (No. Dangerous territory, that.) A floosie. You wouldn't know where he'd been. Well, you would. Everywhere. He was undeserving of a love as pure as Freddie's. So. Finis. No more thoughts in that direction. Catching him with Pamela had been a timely warning. Freddie deserved better. He'd had a lucky escape. So why was choosing an outfit for dinner proving to be so much of a trial? He sat down heavily on the bed, still in his underpants, and put his head in his hands.

Christopher had luxuriated in a long slow bath, slipped into his designer casuals, and was looking for his cocaine when there was a knock at his door. He groaned, hoping it wasn't the Mad Cow calling on his services again. Fucking Pamela had been a brute and animal act in comparison to making love to Beatrice again, which had been wonderful. There had been a tenderness and an innocence to it which he had all but forgotten since their old affair, and which seemed to have reawakened his old feelings for her. Damn Terence Armstrong for taking her away from him. And having had the difference between sex and love-making demonstrated to him within an interval of only a few hours, he was sore and sated, and wanted nothing more than a little snort, a couple of drinks, and a nice supper. Preferably paid for by Frederick. And thinking of whom, Freddie was probably feeling a bit neglected today. Better pay him some attention. He'd sit next to him at supper tonight and make him feel special.

Still buttoning his shirt he opened the door. It was Terence, curse him, who was smiling. Could be a dangerous sign.

'Terence. Hi.'

'Hello there, Christopher. Had a good day?'

'Not bad, you know – just mooched about . . .' Better get off that subject quickly. 'It's a lovely place, isn't it?'

'Fabulous. We're going out to dinner. Want to come?'

'Great, yeah. I was just about to potter out and see what everybody was up to.'

'Well Pamela and I are up to pre-prandial drinks. Want to join us?'

'Terrific. I'll be along in a tick . . .' Soon as I can find my bloody Charlie, he thought, can't face that bloody woman's knowing smiles without. What the hell had he done with it?

'By the way, thanks for seeing to Beatrice this afternoon,' said Terence, smiling most sincerely.

'Sorry . . .?' asked Christopher, trying to disguise his alarm.

'Getting her to drink some champagne. Unusual cure for migraine, but it appears to have done the trick.'

'Oh,' Chris smiled broadly, relieved. 'Oh, well, you know – we actrines. It's a remedy that rarely fails, I've found. If it doesn't cure whatever ails you, at least it helps you forget what it was.' And talking of forgetting – Shit! Was that what had happened? Had he left the cocaine in her room? Had Terence found it? He examined him now through narrowed eyes.

'I'll remember that,' Terence laughed convivially, 'thanks for the tip.' He sniffed and rubbed his nose. 'Seem to be starting a cold. Damn nuisance.' He smiled broadly. 'See you in a few minutes then. I'll go and get Fred.'

Christopher closed the door and grabbed his wallet, riffling through it's contents. No Amex card and no Charlie. Shit shit *shit*! Where the hell was Bea?

Terence, grinning to himself, knocked on Frederick's door. 'What ho, Frederico! Coming out to play?'

Freddie, still in his underpants, peered round his door for protection. His eyes were red and puffy. Poor old Fred. This would never do. Terence pushed his way in. 'Rather sartorial dinner dress, if I may say so.'

'I – I'm not ready. I'm not sure that I want to dine tonight.'

'Not still worried about ruffling Pamela's feathers over her study, are you? I've already squared it with her. She couldn't give a hoot.'

'Good. Well, so long as everybody's happy.'

'Except you, Fred. What's up old chum?'

'Nothing. Nothing. Perhaps I'm overtired. You know how it can be when you finally get away from the office. It all catches up with you.'

Terence was not known for his tender solicitude for his fellow man, but he looked at Freddie now with the same sympathy he had felt for Tom moments earlier. What was happening to him? Were his feelings for Marion turning him to mush? Was it love he was experiencing, and not the usual lust? Shouldering aside a lifetime's habit, he prepared to dispense advice. He smiled at Freddie, a softness in his eyes. 'I know what you need, Fred, and Uncle Terence is the one to provide it.'

'What?' asked Freddie, eyeing him with sudden alarm. He pulled on a pair of chinos at speed.

'A word to the wise, old love. If all this is for Christopher, he isn't worth it.'

'Worth what? I'm sorry, I don't understand.'

'Worth breaking your heart for.'

Frederick exploded into a froth of outraged expostulations. 'Well really – I – heavens – I don't know what to say!'

'Freddie, we've known each other how long? Years. Aeons. Be yourself. Do what you want to do. Nobody cares these days, and in our business, I don't think they ever really did. But pick somebody who's kind, Freddie. You're far too nice for anything less.'

Frederick drew himself to his full height as he zipped his flies. 'I think you are labouring under a false assumption of some kind which I simply cannot fathom, Terence.'

'Am I? Well – good. So you'll come to dinner then?' Terence's eyes flicked over the deluge of discarded shirts on the bed as he left the room. 'I think the cream linen with those trousers, don't you? Open at the neck. It's too hot for a tie.' The door closed behind him.

There was no gracious escape. Freddie would have to go. But he would ignore Christopher all evening with all his might and main.

On re-entering the living room, Terence was amused to see Christopher and Beatrice in an anxious huddle, pretending to pour drinks. They sprang apart guiltily at the sound of his voice.

'You really do look perfect together. We're going to have to find you something, aren't we? What do you think? Classical? Modern? Shakespeare, perhaps.'

Christopher recovered quickly. 'That would be wonderful. I haven't touched the Bard for years. I was only saying to my agent the other day how I'd like to get back on the boards. What do you think, Bea? I suppose we're too mature these days for Romeo and Juliet? Actually, I've always longed to give my Hamlet.'

'Oh I don't know. Ophelia, Bea? Would you drown for your love?'

Beatrice, floundering, was saved by Pamela swanning back in with a shawl. 'What a curious question. One should *kill* for love certainly, but never die for it. Are we ready? I'm famished. Shall we go?'

'Sure, absolutely,' said Terence agreeably. 'Freddie can drive you all in his car. I'll go and rouse the others.'

'There you are, I told you,' muttered Beatrice to Christopher as Terence whistled his way jauntily out of the room. 'He's got a pash on that middle-aged woman in the retro clothes.'

'Mm,' said Christopher, his idée firmly fixe, 'but the coke, Bea, what's happened to my bloody coke?'

Marion and Janice got a fit of the giggles when the latter opened the door to Terence. After settling Tom down for a little nap, she and Marion had been dishing the dirt and washing it down with martini.

'Maybe her and Terry have got one of those "arrangements",'

she said, after describing the Bassett/Miller-Mander kiss from every angle. 'You know, open marriage – but without the ring.'

'That's certainly pretty open,' said Marion. 'Has he got any kids?'

'Don't think so. He was with Suzanne Farleigh for ages, but they never tied the knot, then he went off with whatsername, the American who he directed on Broadway in *Shock!* – Roberta Frink – but she was already married and she went back to him in the end – Steven . . . Steven . . .'

'Stormont?'

'Yeah. Then Terry did marry Angela Manville, but I'm pretty sure she never sprogged. Then he had a rash of young starlets, ending with Bea. Why?'

'I dunno. He seemed to go all misty about the birth, I just wondered if he was experiencing some kind of regret?'

'Well, I should think he regretted scalding himself. Tom certainly did.' They muffled their giggles, lest Tom should hear them next door. He was still in a strop. 'Anyway,' Janice continued, wiping away her tears, 'apart from all that – do you fancy him? Because, honestly Maz, as far as I can see, his tongue is hanging out for you.' She paused a fraction, and grinned. 'If you'll pardon my French.'

And that had been Terence's cue to knock on their door.

Chapter Ten

The dinner had been a strange old event, as Marion and Janice agreed when they met back again in their living-room afterwards to compare notes. For starters, they had contained rather than controlled their giggles when Terence came to call, so they couldn't look at each other all evening for fear of starting up again, which was tricky since they were sitting diagonally opposite each other.

But apart from that, strange undercurrents swirled round their table all evening making them feel, as Marion put it, as if they'd been allowed to stay up with the grown-ups, witnessing, but not understanding, their arcane language. The restaurant had been the swankiest that the Leicester party had ever seen, but even so, the other posh diners had practically swivelled their heads off to rubber-neck Beatrice Miller-Mander, Christopher Bassett and Terence Armstrong when they made their procession to their table.

'It must be terrible getting that all the time,' said Janice. 'You'd be worried in case you'd got spinach between your teeth, or your dress had got hoicked up in your knickers, and that was why they were staring.'

'The price of fame,' said Marion.

'You'll have to get used to that if you go out with Terry,' mused Janice. 'They'll all be going, "Who's that beautiful woman with Terence Armstrong? Have we seen her on telly?"'

'Hardly,' said Marion. ' "Who's that beaten up old bag with

her dress hoicked up in her knickers,' more like — and anyway, who said I'll be going out with him?'

'Don't come the raw prawn with me, Marion,' Janice had retorted. (There was a visiting Australian doctor at work, and she had been learning all sorts of new phrases, her favourite being 'She didn't get lips loike *thet* sucking oranges', which had had her in stitches en route to A and E.) 'Anyway, you *are* beautiful. I've always said so to Tom. You're the only one who doesn't know it.'

'Well, kind of you to say it — though untrue — but still no match for Beatrice. Even you'll admit that.'

'It's not me we're talking about, though, is it? It's Tel. And that is one smitten man.'

'So you say,' said Marion, unsuccessfully suppressing the smile of a cat who's been promised cream.

'*Marion!* You said yourself he put his hand on your thigh at dinner!'

'He was pissed,' said Marion, 'and he was just emphasising a point.'

'Yes, the point being he's got the hots for you!'

'Anyway,' Marion said with finality, 'where had we got to? And pass the gin.'

Where they'd got to in comparing notes was Pamela, who had had a sea change of character all evening — or rather, several sea changes, which had been most confusing. At first she had been charm itself, seeking out the seat next to Marion, and engaging her in an interesting discussion about Benjamin Fox's work. Once Marion had recovered herself from the shock (and the hairs on the back of her neck had been persuaded to lie down) they had got on quite well, agreeing about his innovative brush work and his lush use of colour, and trading bits of information about him which were of interest to them both. Yet all the time, Pamela had been flicking little glances at Terence which seemed to ask, 'Aren't I doing well?'

'Maybe Terry had told her to behave,' offered Janice. 'Bribed her with something, maybe. Said he wouldn't do her stupid play if she wouldn't be nice to his girlie.'

'I'll let that pass,' said Marion, fixing her friend with a look, 'but what was with the mood swings? Can't be PMT at her age, surely?'

'No, she's just a spoilt brat,' was Janice's medical opinion. 'I dunno what she was on about. I lost the plot completely when she was going on to Terry about building materials. I'd been chatting to Chris. Had you gone on to Architecture by then?'

'You thought Architecture, did you?' asked Marion, puzzled. 'I thought maybe it was Dentistry. We'd pretty much run ourselves dry about her dad – my bloody face muscles had got cramp by then, trying to keep up a smile. And she was starting to get – I dunno, a bit tetchy, or distracted – kept rubbing her nose and her eyes were darting about all over the place. I thought I was boring her, which was a bit rich considering we'd spent the whole time talking about her childhood memories of Boring Bloody Benjamin. So I was winding up about his use of Prussian Blue – I'd been really scraping about for things to say – when she bent over to Terence and said something like "Is this better?", smiling at him, almost flirtatious . . .'

'Huh, she's got less than no chance there, with you in the frame,' said Janice, loyally.

'Will you give it up!' Marion exclaimed, though in a tone that said 'please don't'. 'And Terence was agreeing that it was . . .'

'Was what?'

'Better, I suppose.'

'What was better?'

'Do you think you ought to have more gin? I don't know better than what, that's the point – and then she said something – and this is where you must have beamed back in – that sounded like, "But the trouble is, darling, the bridging materials appear to have run dry."'

'That's a really good impression, Maz, you sounded just like her!'

'And then he said something reassuring – I don't know what it was, but did you see him take her hand between his?'

'Between his what?' cackled Janice.

'That's it. I'm going to bed.'

'Ah no, don't, I'm sorry, I couldn't resist. Then what happened?'

'Nothing. She went off to the loo.'

'For the *first* time. My God, she's got a weak bladder. After that she was trotting out every five minutes. I thought to myself, either it's something she's eaten, or that's a woman with cystitis. Anyway, was that when he touched your thigh?'

'Some time around then, yes.'

'What did he say?!'

'Oh nothing. I can't remember.' Be still, oh beating heart.

'Marion!'

'Here, are you going to hog that bottle all night?'

'If you don't tell me, I won't tell you about Chris and Bea,' said Janice, replenishing Marion's glass to the brim.

'He said he liked me.' *I think I'm falling in love,* is what he'd said. Was it possible that she'd misheard?

'Is that all? We know that.'

'Well – now it's official.'

'It's not much of a trade.'

'It's the best I can do. Anyway, tell me about Christopher and Bea.'

'Are you sure that's all?'

'That's *all*! What do you want – a proposal?!'

'Ooh Mazzer, do you think it'll come to that?!'

'Of course not!'

'But if it did . . .'

'If it did I'd eat my hat.' But first I'd have to buy one. Or maybe, buy a veil. No, registry office. I'd look ridiculous in cream taffeta at my age. Enough! Enough!!

'I love weddings. I love hats. That's why I love weddings.'

'I think we're getting pissed. Tell me about Christopher and Bea.'

'I really like you, you know, Maz. At first I didn't think I was going to, I thought you were a right stuck-up snotty cow.'

'Thanks.'

'But now I reckon, if anybody deserves happiness, it's you.'

'So make me happy! Or am I going to have to come over there and beat it out of you?'

'I love it when you talk dirty.'

'That's it. I'm off.'

(*Go, go!* thought Tom the other side of the wall, who had retired to the interesting bit of old wood carving an hour before in the fruitless pursuit of sleep. His legs were still smarting something chronic.)

'Oh no, don't. I'll behave myself, honest. You're right, I am a bit pissed. I get so I can't resist the dooblee ontondree. I'm only teasing.'

'So am I,' said Marion, and settled back down. 'And for the record, I like you too.'

Having thus established their new credentials, the two girlfriends, smiling at each other through glasses of gin, got back to the story in hand.

'Well,' said Janice, slurring slightly, 'It was well weird up that end of the table. The short one called Fred kept ignoring Chris all night, and Chris was falling over himself to be nice to him. I never did get to the bottom of that one. And then, Bea didn't seem to be overjoyed to be sitting next to Christopher, but that was obvious why.'

'How do you mean?'

'Terry's rumbled them, hasn't he? They've been having it off.'

'Are you sure?'

'I told you I saw them snogging, didn't I?'

'Yes, but, a snog's a snog, it's not having it off.'

'They did though, I bet you. This afternoon when we were out.'

'Give, give!'

'It was after all that funny business about the bill.'

'Yes – what was *that* about? I saw Terence with my own eyes put his credit card down – it's the first time I've ever seen a gold American Express card except for on a leaflet in a bank – and he'd been going on all night about how everybody must have everything they wanted cos he was footing the bill.'

'And then he went to the lav . . .'

'. . . And the waiter brought the card back and gave it to Signor Bassett.'

'He wasn't half flummoxed, but he hid it well. I mean — what else could he do? He had to sign it. He could hardly say, no, wait on till my friend gets back from the khazi.'

'I could only think that he must have taken his card out when Terence took out his, as an empty gesture, knowing it wouldn't be taken up.'

'Tight git. He must be loaded. They don't go giving out gold cards to them that's not.'

'Well I hope for his sake he is. Did you see the zillions of noughts at the bottom of the bill?'

'Yeah. I thought my Tom was going to have a heart attack — he'd been muttering on about paying our way.'

'Anyway, cut to the chase.'

'Why does Terry carry his cash like that?'

'Like what?'

'Rolled up in a tube.'

'I've no idea, I didn't see. How do you mean?'

'I wouldn't have noticed myself, but Chris's eyes practically stood out on stalks when Tez got the money out his pocket.'

'When he got back from the loo and found Chris signing the chit? The cash was for the tip, wasn't it?'

'Tez got back, saw Chris signing, and said "Oh thank you Chris, how sweet — I was going to take care of that. Well at least let me pay for the service", and then he got this big note out that was rolled in a tube, unrolled it in Chris's face, and then chucked it on the table.'

'I think I'd been grabbed by Pamela by then. She'd gone into another manic phase, talking nineteen to the dozen and laughing like a mad woman. I don't know what she was on about, but *she* thought she was being very witty.'

'And then Terry went over to the two of you and helped you on with your jackets — he's such a gent, isn't he? And while I was pretending to look at that, and joshing Tom to do the same for me, and fussing over him about his poor old legs . . . I wasn't really – I was on automatic pilot . . .'

'I'll remind you of that ability some day.'

'. . . I was earwigging Bea and Chris, and she said "I told you, he knows – you must have left it in our bathroom."'

'Left what?'

'I dunno. Something incriminating. A dobber, I reckon.'

'Why do you suppose that? It could have been anything.'

'Because then Chris said, "So what? I could have called round for the champagne and left Charlie in the bathroom, all perfectly innocent."'

'Who's Charlie?'

'That's what *they* call a condom, I bet you. That's what I reckon, any road.'

'That's a bit of a wild leap of the imagination.'

'Well he's just as likely to say "what's a dobber?" while we say "what's a Charlie?". Everybody's got their own slang for it, haven't they?'

Marion was unconvinced. 'Anyway, how could a used dobber left in somebody else's bathroom possibly be conceived of as innocent?'

'Yeah, that got me at first. And then I thought, they didn't use it. He brought it round, but he didn't put it on. Because, because . . . Let me finish . . . Because Bea said something I didn't catch, and then Chris said "Did you change your sheets?" Well, if he'd used a dobber she wouldn't necessarily have to change the sheets, would she? The wet patch factor would have been taken care of.'

'Dodgy,' said Marion giggling, 'I can't see that going down too well in a court of law. But anyway – *had* she changed her sheets?'

'Well that's why I'm sure that I'm sure. She said "Why would I bother? I've told you, he doesn't come near my bed. He's never actually *slept* with me, but he used at least to visit. Now he hasn't even done that for weeks."'

'Really?! Well I'll be buggered.' This was very good news indeed.

'Let's hope not, Maz!'

'What's wrong with him? You've got to admit she's gorgeous.'

'Gorgeous, but boring. There you were the other end of the table, wanging on to him and Pam about Art, knowing everything about everything, making them laugh – he couldn't take his eyes off you . . .'

'Maybe I'd got spinach in my teeth.'

'And all Bea talked about, when she talked at all – when she wasn't listening politely to somebody else with her big round eyes all wide and poppy, and her pretty little mouth going "ooh" and "aah" – was clothes.'

'Clothes? What about them?'

'Exactly! That's what you'd say. But she can talk for hours about them. Now can you imagine that'd keep a man like Terry entertained for very long?'

'I suppose not. So you reckon he likes me for my conversation, do you?'

Janice could see she had deflated her new friend, and rushed to make amends. 'Not *just* that. It's obvious he fancies the pants off you as well. I reckon it could be the Charles and Di syndrome when they first got married,' she continued, happy to see Marion smiling again. 'She's pretty all right, but young and innocent and maybe boring in bed. A man of his experience'd much prefer the older woman who's more of a goer. Don't get me wrong,' she added hastily as her drinking companion's face darkened, 'he seems genuinely fond of you.'

Is that all I am? wondered Marion morosely, Just a good old shag? She swirled the notion round her mind for a moment while she stared into her glass. Possibly, she concluded pragmatically, downing the rest of her gin. And if so – well. There were worse fates. Being the fair Beatrice undesired would be pretty bloody hellish.

So much for cream taffeta. It was high time she took herself off to her room for that talking to.

Chapter Eleven

Beatrice couldn't understand where this conversation was heading. When everybody had gone off to bed and she and Terence couldn't help but retire alone together to their apartment, she had expected an explosion of rage, so certain was she that he knew. All the way home in Freddie's hired car she had been concocting a plausible explanation with which to deflect the attack.

I went to bed with a migraine, she'd say, *and I slept. Then shortly before you came back, Christopher called by, to see you. I told him you were still out, but he said he'd wait. He was bored, he'd got no one to talk to.* And you know what he's like, so full of himself, not one to notice that somebody else is in pain. Wouldn't do any harm to put him down, make him seem unattractive to her. *I struggled to be polite, and obviously couldn't refuse him the champagne.* No. Better rephrase that. It might lead Terence to think that if champagne could not be refused, then it might not have been within her gift to refuse — other things — as well. *I was struggling to be polite, and gave him the champagne in the hope that he'd go away, but he opened it there and then and insisted I had a glass because it used to be a tonic, you know, in the olden days . . .* She was proud of this piece of historical knowledge she had picked up from somewhere — perhaps from one of the romances she liked to read. *And do you know, it worked! I started to feel better, and then realised the time, and said to Christopher I was worried you still weren't back. I started to think maybe you'd had an accident in the car — you know what you always say about Italian drivers.* Was this taking too long? Was she gilding the lily? Better stick to the point. *I asked him what he wanted to see you about, and he said 'I've brought him a present' and produced some coke. He's very fond of you, you know, and a huge fan.* That would help things along nicely — at least, it always seemed to work with Daddy. *He said not to worry, that you'd be bound to be back soon, and that he'd prepare you a line as a surprise. He went to the bathroom, and was just about to do that when his mobile rang. It was his agent or something, I think . . .* Better not be too specific until she'd had a chance to brief Christopher . . . *and he needed to check in his diary which was in his room, so he left, meaning to return, and that's when you came back.* Perfect. A good explanation, and one that would put Terence in the wrong too, misunderstanding so generous a gift.

But her story, it seemed, was not to be put to the test, for wily Terence had his own agenda. It was his habit, when bored with an alliance, never to be the one to finish it. He could not be so cruel and still be liked — or that is what he felt. He could not be so cruel and still have a high opinion of himself, was probably more like the truth. So a part of his brain, which he kept secret even from himself, was constantly engaged in defending his integrity while impugning the integrity of others. And this habit was not confined to affairs of the heart — it extended to his work: 'Not in anger, but in sorrow,' was his favoured way of signing off his letters sacking staff, implying it was their unreason that had brought about their fate, and nothing to do with him at all.

So to Beatrice's surprise, alone at last, he turned from locking the door of their apartment, and smiled a heart-softened smile, his eyes all moist and tender.

'Bea,' he said, 'come here.'

What now?!

He took her in his arms and held her close and stroked her hair and gave her little kisses on her cheeks. 'I've been thinking about you so much today. Thinking about us.'

There! It was going to come, she knew it. Finished with in sorrow, not in anger.

'Have you? So have I.' Play for time.

'I've not been easy to be with lately, and I'm sorry.'

This was unexpected. 'No no, you've had a lot on your mind.'

'I have, but I doubt you know quite what.'

'Work?' she offered tremulously, hoping against hope.

'Obliquely, yes. You're trembling! Are you cold, my love?'

'A little.'

'Then sit down next to me and I'll hold you tight and warm you up.' She followed him to the couch where he did as he said, and he covered her legs with a throw.

'Better?'

'Much.'

In their new position she couldn't see his face, which disturbed her, but his voice continued thick and rich with warmth. 'I said it was obliquely about work, and it is. I've been thinking I've been working too much, that I'm missing out, that I have only half a life.'

'Really? In what way?' This was interesting. She often complained she hardly saw him. Perhaps he'd taken it in at last?

'And today, witnessing what I witnessed . . .'

Ah. Now she could see it looming ahead, the iceberg to their Titanic. And would this tiny life-raft of her concoction about the cocaine survive the crashing waves? She mentally rehearsed her story while waiting for him to continue. *The cocaine? It was for you, from Christopher with love. Didn't he tell you? Why didn't you ask? To think that you imagined . . . Impossible, so wrong!* But – what . . .? What was he saying now?

'. . . and afterwards, when I saw that dear little head covered in down, her tiny fingernails perfectly formed . . .'

'I'm sorry?'

'I realised that that was what was missing from my life – from our life together. I'm getting older, and I'm childless, Bea. I want us to make a baby.'

She must be hearing things. Could this be true? It was only her heart's desire! 'Oh Terence! A baby?'

'My darling – would you mind? I realise it's a huge request to make – you'd have to take time out from your career, you might worry about your figure . . .'

'Of course not! Oh Terence, I'd love it!' And marriage, with a ring on her finger and bells on her toes. The dress! Who would make it? She couldn't wait to get back to London, to start making plans. A wedding list at General Trading must be set up forthwith – her mother would be over the moon, and Daddy would close his study door and say 'Silence! I am writing the most important speech of my career! An oblation that must be wrought from finest prose . . .' Yes, well he did go on. What a pity she was already hyphenated, so she couldn't wear her husband's name like a badge – Miller-Mander-Armstrong was going a bit too far. Or was it? Did it not have a certain distinction? She'd check with Mums.

She was startled from this rapid reverie when she found herself being led gently by the hand into her room. 'No wait!' she cried. 'What – now?' He sat her on the bed and crouched at her feet to take off her shoes, gazing up at her with adoration.

'I just want to make love to you, to share my love with you. And to sleep with you Bea, to hold you in my arms all night . . .'

'That's wonderful! Let's go to *your* room!'

'Do you know what's been the missing link,' he continued, as if she hadn't spoken, 'the thing that's held me back? I realised it myself today. Trust. I have never been able to trust anybody as I realise now that I trust you.' He was kissing his way up her legs.

'That's lovely, darling.' The sheets, the sheets! Grab at straws! Change the subject! Move away from the bed! 'By the way, did you find the present from Christopher?'

That stopped him. 'Present? From Chris?'

'The cocaine, in the bathroom. He left it for you when he called in.'

'Heavens! Thank goodness for that. Do you know what I thought when I saw it, darling?' He was laughing, kneeling on the floor, his warm hands on her thighs.

'No darling, what?'

'I thought I'd so depressed you with my horrid self-absorption of late, that you had resorted to lonely and clandestine drug taking!'

Now she laughed too. 'Oh no, darling! How funny!' What a relief!

'So Christopher stayed when he came round for the champagne then?'

Was there an edge to his voice? She'd pass it off lightly. 'Oh, you know what he's like. He'd come to visit you for some amusement and finding you were out – I think he must have been bored with being on his own – he insisted on me having a glass with him while he waited for your return.'

'Really? I hadn't realised we were that close.'

There *was* an edge. 'Oh he's awfully fond of you, and you know – he's a huge fan.'

'That's nice.' He was mollified enough to kiss her neck and smooch her ear.

'Darling?!'

'Mmm?'

'Let's shower.'

'Okay.'

He allowed her to go free, and she all but danced into the bathroom and away from the scene of her so recently committed crime. Now all she had to do was think of a good reason to go to his bed afterwards, instead of hers. He'd followed her to the doorway, and she turned on the shower and started to undress.

'He must have thought me awfully strange when I went through that pantomime with the rolled-up note. I was doing it for your benefit, to tell you I knew about your secret career as a drug addict!'

'Really? I didn't notice. Mm, lovely – it's nice and hot.'

'So he stayed for a while and you had coke and champagne? That's nice.'

'Only a little, just to keep him happy. Aren't you getting in?'

He started to undress. 'Of course. I'll just hang my clothes up and turn down the bed.'

'No!'

But he had already gone, his voice trailing jokily behind him, 'I know, aren't I a stick-in-the-mud? But old habits die hard. If you'd wanted more impulsiveness you should have chosen someone younger.'

She dashed from the shower clutching a small towel to her breast, her body streaming pools of water onto the lush cream of the bedroom rug. Too late.

He straightened up, his body rigid, the covers drawn back in his hand, and turned from the bed to face her. His look was not of anger, but of sorrow.

Chapter Twelve

By the time Marion made it to her new bed she realised she was far too tired for the talking to she'd promised herself. She hadn't slept well for days, first dreading the holiday, and then living it. She took one look at the study's frescoes, her mind awash with gin, and realised that this was not the time or place for a serious audit of her expectations of sex or love. She reeled on to the bed, managing to pull most of her clothes off and most of the covers over her, and promising herself like Scarlett O'Hara that she would think about it tomorrow, she fell into a deep and dreamless sleep not unlike a coma.

Five minutes later, or so it seemed, she was woken by Janice who had thundered into her room unheard and, alarmed at getting no response from singing, shouting or shaking, was now slapping her round the face.

'Jeez! Whassmatter?! Leemeelone.'

'Oh, thank God for that! I thought you'd arrested.'

'I'll have you arrested. Go away.'

'Drink your coffee, you'll feel better.'

Marion's head hurt and her tongue was glued to the roof of her mouth. 'I'll never feel better.' She struggled to open her eyes experimentally. Too bright.

'No going down the covers again!' shouted Janice, whipping them off her.

'What the hell . . .!' Marion expostulated furiously, sitting up. Janice took her hand and curled it round the mug of Nescafé.

'Drink your nice drink for Nursie.'

'Bloody hell Janice! Have you never heard of hangovers?'

'I've heard of them, yes, but I never seem to get them myself.'

'Here — take mine.' Marion closed her eyes again while she sipped the hot liquid. 'Yeuk! I don't take sugar.'

'You do this morning, it'll do you good.' Impervious, Janice beamed back at Marion's spiteful glare. 'I half expected to find Terry had come down your secret passage in the night, nudge nudge, wink wink, know what I mean?'

Marion rubbed her sore ribs where she'd just been elbowed. 'It's too early for this.'

'It's ten o'clock! You've been out for the count.'

'So what, I'm on holiday, what's the rush?'

'It's the third day. The car's got to go back so we're having a daytrip, else it'll have been a waste of money renting it. Don't you want to come?'

'Uh. Okay. But no more talking till we're in the car, and then only quietly. No singing!'

'All right crosspatch,' said Janice, annoyingly doing exaggerated quiet walking over to the door. 'The bathroom's all yours — Tom and I have had our turns. Don't be long. We'll see you at the car. We're going to have a quick explore of the grounds — it's a shame to waste the sun. And don't forget to bring a towel and your cozzie. Don't worry about sunburn cream — I bought a jumbo economy factor fifteen.'

'This is no talking, is it?'

Janice laughed as she went through into the living-room, shouting to Tom that the monster had risen from the black lagoon, and after a couple more minutes of shouting and thundering about, the front door slammed shut behind them. Silence at last! Marion would have liked to have lain there with her eyes closed for just another hour, but fearing loud reprisals she gingerly swung her legs out of bed to see if they would work. Just. She staggered into the shower and slumped against the wall while the cascade of warm water on her back slowly brought her round.

It wasn't until she was dressing in her embroidered crimson cheesecloth and wondering to herself which paintings she wanted to see and where – Siena? Florence? Perugia? – that she suddenly registered what Janice had said about swimming costumes. What on earth was she talking about? Why would you want a swimming costume on a day out in Tuscany? Filled with a sense of terrible foreboding, she slung her woven Indian bag over her shoulder and hurried out of the apartment to face what was undoubtedly going to be Trouble.

Even in her anxious state, as she walked down the wide stone stairs to the entrance hall below she couldn't help imagining some of the comings and goings here over the last seven centuries. Youths springing up the steps two at a time in doublet and hose to press their suit with the master of the house and improve their fortunes; soldiers in armour leaving their sweating horses in the hands of ostlers while they hurried, as quickly as their chain mail would allow, to announce the presence of the enemy over the other side of the hill; daughters and wives trapped here, miles from their peers, trying to amuse themselves within the parameters of what was deemed fitting for a lady, their disconsolate hands trailing half-finished tapestries, their heads full of plans to learn secretly to read. With such a sense of time passing she wondered if in future centuries somebody might divine her own presence here once, walking down the stairs with exaggerated care, her body a processing plant for alcoholic toxins, a middle-aged woman dressed in the garb of her youth. 'No' was the obvious answer, she decided, as she reached the massive entrance doors and struggled with the latch. Even her contemporaries would find it hard to imagine.

Tom had done all the exploring of the grounds that he had wanted, and was now sitting in the driving seat of the tiny Fiat, drumming his fingers on the steering wheel waiting for the off.

Women! He'd been awake since eight o'clock and had been mugging up on the road map so as not to be caught out this time, and now it was eleven. He was ignoring Janice, who was lying sprawled on the grass in front of the car with her skirt pulled up to her bottom, 'soaking up the rays'. He'd pointed out the sign that told you quite clearly in English and every kind of foreign language you could care to mention, that walking on the grass was absolutely not allowed, but Janice had retorted that she wasn't walking, she was lying, and who was that hurting anyway? He put this down to Marion's influence and was not impressed. He was even less impressed when he caught sight in his driving mirror of the bad influence herself swanning out of the Palazzo wearing a riot of red from another decade. Did she have to look so conspicuous? Nobody wore clothes like that now and in fact, among the people he knew, nobody had worn clothes like that then. He only hoped that Janice would not be influenced by that too. He'd sooner be dead than married to anybody who wore kaftans and leather thonged sandals. He pipped the horn crossly to tell Janice her 'friend' had deigned to join them and revved the tiny engine aggressively.

Marion tore open his door and glared at him. 'I'll drive,' she said shortly.

'Don't worry, I'll drive,' Tom replied stiffly, avoiding her eyes by staring intently through the windscreen.

'I'm not worried,' she countered, refusing to budge. 'I'm driving and that's that.'

'Oh come on Maz, let the boy have his toy,' said Janice as she joined them, pulling down her skirt. 'And fair's fair, you did get to drive the Merc yesterday. Look, I'll sit in the back and you can navigate from the front.' The front passenger seat still being no more inclined to give an inch than either of her two holiday companions, Janice squeezed herself over the top of it and somersaulted inelegantly in a flurry of bare thighs and striped knickers, shrieking with laughter all the way. The paracetamol that Marion had taken with her Nescafé was no match for this.

Having been reminded of Terence by Janice's allusion to his

Mercedes, she fervently hoped he wasn't watching these shenanigans from a window in the tower. As graciously as she could muster under the circumstances, she walked round to the passenger side and got in.

'That's better!' Janice bounced up and down on the back seat. 'All set? Don't forget your safety belt, Maz,' she added, as Tom did his usual kangaroo start out of the drive. 'By the way, I had an explore and there's no swimming pool here, so we'd better make the most of today.'

Marion swivelled round as best she could in the cramped car the better to eyeball her. 'Where do you think we're going to swim, pray tell?'

'I don't mind,' said Janice accommodatingly. 'Anywhere'll do so long as it's the seaside. Isn't Pisa on the coast Tom?'

Tom grunted noncommittally. He *thought* he'd memorised the map, but just now, in his mind's eye, he couldn't place Pisa at all.

'The seaside?!' Marion exclaimed. 'When you're in *Tuscany* near the *Umbrian border* for God's sake? What about the art and the architecture in Florence, Siena, Perugia, Orvieto – even Cortona, just down the road!'

'Do they have sea?'

'No!'

'Well I want to swim and sunbathe. I've brought the Lilo.'

'There's no way I'm going to waste what will probably be our only day out, lying on the beach!'

'Is there art and architecture in Pisa?' asked Tom, trying to head off a row.

'Of *course* there is,' said Marion nearly at her wit's end. 'Quite apart from the Museo Nazionale di San Matteo, the Museo dell'Opera del Duomo, the Campo dei Miracoli, surely even you have heard of the Leaning Tower?!'

'There's no need for sarcasm, Marion,' Tom said stiffly. 'I merely wanted to make sure you'd have plenty to see. We'll drop you in Pisa while we go to Viareggio.'

'*Viareggio?!* What on earth do you want to go to Viareggio for?'

'It's on the coast isn't it?' asked Tom doubtfully.

'It's on the coast, but it's a hell-hole!' said Marion, who had never actually been there.

'Why, what's it like Maz?' asked Janice, who wanted somewhere nice.

'It's touristy,' said Marion damningly. 'It'll be wall to wall umbrellas and sunloungers.'

'Fantastic!' said Janice. 'Nice sand?'

They drove in complete silence after a while, each lost in their own thoughts. Having failed to enthuse either Marion or Tom into a game of 'I Spy', Janice had amused herself by calling out the place names on the road signs in a cod Italian accent.

'Chiusi! . . . Arezzo! . . . Terranuova Braciolini! . . . San Giovanni Valdarno! . . .'

It was Tom who cracked first.

'Janice!! For crying out *grief!*'

'What?'

'We can all read! Can't we just have a bit of peace and quiet?!'

Janice chuckled. 'Ooh. Mr Grumpy.' She leaned forward and chubbed Marion's shoulder. 'Marion doesn't mind, do you Mazzer? I'm only practising my Italian.'

Marion unclenched her jaw enough to say, 'Actually Janice, for once I am in complete accord with Tom.'

Janice flopped back into her seat, deflated and hurt. 'Well bugger me!' she sniffed. 'You *try* to be cheerful . . .'

Marion couldn't wait to be rid of them for the day as they came into Pisa, so as soon as Tom started to get twitchy about 'getting lost in the city centre' she told him to pull over and let her out. 'Look, look, there's the sign to Viareggio, just follow that.'

'But will you be all right here?' asked Tom guiltily.

'Yes,' said Marion, 'I shall be more than all right, thank you.'

'Shall we meet you somewhere in the car and all take it back to the airport together?'

'No, the privilege is all yours.' She was unbuckling her seat belt and out of the car in a trice.

'How are we all going to get back?' asked Tom, nervous now at the thought of public transport Abroad.

'Bus and train I imagine and a taxi the other end. Don't worry about me, I shall take care of myself. You just enjoy yourselves at the seaside.' She slammed the door and walked away without a backward glance.

'Hungover,' said Janice, still smarting at Marion's rebuff. 'Come on Tommy, let's leave Miss Mardy Arse and go and play buckets and spades.'

Marion and Frank hadn't stayed long in Pisa — only a couple of weeks — but after a bit of brisk, angry walking, she realised now that she was following her memories. How apposite then that her feet should take her to the Piazza del Duomo or the Campo dei Miracoli, as the tourist industry dubbed it — the Field of Miracles. For how else could it be, other than by a miracle, that she could remember the layout of a city she hadn't visited for decades? Unnerved by this, she decided she needed some sustenance before she could cope with any more time-warp experiences, but just as she was about to sit at an outdoor table of a pretty little bar she happened to be passing, she suddenly realised that this had been *their* bar. It was almost as if Frank was there, invisibly at her side, guiding her steps. This was all too much on an empty stomach, and exactly what she had promised herself yesterday that she would learn to grow out of. Frank was dead, and so was that part of her life, she told herself firmly as she grabbed a mozzarella panino and an espresso macchiato to go. But *where* to go, to get away from memories, to escape the inside of her own head? Nowhere, apparently. She caught herself just in time, before a full-blooded descent into the pit of depression, and squaring her shoulders she decided to breakfast in the Piazza itself. If she couldn't escape her memories, she would purge herself by wallowing in them.

So coloured by Frank were all her memories of Italy, she had forgotten how beautiful this vast green pasture with its bleached white buildings was. Finding herself a small patch of shade near the Baptistry – the sun was now at its midday zenith – she gave herself over to gustatory delight and a visual feast. There laid out in front of her was the famous picture-postcard view: the Romanesque drum of the Baptistry topped by the Gothic workings of Nicola and Giovanni Pisano and crowned by Cellini di Nese's dome – two hundred years and two artistic movements in the making; behind that the Romanesque Duomo, to which its architect Buschetto gave his life in the eleventh century, his very bones built into the façade that his successor, Rainaldo, designed and built; and peeping out drunkenly from behind (which made Marion feel even more woozy) the Campanile, or Leaning Tower, where Galileo Galilei had reputedly dropped his two mismatched balls to make his point about gravity's impartiality concerning weight. Meraviglioso, thought Marion, as she sighed with pleasure, chewing her panino. Why on earth did I stay away so long? I think you know the answer to that, she answered herself sternly. Because you've been stuck in the pain of the past, and have forgotten the pleasures.

After a thorough examination of her lap to make sure she'd eaten every crumb, and having smoked a couple of fags, she felt ready to plunge inside the buildings' interiors and to wander down memory lane. She began with the Baptistry, and joined a throng of tourists gathered round the marble pulpit to pay homage to its creator, Nicola Pisano, rather than its subject, Christ. The enduring nature and power of art never ceased to amaze her – not just that this sculpture was still here seven hundred years later, carved by the artist's own hands, but that he himself had borrowed images of classical antiquity from the vases and sarcophagi of the ancient Romans and Greeks, copying the faces of their pagan gods and transmuting them into Madonnas and saints, converting them to Christianity long after their adherents were dead and unable to defend them. They must be turning in their graves.

An American tourist was putting the magnificent acoustics to the test by leaning over the ropes to holler his name (Marion was only glad that Janice wasn't here) and to listen to its echo as it gradually faded away. When she and Frank had visited, they had serendipitously coincided with a choir practice which had drawn them from hundreds of yards away. It had been Verdi's Requiem, and the memory of it and the irony which transpired to haunt her, made Marion gasp now and hurry out again into the sunshine. It was in Pisa she had discovered she was pregnant. She had told Frank that very day.

As far as wallowing went she was doing very well, she told herself, as she lit another cigarette with trembling hands, leaning against the outside wall. She just hoped that the purging part would kick in soon; this was really too painful to take. She remembered now a double irony — that Frank had been amused at the choirmaster's inappropriate choice of music, when the two of them had suddenly so much to live for. She could see him now as he threw back his magnificent blond mane and laughed, revealing his beautiful white teeth — could almost feel his arms around her as he shared the joke. What a pillock. He'd been wrong.

Now this was new. Was this purging? She'd never felt angry before, at least not with Frank. But hey — why not? She'd complained to him enough times about his habit of striding on ahead of her, caught up in his own enthusiasms, and look what had happened — death. If he'd only been at her side crossing Whitehall he'd have been here now, and so would Jake. Or would they? Would they still be together after all these years? So few of her friends' relationships had survived the Assault of the Younger Woman when they were in their thirties; would Frank have been any different from his peers? Would he have strayed from her side? Having given over her entire adult life to the cult of the bereaved wife and mother (in all but name) Marion tried on Spurned Divorcée for size. It felt infuriating and insulting. If he'd done that, she'd have pushed him in front of oncoming traffic herself.

Yes, she thought, suddenly laughing, this seemed to be purging all right. She felt better enough now to plunge into the Duomo to look at Pisano Junior's pulpit ('What do you want to be when you grow up, Giovanni?' 'I want to make marble pulpits like my Dad.' Extraordinary), and was reminded by the guidebook that this, arguably his best ever, had been dismantled, crated up, and forgotten about for three hundred and fifty years when Gothic had gone out of fashion. So much for art critics, she thought.

The cathedral was teeming with tourists following the raised umbrellas of their guides, and Marion smiled to herself, imagining the uproar that would be caused if Jesus the temple anarchist were to walk in now, overturning tables and chucking out everybody who was trying to make an honest buck. She picked her way through them to view the huge thirteenth-century mosaic in the apse which had been completed by Cimabue in 1302, who had added the figure of Saint John Evangelist. She wished her sixth form were with her now to see for themselves how he had brought the dimension of human feelings into art for the first time, influencing all who came after him.

She whizzed round the Camposanto whose frescoes had been mostly destroyed in 1944 by incendiary bombs dropped by American warplanes, and remembered the outrage Frank had felt about that in his pacifistic youth. Would he have dodged the Vietnam draft if he'd survived? They'd talked about it endlessly, and he'd always said he would, even if it meant going to prison. Marion had pictured herself romantically as Joan Baez, standing by her man, her long hair cut short to show that this was serious, singing songs of protest to cheering youth. How naïve they seemed now, from this perspective.

How would Frank have picked his way through the avaricious eighties — would he have remained pure in thought, word and deed? Marion was beginning to be bored by this endless line of self-questioning, which was progress of a kind, she thought. Let's face it, she told herself briskly, as a working architect he'd have gone the way that Mammon pointed or gone bust, simple as that. Just as the Gothic architects, funded by the Church, had built churches, so architects in the late twentieth century, funded by Business, built business centres. Would she still have loved him had he done so? Would she have helped him pick out his Armani suits? She pondered this for a while, grappling with the dimensions of time. No, was the honest answer. The Frank that she had loved belonged to a different time, a time of innocence, his youthful ideals intact. It was almost sacrilegious to his memory to imagine him yuppied up.

So there it was. Revelation came at last, while she stood in front of a fourteenth-century fresco damaged by a twentieth-century bomb, appropriately called *The Triumph of Death*, by Artist Unknown. She had wasted some of the best years of her life mourning the death of her own youth and innocence. How very stupid.

Curiously, though this honest self-assessment was damning in the extreme, she was filled with a new energy to *live* – really live, to make up for lost time. She'd have an ice cream, then go to the Museo Nazionale di San Matteo to soak up the best of Pisa's paintings. Then she'd find somewhere fabulous to eat. This day was hers, to do exactly what she wanted. This day, and the rest of her life.

Janice, who lived every day as if it were her last, was lying flat on her back in a veritable conurbation of sunloungers, third row back from the sea. This was the life! And it was nice to be just her and Tommo on their own. They'd found their way to Viareggio with no problems at all (except for the parking which had been a bit fraught), and Janice, landlocked Midlander, was as excited as ever to see the sea, even if they had had to take out a second mortgage for the privilege of lying next to it. What rip-off merchants these Eyeties were, bagging every inch of sand with their brollies and chairs! Tom had been quite cross at having to part with such a bundle of cash. Still, it was nice to lie in comfort, and they'd economise on their lunch. Any minute now, as soon as she was dry again, she'd go off and find a supermarket and buy some crusty cobs and a tin of corned beef. The beach vendors were charging as much for a cheese roll as she and Tom usually paid for a three course meal at home.

Just thinking about food was making her tummy rumble. She was thirsty too – God it was hot! Fabulous. Her hands explored her swimming costume. Not too wet – it'd do. She sat up, squinting against the sun, and pulled her clothes on.

'I'm off shopping for the dinner then,' she told Tom, who was lying face down at her side. 'Any special requests?'

'Only if they've got an English paper that doesn't cost an arm and a leg,' he said.

'Shall I put some more sun cream on you before I go?'

'No!' It had been embarrassing enough the first time, with her hands going places the sun couldn't possibly reach. 'I'll be all right – I'm going in the water in a minute.'

'Well you just mind you don't get burnt. And keep those scalds in the shade.'

'I am doing – why do you think I'm lying on my front?'

'Aah – does it hurt?'

'A bit. It's okay.'

'My brave little soldier.' He looked so cute lying there in his trunks. She flopped down on to her knees to plonk a great snog on his mouth.

'Are you going then?' he asked pointedly when he'd fought his way out for air.

'Yeah, I'm starving, are you?'

'Mm.'

'See you later then.'

'Bye.'

'And no talking to strange women while I'm gone!'

'No.'

'Won't be long.'

'Okay.'

'Don't get lonely.'

'I won't.'

'See you in a bit.'

'Yes.'

'Shall I get you orange or Coke?'

Bloody hell! 'Anything — whatever you like.'

'Back in a tick.'

Tom watched her finally depart, her sandals spraying sand as she walked, nodding and smiling to everyone she passed. He was not a happy bunny. He'd just been nodding off for a nice snooze, and now he was totally awake. He glanced round at his neighbours, feeling conspicuously pale. Everybody was so beautiful, and so brown, and there were so many of them! He felt even more self-conscious now he was on his own. He'd felt dreadfully exposed when Janice had marched them down the ranks of sunbathers looking for the perfect spot, and even worse when he had had to take his clothes off standing up under the umbrella for all to see. Hadn't bothered Janice, of course. She'd had her clothes off and had run down to the sea before you could say 'Mind out for jellyfish!' She seemed to be genuinely oblivious of the fact that she was white and wobbly, and that she was drawing attention to herself by her screaming and laughing and splashing in the waves, shouting at him to blow up the Lilo and 'Come on down!' He'd inflated the Lilo from a prone position, but refused to take it to her, telling her when she arrived back to chivvy him, dripping salty water all over his back, that he preferred to relax first. If only!

And now he'd got Janice from under his hair, some kids had switched on a ghetto blaster right next to him, playing House. Maybe it was time to go into the sea. He willed himself to sit up, but couldn't bring himself to. The reason he was lying face down was not, as he had told Janice, in order to protect his scalds, but to hide the little tummy that had sprouted over the last few months (did she have to fry *everything*?), and because the red marks where the boiling water had landed on his legs made him look as if he'd got some dreadful lurgy. God it was hot though. Bloody hell!

After a few more minutes he could take it no longer, and he devised a plan. He'd carry the Lilo in front of him down to the sea, then float about on that for a bit. He could stay out there longer like that – he wasn't too strong a swimmer and you looked daft splashing about in the shallows on your own for very long.

It took a great deal of self-discipline not to scream and run when his feet touched the burning sand, but gripping the Lilo tightly to his chest and gritting his teeth, he walked sedately enough to the water's edge and stood tentatively in the tiny wavelets, acclimatising his skin to the shock of the temperature change. At least it was less crowded down here, and would have been a bit quieter too if those oiks on the water-bikes hadn't been racing each other and pratting around. Still, they were much further out than he intended going, and they'd probably get bored in a bit.

His feet and ankles now being at home in the coolness of the water, he slowly waded in up to his knees. Ouch – it stung his burns! He put the Lilo down and tried gingerly to sit on it without getting wetter, but it kept floating away behind him. The only way, obviously, would be to straddle it, and then lower himself down into a lying position once he was safely aboard. As he did so, his weight in its centre caused it to sink, and the two ends came up and slapped him wetly round the head. Gordon Bennett! Why was everything so frigging difficult, even trying to relax?! Finally he managed to get himself lying on his front, gasping as the water hit his chest and wondering, as he did annually, what it was about holidays that had everybody killing themselves all year in order to afford one. Personally he would be happier pottering round his own garden or tinkering in his shed.

After a while, with the sun on his back cooled by a light breeze and the sea causing the Lilo to undulate gently beneath him, even he had to admit that this was not unpleasant. This close to the beach there were still too many people in the immediate vicinity for his comfort, but he found that by paddling with his arms he could float effortlessly away from them into his own private patch of water. He put his head on one side and gazed out to sea. The water-bikers had raced off to

disturb other bathers further up the beach now, and they had been replaced by some muscle-bound show-offs on windsurfers, but that didn't matter – at least they were quiet and some way away. He felt jealous of their younger, toned bodies as they leaned them this way and that to guide their craft, and he vowed that he would rejoin Greg Jones's early-morning jogging sessions when he got back to school, and maybe even join a gym. But for now, just floating and relaxing was all that he required. Not unpleasant at all.

It took Janice a good while to find a supermarket, and even longer to convert the price of everything from lire into pounds. She bought two peach yoghurts, half a dozen cobs, a tin of corned beef and some measurement or other of tomatoes – she still thought in pounds and ounces, even at work where it was all kilos and grams. She picked up a can of orange and of Coke so that Tom could choose, and then set about planning their tea tonight and their dinner tomorrow. She didn't want to get too laden down because of having to bus it back after returning the car, but she knew they needed loo rolls, and the shop had an offer on tins of tuna chunks. She loaded up her basket and took it to the till. What a price! Oh well, she assumed that Snotty Cow Marion (as she had taken to calling her again in her head since the incident in the car) would want to share, so at least she'd get a third of the money back tonight.

Tracking down Tom's paper proved trickier, but finally she found a two-day-old *Daily Mail* in a shop in a hotel (she'd had to go in to borrow the facilities). Two pounds fifty! What a rip-off! And it had nothing to say except bad news about interest rates and famine in foreign parts. Oh well, if it made Tom happy she'd get it and lie about the cost. He was worth it, and they were on their hols.

Struggling back to the beach with her carrier bags she thought it would be a close run thing between eating first or throwing herself immediately in the sea. It was so hot in the streets with the heat of the sun bouncing up off the pavements. At first, when she had reached the promenade and was faced with the vast acreage of colourful sunbeds and umbrellas, she panicked and couldn't remember where they'd parked themselves, but after plunging on to the beach and trudging a couple of hundred yards along the third row from the front, she at last recognised a fat Italian mamma with her brood of bambinos, who had agreed with her sign language on her outward journey that it was indeed a lovely day. Twelve brollies later she saw her and Tom's towels spread out on their sunbeds, and plonked herself down with relief. The Lilo had gone, so he must have finally unwound enough to go into the sea. Poor old Tommy, she thought fondly, he doesn't like change. Every year it was the same. He never got used to being away until it was almost time to go back. She scanned the sea for him but couldn't see properly round the brollies in front. Oh well. She'd make up a quick corned beef cob just to take the edge off her hunger, and potter down to the water in a minute. Blimey it was hot! She took off her skirt and top, slapped on some more factor fifteen, and got to work on the tomatoes with Tom's Swiss army knife. She might as well do all the cobs while she was about it. Yum. It was really nice bread.

She was suddenly conscious of a huge palaver going on around her, with everybody pointing and running down to the sea. What was it? Was it a shark — did you get those in Italy? Anxious now for Tom's safety, she ran down to the water's edge to join the crowd. She couldn't see Tom anywhere — nor, thank goodness, the triangular fin of a shark — only some fool on a Lilo who had floated out miles too far and who was being persuaded to ride pillion on a water-bike for a lift back to shore. It wasn't . . .! It couldn't be . . .! He was always so careful . . .! It was.

As far as conspicuousness went, Tom bitterly reflected, as he clung on to his pink Lilo with one arm and to the gym-hardened six-pack of the water-biker's diaphragm with the other, he'd made it to the top. All he'd wanted was a little bit of peace and quiet. Was that too much to ask? Okay, so he'd fallen asleep and drifted out which had been silly – but he'd have been fine if the water-bikers hadn't have thought they were at Le Mans; he could have paddled back. One minute he was warm and drifting pleasantly, the next he was drowning in the cold deep sea. Stupid boys. If they'd been at his school he'd have kept them in for a week. And why had everybody needed to come down to the water to gawp, the morons – didn't they have anything better to do?

Oh God, there was Janice, her arms going like a windmill, running through the waves towards him, screeching – what? Cheese? Did she really think that at this precise moment he gave a toss what she'd got for his dinner? Oh no, no – she'd got the Instamatic. Don't shoot! Shit. He'd never be allowed to live it down. Quietly drowning would have been preferable.

Chapter Thirteen

Meanwhile, back at the Palazzo, Terence's sorrow had turned not to anger, but to internalised rage. Indeed, so furious had he been whilst shaving that he had even forgotten about his embryonic moustache, and half of it had disappeared inside his Remington before he'd realised his mistake. Cursing, he shaved the other side off viciously, to punish himself for his stupidity. *Why* had he told that particular lie last night? Why had it gone so disastrously wrong? If there was any justice in the world Beatrice would be on a plane right now, flying home in shame, not twirling girlishly round him whenever he looked up, and wanging on about weddings.

The wet patch had been dry. Damn the Italian summer weather! And damn those awful floral sheets which left no trace of the recently committed crime to the naked eye. He could hardly have insisted on a lab analysis, could he – although that thought had flashed wildly through his head. He'd set it up so perfectly, to put all the blame on Beatrice when he finished with her, to make himself the innocent cuckold. It was perfect script writing – the set-up, then the sting. 1: Hero says he wants to have baby because he feels he can trust his partner's fidelity. 2: Discovers the sodding wet patch in her bed. 3: Tears and recriminations (not in anger but in sorrow). 4: Hero, alone now, turns to new heroine for solace.

Instead, this. 1: Hero (stupid stupid *stupid*) says he wants to have a bloody baby because he finally trusts his partner's fidelity. 2: Throws back her sheets and turns to her accusingly. 3: She joins him at his side, peers at the sheets and says 'What?' 4: Hero peers at dry, unstained sheets, blusters about thinking he saw a spider. 5: Heroine, an arachnaphobe, screams blue murder and insists on going to *his* bed to make babies.

God, he'd put himself in a terrible fix. After all that bollocks about being in love and missing out on half his life, how was he to explain that he couldn't get it up? Last night had been okay – he'd pretended to be more drunk than he was, and allowed Beatrice to be graciously forgiving. But this morning there had been no getting out of it. The image of Aunty Ivy's pink rayon petticoat had had to be conjured up and pressed into service, and even that had only just worked. Now what was he going to do – he couldn't go on like this for ever. And what if she was pregnant already? He wouldn't put it past one of his sperm to have front crawled like crazy to its target and embedded its stupid fat head in one of her eggs.

Breakfast was fifteen kinds of hell. Pamela was so cranky with her coke hangover she could curdle milk at a hundred paces. God that woman was voracious! There must have been two grams left in the bag when he pressed it into her hand at the restaurant, and when he asked her for it back at the end of the evening, she'd said it was all gone. Of course, she was probably lying. And Chris was still obviously sulking about having to pay the bill – something which Terence would have enjoyed if everything had gone according to plan, but now, with his own problems, was just another irritation, watching him mooch about in Chekhovian dolour, playing with his eggs. Eggs! Why eggs, this morning of all mornings? As for Freddie, still avoiding Christopher, still with his head up his own arse – did he always chew everything seventy-three times like a ruminative cow, or was he just trying to be annoying?

And then there was Bea, arriving late to table looking radiant and smug, wanting to feed him little intsey bits of buttered toast and be all coupley-cosy. Why didn't she go the whole hog, for

God's sake, and wear a T-shirt saying 'I shagged the King?' She looked different this morning, her face seeming to have plumped out, the haunted nervousness gone. Terence wanted to smack the look of self-confidence off her stupid bovine face. Did she really think for one moment that she would ever be Mrs Terence Armstrong? She must be mad! Thank goodness he and Angela had never got divorced – it suited them both to tell their lovers that their ex was being tricky and would never give consent. He cheered up slightly, remembering this old chestnut. He'd haul it out later, when the time came. But in deepest, deepest sorrow, of course.

His cheerfulness was short-lived, however, when he heard a car in the drive outside, and going to the window (as much to avoid having any more buttered toast popped into his mouth as anything) he saw Marion disappearing with Janice and Tom in their little Fiat. Wait for me! he'd wanted to shout, don't leave me with these dreadful people! Where were they going? He bet it would be fun.

After a while Pamela announced that she was going back to bed, and for once she didn't look smoulderingly at Chris when she said it. She said she had a headache, and Terence didn't doubt it.

'The hell of it is,' she said, turning in the doorway, her hand rubbing her aching sinuses, 'is that there are people coming to dinner tonight. Joe and Evadne McCorquodale, Frederick – I invited them for you, since you so enjoyed their company last time you were here.'

'How marvellous,' said Frederick politely. 'Shall I cook?'

'Would you be so dear?'

'Of course, it will be my pleasure. I was already thinking of driving into Cortona today, so I'll do some shopping while I'm there. Shall I do my risotto al pomodoro con melanzane?'

'Anything,' replied Pamela, quickly bored now she'd palmed the domestic chores off on to somebody else. 'You're so talented in the cucina, I'm sure whatever you present us will be a gastronomic triumph.'

Frederick beamed with pleasure as she took her leave, and instantly fussed about with notebook and pencil to make a list.

'I'll come with you,' said Christopher at once. He still didn't know where he stood with Terence after yesterday, and he looked to be in a dangerous, seething kind of humour this morning. And apart from anything else, having been landed with the bill last night he really needed to buddy up again with Freddie to save himself from more expense.

'We'll all come,' said Terence quickly, and Beatrice chanced a pout. Anything would be better than being pressed into service by the brood mare again, he thought uncharitably. And anyway, Marion might be there.

Freddie wanted to visit the Museo Diocesano first, having missed it on his last visit, and the others, knowing nothing of Tuscan art treasures and caring even less, were happy enough for him to be in charge. It turned out to be housed in a deconsecrated church in the shadow of Cortona's Duomo.

'Are you sure that's it, Freddie?' asked Terence, looking doubtfully between the two. 'Shouldn't we be going into this big one here?'

'You can if you like,' Frederick knowledgeably replied. 'There is an Andrea del Sarto *Assumption* which is worth a look, and I personally found Berrettini's *Death of Joseph* to be quite moving on a human scale. But in the main it is a fairly disappointing collection of seventeenth-century work.' There was also a rather queeny looking Christ on one of the altars, but he would forgo the pleasure of going back for another look at it, given his present company.

'Right,' said Terence, completely lost. 'We'll come along with you then.' How he wished that Marion was here to be his guide.

Inside the church, Frederick stopped to admire a battle scene carved on a marble sarcophagus. 'Quite a mélange of myths,' he noted succinctly to himself.

'What are they, Freddie?' Christopher enquired, feigning interest at his side.

'Well, here, quite evidently are the Lapiths at King Pir-ithous's wedding, fighting the drunken Centaurs . . .'

'Is that Lapith as in Lazuli?' asked Beatrice brightly. Terence sniggered. 'Thinth when did you have a lithp?' he asked cruelly, which was pretty rich since he had no idea who the Lapiths were himself.

'I think you mean *lapis* lazuli,' said Freddie kindly, 'from the Latin, meaning stone. The Lapiths were Greek, belonging to a mythological race in Thessaly.'

'Oh,' said Beatrice, 'I see.'

'And who are these chaps?' asked Christopher, pointing to some pretty youths, who he was sure held more interest for Freddie.

'Dionysians,' said Freddie, blushing, 'fighting the Amazons.' He moved swiftly on into the nave.

'Gosh, how yeuky!' Beatrice exclaimed as they fetched up in front of Lorenzetti's haemorrhaging Christ dangling from his cross.

'That's where our Protestant culture makes everything so mimsy,' mused Terence just to be superior. 'The Catholics have got it right. It makes his sacrifice seem all the more human, showing such eviscerating pain.'

'That's what I think too,' said Freddie, beaming. 'One can so easily forget the Son of Man, and think of Him exclusively as the Son of God, protected from human suffering. Whereas with this amount of blood and corporeal anguish . . .'

Now that Terence was safely chatting to Freddie, Christo-pher moved away from him to join Beatrice, who was examining some old font. Quite apart from anything else, he needed to find out what had gone on last night and if he was in the clear. But also, Bea was looking even more beautiful this morning – irresistible, in fact. Images of their love-making flooded into his mind, making him ache with desire.

'How did it go with Terence last night after we'd left you?' he asked her in a hushed tone while surreptitiously fondling her bottom.

'Wonderful,' she breathed, taking a little sidestep to detach herself. 'He wants me to have his baby.'

'Really?' asked Christopher, astonished. 'Are you sure?'

'Of course I'm sure,' she hissed, moving away to gaze milkily at Sassetta's *Madonna and Child with Saints*. To his intense surprise, Christopher felt gutted. Was this dog-in-the-manger stuff, he asked himself, or real honest-to-God, red-blooded jealousy he was feeling? He was used to girls pursuing *him* after he had slept with them, not the other way round. And yesterday afternoon had been so nice. At least, it had been for him. Hadn't it meant anything to Beatrice all?

Terence, irritated beyond measure at seeing Beatrice looking broody at Mary and Jesus, her only begotten son, found great solace in della Gatta's version of the Virgin, appearing to do a striptease in mid-air to an awestruck crowd below. 'What's this, Freddie?' he asked, laughing coarsely and speaking loudly to knock the self-satisfaction off Bovine Beatrice's face. 'Why's Mary taking off her corset and waving it at that bloke?'

'It's Doubting Thomas,' replied Freddie pointedly, pursing his mouth, 'refusing to believe in the Assumption, just as he had refuted the Resurrection. In order to prove that God was rewarding the Virgin Mary for the Immaculate Conception by taking her living body to Heaven in her sleep, and not just her soul, she removed her girdle in mid-ascent and threw it down to Thomas as physical evidence. It is still in existence, kept as a holy reliquary in Prato, for other doubters to see.'

Terence burst out laughing. 'Really? And where are her knickers kept?'

'Of course it may be amusing to modern thought,' replied Frederick stiffly. 'It all started with the Crusades, of course – a kind of reliquomania.'

'What, like women at Tom Jones's concerts throwing him their their underwear in the hope that he'll return the favour?' chortled Terence.

'It's rather sad if that is the modern equivalent, isn't it?' Freddie said. *Why* were people such *Philistines*? Was it going to be like this all morning? He was dying to see Fra' Angelico's *Annunciation* about which he'd heard so much – the delicate feathers on Gabriel's wings, the carpet of wild flowers – but not in this company. Back in London, when he was planning this trip, he'd dreamed of bringing Christopher here on his own to see the master's work. Now it was all spoilt, what with Christopher getting up to mischief with Pamela, and Terence practically calling Freddie a poufter to his face. Where was the romance in that?

'Look,' he said now, desperately, 'if you all want to have a look round Cortona, I could meet you later, for lunch. It's a shame to waste the sunshine . . .'

'No no, this is fascinating, Freddie,' said Christopher, flirting again (but this time to punish Bea).

'And it's so wonderful to be with somebody so . . . so . . .'

'Articulate?' asked Terence, with heavy sarcasm.

'Erudite, I was going to say,' retorted Christopher, his eyes narrowing to tiny slits. 'But of course, if Terence and Beatrice want to go off and trot round town . . .'

'Well . . .' said Beatrice, thinking of the tempting shops.

'No,' said Terence.

And so it was with heavy heart that Frederick, feeling like a tourist guide for Texans, was followed by his party to the altar, to gaze on the Archangel Gabriel, painted by his hero, the Domenican friar. Not for the first time, looking at exquisite religious work, he thought to himself how much happier he would have been had he been born during the Renaissance, living a monastic life and quietly illustrating manuscripts.

'What's the story here then, Fred?' asked Terence.

'Well, as you can see, the Annunciation of the birth of Christ,' he replied. Surely he didn't need to explain what that was? 'In the background we have Adam and Eve being expelled from Eden, the finale, if you will, of Man's fall from grace – and here comes his salvation – Gabriel sent by God to tell Mary that she is to be with child.'

'How romantic,' breathed Beatrice.

'Who's it by, Freddie?' asked Christopher, wishing she was

feeling romantic about him. 'Was it somebody important, did you say?'

'Fra' Angelico,' said Freddie reverently. 'The Master.' He was all for people learning, and unless he was greatly mistaken, they seemed to be interested enough. 'You see his glorious use of primary colours, and his command of such minute detail, as for instance in this carpet of wild flowers.' He stood back for a moment, taking in the whole. 'Actually, I think it is most definitely the best of his work that I have ever seen. He combines breathtaking technique with a true understanding of the Bible, a religious awe. Even if one were a complete rationalist, I think, gazing on this, one might be persuaded to believe in angels.'

'Oh yes. Such beautiful wings,' said Beatrice dreamily. 'He must have had to study lots of birds. Do you like Sir Peter Scott?'

An extremely fine lunch (seared vegetables drizzled with extra-virgin olive oil followed by spinach gnocchi in an exquisite duck ragù) soothed Freddie's jangled nerves, but he started to twitch again over his espresso as he checked and rechecked his shopping list for the evening's meal.

'Don't worry, Freddie, I'll help you,' said Christopher, whose idea of cooking was to zap prepared morsels from Harrod's Food Hall in his microwave.

'We'll all help,' offered Beatrice. 'It'll be fun!'

'Who are the McCorquodales?' Terence asked.

'They are American friends of Pamela's who live across the valley,' Freddie replied. 'Joe is an archaeologist specialising in the Etruscans, so of course he is fascinating to talk to. He's currently working on a dig nearby where they've had some extraordinary finds.'

'Super!' said Beatrice. 'So what are we going to eat?'

Terence rolled his eyes and wondered what Marion was doing now, and if she'd be back in time to be inveigled into joining them for Freddie's feast. He thought he'd go quite mad if he didn't see her again soon.

Chapter Fourteen

Janice and Tom had taken the scenic route back from Pisa, having taken five buses (two by mistake) between the airport, where they had returned the hired car, and Claudio's shop and bar, which was the closest to the Palazzo that the bone-shaking local bus went. To their great surprise they found Marion sitting outside drinking grappa with some local men.

'Hiya!' said Janice, who had enjoyed her day out so much she was prepared to forgive and forget. 'What a palaver getting back! I was looking out for you all the way. Did you have a fabulous time?'

'Terrific,' said Marion. 'Do you fancy a drink?'

'Ooh yeah! What's that you've got?'

'Grappa — do you want to try?'

Janice took the proffered glass and took a deep swig. 'Bloody hell,' she coughed, to the locals' amusement. 'It's like nail varnish remover. I think I'll pass on that. But I could murder one of them pink things Terry got us yesterday.'

'I'll have a beer,' said Tom quickly. He'd had enough shocks to the system for one day.

'How come you got here before us?' Janice asked. 'We left at five, but it's taken us hours to get here.'

'I hitched,' said Marion, nodding towards one of the men she'd been drinking with. 'I was lucky that Antonio had gone up to Pisa in his truck and that he was on his way back when I stuck out my thumb.'

'What are you like?' exclaimed Janice. 'You could have been raped and mugged!'

'But instead I got a nice ride back in good company,' Marion replied. 'Cheers.' She clinked glasses with them and drained the last of her grappa.

'Un altro?' enquired Claudio.

'Perché no?' said Marion, devil-may-care. She turned back to Janice and Tom. 'I was just about to order some food. Do you fancy eating here?'

'No, don't do that, save your pennies – I've bought some provisions.' Janice pointed triumphantly to her heavy plastic carrier bags. 'I'll make us all a snack when we get back.'

Marion didn't need to look at the shopping to know that she would be staying put. 'Not for me, thanks,' she said. 'Claudio's wife Maria is in the kitchen tonight and apparently has made her legendary rabbit stew. Why don't you save the food till tomorrow?'

'Oh no, I couldn't!' Janice exclaimed. 'Not rabbit. I always think of *Watership Down*.'

Marion caught herself before she could make a withering comment. She lit a cigarette and smiled. 'So how was Viareggio?'

Tom held his breath. He had had words with Janice about the taking of photographs of people when they are in embarrassing situations through no fault of their own, and the making of silly stories for cheap laughs from same.

'Fantastic,' said Janice. 'Really brilliant. Wasn't it Tom?'

He smiled at her approvingly. 'Very nice indeed.'

'What about you – did you have a nice time looking at your art?'

'I had a great time,' said Marion, and then added, 'Listen, I'm sorry about this morning. I'm not at my best first thing after a tankful the night before. I get a bit . . .'

'Snotty,' Janice provided.

'Not to put too fine a point,' Marion conceded.

The scents of the rich meat stew being prepared within were starting to waft without, and Tom's tummy was starting to rumble. He downed his beer. 'Shall we make a start back, Jan?'

'Yes, okay,' his wife replied. 'Are you starving hungry?'

'Getting there.'

Janice bent forward to Marion conspiratorially. 'I'm dying for a tinkle. What's the lavvy like?'

'You'll survive it,' said Marion.

'Do you want to go, Tommy?'

'I'll be all right thank you.'

'You can always go in a hedgerow on the way back. Don't you envy them Maz?'

'Mm,' said Marion. Of course she envied them. Their power, their freedom – but their ability to pee standing up? Not really. Not on an everyday basis.

After they had watched Janice all the way into the shop, Marion and Tom found themselves uncomfortably alone with not much to say to each other.

'So what are you reckoning on doing tomorrow?' she asked, to break the silence.

'Not sure,' he said. 'What is there?'

What indeed, without a car? The holiday suddenly seemed very long. 'Well, Cortona isn't far. Not too long a walk, I shouldn't think, if we could find a way across the fields.'

'Is there much to do there?'

'There's some very interesting stuff to see in and around. It's a medieval city, but with Etruscan roots. A couple of galleries, one of which is stuffed with Etruscan and Roman finds, and the other has some very important works of art from the Renaissance . . .'

'Oh well,' said Tom, with what sounded like resignation, 'I suppose it'll be worth a look.'

'Yes,' said Marion, and they fell into silence again until Janice bounded out to rejoin them.

'You'll never believe it!' she cried to Tom. 'Here's us been lugging all that shopping back, and Claudio's got an offer on tuna chunks as well!' She scooped up her carrier bags and Tom stood up to go.

'Are you sure you'll be all right getting back?' he asked Marion doubtfully. 'It'll be getting dark any minute.'

'I'll be fine,' she reassured him. 'You go back and enjoy your supper. I'll see you later. Won't be long.'

She watched them lurch off down the road, hampered by their groceries, Janice trying to claim Tom's hand in hers. Something had to be done. Transport had to be found. She needed her freedom to explore, and to escape them. She'd made up her mind today, after shaking off the yoke of Frank, that whatever Terence might have to offer, she would take. But when she thought about it, however improbable it might be that he wanted her more than he wanted Beatrice, it was hardly likely that he could carry on an affair under his partner's nose. No, that salvation couldn't be relied on. What should she do? Draw on her meagre savings and blow it all on a hired car for the duration? A horse! A horse! Her kingdom for a horse!

Pamela had ordained that they would dine al fresco, a charming idea which necessitated Herculean labours from Terence and Christopher in negotiating a trestle table and chairs down two flights of stairs, and had Freddie working off his calories between courses as he struggled to provide a seamless service between kitchen and diners.

Between them, Pamela and Beatrice had made the table into a thing of beauty, with white linen and cut glass, candelabra and bowls of flowers. Terence, sitting back in his chair after a feast of antipasto and risotto, watched the candlelight play flatteringly on the animated faces of his fellow guests, and decided to use this scene in his next film, which was to be an adaptation of Chekhov's *The Seagull*, updated for the modern viewer. He wished he'd fought harder now for a bigger budget, so he could have shot it here instead of at home. Nottingham in November – brrr!

He must have been mad to agree. Oh well, the artistes would just have to be underdressed in thermals and lump it.

The McCorquodales did not hold his interest for long after they had been introduced. They were an odd couple, Joe tall and craggy in his late middle age, and Evadne short and round with a halo of peroxide frizz – a dumb blonde if ever he'd seen one, and well past her sell-by date. Everybody was deferring to Joe, fresh from his dig and talking excitedly about his latest finds. Evadne said nothing, but beamed and nodded at everything hubby had to say. Terence was sure that he was fascinating to listen to if you liked that kind of thing, but his own interest in history extended only as far as research for the plays and films he directed. So far he hadn't encountered any ancient Etruscan literary masterpieces, and he doubted that he ever would. He was bored. When would Marion return? He glanced up at the tower for the hundredth time, and was rewarded at last by a light shining from the first-floor window. How come he hadn't heard their car? He excused himself from the table.

'I'm going inside for a moment. Do you need anything bringing down, Freddie?'

'I don't think so, thank you. I shall go up myself in a moment to check on the chicken.'

'Good God, is there more? You're spoiling us.'

He was rewarded by Freddie's bashful dimpled smile as he slipped away. Fantastic. He'd bring Marion down to join them for dinner. And Janice and Tom, of course.

Upstairs, he knocked jauntily at their door, and moments later Tom appeared.

'Oh. Hello.'

'Hi, Tom. How's the legs today?'

'Bit sore.'

'Mine too. Had a good day? You've been off jaunting.'

'Yes thanks.'

'Anywhere nice?'

'Not bad.'

God, this man would do well under interrogation. It was like trying to squeeze information out of a breezeblock.

'I saw your light on. We're having supper outdoors. Come and join us.'

'No thanks, Janice is making us something here.'

At that moment she appeared from the kitchen, a Swiss army knife in one hand and an unblemished tin of tuna in the other.

'Terry! Hiya! I thought maybe Tom was talking to himself – he does sometimes, don't you me duck? Here, do this will you? I can't get this bleddy tin open for love nor money.'

'Don't do that,' said Terence, preventing Tom from taking the can. 'I was just saying – we're having dinner outside. Freddie's cooked a feast enough for an army. Come and help us out. Look – doesn't it look pretty?' He led her over to the window to look down on the scene below. He must remember this shot for the movie. Maybe he'd use a crane and have a long slow track in . . .

'Oh, yeah!' said Janice. 'Doesn't it look romantic! What are you having to eat? Are you sure there'll be enough? We could bring a couple of cans down if you're short.'

'Not necessary, but we'll take some plates and glasses and these chairs,' said Terence quickly, avoiding Tom's disapproving look. 'We've got everything we need except fun company! Where's Marion – in her room?' he asked, as if it was an afterthought.

'No,' said Janice, grabbing plates and rummaging in the cupboards for something to contribute to the feast. 'Have you got a pudding? I've got a couple of yoghurts and a packet of chocolate marshmallows here.'

'I really don't think we'll need them. In the bathroom?'

'Ay? Oh yeah, help yourself.'

'No, I meant is Marion in there?'

'No,' said Janice, cramming things into carrier bags. 'There we are, that'll do – I'll bring the Ryvita as well. Can you two manage the chairs? Mind your back, Tom! Takes nothing to put it out, Terry, and then he's flat on his back in agony for a week.

Are you all right for booze? Marion and me put paid to the gin last night.'

'We've got plenty,' said Terence, puzzled to find himself descending the stairs with everything but what he'd come for. 'So where is she?' he added desperately.

'Maz? She's in the village having her dinner at Claudio's bar.'

Damn and blast it! Now what was he supposed to do – talk to Boring Tom all night instead of Boring Joe? Oh well, at least Janice couldn't fail to liven things up, he supposed, and there was always the possibility of grabbing Marion to join them when she finally deigned to return. What was she thinking of, a single woman dining alone? Who was this Claudio, and how attractive was he? He suddenly remembered her irritation in the trattoria yesterday, and heard himself telling her he'd kidnap her to keep her amused. Of course. She must have had a frustrating day with Janice and Tom. He must think of a way of kidnapping her tomorrow.

The convivial chatter at the table died to a frozen silence as Terence led Janice and Tom into the charmed circle of candlelight. He was amused to see Pamela's jaw drop in disbelief at what he'd done.

'Hiya!' Janice called, oblivious of the atmosphere. 'Hiya Pam! Hi Bea – don't you look nice? Hi Chris, how are you doing? Here you are Fred, we've brought some goodies. Ooh what's that you've been eating? Rice pudding and prunes?'

'Risotto with aubergines, actually,' said Freddie, his heart in his boots at this unwanted disruption. What would Pamela think? He peered into the carrier bag which Janice had shoved in his hands. What *were* these strange offerings, and what on earth was he supposed to do with them?

Janice cackled. 'Rice pudding and prunes! What am I like? Is it nice? It looks lovely, doesn't it Tom? Hiya – I'm Janice and this is my husband Tom.'

'Joe McCorquodale,' said Joe, standing politely and shaking her by the hand. 'My wife, Evadne.'

'How do you do, Janice. Tom.'

'Ooh – Americans! Are you on holiday too?'

'No, we live here,' said Evadne as Janice settled down beside her. 'Joe's an archaeologist, currently working on the Etruscan site down the road.'

'Oh. And what about you, what do you get up to while he's doing that?'

Everybody listened to the reply which was to change the tenor of the evening. Nobody had thought to ask Evadne anything about herself, since Joe was so obviously the star guest.

'Me? Well, just now I'm writing a self-development book on psychic power. You know – that accursed phrase "New Age"? Pretty silly really, since most of it has been practised since time out of mind.'

'How amazing!' exclaimed Janice. 'So there's your husband digging up the past, and you delving into the future. Between you you've got it covered!'

'I guess so,' Evadne laughed.

Freddie was surprised. 'I thought you were researching ancient religions, Evadne?'

'Well yes, I was,' she replied. 'And I still do, for myself. But try getting research grants to study goddesses and divination in matriarchal religions!'

Joe shifted in his chair and looked abashed. 'Academia is still pretty male dominated,' he conceded. 'Crazy really in this day and age.'

'So you've become a goddess yourself?' said Terence, at last interested. Trust Janice to make the party go with a swing.

'That's right!' said Evadne. 'There I was knowing all this arcane ancient stuff about how to divine who was going to win the battle, and whether it was gonna be a good year for corn . . .'

'How *do* you do that?' asked Pamela, whose olive grove glistened silver in the moonlight behind them.

'Well, it's not really a thing you could do now without animal rights activists burning you in your bed,' Evadne giggled.

'You split a goat in half, throw its entrails in the air, and see what shape they make when they land.'

'You can see why they changed over to tea leaves,' agreed Terence. 'So how did you discover you had these powers yourself?'

'My daughter back home sent me a tape. I was at that stage of my research where I wanted to tie it in to a modern context, and over the last decade or so we've seen a lot of this old wisdom regain popularity. Barbara Ann had been to a sweat lodge for a weekend and had all kinds of out-of-body experiences. I was listening to the tape with an academic interest when I found myself going into a kind of a trance and hearing voices in my head.'

'What did they say?' asked Beatrice, leaning forward eagerly.

'Well, the voice on the tape had told me to hold a question in my mind while I concentrated on my breathing and so forth, and of course, the biggest question in my mind was "Where's the next buck coming from? How can I continue my research? How do I get all this knowledge out into the public realm?" And I suddenly saw this shining light, and this voice in my head said, "Don't dream it, be it." So I said, "What? Nobody works harder than me! I'm not a dreamer, I'm a doer!" I was pretty mad at that. I had gone down every avenue I could think of to get funding. And then this light kind of . . . broke open — the rays parted — and behind it, this scene was playing out. There was this High Priestess standing on the steps of a temple before a great throng, her arms above her head, her head thrown back, "They come, they come!" she cried. And suddenly, from out of nowhere a great horde of warriors came, slashing at the crowd with their swords, cutting their way through to the temple, to the High Priestess herself. Other Priestesses and a couple of Eunuchs flung themselves in front of her, to protect her, but they too were cut to the ground. It was terrible to watch! Blood everywhere, and the dreadful, dreadful cries of the mortally wounded.'

'How simply awful!' exclaimed Beatrice. 'But what did it all mean?'

'What I was witnessing was the advent of the male religion come to root out the Goddess,' said Evadne, 'which, as a matter of fact, is the stuff of my study. And there she was, this High Priestess, this last defender of the faith, faced at last with the destruction she had foreseen, standing bravely and defiantly before this brute male commander, his great sword lifted to strike at her neck. And in that moment, which lasted an eternity, as the blade swung towards her, she cried out from her heart, "I shall return!" And I saw her face, like a piece to camera, like she was looking directly at the lens, directly at me, and the voice said, "I *am* you!"'

'*You* were the High Priestess?' asked Terence, just to be sure. It was all a piece of absolute twaddle, but magnificently performed. She had indeed become the High Priestess during the telling. He glanced at Joe to see how he felt about all this, and saw that he had become one of the felled Eunuchs.

Evadne inclined her head in a regal nod. 'And I have returned.'

'Blimey,' said Janice, breaking the silence. 'So do you read palms?' She shoved her pudgy hand under the High Priestess's nose. 'Go on, do mine. I had it done once by a gypsy in Skegness, didn't I Tom? She was brilliant – she told me everything about myself, and everything she said was true.'

'We mustn't disturb you at a social occasion,' said Freddie disapprovingly. How embarrassing for poor Joe! What on earth had happened to Evadne since he'd last met her? She must have had a breakdown. Surely such mania must be grounds for a divorce?

'No trouble at all,' Evadne smiled as she bent to her task. She inhaled deeply, taking Janice's hand in hers, and breathed out slowly through her mouth, her eyes half closed. 'You are a young soul. This is only your second or third incarnation. You were a milk maid in a former life, on a large estate in the country. You fell in love with a farm worker – I see him splitting logs and building fences – and were engaged to be married when he was called to war, and was killed. You died of a broken heart. You had unfinished business together, so you came back at the turn of the last century. You were a parlour maid . . .'

'Always a peasant then!' said Janice cheerfully. 'Sounds like me!'

'. . . and you had caught the eye of the local undertaker's son – I see him building coffins, see him stroking the wood . . .'

Janice nudged Tom. 'You haven't changed then!' He squirmed in his seat. This American woman was bonkers. He'd have given anything to be upstairs now, eating tuna and Ryvita with Janice in companionable silence. He was starving hungry and so far they hadn't been offered so much as a bread roll.

'You fell in love and became engaged. But you had a dark secret. The son of the family you worked for used to visit you in your room at night, against your will. You became pregnant. Desperate, you told your employer's son, who sent you to a disreputable drunken sot of a doctor who performed a barbaric abortion. Two days later you died in the arms of your fiancé, having told him all. He swore he would avenge your death. He challenged this bounder to a duel, and died of his wounds.'

'My hero,' said Janice, smiling affectionately at Tom.

'Was duelling still legal in England at the turn of the last century?' asked Christopher, who had already cast himself in the role of the honest coffin maker's son for the movie. It was a good story. Surely Freddie could find a writer to make it into a starring vehicle for him?

'No,' Freddie supplied succinctly. This was stuff and nonsense from beginning to end. Ill-digested Catherine Cookson. Imagine the son of an undertaker becoming affianced to a maid – parlour or not. The merchant classes would *never* have intermarried with their servants.

'It wasn't in England,' Evadne slowly opened her eyes. 'It was in France. It was seen as a 'crime passionnel', and the son of the house went on to lead a long and prosperous life.'

'How truly sad,' said Beatrice, who had believed every word. 'But how wonderful that you have both come back and found each other again.'

'You know, you've missed your vocation,' advised Terence. 'You could fund your research by writing period fiction. That last story would make a cracking musical.'

Pamela's eyes flickered in alarm. That was all she needed, Terence Armstrong getting interested in somebody else's story. Damn Evadne McCorquodale, coming here and pinching her contacts.

'Do you think so?' asked Christopher, equally alarmed. 'I was thinking what a good film it would make.' Despite dozens of lessons with the very best teachers he couldn't sing a note in tune.

'But what about now?' Janice wanted to know. 'Do you only get past-life stuff — don't you see into the future?'

Exactly, thought Freddie, Terence, Pamela and Tom. Anybody can make up silly stories about supposed reincarnations that couldn't be disproved. Now get out of *that*.

'Reincarnation is what interests me most,' Evadne admitted. 'I do get some present life stuff, but I don't usually pass it on. It could do such harm, and to be honest, I don't know how accurate my impressions really are.'

Ha, thought Freddie triumphantly, Gotcha! 'Would you like some more wine, Joe?' he asked. Now they could get back to the more interesting topic of his latest Etruscan finds.

'That's very kind.' Joe offered his wineglass, looking Freddie in the eye with a faded boyish twinkle. Was he flirting? Freddie's heart banged loudly in his chest, pumping every drop of his blood to his face. His hand trembled and he spilled some wine. Oh God! 'I'm so sorry, how clumsy,' he said.

'Not at all,' Joe assured him, licking the wine from his fingers. He'd suffered worse embarrassments. Quite recently, in fact.

'No, but go on,' Janice urged Evadne, ever the terrier on the scent of a trail. 'I don't mind if you get it wrong. Have a stab at it.'

'Okay,' said Evadne, 'but don't blame me if it's way off track!' Again she closed her eyes and breathed deeply. 'Look, I'm just going to speak my impressions. You can decide if they make any sense.'

'Great,' responded Janice encouragingly. 'Impress away!'

'I'll just go and check on the chicken,' said Freddie, rising noisily from the table and breaking the mood. It was more than he could bear to watch.

'Could you use some help?' asked Joe, following in his wake.

'Sshh!' said Beatrice, completely rapt. Terence just knew that she was going to ask to be next, eager to have confirmed that he and she were in fact twin souls. Women were so susceptible to this kind of tosh. If there was any unfinished love business for him it was with Marion, not this silly young girl. Where was she? If she didn't come soon he'd drive to the village to get her, let Beatrice make of that what she would.

Evadne's deep breathing was getting quicker and noisier. 'Are you all right, Ev?' asked Janice. 'Don't hyperventilate whatever you do, not on my account. It's only a bit of fun.'

'You deal with the public in a caring role,' pronounced the High Priestess in strange guttural tones. 'You're in healthcare — or should be. A nurse maybe. You've had your own health problems, but that's all okay now. You're happily married at last, and Tom is still in wood. I see him with a lot of children, but they're not his — he's a teacher!'

There was a collective intake of breath around the table.

'Spot on!' exclaimed Terence, despite himself.

'On the knob!' agreed Janice, more colloquially.

'You have no kids, but there's a baby around here somewhere, connected to you. Could you be pregnant?' Evadne asked suddenly, opening her eyes, and returning to herself.

'Not a chance,' said Janice. 'I've had it all taken away. That was the health problem you mentioned that's sorted now,' she confided.

'Could it be somebody else's baby you're picking up?' asked Bea, breathlessly. 'Somebody close by?' Terence froze.

'It'll be Paola Sonelli's,' said Janice. 'I delivered it yesterday. Bloody hell, Ev, you're amazing!'

'Well, what do you know?' beamed Evadne. 'I must be improving. I've been practising so far on poor Joe, and been way, way off. Last week I was convinced he was about to fall in love with somebody else!' She laughed heartily. 'Boy was he mad!'

Upstairs, Joe and Freddie were going through the motions of looking at chickens.

'I think just another few minutes,' Freddie blustered, his face still burning. 'I should have put them on earlier, but what with dashing up and down stairs . . . Pamela's idea, but worth the trouble. It's lovely to be out . . . Side,' he practically shouted. 'Nice to be outside on such a fine evening.'

'Yes,' Joe agreed, equally shy.

'I was very interested in hearing about your latest exciting finds,' Freddie continued, clattering pots and searching vainly for the carving knife he'd sharpened specially a few hours before. 'Where's the knife, where on earth is the wretched knife?'

'Here?' asked Joe, calmly offering it to him with a smile.

'Yes,' said Freddie, unable to look at him, 'Thank you. Now which of these serving dishes did Pamela say to use? Heavens, they're all dusty, and I haven't even dressed the salad.'

'May I?'

'Well . . .' Freddie was more than a little finicky when it came to culinary skills, 'Perhaps you wouldn't mind washing this dish while I do that myself?'

'Not at all,' said Joe, amiably taking the dish to the sink. 'Although you could trust me. My mother was French, and was very particular about tossing it by hand . . . the salad! the salad! using her hands to – to turn it, get it coated, evenly, each leaf, without implements, which could bruise it – you can't be too careful . . . it repays the effort . . .' He wished the ground would swallow him up. Gee, this felt awkward.

'Yes,' Freddie concurred, pouring the oil drop by drop. His mouth had gone peculiarly dry and the back of his neck was tingling. Too much wine, he thought, must drink more water.

'Well, that seems to be about it,' Joe said, drying the dish. 'Will I set out the chickens? Do you think they'll be done?'

'I should think so,' Freddie answered, giving all his attention to the salad, 'Perhaps you could prick them . . . with a fork! . . . prick them with a fork, and make sure that the juices . . . the er . . . run clear. That they're not pink.' Good God, why did everything they said sound like a double entendre? Thank heavens that Janice person wasn't here with her ribald sense of fun. What on earth was going on? He liked Joe of course. Very much. He liked his academic mind, his contemplative seriousness, his cultured sensitivity, he admired his work. But he had never thought of him in *that way*. Had never thought of any man his own age *like that*. (So hypersensitive and uncomfortable with this side of himself was Freddie that he even thought about the subject in italics.)

He sneaked a look, to see Joe examining the chickens with utmost care. It was so nice to have help in the kitchen! And his shoulders were so broad, his hands so sensitive . . .

'I was wondering . . .' said Joe, transferring the chickens beautifully on to the dish.

Oh no! Freddie simply wasn't prepared for this. 'There's a sprig of sage on the chopping board — could you pop it on as a garnish?' he broke in anxiously.

'Well hey, let's talk about two minds beating as one!' Joe exclaimed, turning to face him at last. 'That was exactly what I was wondering!' The two men looked at each other for a fraction of a second longer than was absolutely necessary, and smiled warmly.

'Voilà!' said Joe, placing the sage delicately and presenting the dish for Freddie's approval. 'Ça va?'

'Parfait,' said Freddie, and together they descended the stairs in silence.

'Evadne's a good person,' Joe declared suddenly as they let themselves out of the Palazzo. 'And a good scholar.'

'Of course,' said Freddie hurriedly.

'She's been unfairly thwarted at every turn to get funding,' her husband continued, 'while I . . .'

'Most frustrating for her.'

'I admire her pragmatism, getting involved in this . . . new interest. It sells.'

'Yes. A marvellous idea,' Freddie lied.

'And to be honest, some of her predictions are uncannily accurate.'

'Really?'

'But then she's always been very perceptive. It was she who saw straight off that we were destined to be married. We were both recovering from our second divorces when we met.'

'Ah.' They were nearing the table, and Freddie was relieved. He wasn't used to this kind of confidential talk.

'I was wondering . . .' said Joe.

'Yey hey!' shouted Janice, seeing their approach. 'Grub's up! Thank God for that! I'm starving!' She wasn't the only one who was relieved to see them arrive. Things had been going pretty pear shaped, prediction-wise.

'Look, I'm sorry,' Evadne continued to a distraught Bea as Freddie carved the chickens. 'I should never have started this. And just because I can't see a baby right now, or a wedding, it doesn't mean there won't be one.'

'No. Quite,' said Bea, rallying.

'Joe can tell you how wrong I can be, can't you honey?' Evadne asked.

'Mm,' said Joe.

'And you're an actress,' Evadne went on, trying to dig herself out of the hole she had prophesied herself into. 'Maybe I was picking up on the story of your next role.'

'Sounds like a great script, full of romance and betrayal,' Terence mused mischievously. 'You must have your agent look out for it, Bea. Both of you,' he added to Christopher, 'since you are obviously destined to co-star in this.'

'Of course!' said Evadne gratefully. 'That's where I must have made my mistake. I'm truly sorry, Terence, for the mix-up.'

'Not at all,' Terence reassured her, enjoying himself enormously. 'And anyway, what you say is true. Beatrice and

Christopher *have* been lovers in the past, both on and off the screen, haven't you loves?'

'An awfully long time ago,' protested Christopher, avoiding Pamela's penetrating glare.

'Blimey, you theatricals!' said Janice admiringly, '*Hello!* doesn't tell the half, does it?'

'Chicken?' asked Freddie of everyone. Heaven alone knew what Evadne had said since he'd been away, but the air around the table was positively swirling with subtext.

'Yes please,' said Tom.

'And I'm rather attracted to what must be my part in the story,' said Terence, unwilling to let the subject go, 'and the deus ex machina sweeping me off!'

'What *is* that?' asked Janice, her mouth already full.

'An unlikely plot device that comes from out of nowhere,' Terence informed her, 'to resolve the story, or push it on in an unexpected direction. It's Latin. Quite literally it means "God coming out of a machine", doesn't it Freddie?'

But Freddie, his mouth opened to reply, was silenced as they all were, by the roar of a fast approaching motorbike and a squeal of brakes.

Chapter Fifteen

Marion had thought that her new mode of transport, which she had hired from one of her drinking buddies in the village, would raise a few eyebrows on her arrival. But even she was unprepared for nine people running out from the back of the Palazzo, and Beatrice's hysterical screams.

'What? What?!' she said, taking off her helmet and fanning out her hair. 'It's only me!' But apparently that made things worse.

'Blimey Maz, talk about timing!' Janice exclaimed, shaking poor Bea till her teeth rattled in her head. 'Bea, pull yourself together girl or I'll have to clock you one! It isn't God. Only Marion, see?'

'Well well,' said Terence admiringly, smirking from ear to ear. 'What have we here?'

'A Harley Davison twelve hundred,' said Tom, examining it at close quarters, his voice dripping with envy. 'Nineteen seventy-two.'

'Three actually,' corrected its proud (temporary) new owner. 'Isn't she gorgeous?'

'She certainly is,' Terence agreed. Where had this woman been all his life? She truly was remarkable.

'Listen Bea, do you want me to take you indoors for a little lie down?' Janice asked of her patient, who was struggling to control herself for fear of being hit.

'No! No, I'm sorry, I'm fine – it was just a shock. Silly of me,' said Beatrice.

'My fault,' said Evadne. 'No more spooky stuff tonight.'

'We ought to be going soon anyway,' Joe offered. 'It's late.'

'Nonsense,' said Terence. 'With the chicken just served? Let's all go back to the table. And I'm quite sure that Freddie will have made a marvellous dessert.'

'Actually I just bought fruit,' said Freddie apologetically.

'There's always my marshmallows,' said Janice, leading the way. 'Come on Maz – we've got candlelight out here and everything. It's really nice.' She took Marion by the arm and steered her firmly away. 'I'll fill you in later,' she hissed in her ear. 'You'll never guess in a million years!'

'This gravel will have to be raked!' Pamela called after them reprovingly. 'First thing tomorrow morning will do!'

Processing back to the table, Beatrice slipped a proprietorial arm round Terence's waist while Christopher kept his distance. The last thing he wanted was to be embroiled in a jealous love tangle, or worse, a fight. He didn't know what to make of Evadne's prognostications, nor whether Terence really believed the rationale he had given, that she had foreseen a script in which Beatrice and Christopher would co-star. Much as he found himself falling for Bea again, he simply could not afford to offend Terence Armstrong – he might never work again. For the rest of the evening, Chris decided, he would go back to Plan A. He would flirt with Freddie.

Marion was curious about what she had walked into, but everybody was happy to change the subject when they reconvened, so the recipe for the chicken was made much of until every shred had been eaten and the bones picked clean. How many ways are there to say that you simply stuff it with half a lemon and a handful of sage? Freddie thought crossly, not a bit taken in by their fulsome praise. Since Joe's apologia for Evadne he had realised that he had misjudged the situation entirely and he felt rather foolish. Naturally Joe wasn't interested in him, he had merely been embarrassed by his wife and had wanted to smooth things over. And now here was Christopher making doe eyes at him and expressing a sudden interest in the culinary arts which Freddie knew was spurious. Anybody who didn't already know that one cooks chicken for forty minutes per kilo plus fifteen minutes extra had obviously never spent any time in a kitchen, nor ever intended to do so — so why on earth was he pretending?

Pamela, shrewdly watching Christopher's behaviour, knew exactly what he was up to. His flushed look of guilt when Evadne had been in full flood about his love affair with Beatrice was, to her, as good as an admission that he had tasted that particular forbidden fruit recently — and would doubtless taste it again. Personally she couldn't give a fig about his infidelity, but neither did she want to expose herself to the possibility of rejection. She had unwisely kept Patrick, the American summer student with whom she'd been having an affair, at bay since her visitors had arrived. She would keep her options open. In fact, she would reopen one of them that very night.

Janice's chocolate marshmallows brought more food for conversation, some exclaiming in delight that they had never before encountered such a dainty thing, others — or rather, Terence — reminiscing about jelly and blancmange at school parties, about Wagon Wheels and peashooters and Iced Gems and how many Blackjacks you could get for an old penny. Once again, in Marion's company, he was back in his sentimental bubble of blue remembered hills, from which Beatrice was doubly excluded through age and class. It was as if they were speaking in code.

'Do you remember frozen Jubblies?'

'Oh yes,' Marion replied, returning the warmth of his smile, 'I used to buy one with my collection money on the way back from church.'

The air between them crackled with electricity. He couldn't have been more delighted with her reply, nor more pleased to see her, nor wished for a more exciting entrance. Girl on a motorbike! Marianne Faithful! (And remember what *she* allegedly got up to with confectionery.) What a woman! And so full of surprises. He wished that the others would just melt away and leave him on his own with her. She made him feel whole. She joined up his present with his past.

But Beatrice, watching this dangerous adversary who threatened to take away the father of her unborn (and as yet, probably unconceived) child, was not going to be excluded.

'My absolute favourite when I was little was Toblerone,' she rushed in when Terence paused for breath. 'There was a girl at school who'd sneak into the village for you to buy tuck, but you had to give her half, so Mummy used to pack me six of them at the beginning of every term. I used to try to ration myself to one a week, but I never managed it!'

Terence, who had been explaining that he had had threepence a week pocket money which he used to split with his friend Robert since he had none, was less than impressed.

'Unheard-of luxury,' he said, brushing her off, and pitched in again about something called khali that could be bought at the post office stores for tuppence the half ounce. She tried again.

'The coins were really sweet then, weren't they? Mummy kept some sixpences when they went out of circulation. She still puts them in the Christmas pudding every year, but of course, we have to give them back. You got two last year, didn't you Terence?'

'Did I?' he responded crossly. 'I don't remember.' He wished she'd just disappear. She was like a small but irritating gnat.

'You want to watch that,' warned Janice, coming to the rescue. Despite her ambitions for Marion with Terence, she felt sorry for Bea. Couldn't she see that her only hope now was to play hard to get while she weathered the storm, and then see what could be salvaged? She was like a child waving a pop gun in a dangerous war zone. 'People swallow them sixpenny bits by mistake. We had a chap in Casualty one year who jingled like a money box when he jumped up and down. He had about five bob in him by the time it was all counted out. The gastro consultant was really funny – he used to have us in creases. "Well, I hope you enjoyed your dinner," he says to this bloke. "Why?" says the chap. "Cos you certainly paid through the arse

for it," he says!' She slapped the table and guffawed. There was a
short silence, and then they all roared with laughter, even Tom.

'Heavens, is that the time?' said Pamela suddenly. 'I must just
pop over to the college for a moment to sort something out.'

Joe stood up politely. 'Time we were going,' he said. 'Thank
you for a wonderful meal.'

'Don't go on my account,' Pamela called back, as she walked
purposefully towards her prey in the college halls. 'I shouldn't be
gone long. Just some boring arrangements to sort out.'

'Working day tomorrow, early start,' said Joe, helping
Evadne to locate her handbag under the table. 'Not like you
lucky vacationers!'

Everybody stood up in a jumble of goodbyes, out of which
Freddie managed to separate himself. Despite his mix-up about
Joe's intentions he still liked him and admired his work, and
would have given anything to be invited to visit the dig, if only
he could think of a way to ask without appearing to. Sometimes,
being English was exhausting. 'I'll walk you to your car,' he said,
picking up some empty plates. 'I have to go that way anyway.'

Christopher didn't want to be left in the present company
now that it was dwindling. He picked up some plates too. 'I'll
help, Freddie,' he offered, and followed on behind. Really,
thought Freddie crossly, he's become like a piece of chewing
gum on the sole of one's shoe.

'See you, Evadne,' called Janice across the darkness. 'Next
time I'll get you to help me pick my lottery numbers! T'ra Joe!'

'Is she clairvoyant then?' asked Marion, taking a psychic punt
at the evening's mystery.

'Possibly,' replied Terence, smiling, while Janice delivered a
none too subtle kick under the table to Marion's leg. 'Or maybe
just as good a guesser as you.' Beatrice stiffened. Which part of
Evadne's pronouncements did he believe to be true? The bit
about her and Christopher having an affair, or the bit about this
damned woman arriving like a bat out of hell to take Terence
away?

'Now tell us how you came by that wonderful – machine,'

Terence demanded, choosing the word with mischievous care. 'And how on earth you know how to ride it.'

'I've hired it for the holidays from a guy in the village,' said Marion. 'My brother used to have bikes and I nagged him into teaching me. Mind you, that was years ago. But once I saw it, I just had to have it.' She laughed. 'You'd be surprised what you can do with a mixture of bullshit and bravura!'

Terence grinned at her in undisguised admiration. Oh go on, he thought wildly, surprise me some more.

Like many actors, Christopher was no stranger to the world of psychics. There was a woman who did Tarot in Ealing whom he'd consulted several times when he'd been out of work, and each time she'd been right – he *had* worked again. He was glad that Evadne hadn't done him in front of everybody else (except by implication whilst doing Bea), but he was intrigued about what she might tell him in a private consultation, if she'd agree to do one. Escorting her to Joe's car, he dumped his cargo of dirty plates at the door of the Palazzo and managed, like a practised sheepdog, to separate her from the rest of the flock. Hardly a difficult task under the circumstances, since Freddie was engaged in doing exactly the same thing with Joe. Small talk about the evening therefore ensued in pairs at either side of the car, until:

'I was wondering . . .' said Christopher, as he opened the passenger door for Evadne.

'I was wondering . . .' said Joe and Freddie to each other simultaneously as they dithered at the driver's side.

And to their mutual amazement, their wonders ceased. Freddie was delighted to accept Joe's offer of a tour round the dig. Joe was tickled pink that Freddie was about to ask for exactly what he was about to offer, and that their two minds were still beating as one. And Evadne told Christopher that of course she would give him a private session the day after tomorrow, and that would be fifty thousand lire, thank you.

'Nice couple,' said Christopher, as the tail-lights of Joe and Evadne's car disappeared into the Tuscan night.

'Yes,' agreed Freddie, his waving arm now dropping to his side, his smile erased. 'Well, better get back to deal with the pots.'

Chapter Sixteen

Beatrice felt torn, remaining seated as she did while Frederick and Christopher traversed wearily between the table and the kitchen two flights away, clearing away the debris from the meal. It went against her nature and her upbringing to let others do the chores while she remained inactive, but Terence showed no inclination to pitch in and help, and she did not intend to leave his side for a moment while That Woman was around. It was obvious he was infatuated with her. His eyes never sparkled like that for Beatrice any more. What on earth had happened to change his feelings since last night when he had kissed his way up her legs, swearing his love and wanting to make babies? It was all too confusing and hurtful. She started to wonder if marriage to Terence was worth the chase. Would it ever be peaceful and cosy? Wouldn't it mean a lifetime of this, staying at parties longer than she wanted to, in order to ensure that Daddy came home with Mummy to his nest of chicks? She wished that her own mother were here to talk to now. How had she coped in her early years of being Mrs Miller-Mander, in the days when her young husband's voracious legend had run before him, causing him to be known in theatrical circles as Randy Roland? Had it been worth the heartache? And did she feel secure now?

While these turbulent thoughts ran through her head she tried to maintain an outward calm, pretending to listen with as much interest as Terence to the small talk he was making with Marion. What a ridiculous expression! This talk was not small, it was merely the visible tip of a huge iceberg, polite chatter meant to draw attention away from the seven eighths of hidden desire.

Meanwhile, Tom was having his own tussle with hidden desire. He had always admired Beatrice on screen, but being in her actual presence with the candlelight warming her cheeks and highlighting her cleavage was practically more than he could bear, particularly as Janice was up to her usual tricks under cover of the tablecloth, squeezing and stroking a part of him that, at this moment, certainly did not belong to her. Indeed, so great was his discomfort with the current situation, he even wished it did not belong to him either. Gulping down more wine than he was wont to drink in order to dull his senses, he clasped Janice's hand firmly in his to keep it still, while attempting to distract his mind by doing mental arithmetic. He gave up after he had demanded of himself for the third time what was the sum of nine thirteens, which seemed just now to be too abstract a concept, and concentrated instead on constructing an imaginary drawer, twenty centimetres in depth with eight-millimetre rebated dovetails.

It was Terence who finally broke up the party. He had been waiting for Bea to crack, sure that her good manners would prevent her from allowing Freddie and Christopher to do all the work on their own, but she was obviously not going to let him out of her sight. It suddenly occurred to him that the only way he might grab a few moments alone with Marion would be to enlist everybody to trundle up and down the stairs ferrying dirty dishes, so that he might contrive for Beatrice to be upstairs while he and Marion were downstairs, or vice versa. It was worth a try.

'Good Lord,' he cried, as if noticing for the first time that Freddie and Christopher were clattering dirty plates, 'are you doing the dishes as well as the cooking, Freddie? Impossible! Absolutely not allowed!' He stood up and started collecting plates too, which shamed the others on to their feet as he had hoped. He had a half-conceived plan of how he might make his escape the next day to be with Marion, but it needed advance work. And first he must alert her to be ready if he brought it off – he didn't want to go through all that just to find she had gone off on her bike for the day. In the resulting mêlée, however, as he beetled after Marion, Beatrice managed to stay glued to his side like a Siamese twin, climbing the stairs with him with synchronised steps. This wasn't going to be easy, he thought, as he fought down an urge to throw out his foot to trip her. He saw her tumble down the stone stairs in his mind's eye (arse over tit, he thought rudely, in the language of his youth), breaking her lovely neck. A short but tragic bereavement, a moving speech at a memorial service at St James's, and then freedom! To pursue the woman of his dreams.

Pamela's short trip to the college to 'sort out some boring arrangements' was not going at all smoothly. Secretive by nature, she had managed to slink her way through the corridors to Patrick's room without being seen, but had then been confronted by his locked door and no response from within, leaving her exposed and apparently lurking around the student accommodation when the college principal returned to his own quarters from his nightly stroll.

'Contessa.'

'Signor Gambino!'

In ten years they had never given each other permission to use first names. Signor Gambino disliked her intensely, both personally (to the small extent that he knew her) and professionally, but he had grudgingly come to admire her nerve. In his first dealings with her, when the college was negotiating to take over the Palazzo and she was poised on the brink of bankruptcy, she had managed with breathtaking mendacity and avarice not only to squeeze several million lire more out of the Board, but also to maintain a fiction that the handing over of the building was in the nature of a charitable gift. Finding her now to be disadvantaged was a moment of pure joy. He had never seen her caught so conspicuously on the hop.

'Can I help you perhaps?'

'No no,' Pamela demurred, thinking quickly and trying to recover her aplomb. 'Or rather, yes, if you have a pen and paper.'

'You are leaving a note for one of the students?' He fished about in his pockets. 'Not a beautiful piece of writing paper, but perhaps it will suffice?' Wait till he got this one round the staffroom! Gossip was always thick about her continuing affairs with students, but she'd never been caught in the act before.

'Yes. Merely a reminder to return some books belonging to my husband's family that I was persuaded, against my better judgement, to lend,' she said, scribbling rapidly.

'I am so sorry that one of my students has put you to this trouble. It is too bad not to return such valuable treasures. If you would like to give me his or her name I will deliver this note myself.'

'No trouble, Professore, I can slip it under the door.' She returned his pen to him as to a menial who has been dismissed.

'Ah. You know which door?' said Signor Gambino mischievously, as he tucked his pen back in his breast pocket, smiling. Pamela did not deign to reply, but merely held him in her gaze, like a snake.

'Well, that is good,' he said, discomforted. He had the distinct feeling that she had bested him again. 'So I can be of no further service?'

'None whatsoever,' came the double-edged reply. 'Good night.' She watched him until he had turned a corner, and then slipped the note under Patrick's door, irritated to have been discovered. She didn't care for inelegance in any form.

Crossing the lawn with as much elegance as her high heels would allow, she was relieved to see that the dinner party had dispersed, and that the table was even now being dismantled by Christopher and Tom.

'Oh, you've finished clearing away,' she said, heading for her tower without breaking her stride.

'Almost,' said Christopher, as he and Tom struggled to transform the table into its two-dimensional form, 'but if you could just manage to take these napkins and glasses . . .?'

'Good night then,' Pamela continued, affecting not to hear. 'I am *so* exhausted that I shall go straight to my room and sleep.'

There is a God! thought Christopher with exultation and relief. Having to make one more journey up and down the stairs would be a small price to pay to be let off bed duty with Pamela. He was so happy he felt like sharing his good news, but looking at Tom he could see it would be impossible in his present company. That was the trouble with Normals. They were so easily shocked.

Fortunately for Terence there was nothing normal about Janice. Ever alert to personal drama, she could see that he was bursting to have a few words with Marion alone, and that Beatrice was not about to let that happen. Her motives for changing the course of events were twofold. On the one hand she was a hopeless romantic and wanted happiness for her friend, and on the other she loved stories, and how was she going to get the next instalment if it was never allowed to happen? The washing-up was all but finished, and the guessing game for where all the pots and pans lived was now under way. Freddie of course knew where everything was kept, so in order to gain time, he must be dispatched.

'Ay up, Fred, you look knackered mate. Why don't you pack it in — we can finish off here,' she offered.

Freddie was relieved to be given permission to go. He *was* tired — cooking for parties always drained him emotionally and physically — and he was longing for the quiet of his room where he might go over the events of the evening in his mind. Just when he had decided that any flirting had been a figment of his imagination, Joe's invitation to visit the dig the next day had confused him all over again. And he needed his beauty sleep if he were to be up early in the morning and at his best. 'If you're sure?' he asked. Janice was positive. And then there were four.

'Tez, can you go down and have a look that Tom's okay with

the table – you know what his back's like. And them chairs outside need taking back to our flat.'

'All right,' said Terence, reluctant to leave since he was not party to her plot. He shrugged a hapless goodbye to Marion behind Beatrice's back. And so there were three.

'That frock is absolutely gorgeous, Bea,' said Janice, introducing the only topic she knew to be of interest to the young actress, and which might absorb her attention at the crucial moment. 'What is that material? Is it silk?'

'No, it's actually one of the new breed of synthetic materials,' said Beatrice, taking off her apron. 'Great for travelling. You can practically wash it and wear it, it dries so quickly. And it does hang well.'

'Well it does on you,' Janice flattered her. 'But I bet you could wear a sack and look a million dollars. Was it designed specially for you?'

'Oh no, I got it off the peg at Harvey Nicks. I hadn't heard of the designer when I bought it – Sandra Hills? – but now I've got three of her pieces and I love them to bits.'

'Sandra Hills?!' exclaimed Janice, whose knowledge of labels encompassed British Home Stores and George at Asda. 'Amazing! She's fantastic isn't she? Have you got the others with you?'

'Yes,' said Beatrice. 'You've seen one of them, I wore it last night.'

'Oh!' enthused Janice, to Marion's surprise. 'That was fabulous. I might have known it was a Hills. You're not telling me that was synthetic material too?!'

'It is!' attested Bea.

'Never!' said Janice. 'Can I have another look?'

'Of course,' said Beatrice. 'Let's finish the dishes and I'll show you.'

'You won't mind carrying on putting these few away, will you Maz? We'll be back in tick. I just can't wait!'

'No, you carry on,' said Marion, clattering cutlery into a drawer. What on earth had got into Janice? Nothing she had ever worn to date would bring the phrase 'fashion victim' to mind.

'Come on then Bea, lead me into Paradise,' Janice commanded, taking the tea towel out of Beatrice's hands and guiding her out of the room. 'It's the closest I'll ever get to heaven this side of the pearly gates! I love good clothes – I just wish that I could afford them. Do you ever wear Chanel? Oh, by the way Maz, don't forget to keep our glasses and crocks separate – they need to go down with us.' She turned quickly in the doorway, pushing Beatrice through first, and mouthed 'Take them down now!' before continuing her gush. 'You'd look gorgeous in those little suits that Audrey Hepburn used to wear – you've got the legs for it, and the bones, of course . . .'

So that was what she was up to, thought Marion, and laughed as she gathered up the glasses and plates. She really was incorrigible. Thank God.

Slipping down the stairs, she had to squeeze to one side to let Christopher and Tom through, manhandling their table.

'Just taking these to the flat,' she explained unnecessarily. 'I'll be back in a second for the rest.'

'It's open,' Tom grunted. 'Terence is in there, taking the chairs. Can you lift your end higher, Chris? It's banging me scalds.'

'Sorry,' said Christopher. 'Sure.' Banging me scalds. What a curious expression. Whatever could he mean?

When Terence saw Marion entering the flat as he was about to exit, he stopped in his tracks and just stared, unable to believe his luck. The air between them was charged with an unbearable tension. 'Well well,' he said finally. 'Alone at last. Or are we?' He gazed past her shoulder to the door.

'For a couple of minutes,' Marion replied, her wit deserting her. 'Janice . . .' But her tales of heroic exploits were silenced by his sudden embrace and his lips sealing hers.

Time stood still.

Rockets exploded in the night sky.

An orchestra played.

Rocks fell off mountains.

They were shaking when they peeled themselves apart.

'You'd better go,' she said.

'I want you,' said he.

'I know, but . . .'

'I'm going to kidnap you tomorrow. I don't know how exactly, but I will.'

'Okay.'

'Expect the unexpected. Be prepared.'

'I will.'

'Are you coming back upstairs?'

'Better not.' Her legs were still not her own.

Reluctantly he tore himself away, giving her a final look of longing from the doorway. 'As soon as I can I'll . . .'

She could only nod her assent. But to what? she wondered, as he disappeared from view.

Dragging himself back to Pamela's living-room, Terence decided he needed another drink before he could face the prospect of being alone in a bedroom with Beatrice the baby-maker. His heart was still pounding from his encounter with Marion and he was aware that a foolish grin was constantly threatening to move in and make base camp on his lips. The last time he could remember feeling like this, he was wearing a school blazer edged in sixth form braid. Ridiculous! Wonderful! The chase was on, his sap was rising. God, he felt potent! He checked himself. An added reason to get absolutely slaughtered and incapable before Bea could get her claws into him. He poured himself a large brandy, looked at it in the glass for a moment, and then made it larger. Just now he needed brewer's droop like most men his age needed Viagra. He heard Tom and Janice making their good-byes, and before he could get the glass to his lips, Beatrice was there to reclaim him.

'Oh darling,' she said, sliding her arms around him from behind and nuzzling his back with her silly pretty little face, 'surely you don't want any more tonight. Besides, I thought you said that brandy keeps you awake?'

'Not if it's in large enough quantities,' he replied, slugging it back. 'Want one?'

'No thank you,' Beatrice demurred in a thin prim voice, 'I've had enough.' She disengaged herself from him, but couldn't bring herself to leave the room. 'But I'll keep you company.' She threw herself on to a sofa, striving for nonchalance. 'Where did you get to while I was showing Janice my clothes just now?' she asked.

'Clearing up,' he said, and topped up his glass. 'Why?' he added belligerently, fixing her with a dead-eyed stare.

'I just wondered,' she said, squirming. Janice had practically had her entire wardrobe out on display before she had realised that she had relaxed her vigil on Terence and Marion. She knew they'd been together, she just *knew* it. 'Why are you so angry?' she ventured plaintively, embracing the victim's role.

'I can't imagine,' Terence replied through teeth gritted with sarcasm. 'Ah, Christopher!'

Beatrice jumped guiltily at the mention of her recent indiscretion's name, until she realised that he had entered the room. In fact, he had been trying to slide through the living-room unobserved, on his way to a blissfully Pamela-less night's sleep. He stopped now in his tracks, as if stung.

'Hello there,' he said. 'I thought everybody had gone to bed.'

'Just having a nightcap — come and join us,' Terence invited him, smiling.

Christopher didn't need to see Beatrice's small shake of her head in his direction to know that this was not the thing to do just now — the air was positively thick with anger and testosterone. 'No thanks,' he said. 'I'm really tired. I'm off to bed.'

'Sure?' asked Terence, starting to pour another glass anyway. 'Just a small one?' He crossed the room smiling that dangerous smile of his, and put it firmly in Christopher's hand before he could demur. 'Cheers!' he said. 'Your health and happiness.'

'Oh well, thanks,' said Christopher uncomfortably. 'And to

yours.' He raised his glass to Terence and drank. 'Mm, nice stuff.'

'Talking of which,' Terence announced suddenly, 'thank you so much for your generous gift yesterday. You must think dreadfully of me for not mentioning it before.'

'Gift?' asked Christopher, his eyes sliding over towards Beatrice for a clue. To his horror, her eyes were suddenly huge and fixed, her body completely still, as if she were waiting for some fatal blow. What now?

'I couldn't believe my eyes when I first saw it,' continued Terence, laughing. 'I thought at first that Bea had a dark and dreadful secret she was keeping from me! Did she tell you?'

'No, I don't think so,' said Christopher, turning to her for help.

'The coke!' she spluttered now. 'That you left in our bathroom for Terence, as a present.'

'Oh the *coke!*' exclaimed Christopher. 'That I left as a *present!* Yes! Did you enjoy it?'

'Wonderful! Quite perked me up! Such a surprise! And too, too generous, Chris.'

Christopher thought so too, now that he had collected himself. And now he knew where it had disappeared to he wanted it back. Two grams of prime Charlie. A hundred and twenty quid. Not to mention the usual boring bloody performance to get hold of it. 'Actually,' he said, unable to restrain himself, 'I hope you didn't think it was *all* for you. I – er – as a matter of fact it was all I brought out here with me.'

'Oh no,' said Terence, enjoying himself hugely, 'I'm sure there must be some left.'

'We could have a little toot now, I suppose,' offered Chris, willing to be generous all over again if only to get within sniffing distance of his coke. In anticipation, he took out a note and his credit card from his wallet, and suddenly, looking at it in his hand, it dawned on him to what extent he'd been had last night in the restaurant. Terence had had his card all along! He'd put it down on the table on purpose, to punish him. Jesus! Did that mean he knew about him and Bea? What else could the punishment be for?

Over the rim of his brandy glass, Terence noted the light bulb finally go on over Christopher's head and smiled to himself with grim satisfaction. Look at the two of them – Chris with his jaw hanging open, Bea with her eyes popping out of her head – ha! Was there a farm somewhere, where they bred actors for their congenital stupidity? It was almost too easy to be fun. Still, one last little twist of the blade . . . He downed his drink in one, and walked over to the door.

'You two can if you want, it's a little late for me,' he said as he went, finally answering Christopher. 'I'm off to bed. Good night.'

'Night,' said Christopher, completely confused. 'So – shall I come with you to get the coke?'

'With *me*?' asked Terence in a surprised tone, turning in the door. '*I* haven't got it.'

'You haven't?' asked Christopher, dismayed.

'No, no. Last I saw of it, it was disappearing up Pamela's nose at a rate of knots. But then – *you* know how voracious she is about everything. See you in the morning. Sleep well.' And with that, he was gone.

'Hadn't you better go too?' asked Christopher of Beatrice into the shocked silence that Terence had left in his wake.

'I suppose so,' she replied palely, and forced herself to stand.

'He knows, doesn't he?' said Christopher. Her perfume wafted towards him as she made her way to the door and he was reminded of his feelings of earlier in the day. She was so lovely. And if Terence was on to them anyway, maybe there was nothing to be lost in declaring themselves openly, of making a go of it. Maybe it was time he settled down? Certainly, most of his friends had been doing that lately – he'd been to five weddings in the last twelve months, and he'd been starting to feel a little left behind. And one couldn't open the papers these days without seeing a photograph of yet another male star wearing a baby slung across his chest, proclaiming the virtues of fatherhood and family life. It might be rather nice to have someone to come home to.

'Knows about what?' asked Beatrice crossly.

'About us, of course.'

'Don't be silly.' Beatrice wished she felt as confident as she hoped she sounded. 'There is no "us" to know about. Good night.'

Christopher was left alone, holding a glass of brandy he hadn't wanted in the first place. What to do? The less she wanted him, the more he seemed to want her. Was it love he was feeling, or lust? He thought about it for a moment, and then realised that there was no way for him to know. He'd never learnt the difference – hadn't even suspected there was one, until yesterday afternoon. But that didn't mean to say he *couldn't* learn. How to get Beatrice to fall out of love with Terence and in love with him, though? Well – nothing he could do about it tonight. Squaring his shoulders, he drained his glass. And now he was left with another problem. Could he bear to risk a visit to Pamela's room to get his coke back, before the greedy cow snorted the lot?

Beatrice found Terence, to her surprise, checking his e-mail on his laptop in his room.

'Oh darling, don't!' she exclaimed. 'You promised you wouldn't work on holiday. You've already worked far too hard this year.'

'Things don't stop happening just because I come away,' said Terence without turning round. 'Besides, this in itself is a *working* holiday. We wouldn't be here now without Pamela's project.' Meaning *you* wouldn't be here now without my work.

'If the office really wanted you, they'd call you on the mobile,' Beatrice persisted, but more gently. She crossed the room and lightly put her hands on his shoulders. 'Come on, come to bed and let me massage your back.' The back in question stiffened at her touch.

'Beatrice, I am working and I would like privacy, if that is not too much to ask.'

'Darling, what is it? What have I done wrong?' asked the fair Beatrice, trembling on the precipice of tears.

'I would have thought you would be in a better position to answer that than me,' snapped Terence, shrugging off her hands and turning to fix her with angry eyes.

'You aren't upset at what that silly psychic woman said, are you?' she offered tremulously. 'She just got the person wrong. Everything she said was true, but about how I feel about *you*. It's your baby I want, it's you I want to marry!'

'Really?' said Terence flatly, turning back to his work. 'Chris seemed rather surprised when I thanked him for his generous gift,' he continued after a cold sea of silence, an edge to his voice. 'Almost as if he didn't know he'd given it.'

'Oh!' said Beatrice. So it *was* Christopher he was angry about. Well – at least he cared enough to be jealous. Maybe things weren't so bad after all. 'I should think he was just tired and it had slipped his mind for a moment. He's a bit vague at the best of times. You know what he's like.'

'Not as well as you do, it seems. Good night.'

'Terence . . .?'

'Good night, Beatrice.'

After she had left him – pale, he imagined, although he hadn't bothered to turn and see, with a hand held to her throat – at least, that was how she played tragedy on stage – he got back to the matter in hand, e-mailing Fiona, his PA in London. Phoning was too risky with Beatrice in her policing mode at the moment – he couldn't be sure she wasn't lurking behind some arras, listening to his every word.

'Phone me immediately,' he typed after some thought. 'Tell WHOEVER answers that it is imperative you speak to me AT ONCE about making an appointment while I'm here to see a backer for the film.' He sent it off to London and wished it God speed. All being well Fi would check her mail first thing in the morning, and the next day would be his, to court Marion in Rome.

*　　*　　*

Naturally, Janice had been agog to know the next instalment of the saga when she finally escaped from her examination of Beatrice's wardrobe. Returning with Tom to their apartment, she had hauled Marion out of the bathroom still damp from the shower and sat her down in the living-room for a thorough interrogation over sweet martinis. But frustratingly, Marion was withholding everything except name rank and number until she in turn had gleaned everything there was to know about the Evadne story.

'She reckons she's a reincarnated goddess,' explained Janice matter-of-factly, hurrying through her story. 'I dunno about that, but she's definitely one hundred per cent psychic.'

'One hundred per cent cock and and bull, more like,' Tom corrected her, smugly.

'Oh yeah? Then how come she knew you were a teacher and I was a nurse?' demanded Janice while Marion sipped her martini in silence and waited for the marital bickering to stop.

'You fed her the information yourself,' Tom replied smugly.

'No I never!'

'You kept nodding when she was close. It was all guesswork. And you kept saying stuff to me about wood when she was going on about all that reincarnation rubbish.'

'Reincarnation?' asked Marion, now totally lost.

'She told us loads about our previous lives,' said Janice, turning a cold shoulder on her centuries-old love object and giving her entire attention to her new friend. 'Apparently Tom and I have been trying to get together for years, but one or other of us keeps dying, so we've had to keep coming back to have another go.' She glared at him now as he snorted his ridicule. 'Can't think why at the minute, though.'

'Right,' said Marion, wishing she'd been there. From the sound of it, it might even have been worth forgoing her delicious rabbit stew. 'So what was it that upset our Bea?'

'Well, she wanted her turn next, and you could tell she wanted to copy us, you know, to be told that she and Terry were meant for each other and all that. You should have seen her clinging on to him all night, Maz, and he couldn't stand it, you could tell. He's definitely off her. It was obvious he didn't need Evadne to tell him she's been cheating on him with Chris.'

'You're kidding! What did she say?'

'It wasn't so much *what* she said as how she said it. She kept talking about the problems Bea was having at the minute with her love life and how it would all smooth out in an unexpected way in the end. But she kept looking at Chris when she was saying it, you know, counting them as a couple and ignoring Tez . . .'

'Which is why it's all such bollocks,' said Tom dismissively. 'She was guessing, and she guessed wrong.'

'Just cos you've got the hots for Bea!' Janice retorted.

'No I have not!' he spluttered back. Nevertheless he blushed from head to toe.

'You have! You think she's bleddy lovely! You go all stupid when you see her.'

'No I do not!'

'You do!'

'Not as stupid as you went over her frocks!' Tom ineffectually counterattacked. 'What was all that about when it was at home?'

'Oh shut your face. You wouldn't understand.'

'You shut your face!'

Marion suppressed a sigh of frustration. She wasn't going to get any more dirt tonight. She drained her glass and stood up to take her leave. 'I'm really tired. I'm going to bed.'

'Ah, don't go Maz, you haven't told me your end. And there's more I haven't told you about yet!' Janice offered to her retreating back.

'Tell me in the morning,' said Marion, going through into her own room. 'Good night. Sleep well.'

'There you are you see — now look what you've done!' said Janice, furious, to Tom. 'Satisfied?'

'Obviously not,' he snapped, fuelled with the anger of transferred guilt, 'I haven't slept with Beatrice Miller-Mander yet!'

'In your dreams!' parried Janice dismissively as she strode over to Marion's door.

'Not in mine, in yours apparently!' shouted Tom to the thin air into which his wife had just disappeared. He sat for a few minutes on his own listening to the girlie giggles coming from the next room, and muttered to himself about what could have gone wrong. All he'd wanted was to sit with a drink for a while and talk to Marion about the Harley and how much it had cost. It had been years since he and Janice had been on a bike – not since they were courting in fact. He'd been going to ask for a lend – he'd have paid the going rate for the day. Well stuff her. Stuff them both. Women. Listen to them, cackling like witches behind closed doors! And they whinged on about the exclusivity of men's clubs! He staggered to his feet, realising with surprise that he was drunk. 'I'm going to bed myself!' he called. But answer came there none, save for another sudden shout of laughter, which he knew in his water was Janice finally dishing the dirt on the Pink Lilo Experience.

In fact, Janice was much more interested in gleaning the latest instalment of the ongoing romance than she was in being disloyal to her husband.

'So go on, Maz,' she said, bouncing on Marion's bed. 'Spill the beans. What did he say?'

Marion hesitated. She wasn't really used to girlie chats, and when the girlie in question had a megaphone where her mouth should be, discretion was definitely the wisest course. She decided to miss out the bit about the kiss, but she had told her about the possible liaison the next day.

'Expect the unexpected, ay?' exclaimed Janice now, excited. 'What do you think he meant?'

'No idea,' Marion, yawned. 'Do you mind if I go to sleep now? I'm exhausted.' Already in bed, she pulled the covers up to her ears with an air of unequivocal finality.

'Okay,' agreed Janice, and sprang up off the bed. Did she

never tire? 'Ay!' she said suddenly, on her way out of the room. 'What's the last thing you'd expect to happen now?'

'For you to go quietly?'

'No, you daft bugger,' laughed Janice, unoffended. 'Terry to give Bea the slip and come down your secret passage tonight! How else is he going to tell you what he's planned for tomorrow?'

'I think I've got the night off,' said Marion. 'I don't think the unexpected starts till the morning. Switch the light out when you go.'

'That's the whole point of the unexpected,' said Janice, QED. 'Night, Janice.'

'Night,' said Janice amicably. But suddenly before leaving she swung over to the door of the secret passage and unlocked it on Marion's side.

'What on earth are you doing now?!' demanded her friend. 'Just go to bloody bed and leave me in peace!'

'Be prepared!' Janice reminded her. 'You'll thank me in the morning.'

'He won't come tonight,' said Marion. 'And if he does, he'll get short shrift. I'm knackered.'

'Oh well,' said Janice, finally, mercifully, going, 'you never know. Night night, sweet dreams. Don't worry – if I hear screams in the night I'll assume it's friendly fire!'

Marion grunted, closed her eyes and snuggled down in pursuit of oblivion. But no sooner had Janice left her in peace, than her mind was full of the day's adventures. Pisa itself would have been stimulation enough, let alone getting herself sorted out with a Harley – but to actually lay Frank's ghost to rest after so long . . . And it hadn't hurt at all. On the contrary, a lifetime's pain had apparently just melted away – the tight feeling in her diaphragm which was always there had disappeared. So liberating, as if a hard and time worn boulder had been lifted off her chest. And now Terence Armstrong – *Terence Armstrong!* – seemed to think his life was not complete without her. Bloody hell. She was wide awake again. But even that she didn't mind. She reached out and switched on the bedside light, aware that she was wearing a ridiculous smile. She felt so *alive*, so vital, as if each and every cell in her body were out at a street party celebrating victory and liberation. Her eyes settled on her tote bag across the room in which her art materials had been imprisoned. Yes. Why not? She actually wanted to draw.

Chapter Seventeen

It was three thirty in the morning before Pamela's hurried note finally found its mark, and when it did it knocked the smile clean off Patrick Donleavy's face. It was a handsome face with kind blue eyes and a finely chiselled jaw, and it had cost him dear to put the smile back there after recent events. So now, when he returned to his room alone after a pleasant evening in Cortona with a couple of fellow students, and he saw his own name winking up at him in that too familiar hand, he groaned at his own stupidity, plucked the note up off the floor and sat down heavily on his bed to read.

'Dear Heart,' it began. That was rich, coming from a woman whose only known organ was sited nowhere near her chest, he thought spitefully. 'If my light is still on when you arrive back, it means I am waiting for you. Come to me. P.'

Patrick crushed the note in his hand, clutched his head and cursed his dick. When the hell would it learn to keep itself quiet and small and nestled in his underpants minding its own damn business? After all he'd been through at its expense! Wasn't ruining his marriage and losing his kids enough? And hadn't he promised himself – sworn it on the sacred blonde heads of Bobby and Louise – that never *ever* again would he be ruled by its tyranny? His therapist had told him – yes, he'd even put himself in therapy, he'd been so shocked by the results of his folly – that everything could be turned around if he had the will. True, he couldn't undo the damage that he'd done, but here at least was an opportunity for personal growth. Break your patterns, he'd told him (at two hundred dollars the hour), and use this time for yourself. Look at the positive – surely there are things you might have wanted for yourself that marriage and being a full-time father might have prevented you from pursuing?

And when he'd thought of it like that, sure. He'd always wanted to spend time in Europe, and Italy in particular, and he'd got to a stage in his career that even handing over half his pay in alimony didn't limit him too much. He'd been almost excited when he'd discovered the residential summer art course studying techniques of the old Italian masters in Tuscany ('students will be housed in the thirteenth-century Palazzo' – wow!) on the Web. He'd felt mature and ascetic when he'd made his reservation and told his partners at the office he was taking two months off. He'd imagined himself walking through corridors of stone, serious-minded, self-contained, smiling pleasantly but distantly at fellow students on the course. And in the evenings he would withdraw from their company early, after a light supper of some fruit and cheese, to return to his small room with single monastic bed to reflect on what he'd learned each day.

And look what had happened instead. His dick had gotten out of his trousers on the first goddamned night! He hadn't even wanted her for Chrissake – surely she was almost old enough to be his mother? But he had allowed himself to be seduced by her upper class English accent, by her title, by her Palazzo, by Tuscany itself.

Part of what Pamela had told Signor Gambino was true. He had been lured into her apartment by the promise of borrowing rare and fine books, but once there it had been impossible to get out again without paying what she had smilingly cared to call 'a small library charge'. And over the past few weeks he had found to his dismay that it was an arrangement she intended to continue. Well this was an end to it. No more! To hell with politeness! He had drunk enough tonight to give him the courage to call it off. He went over to his window and looked up at her tower. A light still burned in her room. Fine. He'd come to her all right.

Stalking across the lawn, his eyes fixed with loathing on that light, he traced his now familiar steps to the small door tucked behind a flowering bush at the foot of her tower, which led to the secret passage linking all the floors ('known only to the cognoscenti' she had said flirtatiously when she'd shown him), and went up the narrow stone steps for what he vowed would be the last time. Outside her door he hesitated for a moment, wondering if he should knock. No. He'd enter on the offensive, speak his mind straight out, and leave. He grasped the iron handle with resolve and pushed open the heavy wooden door. The light was off. She must have given up on him in the time it had taken him to mount the stairs. Should he go — leave it till the morning? Hell no. He'd come this far. Might as well get it over with.

'I've had enough of this,' he announced firmly. 'It's got to end.'

'What?' said Marion with pounding heart, her eyes as big as saucers in the gloom, her body rigid with fear. She'd dreamt of this happening so many times, but surely this time she wasn't asleep? Or was she? What was more unlikely — that after drawing like a woman possessed for two hours, she'd fallen so heavily into an intensely dream-filled sleep in less than two seconds flat, or that Frank's ghost had tracked her down in Tuscany just when she had thought herself free of him? When she'd heard the passage door open she had assumed that Janice had been right, that Terence had crept softly from his room to tell her the details of tomorrow's tryst. But much as Terence's accent wandered, it didn't go as far afield as California, USA.

'I'm sorry, but my mind's made up,' he continued. 'My life's already complex enough.'

'Your *life*?' asked Marion. Were all the stories true then — was there life after death? She struggled into a sitting position and peered at the figure silhouetted in the doorway.

'Okay, okay, I know it's not exactly for life, just a holiday affair, but that's what I came here to stop.'

'I see,' said Marion. It was hard to tell in the dark, but he seemed somehow to be more mature, his voice deeper than she remembered.

'So that's settled then?' he said.

'I don't know. I suppose so. It's funny you should choose today of all days. I thought I'd got over this. I thought I'd exorcised your – ghost.' It was so strange to be talking to him out loud. For years their conversations had taken place inside her head. Could it be an old acid flash from her student days of dabbling? She'd heard of such a thing certainly, but never experienced it herself.

Patrick was confused too. This was weird. Her voice had changed. Where was the aristocratic drawl? 'You sound different,' he said.

'So do you.'

'Well anyway, so long as that's understood,' he said, anxious to go.

'Frank . . .'

'What?!'

'Can I see you – just for a minute?'

'Pamela?'

'What?!' Marion's hand explored the bedside table and found the light. For a moment they both blinked and stared at each other in horror.

'I – I'm so sorry,' Patrick apologised, recovering himself awkwardly. 'I – thought you were somebody else.'

'Yes,' agreed Marion. 'Me too. Pamela is upstairs in her bedroom, I imagine,' she added, pulling the sheets up over her breasts.

'I'm sorry to have disturbed you.'

'Not at all.'

'Good night then,' he said.

'Good night.' She watched him leave, sitting there, completely bemused. He was Frank to the life, only forty.

*   *   *

Outside in the passage, Patrick leaned against the wall, mortified. Who was that woman, and why was she sleeping in Pamela's office? Of course, she must be one of the house guests that Pamela was expecting. What an asshole! He was so deeply embarrassed he just wanted to run back to his room, but after a moment he forced himself onward and up the stairs. He'd come this far — even had a rehearsal for God's sake — he might as well finish what he'd come to do. But wait a minute. The light in her bedroom had been switched off when he'd looked up at the tower, that was why he'd assumed she was in her office . . . Well tough. He'd just have to wake her up.

Reaching Pamela's floor, he pushed open the secret passage door into the corridor of her apartment and peered round, alert for any sound — he'd met enough of her house guests for one night. Reassured, he closed the door which formed part of the hallway's beautiful panelling softly behind him and walked the few steps to her bedroom. No light shone from beneath the door, nor was there light through the keyhole, so far as he could see. Well good — if he woke her from her sleep, at least he'd have the element of surprise and she wouldn't be able to marshal her formidable powers of manipulation. This was experience speaking. It wasn't the first time he'd attempted to end their arrangement, without even counting the aborted mission downstairs. He would switch on the overhead light from the doorway so as not to repeat his mistake, make his speech clearly and unequivocally without being inveigled further into her room, and leave immediately. He took a deep breath for the plunge. So do it, he told himself, the quicker the better! And with that chastisement he squared his shoulders, grasped the door handle with firm resolve, and walked in.

It would be hard to say who was more surprised in the bright overhead light when Patrick made his entrance into the very web of the black widow. Was it Christopher, in dominant doggy position, who a moment before had been fantasising about making love to Bea, and who was now forced to admit that it was a very different back that he was biting; could it have been

Pamela beneath him, half on, half off the bed, only two thrusts away from her third orgasm, her coitus so cruelly interruptus, and so publicly? Or was it Patrick, mouth already open to make his speech, whose features, near frozen, flickered imperceptibly between euphoria and disgust? For though seeing her being pleasured was even more grotesque than doing it himself, surely this meant he was free!

As usual, Pamela opened on the attack. 'If you can't come on time, don't come at all,' she instructed, literary quotations never being far from her grasp. 'You couldn't have expected me to wait for ever.' She felt Christopher's engorged member shrink to a shadow of its former self and heard him scrabbling behind her for the cover of the sheets. Terrific. Now she was completely exposed. Well, what of it? It wasn't her fault this had happened. She rose laconically, as unashamed as Eve before her apple eating days, and recovered a half glass of warm champagne from the walnut dresser. 'I trust you had a pleasant evening?'

'I . . .' said Patrick, inside screaming for his scrambled wits to reform themselves in rank and file, 'I came to say it's over, but I guess it was dee trow.'

'De trop,' corrected Pamela in perfect French. 'Yes, apart from pronunciation I think you're perfectly correct. Do switch off that ghastly bright light as you leave.'

No! thought Christopher wildly, Not until I've found my clothes and joined you! But alas, that wasn't to be.

Never was parting such sweet sorrow, thought Patrick, elated, as he plunged them back into the darkness where they belonged and put two inches of carved wood between himself and a vision of hell. What a gift, what perfect timing, to finish with the woman and still be morally in the right! The smile that was on his face before he found the note from Pamela returned more broadly as he walked back towards the secret passage door to make his lucky escape complete, and was swiped off again almost immediately when the panelling refused to budge beneath his fingers. Jesus H. Christ, this couldn't be happening. Maybe it was the wrong panel. Frantically, he pushed the wall with both hands in an ever expanding acreage. Up and down the corridor he went, pressing frescoed faces. Why now, why this, why wouldn't it budge – he'd never had this trouble before? What if somebody came out of their room and found him like this, desperate, sweating, clawing at the wall? With great effort he stopped himself to draw a deep breath. He must think his way out of this, pronto.

Marion had never felt less sleepy in her life, despite being dog tired from her extraordinarily eventful day. To have finally buried Frank, only for his modern-day doppelganger to rise fully formed from his grave. The irony of it – the timing! And, more to the point, who *was* he? She suddenly started to wonder if she could have her cake and eat it, and sat bolt upright to think.

This man was gorgeous – far better-looking than Terence Armstrong, and needless to say, much more her type. Would it be retrogressive of her to pursue him – would she still be chasing phantoms? He probably didn't look *that* like Frank in the cool light of day. She knew in her bones that whatever happened between her and Terence in holiday mode here in a Tuscan palazzo wouldn't survive transplantation to the chillier climate of class-ridden England, mostly because of her own prejudices. He belonged, after all, to the class of people she normally wanted to kill. She couldn't imagine having him visit her in the jumble of her unloved semi in Wigston Magna any more than she could see herself, dressed to the nines, hanging off his arm at a West End opening night. But then again she couldn't see Frank II in a Leicester setting either. Although – hmm . . . California (if she'd recognised his accent correctly), to live out the rest of her days? Perhaps she was getting a bit ahead of herself. Getting involved with either of them would merely be a holiday romance, and lest she pushed it to the unvisited nether regions of her mind entirely, she should take into account that this new Frank had obviously been having an affair with Polythene Pam. Yeuk yeuk yeuk! It didn't bear thinking about.

Having given herself the equivalent of a cranial cold shower, she felt released from the giddiness of rocks falling off mountains with Terence and ghost hunting with Frank II, and was ready for sleep. As she snuggled back down into the comfort and sanity of her spinster's bed she decided that tomorrow would be spent alone. She would pack up her sketch books and take them for a spin on the bike. Why bother with the vagaries of sex when you could have the thrill of a Harley Davison thrumming between your thighs?

She had just fallen into the soft warm darkness of sleep again, dreaming of nothing more erotic than the slap and swirl of oil paint on canvas, when the sound of muffled banging drew her back into full consciousness. What now? She lay silent as a stone as she tried to work out what it was, where it was coming from, and whether it should bother her. Could it be Janice and Tom, perhaps, forgiving each other their differences? No – this didn't sound like bonking, more like hammering on a door. But which door? Heaving a sigh, she switched on the bedside light and got out of bed to investigate. It was coming from the living-room, as far as she could tell, and gave no sign of stopping. Grappling with the sleeves of her silk kimono and belting it tightly, she went in search of its origin.

Clearly, once she was in the living-room, she could tell it was the front door of their apartment that was the victim of this rude and untimely assault. Surely it couldn't be Terence already – it was only half past four? Only half past four?! How dare he wake her at this time, when she'd hardly been to sleep! Well, little did he know that short shrift was about to come his way in large quantities. She stormed over to the door and pulled it open roughly, and for the second time that night came face to face with the walking ghost, Frank II.

'Oh,' she said, 'it's you.'

'Listen, I'm really sorry about this, but I'm locked in,' he apologised. 'I thought I'd leave the front way, but the main door downstairs is locked and no sign of any key.'

'Right,' said Marion, 'I'll find mine.'

'Or I could go down the back way if you'd let me through your room. Save you coming down and locking up behind me.'

'Okay.' Marion stepped back into the apartment to let him in. Yes, he was gorgeous all right. That hair, so thick and blond – couldn't you just see your fingers running through it? Those eyes, so deep and blue – you could dive in there and swim and swim, be lost for all time, exploring unknown reefs. And as for those lips – For God's sake pull yourself together woman, she chided herself, don't forget that he is also dumb enough to screw Pamela.

'You seem to be having a bit of a night of it what with one thing and another,' she continued, filling the awkward silence as she rebolted the front door and led the way to her room. 'I'm Marion, by the way.' Stop it stop it stop it! There is absolutely no need to introduce yourself. And do not wiggle your hips like that as you walk ahead of him.

'Patrick. Donleavy.'

So, Patrick. Paddy. Pat. Yes, and what other name begins with P? 'You're not staying here then? You're not one of Pamela's guests?'

'No, no. I'm studying at the college – a short summer course.'

Of course, how perfect for the raddled old bag – a steady supply of students for her to get her claws into. Poor Patrick, what a nightmare, what a waste . . . Hang about though, it takes two to tango, and he is hardly an innocent young boy. 'Really, and what are you studying?' The Kama Sutra?

'The Italian masters.'

The Italian masters?! Tall, blond, hunky *and* interested in art? Thank you God! Yes, and shagging Pamela. Remember the bit about giving with one hand and taking away with the other? Let him go. Throw him back into the she-lion's cage.

'Well – here you are.' She opened the secret passage door for his escape. If he went through it, then it wasn't to be. So prevaricate. 'I didn't realise this went down as well as up. Does it lead to the outside then?'

'Yes. The entrance is pretty hidden behind a bush. It goes all the way up the tower from bottom to top.'

'Useful to know.' Stop playing with your hair — it isn't attractive in a woman of your age, it just makes you look neurotic.

'Don't worry, I won't disturb you again. I'm — sorry to have gotten you out of bed at such an unsociable hour.'

'Don't mention it.'

'And about the mistaken identity earlier.'

'That's okay. More embarrassing for you, I'd imagine.'

'You can say that again,' he replied, attempting a light-hearted laugh. Why hadn't he met *this* woman first? If his dick had to make a monkey out of him, couldn't it have been with her? There was something so attractive about her — not just her looks, although she certainly was a looker — but whatever was in those eyes — intelligence, humour, and something else . . . some promise of an arcane place where a man could find the answer to the secrets of the universe if only he were bold enough and brave enough to try, a place where . . . Oh for God's sake, give me a break! There are frying pans and there are fires, and you only just got out of one alive. With iron resolve, he forced himself to go out through the door. 'Well, good night then.'

'Good night.'

She watched him as he headed down the stairs, noting his broad shoulders appreciatively and the bright gold of his hair, so it was her turn to be embarrassed when he paused halfway and looked back up at her. 'Thanks for being so understanding. Marion,' he said.

'Not at all, Patrick,' she replied. And with that, they disappeared from each other's view; she, pink-cheeked, behind her door and he, red-faced, finally outside in the coolness of dawn. Both of them were smiling. For a moment or three. Then both of them, for their own different reasons, spoke sharply to themselves. Patrick had a reasonably early start in the morning — a lecture on Luca Signorelli followed by a field trip some place to see some of his work — and that, as he reminded himself, glancing at his watch, was what he was here for. He was definitely not here to get into yet more trouble with his dick, particularly not this soon after rescuing himself from the mandibles of the man-eater. Time to go to his room alone and sleep. The crispness of his sheets, changed that morning by an unseen hand, suited this enforced mood of self-controlled asceticism, and with a sigh he arranged himself tidily on his back, his arms by his sides, his legs together, and was soon enjoying the untroubled sleep of the righteous.

Marion, on the other hand, was now far too alert to enjoy anything of the kind. She took up her sketchbook again and went back to the drawings she'd been working on of the pulpits in Pisa. Nevertheless, her mind wandered over her situation, and as she worked she also drew some conclusions. She would definitely not encourage Terence further, and she would definitely not allow him to kidnap her. She would sleep as long as she wanted to, and then definitely go off on the bike somewhere. Maybe Cortona. She'd never visited San Niccolò, for instance, where there was a panelled painting of the Madonna and Child, accessible only by ringing for the custodian and asking nicely for it to be flipped over. Now that was a more proper use of secret passages and panels, and much more nourishing. As for this new excitement, this Patrick, she would stay well away. It was true that on second viewing, and in better light, his features weren't so like Franks's, but there were enough similarities to make a potential minefield of, and she still didn't trust herself enough yet that she had really and truly laid Frank to rest.

She turned her attention back to her drawing, and was appalled to discover that for quite some minutes she must have been doodling drawings of her dead lover's youthful face, and that now her hand was absorbed in shortening the hair and tidying it into a neat parting, drawing fine lines around the eyes, and rubbing out the beard – superimposing Patrick over Frank. *That* was how untrustworthy she was when she wasn't policing her thoughts. She threw her sketchbook on to the floor and commanded herself to lie down and switch off the light for the third time that night, even if she couldn't sleep. There was no question that tomorrow she needed to put herself out of harm's way and be alone.

At almost the same moment that the sleepless Marion was forcing herself to lie down, the sleepless Freddie was telling himself he might as well get up. He had been wide awake for some time, struggling with his first big decision of the day: chinos — navy or stone? It was far too early, of course, but nevertheless he rose now and tried both pairs on, viewing them from every angle for an agonising twenty minutes. Finally the navy won the day — they made a nice sharp contrast to his tan brogues, and had a slightly more slimming effect from behind. Once that was decided the shirt was a piece of cake — the blue-striped Egyptian cotton from Gieves and Hawkes — and to top it off, a green sweatshirt tied loosely round his shoulders like a scarf. Satisfied, he looked at his watch. Perhaps if he dawdled over some coffee in the kitchen while he checked his route to the excavations, he might not be too embarrassingly early, and of course, he had to allow ample time for getting lost. Cars were like some kind of time machine for him. Whatever time he got into one to drive, wherever he was and wherever he was going, he never seemed to get out of it again at his chosen destination for at least an hour and a half.

Now only his Panama hat short of perfection, he caught himself smiling foolishly in the mirror and counselled himself sternly to stop it. This trip to Joe's dig was a cultural and educational exercise, and there was no reason at all to start coming over all fey. Besides which, Joe was a happily married man. Turning from the mirror with a frown now in place of his smile, he picked up his hat in a manly devil-may-care-if-it-creases kind of a way, slung his gentleman's handbag containing wallet, camera and guidebook over his shoulder, and strode briskly out of his bedroom in time to meet Christopher creeping from Pamela's.

'Uh. Hello, Freddie,' Christopher greeted him, shame-faced for the second time that morning. 'Good morning,' said Freddie. How wonderful. He felt no jealousy at all. What a difference a day makes! 'See you later.' He didn't pause in his stride.

'Off out already?' asked Chris.

'That's right,' agreed Freddie, and disappeared down the corridor on the road to new adventures, first stop the kitchen to work out the configuration of the coffee machine.

'Shit,' said Christopher. It was like Piccadilly Circus in here. Still, there was nothing he could do now, and so what if old Fred knew he'd had a shag with Pamela — they were all grown-ups weren't they? Anyway, he wasn't going to let it happen again, and his primary mission had been accomplished. Pam had got out what little coke she had left last night, and at this early hour he had stolen softly from her bed and swiped the remainder. Half a gram was better than no gram at all. He'd hide it somewhere safe and share it with no one. Or maybe with Bea. For now though, the comfort of his own bed beckoned him to its soft embrace. But first a long hot soak in the bath to wash that wretched woman off his skin. He returned to his room and locked the door behind him. He knew Pamela's waking appetites, and he was certainly not going to be her breakfast in bed.

Down below in the front drive, as Christopher's head was at last gratefully moulding its impression into the comfort of his own pillow, Freddie was strapping himself into the Lancia, turning over the engine, and slipping softly through the gates.

At last, for the first time on that long night's journey into day, all the remaining occupants of the Palazzo Fratorelli were completely and concurrently asleep.

Chapter Eighteen

Tom was the first to wake up, at what was for him an exceedingly late hour, suffused with vague feelings of guilt and a hangover. He became aware that he was lying right on the edge of his side of the bed and that Janice was doing the same over her side, which in a bed this size left room in the middle for the Berlin Wall. Why? What had happened? He remembered being tetchy — argumentative perhaps — but could summon no precise details. He was cold and depressed and feeling at odds with himself, just like the bad old days before Janice got her hands on him. What he wanted most was a reassuring cuddle. Did he dare to try? What on earth had he said to drive her all the way over there? Whatever it was, he'd apologise most profusely, no foolish pride. Would she be in a kiss-and-make-up mood if he were to send out an expeditionary force of — let's say . . . his cold right foot — over to her side, to stroke her calf? Because for all her faults, you could toast crumpets on the warmth of Janice's heart. And if you could rouse her response with a gentle yet firm caress (the combination had to be precise and exact) before she was fully awake, she was much more docile than usual. Well, not docile perhaps, but affectionate and cuddly and tender, and far less talkative. At any rate, making love to her when she was still in a somnolent state was just lovely, and the only thing that ever seemed to make him feel whole. The rest of the time it was Mind over here, Body over there, with fiercely patrolled borders. Making love to Janice in the morning was — well — it was more like making love, and less like being ravaged by an eight-armed chimpanzee on heat. An icy awareness seized him.

Where had that phrase come from? And now it had popped into his mind, why did it refuse to leave? Eight-armed chimpanzee, chimpanzee on heat . . . Bloody Nora! Was that what he'd called her last night before he'd fallen into a drunken sleep? No wonder there was a Cold War on! He lay for some time unmoving, still clinging to his edge of the bed, feeling as lonely as if he were the only one left alive in a barren landscape after nuclear war. No way could he risk his right foot on that expeditionary mission now. Nor indeed could he seem to move it at all. It lay in an acute state of tension, completely im-mobilised by the equalising force of the twin commands his brain was feverishly sending. Go over to Janice, now, that's an order! *Stay put, ignore that fool!* Go! *Stay!* Go . . .

A small sigh from Janice and a resettling of her body two yards behind him put that argument on hold. She'd soon be awake and the opportunity for peace negotiations would be lost. It was now or never, and careful as you go! Softly and quietly his limbs stole slowly across No Man's Land. So far so good. And now for that gentle (yet firm) caress . . . Oh yes . . . Oh nice one . . . Ohhh, lovely.

Spookily enough much the same strategy was about to be deployed in the apartment above, although since they had spent the night in their separate rooms, the No Man's Land that Beatrice had to cross was much wider than Tom's, and the danger on the other side much greater. But cross it to the sleeping Terence, she decided, she must. And soon. If you got him at the right moment — and in the right way — you could, in her experience, nearly always guarantee to turn him from a bear with a sore head into a pussycat purring for more. The right moment was now (with any luck), quick sharp, before he woke up. The right *way* was the reason Beatrice was still welded to her bed. It was not something she went exactly potty for, under normal circs. It was something that made most men (and particularly Terence) happy, and most women (including Beatrice) gag. Still, these were not normal circs, and she was an actress, and the show absolutely had to go on. With the self-discipline of her profession, she went over to her lingerie drawer and changed her costume for something less comfortable, applied make-up in the mirror (forgoing lipstick), and launched herself out of the wings.

Terence was dreaming of Marion. He was riding pillion on her Harley, his arms around her leather-clad form, speeding through countryside full throttle. He felt himself grow huge, and then suddenly, magically, he was inside her from behind! Oh God! The bike disappeared and still they were travelling, but this time powered solely by him! If this was dreaming, may he never awake . . .! Faster, faster, the world going by in a blur, driven ever onward by the throb of his massive engine, kept aloft only by the strength of his desire. By the time he was fully conscious, he found that his body was indeed fully engaged. Was this possible? Had his dream come true? His hands went down to caress her hair and – shit! Bloody Beatrice! His engine spluttered and threatened to die. How dare she creep into his bed and take advantage of him in his sleep? But then again . . . ooh . . . she was determined, he had to give her that. Maybe, so long as he let things take their natural course and kept his eyes tight shut, couldn't he just lie back and watch the movie starring Marion that was showing here before? Think of the leather. Think of the speed. Think of the power of that engine, the pounding of those pistons, the endless, ceaseless, throbbing rush . . .

Beatrice was canny, and she had not worked this hard at a chore for which she didn't much care for naught. By the time she had Terence at the top of the rollercoaster begging her never to stop, she had swiftly rearranged herself so that a much more foetus-friendly receptacle was in position to receive his blessings. Please God, make it potent!

Afterwards he seemed so warm with gratitude that she dared

a little cuddle until he fell asleep again, then slipped quickly from his bed to her bathroom, where she promptly stood on her head and stayed there for some long time. Thank heavens for Yoga.

Patrick was into his second lecture by the time Marion started to come round, and she was dragged from her sleep only then because Janice was bouncing on her bed, post-coital and full of the joys of spring. She and Tom rowed rarely, and when they did they both agreed it was worth it for the making up afterwards, not only for the really class sex (Tom called it making love — sweet), but because they always aired their differences and found that they were small. This time, it had emerged, he had been feeling left out and jealous of her new friendship with Marion, and she had had to reassure him where her fidelity lay. 'You know me,' she'd said, 'I make friends with everybody, I'm only being sociable. But you're my biggest and best.' It was something that Tom had had to get used to over the years. He was more the type who made one good friend last a lifetime, and he had married his. He just had to be reminded occasionally that it wasn't a competition. Having been thoroughly convinced of the supremacy of his position in his wife's affections this morning, he could afford to be magnanimous. And she was right — they were all on holiday together and it was he who'd brought Marion along. It wasn't fair to ignore her, however tricky she could be. She was a woman alone, and deserved their pity and companionship. They had decided that they were going to push the boat out and treat themselves to breakfast at Claudio's, and he generously dispatched Janice to invite Marion to join them.

Marion, of course, had other ideas, all of which involved more sleep.

'Why are you so tired then? Did he come last night? If you'll pardon the expression!' demanded the irrepressibly ebullient Janice, undeterred by Marion's usual morning mood.

'No. Will you *stop* pulling the blankets off! Look, you go. I may join you later.'

It was then that Janice spied the drawings. 'Cor Maz, who's he? He's bleddy gorgeous!'

Marion groaned. She should have shoved them under the bed. 'Nobody,' she said.

'I like the way you shortened his hair – he looks much better like that. You're dead clever, you. I wish I could draw.'

'Anybody can. It just needs practice. Now go and have breakfast.' She turned over and presented the blank wall of her back, closing the subject, she hoped. She knew now that she wouldn't find sleep again this morning, but she wanted to be alone with her thoughts.

'Are you going to come then? We're buying.'

'Yeah yeah. Thanks.'

'You can leave Terry a note if he doesn't come by the time you're ready.'

That grabbed her full attention. 'What for?'

'Well if he didn't come last night he'll be here soon, won't he, to tell you where to meet him for the kidnapping.'

Marion sat up straight. She hadn't thought of that. 'I'll see you down there in five minutes,' she said, springing out of bed.

'Yey hey! She's coming Tommy!' Janice called through. 'Don't you want us to wait?'

'No. I'll be bringing the bike.'

While Tom and Janice pottered down the hill to Claudio's, romantically hand in hand, stopping occasionally to point out some flower to each other or to gaze at a view, or simply to cover the other's face in kisses and to re-avow their love, Marion raced round her bedroom grabbing her things for a long and solitary day out, but not before locking her side of the secret passage door. So far she'd been lucky that Terence hadn't bounded through it already – it was almost eleven o'clock. She couldn't believe she hadn't locked it after letting Patrick out. A Freudian slip? The unconscious desire for him to come waltzing back in again? Well, there was certainly no time now for such reflection, and it just went to show what danger she was in if she didn't watch herself. She dashed to the bathroom and scrubbed her face in cold water.

Back in her room, she found that choosing a costume was tricky, now that she had the Harley. She had been very aware the day before that simply riding a bike that size made her a magnet for male attention, but having her cheesecloth skirt up round her thighs made her look as if she liked it that way. And today was to be a completely and totally male-free zone. Which meant, on viewing her limited wardrobe, that the crushed velvet flares it would have to be. Dragging them on and choosing her seersucker blouse by default, it being the only one clean, she thought that perhaps she might buy some more clothes today. She was beginning to feel that, useful as it had been for her outward journey, now she was here she was outgrowing 'hippie' for the second time in her life. It was time to discover what the new Marion wore. Still, she reflected, she had been right not to pack the clothes she'd bought for the holiday. Whatever the new her might prove to be, it definitely wouldn't be beige.

Emerging outside into the warmth of the sun and feeling the better for it, she was too slow to prevent her head, on automatic pilot, from swivelling round to glance over towards the college. *Marion Hardcastle*, she heard herself think in her best school teacher's voice, *you will stop that at once!* There was no need to chide herself over similar sneaked glances at Terence's window, however — she dreaded that he might be watching her make her escape and try to follow. Mounting the Harley, she started her up and roared out of the gates at full speed.

In fact she needn't have worried. The only person watching her leave through their window in the tower was Beatrice Miller-Mander, who was assembling a tray of goodies in the kitchen. She had been about to take Terence breakfast in bed, but on reflection, and smiling happily to herself, she considered all in all that he would be best left to sleep for a while longer now.

It was late for the breakfast trade down in the village, but Claudio was more than happy to oblige, if only he could understand what this funny little English woman wanted for herself and her silent husband. In a place so small and off the beaten track as his, you had to take full advantage of every tourist lira that came your way. Now she was flapping her arms and clucking, to the huge amusement of his children.

'Pollo?' he enquired doubtfully. What did he know about what they ate in the mornings?

'Maiale!' exclaimed Gino, his four-year-old son, chortling with laughter and pointing his fat little finger at Janice, who had now passed on to oinking and snuffling.

'Porchetta?' asked Claudio.

'Marion'll be here in a minute,' Tom said quietly, head down, staring in embarrassment at the tablecloth. 'Just order some coffee till she comes.' But Janice was no quitter, and besides, this was fun. 'What's he say? Porketta? Si, si, porketta – baconi and eggsa and two-o rounds of toasto eacho. Blimey, what do you do for toast? It doesn't make a noise.' Just as she was re-enacting the drama of the pop-up action of a toaster to an enthusiastic audience of children and shoppers, the Goddess herself arrived on her machine. Never had Tom been happier to see her.

'What's this – charades?' Marion asked as she turned off the engine and propped the Harley on its rest.

'Hiya Maz!' laughed Janice, still popping. 'I'm trying to tell him breakfast!'

'Ah, ciao Marianna!' exclaimed Claudio, not one whit less happy to see her than Tom. 'Che cosa vuole la tua amica? Mangiare? Volare?' Her toaster impression certainly made it look as though she was trying to fly.

'Toilette?' shouted young Gino, who had watched Janice's egg-laying mime with great interest.

'What are you after?' asked Marion of Tom. 'Bacon and eggs?' He nodded, unable to meet her eyes, and cleared his throat. 'And toast.'

'Okay, Miss Linguaphone, let's hear you say it!' said Janice, collapsing back into her seat and pulling the giggling Gino onto her lap.

'Uova con la pancetta e pane tostato per tutti e due, e per me . . .'

'Espresso macchiato,' offered Claudio, after one look at her heavy lidded eyes.

'Sì!' laughed Marion. 'E una spremuta d'arancia possibilmente!' she called after his disappearing back.

'Ma certo.'

'Blimey,' said Janice. 'All that for a bit of breakfast! They don't half gob on!'

Marion lit a cigarette as they waited, and Tom tried not to flap his hands at the smoke. He couldn't take his eyes off the Harley. He supposed that Marion would be off soon on a bike ride, and him and Janice would just be stuck here all day. He was starting to regret his pecuniary prudence over the car. If only he could persuade her for a lend. It must have cost a fortune to hire – there was no question they would be able to afford one themselves, even if there was another in the village, which seemed highly unlikely. The breakfast, when it came, bore no resemblance to its English counterpart, but he choked it down to keep Marion sweet. Unlike Janice.

'This bacon tastes reasty. Is it off?'

Marion raised her eyes to the heavens as she spooned sugar into her coffee. 'It's pancetta – it's just cured differently.' If anything should be off it was her. She glanced nervously at her watch. If Terence had seen her leave the Palazzo he could be here at any minute. She gulped down her orange juice, chased it down with the espresso, and called for Claudio, who would take nothing in payment from her. Tom watched in amazement. How come she was so popular with everybody, when with him she was so prickly? First Terence Armstrong, now Claudio – and who was that greasy-looking type down the street, who'd just caught sight of her and waved, and whose shouted greeting of 'Ciao, Bella!' she cheerily returned?

'Who's that?' said Janice, peering down the street, who wasn't one to wonder when she could just as easily ask.

'Oh, Franco – local wheeler dealer. He hired me the bike.'

Tom sat up straight. She was obviously about to go. He had to know.

'I bet he charged you an arm and a leg?'

'Two of each plus the torso, Tom,' smiled Marion, mounting her steed. 'You are looking at caution cast to the winds. I'm off for a ride. See you later.'

'You're not going already? Where to?' demanded Janice, but her words were drowned out by the roar of the engine, and before you could say 'Easy Rider', her friend had hit the road and was gone.

'She didn't even say what happened with Terry,' she complained to Tom. 'I wonder if she's off to meet him somewhere?'

'Dunno,' he said, his eyes now following Franco as he disappeared into what was evidently his garage workshop down the road. 'I wish we had a bike to explore on.'

Janice looked at him fondly and gave him a kiss. 'Aah – just like we had when we were courting?'

'Well yeah,' said Tom, 'only bigger than that.'

They sat in silence for a while, each lost in their own thoughts, and when Claudio came over to mime 'Volete cappuccino?' they both agreed that they did. For stuck here without transport, what else was there to do but measure out their life with coffee spoons? For did they dare disturb the universe? And if so, how should they begin?

Chapter Nineteen

While Janice and Tom inhabited the world of J. Alfred Prufrock, albeit without their conscious knowledge (in fact, if you'd said 'Eliot' to them they may just have answered 'Gould', or even 'E.T.', but more likely 'Winterbottom', for that was the name of the gay theatre nurse at Janice's Infirmary who, with his partner Martin, had been coming to them every Boxing Day for the last five years), Marion was pondering the words of Aldous Huxley. She had been meaning to take it easy today and merely potter along to nearby Cortona, this being the first time out on a bike for years, let alone a monster like this one. But once she was cruising pleasantly along country roads with the wind in her hair and the sun on her back, she couldn't resist driving on and on and up through the lovely wide Valdichiana valley and its ruminating white cattle, until she realised she was almost at Sansepolcro, and therefore only minutes away from what Huxley once described as 'the best picture in the world' – Piero della Francesca's *Resurrection of Christ*. It was a place that Frank and she had meant to visit but never had, so thankfully there could be no sentimental journeying here. Before she knew it, she was parking in the shade of the medieval walls, tugging at her velvet flares self-consciously as she left the bike behind her, and walking through promenading tourists up Via XX Settembre. Shops – there were shops! She'd buy herself some clothes. She didn't care how much of her savings would be eaten up (after the amount she'd splashed out on the bike, anything else would be mere chicken feed), she simply had to get out of historical costume and into — what? Who knew?

But even as she was crossing the street to window shop in a lively-looking boutique, shutters started rattling down all around her and doors were being locked. Good grief, it was one o'clock already, which meant also that the Museo would be shut for the hallowed hour. So — lunch then, she supposed — why not go with the flow? And while she was hunting for a trattoria, she could get the lie of the land. A few blocks further on she discovered Piazza Torre di Berta, which had to be the main square, and walking on past the Duomo and under a bridge that connected two grand buildings, she found one of them to be her quarry, the old Palazzo Communale which was now the Museo Civico, and home to some of della Francesca's finest work. Sure enough it was closed between one and two, but as she was turning away in the hope of finding somewhere to lunch nearby, she noticed that people were still going up an outside stairway to what looked like an entrance, and pausing to gaze in at the top. Well, if she was going with the flow she might as well keep flowing, she thought, and followed them up the stairs.

At the top of the stairs, she found to her delight, she could look through a glass panel into the hall housing Piero's paintings, even when the Museo itself was closed. Now where in England, or come to that, the rest of the world, would the city council assume that you might be consumed by an uncontrollable urge to see an artist's work at any time of the day or night, and that it was therefore their responsibility to give you, gratis, a quick fix? As the people in front of her sighed their satisfaction and relinquished their places, Marion pressed her nose up against the glass and drank in the Master's paintings. And here, opposite her, was Huxley's favourite — the risen Christ. Despite her atheism, Marion was moved. By the grace of the artist's clarity of vision and his use of unpretentious imagery, this Christ was so human, and he spoke so directly of the extraordinary ordinariness of rebirth to his agrarian fifteenth-century viewers; for as he rose, so did the blighted land around him revivify, putting out fresh new shoots, turning brown to green. See? he seemed to be saying, Look what happened to me. So no matter how bad things may look to you now, no matter how bleak your life, there is always hope, always another spring, always the possibility of a fresh start and of a new life about to begin. You don't even need blind faith, or priests to interpret the mystery — just look at the seasons, and know it. This was just the message that Marion was eager to hear. She stayed long at the window, until the discreet coughs of those behind her caused her reluctantly to turn away and descend the steps. She would return after lunch when the Museo reopened, and pay her respects in the flesh.

And now it was in her mind, yes, lunch — she was starving. She'd passed a promising trattoria on her way here. She'd treat herself to a proper sit-down meal and savour every mouthful. Why not, when her winter was over, and the plenitude of spring was in the air? Fortune smiled on her, as did the waiter, who gave her the last remaining table outside, in the shade of an umbrella. Perfect. She could sit here and think her thoughts and eat good food and watch the world go by. Guided by the waiter to the special dishes of the day, she ordered a primo piatto of spinach ravioli stuffed with ricotta and vegetables, and to follow (with an inward apology to the white Chiana cattle) the involtini di vitello. She knew she mustn't drink much — the Harley was hard enough to handle stone cold sober — but she allowed herself to be pressed into one glass of the local wine at her new friend's insistence. It was made from the grapes of his grandfather's vines, he told her, and this year's crop had been the best in a decade. Before she knew it he was back at her side with a small terracotta jug of the Chianti and a complimentary dish of sun dried black olives encrusted in chilli and herbs. He poured the wine with reverence and watched her face transform with pleasure as she first inhaled its fragrance and then took her first sip, her mouth filling with the flavour of dark skinned cherries warmed by the sun.

'Buono?'

'Incredibile!'

And that was all it took, apparently, to make him a happy man. She watched him as he left her for another table, completely contented with his lot. And who wouldn't be, mused Marion, popping a marinated olive into her mouth, to give so much pleasure to so many every day? How different her own life would be, for instance, if after stuffing her pupils with knowledge in class they turned to applaud her with as much incredulous delight and gratitude as she had shown the waiter. It was true that every now and then a pupil passed through who showed genuine talent and élan, and who seemed grateful for her attention, but they were the infrequent exception rather than the rule. Normally the only time they spoke to her with heartfelt passion was to say, 'Miss! The bell went ages ago!' But these were retrogressive wintry thoughts, she reminded herself sharply. Where was her recent mood of resurrection? Obviously throwing in the towel at school and becoming a waitress in Tuscany wasn't going to be the answer, so what form should her rebirth take? For a moment there was a huge blank space inside her head as terrifying as any virgin canvas, and then, before she was even aware of it, she found she was thinking of Patrick. Oh no you don't, she told herself firmly, you have not come this far only to fall into the thrall of another man, not Patrick and not Terence. Think of your own spring, of your own new shoots burgeoning.

Returning to her table with the ravioli, the waiter found her frowning and muttering to herself.

'Va bene?' he asked in some concern.

'Ah – si, si – mille grazie – benissimo!' she replied. He smiled in return, and placed the dish in front of her as if it were a bowl of jewels. Again her eyes followed him as he walked away, chatting to other diners. You can learn from him, she instructed herself as she might instruct her recalcitrant class, What does he do differently to you? After a short pause a hand shot up in the back row of her mind. Yes? she demanded, But be sure it's something sensible – be warned, I am in no mood for nonsense!

He lives in the moment, came the now doubtful reply. Yes, Marion Hardcastle, good. He lives in the moment. So how do you think you can live in the moment when your thoughts, now freed from yesterday, are constantly casting around for the uncertainties of tomorrow? The present is this ravioli, and the pleasure you might choose to take in the single-minded eating thereof. Begin.

She looked obediently at her plate, at the three huge and handsome home-made ravioli glistening green beneath the extra-virgin olive oil and flakes of parmigiano, and was glad to give it her full attention. Taking up her knife and fork, she was delighted to discover that each contained a different treasure – in one asparagus, in another zucchini, and in the third porcini. Now what could the future possibly hold that could come anywhere close to this? Willingly she gave herself over completely to the tastes and textures in her mouth, partaking first of this one, then of that, so that she was more than half finished before she realised that her mind had gone walkabout without her permission, and that a feeling of sadness was creeping over her, driving pleasure away. What on earth is the matter now? she demanded angrily of herself. If you can't concentrate on this then I despair of you! Is this food normal to you then, and unworthy of your attention? Do you eat like this so often in Leicester that it deserves your contempt? Do you take back your plate from the school dinner lady daily and say 'Oh – home-made ravioli again'? But merely entertaining that thought for a moment brought an awareness of what was wrong. For here she was, not only halfway through her pasta, but also halfway through her holiday. In a few short days she would be standing again at her own threshold, and opening the door to the chaos within. The food, so recently ambrosian, turned to sawdust in her mouth. Marion Hardcastle: Living in the Moment – D minus – go to the back of the class.

On automatic pilot she chugged her wine and poured another glass. This was more like her life – slamming back booze on her own to ease the pain. Oh, for heaven's sake, Marion! she chided herself. If you have to do it, at least don't glamorise it – easing the pain indeed! If it's that painful you would flee from it, not embrace it. All you are feeling is the strangeness of change, and change you must, or be lost. If you *must* think and eat at the same time, at least think constructively. Thus chastened, she chewed the rest of the ravioli thoughtfully, and tried to be honest with herself.

— If it's a man I want, why haven't I got one? she asked herself.

— Because I couldn't commit, came the reply.

— And why?

— Because I was living in the past.

— And why?

— Because of Frank.

— Because of Frank?

— Because of me?

— Better.

— Why because of me?

— Perhaps it suited you to be alone. Why else would you base your entire adult life on the thwarted desire of youth? Perhaps you just don't see yourself as others do, one half of the whole picture? Perhaps single is your natural state.

She tried this on for size as she ate. Was that it? Had she used Frank as a shield against the likes of Colin Menseley, for fear of getting in too deep? She tried to picture herself in a life shared with Colin, for argument's sake, since he had been her last attempt. If he were here, what would they be doing now? Well, they wouldn't have the Harley for one thing, and if by some miracle they did, she certainly wouldn't be driving it. But why on earth not? Had not women endured force feeding in prisons, and thrown themselves beneath the hooves of the King's horse, just so that Marion could be enfranchised? And didn't that include doing what she damn well pleased, in a relationship or out of it? Certainly the young generation of Riot Grrrls whose graffiti in the loos was so often criticised in school assembly would assume it as their right, and Marion would endorse that one hundred and fifty per cent. No, the fact was that she wouldn't have had the

Harley if she'd been with Colin because Colin was dull and safe and he would have overruled her extravagance — like Tom he would have counted their pennies with prudence.

This was getting her nowhere. Not only had she finished the rest of the ravioli without tasting it, she was also going up blind alleys. What then would make her happy? As if in answer, the beaming waiter took away her plate and replaced it with another which bore the thinnest slices of tender veal wrapped around whole young artichokes, cooked in its own juice. It looked wonderful. It was time, literally, to change course.

— I want excitement and adventure, the debate continued in her head.

— Good. And?

— And I should stop blaming everybody else for not giving it to me.

— Excellent! So?

— So I must give it to myself.

— That's right. And what form will it take?

— A commitment to myself.

— Mm . . . and more specifically . . .?

A fragment of her conversation with herself last night came to her. She had tried to picture Terence visiting her in her unloved home, and had found it was impossible to let him in. Just thinking of her house now made her flush with shame. She had bought it carelessly ten years before and had never looked at it with a lover's eyes, never given it her attention. She walked through it now in her mind's eye, noting the yellowing paint-work, the threadbare carpets, the mess and the jumble of it all. One room she called the junk room, where things were slung haphazard and forlorn — but how did it differ from the rest of her home? She had made of it a whole junk house. And hadn't she originally meant for the so-called junk room to be her studio?

— I shall redecorate and reorganise the house.

— Excitement and adventure, yes! That should keep you satisfied.

— There's no need to be sarcastic.

— There's no need to be banal.

— I am not being banal! I shall make a space that gladdens my heart to enter, and I shall make a studio and paint. I shall enrol in a life class. I shall remould my life until it fits. I shall buy new clothes and do something different with my hair, and maybe sell the car and buy a bike — why not? And I shall cook for myself — no more frozen pizzas and eating out of tins. And I will visit more galleries, see more movies, read more books. First I will change myself . . .

— And then?

— And then I might see about finding a bloke.

— Marion!

— But not until. I like their company, and let's face it, I am partial to sex.

— Well, better than nothing. Now eat your veal, and mind you savour every bite.

This she now found she was able to do wholeheartedly and with gusto, and the waiter, watching Marion as he watched all his customers, with care and concern, was happy she had at last found something to please her. For Marion's part, food had never tasted so good, and had certainly never disappeared from her plate faster. Before she knew it she was refusing a dessert (she had her mind set on three different flavours of ice cream from a gelateria she had spotted, to be eaten on the hoof as she window shopped) but saying yes to coffee. She needed to clear her head, since the small carafe of Chianti she had drunk far exceeded the one glass she had been going to allow herself. As she lit a cigarette and took small sips of the bitter-sweet espresso she looked around her at other women in the street to see if what they were wearing might do for her new image, but among the summer floral prints and crisp linen business suits there seemed nothing that said Marion Hardcastle, New Woman. Perhaps she should start with the hair? Or just not bother? After all, it was *internal* change she needed — what did the packaging matter? She caught herself about to fall before the first fence, downed her coffee and settled the bill.

Courage mon brave! she told herself, and plunged off into the shopping crowds.

Half an hour later she was staring into yet another boutique window, as unable to bring herself to enter as she had been at the dozen or so before, and thinking that surely now she had earned herself an ice cream break and a return to the Museo, when she became conscious of two young girls behind her daring each other in Italian to ask her where she'd got her velvet flares. She turned and looked at them, and they giggled uncomfortably, not knowing if she'd understood.

They couldn't be a day over seventeen years old, she thought, which strengthened her resolve. Not only was she wearing the garments of her youth it seemed, but also of theirs, which was too embarrassing for words. She must find something immediately that more befitted her age. Doughty Leicester sentiments like 'mutton dressed up as lamb' resounded in her head, but to her surprise the girls were only the more admiring to see that (as they muttered to each other, sotto voce, in astonishment) she was as old as their mammas yet still had an eye for street fashion. She gave them what she hoped approximated to the uncomprehending smile of a foreign tourist so that she may learn more about herself at second hand, but they, embarrassed in their turn, just pointed at her pants and said 'Che bella' and went giggling on their way. She watched them go, teetering on platformed soles, and admired their trousers in return, stylish, timeless, and what's more practical for the bike. So that was that. Blue Levi's it would be. She plunged into a shop.

So good was the salesgirl that when she re-emerged out on to the street for her promised ice cream, she was transformed from head to toe — Levi jeans, Levi jacket, a plain white T-shirt, Ray-Ban shades, and a pair of bike boots. Her outgrown youth she now carried effortlessly on her back together with two new shirts and a linen jacket ('but you must have it, it was made for you' the girl had said), in her new black leather rucksack. She walked back towards the gelateria admiring her reflection in shop windows, feeling taller and less conspicuous, and almost ready for the world except for her hair. She had stopped seeing her stylist ages ago, even before she had finished with Colin, and had kept it more or less at shoulder length with the aid of the kitchen scissors. It was unkempt (especially now, with the long bike ride), straggly, and two different colours of mouse — both brown and grey. Something had to be done, and now, while the mood was upon her.

It seemed that fortune was smiling, for before she knew it she had not only located Fabio's, the trendiest hairdresser's in town, but she was gowned and sitting in a chair with Fabio himself running his fingers through her hair. Her new found self-confidence, however, was soon draining away as he demanded to know what kind of English animal had last been let loose on her hair. She now looked at herself through his eyes in the mirror — a middle aged woman who had let herself go, barely deserving of his valuable attention, and she could almost see herself shrinking in size. No, she replied to his questions, she didn't have anything specific in mind. Imperiously he decided she would go shorter, maybe a bob, and that the colour must be made richer, possibly mahogany. Although she herself was doubtful, she lacked the courage to demur, and so it might have been, had he not asked, almost casually, as he started to cut, 'So, this is for a new job, new boyfriend?', and Marion had said firmly, 'No. This is for a new me.'

His scissors froze mid-air immediately and he looked at her again appraisingly, his interest finally aroused. 'You have a strong face, but it needs something dramatic to show it. Do you like Sinead O'Connor?'

Marion quailed. 'Her music, not her hair.'

'Then, Björk?'

'Likewise, I'm afraid.'

They compromised on Annie Lennox.

Two and a half hours later, with three flavours of ice cream from the gelateria still fresh in her mouth (chocolate, pistachio and peach), the new and improved Marion Hardcastle entered the

Museo with short bleached hair and a smile. Looking neither right nor left she made a steadfast pilgrim's progress to Room 4. The other works could wait. All she wanted now was to pay homage to the painting that had drawn her here and changed her life, della Francesca's risen Christ. For verily, was she not saved? An hour or more she gazed and gazed, wandering over to look at his Madonna, then at the crucifixion, then back again to the Resurrection, until she was replete. Glancing at her watch, she was astonished to see that the day had practically gone, and thinking of the long bike ride in front of her, she decided to head back.

As the kilometres stacked up behind her she suddenly remembered Terence's plans for their day together, and couldn't face the inevitable explanations. It would be too much to hope that she might avoid him entirely for what remained of the holiday, but she certainly wanted to put it off for as long as possible. She was sure in her own mind that she didn't want him now, but she could do without having to persuade him of that — he didn't look like the kind of guy who would take rejection lying down. She thought about dining at Claudio's again, but decided it was too close to the Palazzo for safety. She would go to Cortona, then, and wander about for a bit. If she got a move on, she might still visit the small church of San Niccolò, and see the hidden altarpiece. She felt much more confident on the Harley now, and she relished the wind in what was left of her hair as she pushed it ever faster.

Arriving in Cortona, she decided against leaving it in the town's main car park on the off-chance that Terence might be around, and seeing it, know she was there. Instead she rode it through the thronged and tiny shopping streets, but, looking like she did, caused such a stir that had he been anywhere within a five-mile radius he would have heard the news anyway. Eventually though, and climbing ever upward, she left the gawping crowds behind her and found her quarry and parked the bike outside. Now to see if the custodian would be happy still to see her at this late hour — it was very nearly six o'clock.

She rang the bell, and to her great relief, was allowed inside. 'I wouldn't normally let you in at this time,' the custodian grumbled to her. 'But you're lucky — there's a party booked to come here in half an hour, by special arrangement.' Marion apologised and assured her she wouldn't be long. The last thing she wanted was company in this quiet church. She looked first at the fresco of the Madonna and saints, but then was drawn to the altarpiece and poor old Jesus at his lowest ebb, crucified. Much as she admired Signorelli, she was glad she had seen Piero's Resurrection first, or she might have been depressed. She had never understood why the Christian Church had taken an instrument of torture for its symbol — why remind yourself of a long and painful death, when what he'd stood for, surely, was life renewed and hope sprung eternal? Perhaps she was suffering from Art fatigue — there was only so much you could really see in a day. She asked, as was expected of her, for the picture to be flipped over, and gave an almost perfunctory glance at the Madonna and Child on its other side. What she wanted most, she realised, was to be out in the evening air, to stretch her muscles and to remind herself how glad she was to be alive.

She turned to thank the custodian for her time, but found that she had scurried to the door and was calling to somebody outside. Marion listened, and could hear by the crunch of footsteps on the gravel in the courtyard that the awaited party had arrived early. Indeed, even as she stood there, a couple of well-heeled women of retirement age were leading the way, clutching their sketchbooks and bending the ear of what looked to be their long-suffering guide, who was in turn trying to hurry in those who lagged behind. It was definitely time to go. She smiled politely, apologising as she brushed past the motley collection of nationalities and ages who were still thronging in, and squeezed out of the door.

By contrast to the cool dark interior of the church, outside the evening sun was blinding and she paused briefly, her eyes crinkled against the glare, to replace her sunglasses. She couldn't see the bike at first, and then realised it was because a group of five or six of the visiting party, mostly men and boys, were gathered round it admiringly, crouching down or standing – the younger ones even daring each other to get on. Americans of course.

Even before she could compute this information with other nuggets gleaned within the last twenty-four hours, their exasperated guide had come out behind her to call them in, and Patrick's blond head, previously hidden from view, now rose from his examination of the engine. Her stomach lurched as the group left the bike and straggled, good-natured, towards her. She wasn't ready for this. Swiftly she left the doorway of the church and drew to one side, blending, she hoped, with the walls and thanking God for the radical change in her appearance, while she knelt down with her back turned towards them, and pretended an overweening interest in the contents of her rucksack, her ears straining for the sound of his voice.

'Shall we stay in Cortona again tonight, and go back to eat at that place? Maybe visit a few more bars?' said a man of about his age as they passed beside her.

'Yeah, eating sounds good,' she heard Patrick reply, 'but I'm going to take it easy on the booze tonight – believe me, last night was enough!'

She heard his companion's answering laughter as they disappeared into the church, and the lecturer – for now she knew that the small and irritable man in charge was a college lecturer, and not a tour guide at all – call to two dawdling youths who were obviously more impressed by motorbikes than by art, that they were keeping the entire party waiting. They scuffed their way across the gravel, complaining about their parents sending them to summer school when they could be having a cool time at the beach.

'Who's this guy we're looking at here?' one said disaffectedly.

'Signorelli, Signorelli, you've been looking at him all day!' the lecturer replied in an acerbic tone with which Miss Hardcastle, teacher, could empathise. 'And you'll be looking at him all day tomorrow in Orvieto! Now please . . .!' And at last she was left alone to make her escape. Standing up again on shaking legs, however, she found to be another matter entirely – she hoped she could manage the heavy bike in this weakened state.

She took several slow deep breaths to calm herself as she sat with relief on its comfortable saddle, started the engine, and eased out the clutch. But where to go? She couldn't stay in Cortona for the evening as she had planned, now she knew he'd be there – she'd been lucky enough already that he hadn't recognised her. Perhaps Claudio's after all, and risk discovery by Terence? But even as she left Cortona far behind her and cruised up to his restaurant she could see for herself that it was uncharacteristically full, and that Claudio himself was stretched to his limit, darting up and down the tables outside, which had been pushed together for a large and boisterous crowd. She sat on the bike, the engine idling, as he came towards her, spreading his hands with a shrug, 'So sorry Marianna – an engagement party, been booked for weeks – there's nothing I can do.'

Now where was she to go to put herself out of danger – back to Cortona or on to the Palazzo? Which was the lesser of the two evils – to risk bumping into Patrick or to Terence? Devil, deep blue sea? Rock, hard place? The debate was brief. There really was no question. She had to put herself out of her own temptation's way. She eased the bike out on to the road and sped back towards the Palazzo, which as it turned out was danger enough in itself.

Almost home, she was belting towards a minor crossroad where she now knew from experience she had right of way, when some fool and his wife on a Lambretta cut across her from the road on the left and swept in front of her, causing her to swerve violently. By the time she had corrected the swerve and reduced the speed of both the bike and her pounding heart, she could see quite clearly that the wife in question was Janice, so there would be no prizes for guessing who was the fool.

Chapter Twenty

Terence had had the most god-awful day, although even he had to admit it had started well enough. So confident had he been that his e-mail to Fiona would get an immediate result and that he would have the perfect excuse to slip away with Marion for the day, he had even allowed himself to return Beatrice's affection at breakfast. It was a curious fact, and one he had noticed before, that no matter how intolerable a woman became, as soon as he was within sight of escape, he almost instantly felt quite fond of her again. He supposed it was something to do with pressure. She had sensibly left him alone after her naughty little incursion into his bed, and he had dozed happily for some time before she arrived with a tray of coffee and fresh bread and preserves, all of which was quite delicious. When he had finished eating she had snuggled up on his chest for a while, which was agreeable enough, and had left him without demur when he kissed her lips and told her he wanted to shower and dress. Really he couldn't fault her in any respect. Nor in fact was any human in error. It was the frigging computer that was to blame.

Showered and dressed – even whistling while he did so – he strolled down to the living-room where he asked Pamela with commendable casualness whether there had been any calls for him. The answer coming in the negative caused him no more than mild surprise – Fiona was such a party animal, she often arrived late at the office. Perhaps, by the time she had got in, she had been caught up with phone calls and hadn't had time yet to check her e-mail. He glanced at his watch and was surprised to see how late it was. Allowing for the time difference in London, she should have been at her desk an hour ago. And what of Marion? Here it was, almost time for lunch, and he had given her no word of his plans. Was she still waiting, sitting downstairs cursing him, twiddling her thumbs? After his morning fantasy he was really looking forward to sitting on the back of the Harley, his arms round Marion's waist, but at this rate, if something didn't happen soon, it would be too late to drive all the way to Rome and back, let alone have time to check into a hotel for the afternoon.

And now Beatrice was starting to make irritating noises about what they might do with themselves for the day. On the pretence of slipping back to his room for a map, he sat at the escritoire, opened the lid of his portable PC and logged on to the web, the wide world at his fingertips. His in-box was empty, save for his own e-mail to Fiona, which had been returned, undelivered and unread. What the bloody hell was wrong with it now? Frigging technology. He tried again, and again it was returned. Had he got one of the sodding dots of the address in the wrong sodding place? What was the point of spending thousands of pounds on the latest form of communication when you'd be better off with two frigging cocoa tins and a long piece of string? With difficulty he controlled his temper, moved a dot, and sent again. Shite!!!! Returned again. Try again, returned again; try again . . . nothing worked. The inappositely named Help Menu didn't help him, and nOR DiD THumPPping THE fRIGging KeybOArdDDDDDD. He shut down the computer to serve it right, slammed the lid, and was about to recourse to the dangers of being overheard on the mobile phone (if he could make the sodding thing work), when Beatrice arrived breathless at his side. Pamela had invited them to go with her to visit some friends for the day, and the big news was that they had a swimming pool, gushy gush! Even she could see, though, that there was danger in his eyes when he looked at her.

'Anything the matter darling?'

'No.'

'Bad news from the office?'

'Not a thing.'

Wisely she had withdrawn to get her swimming things and plan her wardrobe, pre and post swim. Did he dare risk a saunter down the secret passage to Marion's room, he wondered? And if he was caught, how would he explain that one away? He hedged his bets and threw open his bedroom window, leaned out dangerously, and looked down at the driveway below. The bike was gone. Damn it to hell. He couldn't blame her he supposed – she must think he'd been all talk the night before. Curses! Another day wasted! Another whole day of Bea. He grabbed a towel and his trunks and stomped downstairs, where his temper was not a bit improved to find that Christopher would be coming with them. Freddie, apparently, had gone off early on his own. Sensible bloke.

And worse was to come. It quickly became apparent when they arrived at the opulent house of Pamela's 'friends' that she had not invited them along out of the kindness of her heart (as if!), but that they themselves were her admission ticket – they had been brought along as famous trophies to enhance her stature in the eyes of Mr and Mrs Dull and win her a place at their table. Why? They must have had something that Pamela wanted, but it certainly was not wit or charm. A few other lunchers had been gathered for the occasion, all in various stages of unattractive disrobement around and in the pool, and all stopped dead to gawp at the entrance of Pamela and her prizes. Chris and Bea were in their element, of course, and stripped down to their bathers at once, under the fascinated gaze of admiring eyes.

Terence found a shady spot and refused no drink that came his way. He thought he might have a nap to ease the tedium, but Mrs Dull (for the life of him he couldn't remember her name after they'd been introduced) insisted on bringing him titbits from the buffet table and sitting by his side. She was a theatre buff (wouldn't you just *know* it), and she and Mr Dull had seen everything that was anything and sat on two theatres' boards, one in London and one in the town of their Home Counties retreat. She was, she said, his greatest fan, and then went on to list all the productions she had known and loved, most of which weren't by him at all. They had met Name Drop at an awards dinner and Sir Name Drop at a first-night party, and regularly dined with Dame Name Drop whenever she was in town — did Terence know her? (Know her? He'd had her.) After what seemed like days of listening to her prattle, and thinking that he was in great danger of either throwing himself to the floor and frothing at the mouth, or of savagely beating her even more senseless than she already was, he excused himself and went indoors in search of a bathroom, just to get some peace. It wasn't until he had locked the door and splashed his face with cold water that he suddenly realised he was now free to call Fiona on his mobile.

His mood, when he returned outside, was so much improved that he allowed himself to be cajoled into a spirited game of water polo in the pool, where he scored three goals straight off. Indeed, he was in the actual act of pushing home the second of these when he heard the satisfying sound of his mobile phone ringing in his jacket pocket on dry land, and when he stopped to wipe the water from his eyes, he was even more gratified to see that Beatrice was helpfully taking the call and bringing the phone to the water's edge.

'Darling, it's Fi,' she said, looking worried.

'Really?' he replied disingenuously. 'I wonder what's up?'

Back in his London office, Fiona had invited her PA pals in from across the corridor and put the call through the conference speaker so they could all enjoy the joke. The worst part was muffling their giggles while they listened to the boss doing a brilliant one way impro down the line.

'But I'm on holiday,' he protested to nobody at all, 'and I told you that under *no* circumstances . . . Oh I see . . . Yes, yes . . . So I have to see him tomorrow or not at all? . . . In Rome? . . . Well fine, I'll take Beatrice and we'll make a day of it . . . Oh no, you're kidding? . . . And how much is this worth to us? . . . Right, right, no you're quite right, it has to be done . . .'

After he'd rung off and the girls could giggle out loud, Sara, the new girl, wanted to know what he was up to now. But Fiona, who knew him like the back of her hand, said the real question was not what was he up to, but who was he up? They all laughed till they were fit to be tied.

In Tuscany, Terence was now improvising the nonexistent other half of the call for Beatrice's benefit, still standing waist deep in the pool, the polo players waiting patiently for their demon striker to return. 'He's worth millions to us in potential backing for the film, so I'm afraid I just can't say no. I said I'd take you, but apparently he's arranged to pick me up by helicopter from a local airfield here, and there aren't any seats left. From the sounds of it he's on such a tight schedule, we'll probably be doing half the business in the air! I'm sorry darling.' Beatrice pouted and was close to tears. This happened all the time. 'But the holiday's almost over,' she complained. 'I know, my love,' Terence said, and pulled her down to him at the water's edge, and kissed her. 'We'll just have to make the most of today.'

Rejoining the game moments later, with the scent of one of the world's most beautiful women still in his nostrils, and the promise of spending the next day with the object of his dreams, scoring the third goal was a breeze. The fact that Christopher was on the opposing team's defence was the cherry on top of the icing on his cake. He tried hard to maintain this mood, knowing he would soon be free. He even managed to stay smiling when it was presented to him, fait accompli, that they would be staying on to spend the evening with the Dulls.

At around seven, a second wave of guests started to arrive and the party expanded. The buffet table was cleared and refilled with salads and vegetables of every kind, and the air was filled with the aroma of roasting meat and fish as a team of barbecue chefs worked, glistening in the heat, to satisfy fresh appetites. The Dulls were certainly getting their money's worth from their celebrity guests, and Terence started to suspect that this must have been planned for ages, which meant that Pamela played her cards even closer to her chest than he did himself. What was the woman like?! She'd surely taken quite a risk leaving it until the last minute to invite them along if his suspicions were right. What would she have done if they had claimed a prior engagement for today and not come with her? After a moment's reflection he realised that she would have done exactly the same as he would in her shoes – she'd improvise. He made a mental note to himself that if his company did pursue the rights to her father's book they would have to watch her like a hawk during the contractual negotiations, otherwise she would have the skin off their back before they even felt the sting of the flaying knife. Terence couldn't help but admire her skill. She reminded him in part of his ex-wife Angela, who was far too similar to him for their marriage to have worked, but by God she'd given him a run for his money. When he thought of timid little Bea trying to usurp her place in his marital bed . . . absurd! Where would be the challenge in that?

Thinking of her now, his eyes sought her out over the prattling heads of Mrs Dull and her best friend Mrs Deadly, who were currently trying to outdo each other in dramatic criticism for his benefit. There she was, looking quite beautiful, even he had to admit, dutifully queuing at the barbecue for the Thai king prawns he had asked for. Would she never learn that the only way to hold his interest would be to play hard to get? It wasn't as if she had to look very far to realise how unattractive availability could be, for glued to her side was Christopher trying vainly to get her attention which she repulsed, and behind him was Pamela, who was trying vainly to get *his*. Terence laughed as he absorbed the nuances of their group (which Mrs Deadly and Mrs Dull took as appreciation of their bon mots). It was for all the world like watching the ill-matched and frustrated would-be lovers in *A Midsummer Night's Dream*. As much as he enjoyed the sight of them collectively making fools of themselves over each other, some distant alarm bell rang, subdued but insistent, in the back of his mind. He suddenly realised with horror that he could just as well be watching himself with Marion. Had he been too eager — was that why she had gone off without him? It was a timely warning, he thought, and he promised himself he would behave more coolly at their next meeting. Of course there was still the thorny problem yet to come, later at the Palazzo, of how to slip Bea's leash long enough to tell Marion of his plans for her tomorrow. Now that was going to be a poser. How to appear off-hand and distant while making a secret assignation in the middle of the night?

While Terence puzzled over this conundrum, Chris was doing mental gymnastics over his own. With Terence now mercifully being taken out of the way tomorrow on business, how was he going to shake off Pamela long enough to take advantage of Beatrice being on her own? For the more he was with her, the more he realised that this unfamiliar feeling in his chest must be what others talked about as love. How else could he explain away that he had caught himself earlier, while dozing happily in the sun, making a mental list of wedding guests and even arguing the toss between the expediency of a registry office or the more romantic setting of a church? He was even picturing a baby Bassett in Beatrice's fond maternal arms, himself gazing on them, puffed with pride. Was this nature's way of reminding him that he was nearly thirty-four, and had yet to pass down his genes? Whatever was driving him was driving him hard, and he felt he simply had to have her to himself to persuade her of her folly in thinking she wanted Terence instead of him. He suddenly remembered his appointment the next morning with Evadne. Of course — she had known the truth. He would take Bea with him to hear from a psychic what he himself already knew — that their destiny was shared. But where to go afterwards to cement their union, and how to escape Pamela? He needed transport for a quick getaway, and his funds were low. Well, needs must. He *had* to have her. He would have to dig deep into his pocket and hire a car. He felt his ardour almost dying at this thought, but then to his astonishment the moment passed and he felt passion surge even more strongly. This *must* be love. He had never been foolish about money before.

Chapter Twenty-One

After the bikers had parked up at the Palazzo and Janice had seen Marion's hair and screamed and thrown her arms around her and told her she looked bleddy lovely, Marion couldn't begin to find the words to remonstrate with Tom about her brush with near death and his part in it, so in the end she didn't bother. Besides, both he and Janice were so chuffed with themselves about using their initiative, it would have been cruel to deflate them. They had done some tough bargaining with Franco (and looking at the scooter, thought Marion, so had he) and had been as excited as kids when they handed over the hard won funds of the Department of Education and the NHS in exchange for the adventure of the open road. They'd spent the day 'just pottering about, just like when we were engaged' and had found a market in a nearby town. The storage unit underneath the scooter seat was stuffed with goodies, and Marion helped to carry them up. Both parties had thought to buy booze.

'I've bought the ingredients for spag bol,' said Janice as they entered the apartment, 'seeing as we're in Italy.'

Marion couldn't bear to think what that might be like, Janice-style, so at once she volunteered to cook. She felt good chopping onions and tomatoes, if a little rusty, and congratulated herself on putting into practice so quickly what she had promised herself earlier in the day. She'd been eating convenience food at home for ages as part of her general decline, but all that was going to stop. From now on, self-nourishment would be her byword, in all its forms. The frying meat sizzled satisfactorily as she deglazed the pan with red wine, and a cloud of fragrant steam came up to tantalise her taste buds. This was fun.

''Fraid I couldn't find any Oxo,' said Janice, 'so it might be a bit insipid. But we brought some Marmite with us if you want it.' Marion demurred, and was even more glad she'd elected to be chef. While they waited for it to cook, they all repaired to the living-room with large gin and its where they made a convivial group. Tonight, even Tom seemed happy, and though Janice was bursting to know the latest in the Terence saga, she wanted to keep it that way. She was in a bit of a cleft stick, not wanting him to feel excluded again, but conscious of the fact that Marion would be unlikely to want to dish the dirt in front of him. Her mind circled around the subtleties of the situation for a while, and then decided that, as always, direct was best.

'So come on Maz, what's going on with Terry? Did you do him, I'm dying to know? Don't worry about Tom, he's an honorary girl, aren't you my dove?' Nothing Marion had ever encountered in Mr Cowlishaw, Woodwork, could find resonance with this surprising assertion, but she buried her face in her glass for a moment to hide her smile, and noticed that Tom, after a struggle to control his own features, was doing the same. She doubted though, in his case, that it was a smile he was trying to suppress. But all in all, by unspoken agreement, it seemed that amnesty was in the air, and she would not be the one to break it.

'To be honest, I've gone off the whole idea,' she said. 'I spent the day on my own, looking at paintings and buying these clothes.'

'So who's the hair for?' Janice challenged her. A woman didn't do that sort of thing for no reason, she knew.

'For myself.'

'Blimey.' Lying cow. Maybe there was someone else? 'I was telling Tom about your drawings. They're brilliant, especially the ones of that bloke.'

'They're just rough sketches, nothing much.'

'So who is he, Maz? Come on, tell Janice. You know you want to.'

'Just somebody I used to know. He's dead now.' The words were out of her mouth before she had time to think, but it felt good to say it at last. Young Frank was finally dead. Nevertheless, the subject must be changed. 'So come on, tell me, where are you planning to go tomorrow on the scooter? Back to Viareggio?'

'We might, or we might go to this lake we heard about – it's nearer, and you can still swim.'

'Trasimeno?'

'That's it! Do you want to come?'

'Mm. I don't know. I might.' Marion couldn't imagine a worse fate than to go paddling with the Cowlishaws, particularly since the time now left of the holiday was diminishing fast, but a fragment of conversation overheard outside the church of San Niccolò was burning a hole in her brain, and she knew she had to protect herself. On no account must she allow herself to go anywhere near Orvieto.

'So what's made you go off Terry?' asked Janice, still searching for some drama in the conversation.

'Well, for one thing he's already got Beatrice Miller-Mander,' Marion replied.

'Quite right,' said Tom, and then blushed. Janice looked at him but decided to let it go. Let the man have his fantasies. She, after all, had the man.

'And for another?' she asked.

'I just don't fancy him.'

'You've changed your tune!'

'Not really. I was just flattered to be pursued, I suppose.'

'And it's not every day you meet a celebrity.'

'True, true.'

'So why d'you buy new clothes?'

'Because I needed some, Janice.'

'She did,' confirmed Tom, and blushed again as both women

turned to look at him. 'I mean, speaking as a man.' Worse and worse, he could tell. 'Shall I go and put the pasta on?' he said, rising to his feet. Neither of them rushed to stop him.

Over dinner, which wasn't bad all things considered, thought Marion, she managed to steer the conversation round to less dangerous territory, pretending a burning curiosity to know how Janice and Tom had met, and feigning great interest in the tale of how the sawn-off tip of his thumb had led to romance in A and E. As the wine flowed, replacing the river of gin, so did their laughter and merriment, so they didn't hear the sound of Terence's car pulling up outside — heard nothing, in fact, until the knocking at their door.

'What d'you bet it's Tez, Maz?' demanded Janice, slurring her words, as Tom wove his way over to answer it.

'Sshh!' said Marion, slumping down in her chair. 'If it is, I'm not in!'

It was Christopher, looking tanned and beautiful after his day in the sun, and in a state of excitement. 'Hello there. Tom, isn't it?'

'Ye-es?'

'Is that your scooter outside?'

'Why — what's happened?!' Tom said in alarm. It was costing enough already without having to pay for accidents.

'Nothing, nothing. I was just wondering where you hired it. It's so dinky. Did they have any more? Was it frightfully expensive?'

'Hiya Chris!' shouted Janice. 'Come in and park your arse, we're having a drink!'

'I'd love to, er — Janice? But I'm really tired,' said Christopher, politely taking one pace inside to show willing. 'Oh, Miriam, you've changed your hair! What a difference! You look fantastic — so cool!'

'It's Marion,' said Marion shortly, but only to cover her pleasure at being admired by one who knew. Cool, ay? Not bad. Tom, too, was more than happy to be envied by a film star, and particularly so since his scooter seemed to have pre-eminence in

Christopher's mind over Marion's Harley. He'd been feeling a bit naff about that up until now. He described in great detail, man to man, how to find Franco and how to bargain him down, and anybody would have thought that he'd discovered him himself.

'Well thanks then.' Christopher displayed his fine teeth in a smile. 'Sorry to have disturbed you. Good night.'

'Night Chris!' called Janice after his retreating form. 'Sleep tight, mind the bugs don't bite!' She watched him, admiringly, all the way out of the door. Like the Cheshire Cat, his smile was the last of him to disappear. He really was handsome and hunky – she couldn't half give him one. She staggered up to refill her glass, and then changed her mind. Bed. Now. Tom would have to do. 'Actually, I'm feeling completely knackered myself. It's all that fresh air on the bike.'

'Me too,' agreed Marion, glad to be allowed at last to be on her own. And in fact, she realised, she was exhausted. There had been far too many late nights over the past few days, and far too few late mornings. She took her turn in the bathroom and then retired to bed, first checking that the secret passage door was still locked on her side against intrusion. If Christopher was back then presumably so was Terence, and she could do without another close encounter. She closed her eyes, and no sooner had she relaxed her vigil on her conscious mind than her dreams were full of Patrick, galloping with her on a bare-backed horse, their naked flesh as one, the wild wind in their hair.

By the time Christopher arrived upstairs in Pamela's apartment everybody had disappeared to their rooms. Well that was fine. He'd set his alarm clock for reasonably early the next morning and sneak in to Beatrice after Terence had left. They could stroll down to see Franco together – he'd probably get a better price on the bike hire if Bea was by his side. The only potential fly in his ointment would be if Pamela were to pay him a visit in his bed between then and now – he shuddered at the thought. Being used as a stud by the ugly old hag had been bad enough before last night, but when they had been caught mid-shag by that American guy, whoever he was, Chris had seen himself through the fellow's eyes in the glare of the overhead light and been doubly disgusted. There was no question about it – Beatrice had to marry him. She must save him from himself – he needed to be protected from this kind of thing. He turned the key in the lock of his bedroom door, then, fearing it might prove to be too insubstantial against a determined sally from Pamela, dragged a chair over and jammed its back under the handle. Let her wail like a banshee, he would not let her in.

Had he but known it, he was safe. Even Pamela needed a night off now and then. Exhausted, she was currently in pursuit of nothing more than sleep, but it eluded her. All she could see, behind closed eyes, were unbalanced figures dancing down columns in black and white. Her bank statement had arrived that morning, in amongst the bills, showing more money pouring out than was currently trickling in. She was horribly aware that the subject of her father's book had not been discussed since the night of Terence's arrival, and she was starting to feel ripped off. What if he had no intention of making it into a musical with Johnny Jarmain, that he was here just for a free ride? (How else could she judge people if not by her own behaviour?) She had somehow to get him to talk about it seriously and at length, to rekindle his interest, to get closure before he returned to London. Perhaps she should suggest some big-name casting to guarantee success – at least for the male lead? Glad to be released from the worry of money, her mind now roved pleasantly over the physical attributes of a galaxy of stars, and she let herself imagine entering their dressing-room after the first night, one by one, their faces still glistening from the grease paint, their manly forms stripped to the towel around their waists. Mm, this was fun. She made a mental note to talk to Freddie about including casting rights in her contract.

At the moment, however, lying on his bed in the room next door, a smile transforming his usually anxious face, Frederick was sifting through his own day's events, already become history in their turn. His day with Joe had been perfect in a way he had never even dared to dream. Together they had pored over Etruscan artefacts, gone deep into the secret hidden realms of ancient life and myth. He had listened, fascinated, to Joe's theories of what had happened here two and a half thousand years before, of who this race had been and what was its ethnogeny (Joe subscribed to the hybrid theory – local Villanovians intermixing with Asian travellers from what is now known as Turkey), had admired Joe's strong but sensitive fingers as they reverently handled shards of vases, fragments of tombs, looking for meaning in the clues. Best of all, he had loved Joe's scholarly humility, an entirely unbigoted view that this, his life's work, was at best informed guesswork, that any deductions were coloured by the observer's own small realm of experience. The meaning of the past was always ambiguous, as mysterious and unknown as the future, full of subtlety and shifting shapes, and one could never say with certainty what was in another's mind. But tonight, Frederick Mayer was happy and fulfilled. He felt as if he had finally come of age, after a lifetime's adolescence of romantic delusion. Of two things he was entirely sure: that tomorrow would be as wonderful as today because it would be spent again with Joe, and that at last, the feeling that he felt was love, most deep and true, without a trace of torment. What did it matter that Joe was married, that here was yet another relationship that could never be? At last he was in love with a real grown man, not a blazer-wearing, boater-toting, punting poet, confected in his masochistic teenage dreams. He knew that Joe liked him and seemed to enjoy his company from the way his smile went right up into his eyes when he turned to him to speak. Was that not cause enough for happiness?

Upstairs, Terence was allowing himself to be seduced again by Christopher's object d'amour – it was the least he could do given that she would be deprived of him all the next day. Yet again he felt more comfortable in her company, knowing he would be free of it tomorrow. While Beatrice's head was full of him (quite literally as it happened), he allowed his thoughts to wander back to Marion. Watching the unconsummated dance of Chris and Bea and Pamela all evening, he was confirmed in his feelings that all out pursuit would be counterproductive. He would go to her the next morning while Beatrice was still asleep and appeal to her as a friend, not as a lover, to spend the day with him. He'd seen that she was an inverted snob – he must capitalise on that. He'd trash the shallow upper classes whose company he'd been forced to endure for the past few days, and beg her to rescue him from brain death for a day, just for a meaningful conversation with no strings attached. He could suggest they went to see the paintings in Perugia – wasn't that where Freddie had wanted to go on their first day, when they'd ended up instead watching Paola Sonelli give birth? He would ask her to show him round, to be his guide. That should do it, he hoped. The next day didn't bear thinking about if it were not to be spent in Marion's company. He decided not to go down the byways of that negative mental path, particularly considering the current, pleasant, corporeal distraction that was in the here and now. Why fight it? He let his mind become as fully engaged with that part of his body as Beatrice presently was. Lovely. Lovely. Even lovelier if he allowed himself the fantasy of another's mouth at work. Huge, huge, he was growing massive, at least twice his normal size. Under the bedclothes Beatrice noted the change in his response and congratulated herself. She'd finally got his full attention. Soon it would be safe to change position and go baby hunting again.

In the apartment two floors below them, where Marion, unaware that she was engaged in Terence's mind in other, more active pursuits, dreamt blissful dreams of walking barefoot, hand in hand, in dewy meadows with Patrick/Frank, Janice and Tom were finally unlacing their limbs and settling down to sleep, content and satisfied and still the worse for drink. Unknown to the other, both had been secretly indulging in wild extra-marital affairs while conjoined in connubial bliss. While Tom had been overpowered by a passionate and determined Bea, Janice had been playing doctors and nurses with Chris. Where was the harm, they both thought to themselves guiltily, so long as it wasn't often, and all in the mind? They cuddled up closer, switching out the light, reassured and comforted by the familiarity of the shape and smell of their true-life chosen partner. Holidays were nice, but it was always good to come back home.

Presently, for the fourth midsummer night, the fortified walls of the tower held the motley party and their dreams, safe from attack. Across the courtyard, Patrick, just returned from his evening in Cortona, looked out from his room to Marion's window and saw only darkness where he had hoped to see light. He had been unable to stop thinking about her on and off all day, had seen her everywhere he'd looked, in the paintings, in the crowds – even in the shape of the back of the woman with the short blonde hair he'd noticed, squatting outside the church of San Niccolò. And what on earth did he suppose he would have done if her light had been on, he asked himself – he, who had sworn a vow of chastity to keep himself out of harm's way? Shaking his head in despair at his folly, he grabbed the curtains, pulled them together, and told himself that he should do the same. He would *not* think about her any more. He did *not* want to get involved. He tore his clothes off and forced himself under a cold shower, staying there, shivering, to brush and floss his teeth. Thank God he had the structure of the course to protect him from himself, and that tomorrow his class would be going off to visit Orvieto. Otherwise he might have been tempted to hang around the Palazzo all day in the hope of seeing her again. Which actually, when you thought about it, as ideas went . . . was very bad.

Was he sex mad, like his ex-wife had said? Did one little scratch of a ten-year itch mean he was incorrigible? Maybe. Look what a pushover he'd been for Pamela. Maybe he was, as Kathryn had screamed the night she'd found out, just like all the other guys, just a prick on legs. He didn't like the sound of that. It made him feel stupid and primordial, and not how he liked to think of himself – as a man of scientific reason and artistic sensitivity. As a punishment he made himself stay under the stream of cold water while he went round his molars again. Practical tasks were the key to change. Distract the mind. He would floss that girl right out of his teeth.

Chapter Twenty-Two

As was proving to be the norm on this holiday, Marion was dead to the world the next morning until Janice starting bouncing on her bed. She and Tom had decided on Lake Trasimeno as their day's biking destination, and they wanted to know if she'd come. There was a cup of milky Nescafé and a bourbon biscuit on the bedside table by way of a bribe to wake up, both of which had zero effect.

'I'll get up in a minute,' Marion protested, her eyes still closed. Her head hurt. This night-time drinking would have to stop.

Janice was undeterred. Next in her repertoire came the bed-stripping dance, to the tune of 'The Sun Has Got His Hat On', rendered allegro, fortissimo, and con brio. Marion wanted to kill. She pitied the poor patients on Janice's ward. Go in for a bypass and come out needing ECT.

'*Look*, I'm on *holiday!*' she shouted, sitting up. 'Give me a bloody break!'

'Exactly, and you don't want to sleep it all away, do you?' asked Janice brightly as she swooped up and down the room wearing Marion's sheet. 'We've only got two days left after this.'

'Give me back my covers,' said Marion petulantly.

'Come and get them,' sang Nurse Cowlishaw, and danced out of the door, à gavotte. Marion knew that wouldn't be the end of it. There was nothing for it but to get up. While doing her shopping the day before, Marion had thought to buy espresso coffee and a small stove-top macchinetta, but Janice wouldn't let her near them until she'd had a shower.

'But it'll help bring me round,' she said pathetically as she was frog-marched to the bathroom.

'No it won't, you'll take it back to bed. Shower first, and Janice'll make your nice coffee, ready for when you get out. How do you do it?' she called, returning to the kitchen and taking the percolator apart. 'Does the Nescaff go in the top?'

Marion shouted anxiously for her to leave it. She turned the shower on full blast and warm, and slumped against the wall, still sleepy, under the spray. What was she going to do with the day? She knew she couldn't face Lake Trasimeno with Janice and Tom, but could she trust herself not to drive to Orvieto if she were left to her own devices? Only two days left of the holiday after this, and then a return to Leicester for the rest of her life — it didn't bear thinking about, not even when she tried bravely to imagine the promised excitement of tidying and redecorating her house. In fact, particularly not then. She caught hold of herself before she could disappear down the hole of depression which was opening up in front of her. Think of the present, she told herself firmly — wasn't that what yesterday's Resurrection lesson had been all about? Now what would you, Marion Hardcastle, like to do today to please yourself? How about going to Perugia? A lovely town, some wonderful paintings, the beautiful fountain carved by Pisano and son — and, more importantly, in completely the opposite direction to temptation in Orvieto. She started to soap herself briskly, trying to imitate Janice's zest for life, but the warm water merely made her sleepier, and before she knew it she was lost in a daydream of magical possibilities.

She was standing, in her mind's eye, in front of the gold mosaic façade of the Orvieto Duomo, shining incandescent in the bright rays of the sun. So absorbed was she in the spectacle that she didn't notice Patrick until he was almost upon her. Their eyes locked with an intensity that melted all peripheral vision into a hazy golden blur and they kissed, their arms around one another as if they would never let go, their bodies pressed close. She could smell the sun in his hair. At last he took his lips away from her mouth and pressed them against her ear. 'Come with me,' he said simply, and she did.

They were standing on the verandah of his (modest but beautiful) Californian whitewashed clapboard cottage, perched high on top of spume-sprayed rocks at sunrise, looking out to sea. He was an artist, and so was she. Their easels stood behind them, a shared palette of oils already squeezed from coloured tubes and glistening in the early morning sun, but work could wait . . . They were walking on the beach, their fingers entwined, the white-topped curling wavelets kissing their feet. The water swirled around their bodies as they lay down on the sand, their hungry lips and hands exploring . . .

No no no, no no no *no*, Marion Hardcastle, thought Marion, brusquely turning off the shower and briskly towelling herself dry. If that's the track your mind's running on, then a lakeside picnic of sardine sandwiches with Tom and Janice Cowlishaw is more than you deserve. And really – is that the best you can do? A painter indeed! Talk about Mills and Boon wish-fulfillment fantasies! But he's studying the great Masters at a Tuscan art college, a voice which tried to sound like reason whispered in her head. Exactly, her more sensible side countered – and how do you think he could afford that if he was a working artist? He could be very rich and famous. Oh for God's sake, will you give it up! Anyway, it's more likely he's an architect if he's in the arts at all, she continued in her schoolmarm voice as she assiduously dried between her toes, building ultra-modern office blocks or suburban condominiums . . . Or should that be condominia? Condominii . . . ?

She was standing at the vast and panoramic window of the minimalist penthouse loft he'd designed himself, his arms encircling her from behind, her head leant back against his chest so she could feel the softness of his silk shirt on her cheek, gazing out onto the luscious sunset colours which bounced from building to building, and bled out into the sea . . .

'Ay Maz — hurry up, get dressed!' thundered Janice, shouldering her way into the bathroom, and stampeding, elephantine, over Marion's dreams. 'Terry's here to see you — he's been banging at your passage door!'

'You're kidding!'

'Well, he said expect the unexpected!'

As far as bringing Marion back to earth went this was as effective as slapping her around the face with a wet kipper, and about as welcome. She had escaped Terence's attentions so well the day before that she had almost forgotten about him. Now what? Was he going to propose to kidnap her today too? An image of their last meeting flashed into her mind as she pushed Janice back out of the tiny bathroom and looked in panic in the mirror to do her hair and face. Their passion, a mere thirty-six hours ago, had dislodged rocks from mountains, caused an orchestra to play. She had snogged him, knees trembling, with fireworks exploding around their ears. How the bloody hell did you backtrack from that? She dressed quickly. It would have to be faced. Thank goodness she'd brought her clothes with her into the bathroom — at least she wouldn't have to have this meeting in her nightie. She was trying to think positively.

For a moment Terence didn't recognise her when she walked into the living-room, where he was chatting happily with Janice and Tom. He stopped mid-sentence, his mouth still open, staring at her long and hard.

'Marion!' he said, after he had recovered himself. 'Heavens — what a transformation!' Where were the hippie clothes, the long unruly hair, the intimations of his youth? She had seemed so real to him in his intimate fantasies of late, that he felt almost betrayed by the change.

'Doesn't she look fabulous, Tel?' asked Janice, beaming at her, only to be rewarded by a furious, blood-freezing glare from her friend. 'Oh, right,' she said suddenly, rising. 'Better go and sort things out for the trip. Tom.'

'I've got me trunks on underneath,' her husband replied,

staying comfortably in his chair. 'I don't need anything else.'
Terence and Marion stared hard at the floor.

'Well come and help me in the bedroom then,' said Janice,
pulling him by the hand.

'What with?' he protested, as he disappeared reluctantly
through the door. 'We should be making tracks!' Surely she
wasn't going to jump on him now, with company in the living-
room?

'Terry and Maz want to be on their own to talk,' Janice
hissed to him outside, in what in her scale of volume was a
whisper, but which carried into the awkward silence of the
living-room as if it had been sung from a minaret by a muezzin.

Marion cleared her throat. 'Well,' she said, unable to look
Terence in the eyes, as the silence enshrouded them again in
unwanted intimacy.

'Well,' he agreed. 'How are you?' Something about her this
morning told him that it wasn't just her hair that had changed.
He decided very definitely against taking her in his arms.

'Fine thanks,' she said, wandering around the room adjusting
ornaments. 'And you?'

'I'm really sorry about yesterday,' he apologised. 'Things
didn't work out as planned. And by the time I could get away to
tell you, you'd already gone.'

'Oh, that's okay,' said Marion. 'Not a problem.' Of course,
she thought, he thinks I'm in a strop about being stood up.
'Really, no problem at all.'

'I'm free today though,' Terence offered quickly, acutely
aware that he had made his goodbyes to Beatrice in her bed
almost twenty minutes before. 'If it's not too late?' he persisted.
He suddenly had the nightmare vision of Bea looking out of her
bedroom window and seeing that his car still hadn't moved.
Would she charge down the stairs to find him, come crashing in
here?

'Well actually . . .' said Marion.

Terence tried to calm his rising panic. She was going to say
no, and that couldn't be. His fears the day before were obviously

not without foundation — he had been chasing her too hard and fast and put her off the whole idea. Seamlessly, he hoped, he moved on to the plan he'd devised in the early hours of the morning — seduction by stealth. 'I can't begin to tell you what an awful bloody day I had yesterday,' he said, his old Derby accent ever thickening. 'I got hauled off by your friend Pamela to ponce about round a swimming pool with a load of fat cats from England! God, talk about brain dead! I could have killed for a proper conversation!' He became uncomfortably aware that his speech had become stilted with exclamation marks in his efforts to be offhand. A change of tack was called for. He lowered his voice to lure her into a conspiratorial club of two. 'How was it for you? Did you have to spend it with the rude mechanicals?' The tension eased and Marion smiled.

'No, I shook them off,' she said, 'and went to Sansepolcro on my own.'

'And changed your image!' Terence joshed, chancing a little intimacy.

'Changed my image, had a nice lunch, looked at some paintings . . .'

'Just what I was hoping we might do together today,' said Terence, seizing the moment. 'I thought perhaps we might go to Perugia at last. Without being sidetracked by the miracle of birth this time!'

'Oh!' said Marion. Bugger, she thought. That was *her* plan out of the window then.

'Unless you've got something else on?'

Marion hesitated, not knowing what to say. Of course she wanted to go to Perugia, but not with him. And if she lied and said she was going to Lake Trasimeno with Janice and Tom then he'd only propose he came along too. There was nothing for it but the truth. 'Actually, Terence . . .' she began at last, her eyes looking everywhere but at him, 'I—'

'Listen,' he cut in quickly, aware that she was about to plunge them past the point of no return. 'Marion — the other night . . .' Now it was his turn to avoid her gaze. 'I'm sorry that things got a bit out of hand between us.' He allowed a little ruefulness to creep into his voice. 'Too much to drink, I suspect. That, and the candlelight, and being bored out of my brain until you appeared.'

'That's all right,' said Marion awkwardly. Now what was he up to? Should she take him at face value, or was this just another ploy?

'I really like you. As a person,' he continued. 'I just wouldn't want you to get the wrong idea.'

'Right. No. That's okay. But—' How to retreat now, when the enemy has thrown down his sword?

'But you don't believe a word I'm saying,' said Terence with a smile. 'I can't say I blame you. I've been coming on pretty strong.'

'Oh no,' she demurred automatically. But why did she feel like a fish on the end of a line?

'The fact of the matter is, Marion, that I've got used to living in a fast and superficial world. You've seen a little of it. It's all "Give it me now" and "I've got to have it" – very immature. We're like demanding two-year-old toddlers.' He looked her in the eyes and laughed, inviting her to share the joke against him and his peers, and Marion obliged. Now he was getting somewhere. Softly softly, Terence old son, he told himself. 'And then somebody like you comes along – well, not somebody like you – You – you're pretty original – and you remind me of who I was, where I've come from, of another world I left behind. It feels so comfortable, so familiar, I get confused. It feels as if I know you better than perhaps I do.' What was that phrase he had thought of a couple of days ago, when he'd first turned up on the bike . . . something about joining up his present with his past? Yes, that was it. It was too good to waste. It's almost as if time has fragmented me, if that doesn't sound too grand. Inside I'm still the same old Terry Armstrong from Belper, ordinary bloke, debunker of myths, but outside, I have *become* a myth – Terence Armstrong plc, capital T, capital A . . .'

Lower case plc? thought Marion mischievously, but nevertheless she was interested to know what came next. Certainly she wasn't disappointed by the string of adjectives that followed, appended to her name.

'And then you come along, Marion — intelligent, subversive, funny — I loved the way you dealt with Pamela on that first morning, bearding her in her den, not impressed by any of it, telling her where to get off! And it reminded me of who I used to be, the mates I used to hang around with, how we used to be so irreverent, cocking a snook at authority, and it just somehow makes me feel *complete* — as if you join up my present with my past.' Having delivered what was without a doubt, to his mind, one of his best lines ever, he now stopped to watch her melt. What woman could resist?

Marion, as it turned out. He knew he'd suddenly lost her by the way her smile disappeared behind a darkening of the eyes, but he was at a complete loss when she stood up and walked over to the door to hold it open for his exit. There seemed to be nothing for it but to trail haplessly in her wake.

'I——?' he faltered, confused and lost for words as he stood in the open doorway, mysteriously on his way out.

'Sorry Terence — it sounds a bit of a responsibility for an anarchist like me,' she said. Now there was a twinkle in her eye again. Was she trying to not laugh? 'And I've just come to a stage in my life where I don't want to be responsible for anybody but myself.'

'No no, of course not,' he agreed hastily, 'I'm not suggesting . . .' He wanted to kick himself. He'd gone against every acting note he'd ever given in his long and illustrious career. *Why* had he overdone it when he'd had her in the palm of his hand? And what the frig was he going to do now with the day he'd engineered so carefully to be free? Go back to Beatrice and tell her the meeting was cancelled? 'That obviously sounded much heavier than I meant it to be — I meant as a friend, nothing more,' he said, apologetically. He could almost see his words come tumbling back at him, as if he were frantically trying to run back up a hill of scree. He willed himself to relax as he strolled out through the door and sauntered down the first few steps of the stone stairway, giving her some space. 'Look, have a think about it. I just thought it would be pleasant to spend the day in Perugia, looking at the paintings, nothing more . . . I'm going down to Claudio's for some breakfast. Take your time, see how you feel, and then join me for a coffee? At least let me buy you a coffee.' He managed to laugh in what he hoped was a fairly convincing impression of light-heartedness, and skipped down the rest of the stairs without looking back.

Closing the door behind him, Marion at last allowed herself to laugh. How could she ever have been taken in by that? She realised now that Terence posed no threat to her at all – she absolutely and utterly didn't fancy him, and he'd be too desperate for her approval to try another move. But even so, she thought she would prefer to spend the day alone rather than in his company – it would be too exhausting, watching him try so hard. Coffee sounded good though, but some of her own, made in her new little espresso pot. Still smiling broadly, she made her way to the tiny kitchen, where she found that Janice had beaten her to it.

'I finally figured it out,' she said triumphantly, handing a cup to Marion. 'The coffee goes in that little funnel, doesn't it? But I can't say I know what all the fuss is about. Tastes just the same to me as when I make it in a mug.'

It tasted just the same to Marion too. 'You used Nescafé?!'

'Course I did! That's one area I *don't* stint myself on, call me extravagant if you will,' said Janice with an epicurean air, as she stuffed a can of tuna chunks into her beach bag. Suddenly Marion felt far more of a twin soul with Terence than she had thought possible a moment before. 'Anyway, what's going on – is Terry coming with us? Shall I pack another tin?'

'No, I've decided to do my own thing.' Marion put her still full cup in the sink and turned tail. 'See you later. Have a nice day.'

'Maz! Marion – don't you want your coffee?' Janice shouted, running after her with the cup, but she was already out of the front door. 'Bleddy hell, I go to all that trouble figuring out that stupid pot, and then she doesn't want it,' she complained to Tom, as he emerged out of the bathroom, looking pleased.

'More fool her,' he said, taking the cup from her and knocking it back in one. 'It worked for me. I finally got a result!'

Outside in the driveway Marion grumpily stowed her bag on the Harley and wondered where the hell to go now. She was desperate for that espresso. Maybe she should join Terence at Claudio's as he'd asked, try to put him off the idea of going to Perugia, convince him she wanted to be on her own. She felt the day slipping away from her, out of her control, the two towns she would have liked to visit now off limits because of one bloke she'd got the hots for and another who'd got the hots for her. As she mounted the bike and turned the engine over, she saw the two women she'd seen the day before in Patrick's group at San Niccolò's saunter from the college buildings to stand in the shade. They seemed cross, and were looking this way and that, consulting their watches. They must be waiting for the minibus to take them to Orvieto, Marion realised, and that meant that at any minute Patrick would appear. After her vivid fantasy-life in the shower, it didn't matter now quite so much where she went, merely that she went, and fast. She gunned the engine and roared out of the drive, spraying more gravel than she needed to, just for the pleasure of annoying Pamela.

Driving down the little lane that led from the Palazzo to Claudio's and all routes out, she found it was impossible to stay feeling tense on the back of the Harley. Apart from anything else, just sitting on it forced her, quite literally, to be laid back. She'd have that coffee with Terence, and if he couldn't be persuaded against going to Perugia and leaving it for her sole enjoyment, she'd strike off on her own to Montepulciano. Not much in the way of paintings there, but magnificent architecture and the opportunity to buy a couple of bottles of vino nobile as a peace offering to Janice later that evening. She knew she'd pissed her off by withdrawing from the womanly intimacy so generously offered, and now she had escaped it for the day she could afford to feel magnanimous. On such a day, riding through beautiful

Tuscany with the sun on her back and the scent of sage in the air, she could do without enemies.

She was aware, as she parked the huge bike in front of Claudio's little café and shop, of several pairs of eyes watching her, and she felt twin sensations of self-consciousness and pleasure. She kept forgetting that, in the normal run of things, a woman of her age with cropped white-blonde hair riding a seventies Harley was, to say the least of it, unusual. She herself could hardly credit that she had gone for so striking and eye-catching an image, having lived for so long in a chrysalis state of mousey brown hair and passion-killing cardigans, trying to eschew the attention of others. She remembered now to her surprise that it was not unpleasant to be admired, and she congratulated herself on the success of her holiday experiment so far. It seemed to be restoring some of her old self-confidence. Nevertheless, she was glad she had the refuge of her sunglasses to hide behind as she crossed the few yards to join Terence.

'Hello there!' he said, rising to kiss her on both cheeks before settling her into a chair at his side. He, too, was conscious that her arrival had stopped the rest of Claudio's customers dead in their tracks, and he was delighted to be the one who was in the enviable position of welcoming her at his table. 'I'm so glad you came. What a glorious day. Will you have breakfast, or just coffee?'

'Coffee and juice I think,' said Marion, rummaging around in her rucksack for her cigarettes.

Terence looked around in vain for service. 'It's rather busy here this morning, I'm afraid. It took ages for me to get served. It seems that there's only the one chap to run the shop inside and to serve out here as well. Every time one of the local ladies comes in for her groceries we lose him.'

'No problem. Good for Claudio if he's having a crisis of success,' said Marion, her head still buried in her bag, as much to allow the other customers to satisfy their curiosity about her and get bored before she was forced to look up again, as to find her elusive fags.

'Are you looking for a cigarette?' asked Terence, oblivious of Marion's ulterior motive. 'Here, have one of mine – untipped, though, I'm afraid.'

'It's okay – got them,' said Marion. The sensation of being scrutinised had still not fully abated, and she flipped open her packet and took a moment to select which of the identical cigarettes she would choose before having to raise her eyes and accept the light that Terence was now offering, his lighter poised. She inhaled the first breath deeply, and just as she felt brave enough to look up, lean back coolly in her seat and to nonchalantly exhale, she found to her sudden amazement that she was in astonished eye to astounded eye contact with He Who Must Be Avoided At All Costs. Patrick himself was sitting but two tables away. Naturally she choked.

'Marion?' he asked doubtfully, after a moment's hesitation.

'Patrick,' she replied, her breath fighting to escape her lungs while she strove to imitate composure. 'How are you?'

'I'm fine,' he said, and joined them, nodding politely to Terence, to stand awkwardly by their table. 'I wasn't sure if it was you – you look so different!'

'Oh, yes,' said Marion, completely off balance, her hand straying automatically to stroke her head. Thank God there were no long strands to twiddle with girlishly any more, she thought. Her mouth had gone all funny, and she couldn't be sure whether she was grinning foolishly or grimacing horribly. Making it work and trying to look natural was proving to be a struggle. 'I fancied a change,' she said lamely. Terrific. She had regressed to silly sixteen in a mere moment. She forced herself, with a great effort of will, to grow up fast and remember her manners. 'Erm, Terence Armstrong – Patrick . . .'

'Donleavy,' Patrick supplied, leaning forward to shake Terence's hand. 'How do you do.' Terence returned the greeting, sizing him up. Who was he to Marion, he wondered, and why had she suddenly gone all doolally? Was it because of this Patrick (who was not bad-looking, he noted churlishly), or because she had been spotted with Terence by somebody she knew? Certainly there was sexual tension in the air – as a long and practised observer of such things, he could almost smell it. Was it for him, or for this American idiot with the hair and the teeth? There was only one way to find out, he decided, and he gestured to a chair. 'Won't you join us?'

'No I can't,' demurred Patrick. 'But thanks. I'm off on a field trip to Orvieto, and the college minibus will be here any moment to pick me up. I usually breakfast here, so I have this arrangement with the driver for him to come get me. They're a nice bunch, but you can have too much of being part of a group when you're in their company all day.' Why am I going through this tedious explanation? he asked himself, They don't want to know all this. He was aware too that, though it was Terence who had asked the question, it was Marion to whom he was replying. No wonder the blonde woman outside the church had reminded him of her – it *was* her. And the bike was hers. Incredible. She was like no other woman he had met before – so full of surprises, and even more stunning than the first time they'd met. The memory of the occasion for that meeting returned to fill him with shame. What was he thinking of? Marion must think him a moron, chasing after Pamela in the middle of the night. He suddenly found himself dying to escape, and looked round hopefully for the minibus.

'You're studying at the College at the Palazzo?' asked Terence. So that's where she'd met him. But where? In the grounds, or had they shared a meal, spent an evening together – or the day? Where the hell had she been yesterday while he was with the Dulls? Canoodling with this Californian?

'That's right,' said Patrick, still checking the road for the means of his rescue. 'Renaissance Masters. It's a good course. In depth. I'm learning a lot.'

'Is that for business or pleasure?' asked Terence.

'Oh pleasure, pleasure,' Patrick replied. The word felt fleshy and rude in his mouth under the current circumstances, in Marion's company, and he wished he hadn't said it twice. Well, at least now he knew he was safe from making a fool of himself over her. Clearly she wasn't available. This guy was so territorial he was obviously her boyfriend.

'Here's your minibus,' announced Marion, who had also been scanning the road, as eager for him to go as he was himself. Less than an hour ago she had been beneath his naked body making love in the surf. She couldn't bear to be in his company a moment longer, not least because, in the light of day, he was even more gorgeous than in her fantasies.

'Right,' said Patrick with some relief. 'Well, goodbye. Have a nice day. Good to meet you, Terence. Marion. See you again, I hope.' Now *why* had he said that, he asked himself brutally as he walked away from them towards the bus, and, conscious that they watched him as he went, why in hell hadn't he chosen a more becoming shirt this morning, and a pair of jeans that fitted better over his butt? Thank God he was going to Orvieto, he told himself, as he climbed up into the bus, otherwise, with so little control over himself, he might find himself arm wrestling with Terence for the pleasure of Marion's company. There was that word again. Pleasure. Kathryn was right – he really must be a prick on legs. Settling into his seat he put his arm up for a perfunctory wave, but found to his disappointment that Marion was looking through her bag again and no longer watching him.

'Who was that?' asked Terence nonchalantly when the bus had rattled out of view and Marion finally lifted her head again, this time to look for Claudio.

'Patrick?' she replied, just as nonchalantly. 'I don't really know him, we hardly met. He's a friend of Pamela's, I think. Ah, Claudio!' she called, catching sight of him emerging from the shop, 'Espresso macchiato per favore! E una spremuta! Terence – do you want anything else?'

'Er – cappuccino,' said Terence, although he had drunk enough coffee while he was waiting for her to arrive to last him a week. So *that* was why she had been so jumpy when Patrick had spotted them together, he thought, she was worried it would get back to Pamela and therefore to Bea. Perhaps his chances with her were better than he'd feared. He started to wonder if there were hotels in Perugia, as there were, in his experience, in Rome, London, Paris, New York, where one could rent a room for the afternoon. He could absent himself for a moment while she was looking round a gallery and phone Fiona, who could make some enquiries and do the booking. He'd get her to arrange a nice hotel lunch where he'd make sure Marion had plenty of wine to get her in the mood, and then, bingo. If he couldn't get a woman from a hotel restaurant to a hotel bedroom, his name was not Terence Armstrong. Most of all he was looking forward to the foreplay of riding pillion on Marion's bike, his arms around her, his body pressed against hers from behind. But first, he must find a place to park his car far away from anywhere that Beatrice might see it. Given that it was supposed to be in a small airfield somewhere, awaiting his return by helicopter, it would cause unimaginable ructions if Bea were to see it here, at Claudio's. But he was getting ahead of himself.

'So tell me,' he said, giving Marion what he hoped was a winning smile, 'will you come to Perugia and show me around? As friends, for companionship,' he added mendaciously, in case she hadn't believed him the first time.

'Okay,' Marion conceded, after the briefest hesitation. For what else could she do, she asked herself? If she weren't policed all day now by an outside force, she just knew that wild horses would come and drag her to Orvieto. Better the devil she knew, by far, she thought, looking at Terence's satisfied grin, and particularly this silly devil, who could not tempt her at all.

Terence found his plans going pear-shaped almost at once. His attempts at a convoluted tale as to why he had to find a secluded spot to park his car for the day were cut short when Marion told him there was no way she would be driving him to Perugia on her bike. If he had been an experienced pillion rider, she told him, she might have taken the chance, but since she herself hadn't ridden for so many years their combined inexperience would make them certain candidates for death on the Italian roads. Nor would she consider (although he offered this reluctantly, unwilling to give up the idea of fulfilling his fantasies, at least in part) leaving her bike and driving with him in his open-topped car. He felt like a child who had been expecting a mountain bike from Santa Claus, only to find that roller skates had been left instead. There was some pleasure to be had following in Marion's wake, watching her body lean into bends in front of him on the winding roads, but still he sulked all the way on the green and pleasant route through the heartland of Italy, ignoring the blue waters of Lake Trasimeno glistening in the sun, the breathtaking views of rolling hills and hilltop towns, the churches, the towers, the panoply of history laid out before him, if only he had eyes to see, of ancient tribes, of marching Romans, of holy wars and religious martyrs.

Ahead of him, at one with her Harley, Marion saw it all and was in biker's heaven, savouring the opportunity, soon to be lost on arrival in Perugia, of sharing the sights and her insights with no one, of having to say nothing, of having to take account of nobody else's desires but her own.

Chapter Twenty-Three

Back at the Palazzo, with his bowels satisfactorily evacuated for the first time since leaving the comfort of his own bathroom in Leicester, Tom had finally persuaded Janice that she had packed enough lunch to keep them for weeks, and after a couple of false exits concerning a forgotten bikini and a certain pink Lilo (whose inclusion in their equipment list Tom vetoed to Janice's protests), they were astride the scooter and ready to set off for the shores of Lake Trasimeno. They had studied a tourist guide that they'd found in the apartment and had decided on the town of Passignano sul Trasimeno (which Janice insisted on pronouncing Passing Nayno even though Tom kept telling her it should be Pas*sig* Nayno), and after yet another quick squint at the map to check the perfectly straightforward route, Tom gingerly set a course across the Palazzo's gravel drive, gouged and sprayed into huge furrows by Marion's comings and goings on the Harley. That successfully negotiated, they were soon happily coasting down the little lane and were nearly at Claudio's when Janice started shouting and waving dangerously, and pulling at Tom's shirt to stop. So great was Tom's concentration on the road apparently, he hadn't noticed that they'd just passed Christopher. After a wobbly stop procedure and a few harsh words, they waited on the bike until he'd caught them up again.

'Hiya Chris! Going down to Franco's for your scooter?' asked Janice cheerily, and Christopher agreed that he was.

'You going off on a trip somewhere for the day then?'

'Yes, maybe,' he replied vaguely. Being almost a household name, Christopher was not about to tell every Tom and Janice Cowlishaw about his appointment with Evadne, and he himself wasn't at all sure what to do with the rest of the day after (with luck) she had told Beatrice that her destiny lay with him. It was important to find somewhere quiet and romantic, away from Pamela and the Palazzo, where he could continue to press his case before Terence came back from his meeting. 'Where are *you* off to?' he asked, chiefly so he'd know where to avoid.

'Passing Nayno,' said Janice cheerily, while Tom raised his eyebrows and bit his lip. 'It's a place on a big lake called Trasimeno – it's only about ten mile, isn't it Tom?' Tom nodded. 'We found it in the guidebook,' she continued. 'It's too hot not to be near water, isn't it? And we've done Viareggio already. Bit too far on a scooter anyway, isn't it my dove?' Tom nodded again. 'And I've never swum in a lake. We were going to, in the Lake District when we went there, weren't we Tommo, but it rained the whole fortnight. We got just as wet without going in!'

'A lake?' mused Christopher. That sounded promising, as long as it was big enough to find a spot far from these people. 'In which direction?'

Now it was Tom's turn to speak, which he did so clearly, slowly and precisely in describing the exact route, with all the road numbers and towns passed through on the way, that by the time he had finished Christopher had absorbed not a word. Janice, not a big orienteer herself, recognised his blank look when Tom had finished, and dug about in her beach bag for the guide. 'Here, have this, Chris – it tells you all about it. We don't need this any more, Tommy's memorised the route a thousand times this morning – haven't you Marco Polo?' Tom watched in agony as the book changed hands. It was true he'd worked hard on memorising the route, but there were all those similar-looking foreign names that might trip him up, and what if there was a road diversion for whatever reason, and they got knocked off course? But his ever-generous wife was still rabbiting on to this silly spoilt actor, pressing the book on him despite his polite refusals. 'If you're up for a big drive, you can go all the way round the lake, see — it's about forty miles though, round trip.'

'That's really sweet of you — Janice?' said Christopher, riffling through the pages of colour plates. 'I'll return it this evening if that's okay?'

'Yeah, great,' Janice responded. 'Might bump into you at the lake later anyway.' Chris nodded and smiled, certain that she wouldn't. Forty miles of shoreline was surely enough to avoid them, he thought comfortably, and there was bound to be a little bay away from the crowds somewhere where he and Beatrice could be alone.

'Well, best get on,' he announced. He'd zipped into Beatrice's bedroom half an hour ago with the idea of asking her to come with him to Franco's, but she was still snoozing and reluctant to get up. She'd sounded depressed — he supposed about Terence being away for the day — so he'd told her to wait for him, that he was coming back with a surprise. At this rate the surprise would be that there were no scooters left.

'Yes, us too,' said Janice, grabbing hold of a couple of handfuls of Tom's spare tyre. 'Come on James — to Passing Nayno, and don't spare the horses!'

Tom started up the little engine again, and with a flurry of waves from his back-seat cargo, they continued to weave their way down the small lane in a cloud of dust, most of which made a home, almost immediately, in Christopher's eyes. At Claudio's junction Tom paused for a moment before turning on to the Big Road, to remind his pillion passenger of the drill.

'No clinging on too tight, right?'

'Is this too tight?' asked Janice, her arms around him from behind.

'No, that's okay.'

'Okay then.'

'And sway when I sway, in the same direction – none of this leaning away from bends.'

'I got better at that yesterday,' said Janice indignantly. Honestly, if he was going to be this bossy, where was the pleasure to be found?

'I know you did, I'm only saying. And if you want to tell me something or point something out, *don't* pull me, just shout. Okay?'

'Okay, okay,' said Janice, her holiday spirit fast disappearing. 'We didn't have to go through all these rules and regs every time when we were courting.'

'Yes, but we weren't Abroad then,' said Tom, 'driving on the wrong side of the road.'

Janice relented. She could see how confusing that might be. 'Roger wilco,' she said gaily, and Tom, with a perfectly executed hand signal, pulled out on to the Big Road along the same route that Marion and Terence had carved out only twenty minutes before.

As Big Roads went this one was pretty small, and Tom was soon feeling more confident, counting off the memorised place names as they passed through them, and even finding time to enjoy the sights that Janice drew to his attention, by voice only, as they'd agreed.

'Look at that tower, that house, that church!' she'd scream.

'Yes,' he'd bellow.

'In't it beautiful?!'

'Lovely!' And it *was* lovely, the sun on their faces, the beautiful countryside, welded together on the back of a machine – it reminded them both of their youth, of the rides to country pubs and fumbles in fields, of how much they'd been in love, how happy they'd been to find each other at last, at the ripe old age of seventeen and a half. They could see the Lake before they arrived, winking its blueness cheerfully through the green of the hills and fields, which excited them no end.

'It's like that time we went to Rutland Water!' Janice shouted, almost forgetting her promise about pulling and shaking the driver.

'Yes!' Tom screamed back, smiling at the memory. And in this happy and companionable way the ten miles to Passignano were covered, as he noted with pride when they stopped in the town, in less than an hour.

The same amount of time, as it happened, that it took Marion and Terence with their separate modes of conveyance to cover three times the distance to Perugia. Just as Janice and Tom were starting to get nervous and tetchy with each other about where to 'park their bums' (Janice's phrase, naturally) on the lake shores, Marion and Terence were parking their vehicles at the foot of the hill that led, via steep steps and winding, cobbled alleys, up to the ancient and quarrelsome city which had been fought over by the Etruscans, the Romans, the Goths, the Guelphs, several Popes and the Swiss Guard – not to mention the internecine battles between opposing noblemen and the citizens themselves; or the medieval citizens' favourite game of pelting each other with rocks to see who died first; or indeed the thirteenth-century monk who popularised it as a European centre of excellence for flagellation. In short it was not the most auspicious place, if Terence had but known it, to begin a conquest of any kind, least of all of a romantic nature, and especially not of a woman who had just spent the last thrilling hour flying through the wind on a machine made in heaven, thinking about a certain blond Californian and wondering if she really *did* need to hold herself back against her own burgeoning desires, when he was just so gorgeous, studied art for pleasure, and had possibly even been placed exactly where she would find him by the hand of Fate.

During the hair-raising drive where Marion had set such a spanking pace fuelled by her feelings for Patrick, Terence had managed to juggle gearstick and steering wheel for long enough to phone Fiona in London with his request – find the hotel with the best restaurant in Perugia and book a table for two for lunch, a room for the afternoon, and ring him back pronto. He could almost hear her eyebrow rise in the Convent Garden office, but she'd said nothing – just sounded rather starchy for a while. He must take her back some perfume, or he'd get that lecture again about her being a Personal Assistant, not a pimp.

There was silence between them as they made their way up the steps to the town, Marion's expression hard and grim to protect the softness of her feelings inside, and Terence waiting patiently for Fiona to call him back on the mobile, the sooner to start his seduction. Before either of them were ready to leave the cool dark interior of the winding alleys, they found themselves blinking against the bright hot sunlight of the wide, bustling promenade of the Corso Vannucci, surrounded by tavernas with tourists by the tableful, shoppers, strollers, groups of every nationality being instructed by their guides, gypsies, New Age travellers and their dog, Spot, and even a few Perugians. Already it wasn't altogether what Terence had had in mind.

'Well, where would you like to start?' asked Marion, remembering that she was supposed to be giving him a guided tour. 'The Pisano fountain and the Duomo, or the National Gallery and the Palazzo dei Priori?'

'You've been here before then?' asked Terence, glad at last to start a conversation of any kind. He sensed that Marion was full of an agenda so hidden this morning that he couldn't even begin to guess at the depth of its mystery. Nor was he about to find elucidation, for 'Mm,' was her noncommittal reply. He decided they both needed a little relaxation. 'How about a Campari somewhere before we make a start?' he ventured, and to his relief, Marion thought that was a great idea.

Shade was what they needed too, for already it was ridiculously hot, and after a brief saunter up the Corso and finding no room at any of the inns, the two cool-blooded Anglo-Saxons were ready to drop. Terence felt doom surround him, but mercifully after a couple of hundred yards they arrived at a clutch of umbrella-shaded tables where some people were making to leave, and gratefully he pounced upon their empty chairs. He was rewarded by the ghost of a smile from Marion as she settled herself at the table, almost as if she wasn't really here with him at all, but was somewhere far away. Booze was needed, and fast, he told himself, as his eyes darted about for someone to take his order, but to his surprise Marion beat him to it, waving to an unseen waiter and calling for 'due Camparisoda, per favore' in her sexy Italian, while at the same time managing, successfully this time, to locate her cigarettes in the depths of her bag and light one. Now that was better. This was the Marion he was after.

'So where do you recommend we start?' he asked, while he watched her, enthralled, mop her moist neck and throat with a napkin. 'What's in the National Gallery?'

'Well, a lot of Perugino, not surprisingly,' she replied, almost visibly shaking herself into the present. 'The most wonderful della Francesca — the Polyptych of Sant'Antonio?' Terence nodded wisely as if he knew what the hell she was talking about — 'And of course several fifteenth-century panels of 'The Miracles of Saint Bernardino of Siena' which are fun — almost like an early Superman comic strip — the jury is still out as to who painted those — Fiorenzo used to be credited, but some say it was Perugino and Martini. Saint Bernardino used to preach here to blood crazy penitents — ironically teaching love and peace. His pulpit is on the outer wall of the Duomo over by the Fontana Maggiore . . .' It didn't matter to Terence what she was saying, it was the way she said it: the lovely roll she gave to the Italian 'r', the way her hands couldn't help but join in the conversation, her enthusiasm for her subject which lit her eyes with a sparkling intelligence. He fingered the mobile phone in his jacket pocket, and willed Fiona to ring *now*. He couldn't wait to take Marion in his arms.

With the arrival of the Camparis came a wonderful burst of Italian conversation between Marion and the waiter, where Terence could watch her with undisguised admiration as she rattled off a torrent of tantalising words. 'What was that about?' he asked her, smiling, as the waiter took his leave. 'We were talking about the weather,' she said, returning his smile. 'He thinks we might be in for a storm. Cheers.' She lifted her glass to salute him, and it was as much as he could do to stay in his seat and not take her on the table there and then.

'So tell me about when you were last here,' he said conversationally, to calm himself as they sipped their drinks. He saw Marion's eyes darken before she lowered them, out of his gaze.

'It was when I was a kid,' she answered after a moment's pause. Should she tell this story, this most private piece of her history? Why not? Perhaps if she did, she might finally bury Frank here. 'In another life. I was in love with a guy and we travelled around, then he died.'

'I'm so sorry,' said Terence, and he meant it. The last thing he wanted was to plunge her thoughts into an unhappy past. 'How awful for you.'

'It was a long time ago,' Marion shrugged. 'And besides, the wench is dead.'

'And you've not been back here since?' he asked.

'That's right.'

'Then we must make sure not to leave here without new, good memories to take away with you,' said Terence, ever alert to an opening. If he could persuade her to that way of thinking then everything they did could be blessed with the giddy spirit of shedding the past and starting life anew – a certain recipe, in his past experience, of getting a woman to connect with the present pleasures of her loins to distract herself. 'Let's drink to that!'

'Sure,' said Marion, and glugged down her Campari. But she was aware, by the surprising lack of the old pain in her chest when she had spoken of Frank, that she was already on the mend. The new, good memories she really wanted to make were over in Orvieto at this moment, and out of her reach. *Should* she deny herself that pleasure? Couldn't she give herself the gift of seeking out Patrick that night, of seeing where it might lead? She wriggled in her seat at the thought of it, the images of her fantasies returning. This wouldn't do, she told herself, getting hot under a place so much further down than her collar while she was sitting here with Terence the Obsessed. 'Well,' she said briskly, calling for the bill, 'shall we make a start? I fancy the Gallery first — okay with you?'

Terence agreed that it was, but he would have been happier if she'd fancied *him* first. And where the frig was Fi? But he chucked a handful of money on the table and followed Marion along the Corso to the Galleria Nazionale, where he paused a moment to switch his phone from the Ringing signal, to Vibrate. It was a feature he used often when directing films or watching plays, so that it rang silently and he never had to switch it off. He only hoped that this time when it finally throbbed its announcement against his thigh it would not be the only good vibration of the day.

So far were his thoughts from Beatrice that perhaps he wouldn't even have minded if he could have seen her at that moment, her lovely bare arms around Christopher, her breasts pressing through their thin shirts against his back, riding together on the rented scooter towards the High Priestess and her prophecies. And indeed, he had no need to worry just then, for despite her close physical proximity to Chris, Beatrice's thoughts were only of Terence.

Her depression had lifted immediately when Chris had returned with the scooter and announced that he was taking her to a lake for a swim, after . . . (a dramatic pause) . . . a session with Evadne, and she had bounced out of bed in a trice. She had been shaken at the al fresco dinner the night before last when Evadne had not seen a baby and marriage in her near future, when she'd seemed to be so accurate about the other couple, whatever their names were — Janet and Tim? And there hadn't been time to get her to reconsider her psychic impressions, for almost immediately afterwards the accursed Marion had appeared from out of nowhere on her flashy motorbike, just like the deus ex machina that Evadne had foreseen for Terence. The coincidence had been nagging away at her ever since, filling her with doom, so Christopher's surprise present of a private session was simply perfect — a whole hour to find out exactly what she had to do to get the future she wanted so passionately, and moreover, that she richly deserved. For hadn't she always been a good girl, putting up with Terence's mood swings and infatuations, and was not goodness rewarded? And besides, she thought, suddenly cheering, maybe she hadn't been pregnant then, but maybe she was now — she'd certainly been working hard enough for it over the last couple of days.

For the first time in ages she felt hopeful and happy. Trust Chris to find this lovely little scooter — so much more fun than Terence's Merc. And how clever he was to find out about the lake — it was so hot today, swimming in a cool lake would be simply delicious. Chris was so sweet. If she hadn't been crazy for Terence she might seriously consider him as husband and father material, despite him being an actor — her mother had always made her promise not to repeat her own mistakes. He was certainly better-looking than Terence. And kinder. And much more adventurous and generous in bed. So why did she always end up fancying the bastards instead of the nice guys? Perhaps Evadne might tell her. Her feelings were so strong for Terence, it *felt* predestined. Maybe when the psychic had more time to concentrate exclusively on her, she would reveal their past history over several lifetimes, some unfinished business like Janet and Tim. So excited was she at the thought of this, that her arms tightened affectionately around Christopher, and he too, unaware of the cause, dared to feel hopeful and happy as he steered the little Vespa towards Evadne and the future. Or so they thought.

Pamela was still sleeping when the telephone rang, having woken several times in the night filled with the fear of impending poverty — it has to be said that she felt this every time she was down to her last fifty thousand pounds. At six o'clock she had taken a sleeper in despair, and now at eleven her head was filled with cotton wool, as was her mouth. She blinked against the harsh sunlight that fell across her face, and after a moment of confusion traced the horrible noise to the instrument on the bedside table. Why the *hell* couldn't someone else answer the damned thing, she thought viciously, did she have to take care of *everything* herself? She growled 'Pronto' into the phone as if it were an insult, and heard the anxiety in Evadne's voice.

'Pamela?'

'Yes?'

'Sorry to disturb you. It's Evadne. Is Christopher there?'

'Christopher? I've no idea. Why?'

'It's just that we arranged for him to come for an appointment this morning, and I suddenly find I can't make it. I wonder – would you mind awfully . . .'

Yes, Pamela minded awfully, but she pushed back the covers and stalked out of the room. He wasn't in his bedroom, and neither was Freddie, who might have known his whereabouts, in his. There were signs of coffee having been made in the kitchen, but some time ago – it was cold. Now she was curious, and called out their names as she hurried from room to room. No Christopher, no Frederick, no Terence and no Beatrice, and no note to tell her where the hell they were. Well fuck them! How dare they all disappear and leave her alone. Weren't they guests in her house? Hadn't she generously invited them into her home? Right then. If they were going to treat her like a landlady, she'd behave like one. They would all be presented with bills when they left with everything itemised down to the sugar and milk. Returning to her bedroom to get dressed, she had almost forgotten Evadne until she thought she heard a tiny buzzing noise, rather like an angry wasp. Looking around her for the source she saw the telephone receiver half covered by the bed sheets, and lifted it to her ear.

'Evadne? He's gone. He must have already left.'

'Oh no! Well, will you tell him when you see him that I send my apologies, that I had to go out?'

'I am not a message service,' said Pamela tartly, and put down the phone. Alone, alone – what was the point of having house guests if they left you alone? Her anger hardened into nastiness, her eyes narrowing. Hadn't it always been the way, ever since she could remember, always having to be completely self-reliant? Her back straightened, she held her head higher. Fine. She had only herself to please, so what would be her pleasure? Her mind roved over the possibilities. Ha! She would reclaim her office for the day – she assumed that the dreadful tourists would be out too, and even if they weren't, she was ready for a fight – and she would work on her father's biography. She had to do something constructive about her financial fears, and if she could send Frederick back with some of the manuscript in his hands, perhaps he would be able to get her an advance. And when she had tired of that, she would have some fun writing out individual accounts for her erstwhile friends. There was coffee, bread, toilet tissue, soap . . . use of electricity . . . Already she was feeling better.

Evadne, on the other hand, standing in her living-room and returning the now dead telephone receiver back into its cradle, had taken a decided turn for the worse. The revelation she had received on waking was so extraordinary, so out of left field as dear Joe might say – *would* say, inevitably, later that night when she told him, as she must – that she had forgotten completely about Christopher's appointment until this moment. She could no sooner concentrate on anybody else's future now than she could fly to the moon. In fact, since she had been practising psychic flying, that would be easier to do by far.

If only she hadn't rushed to fulfill her own prophecy for herself as soon as it had been revealed – but there had been no gainsaying the urgency of the voices in her head, she had had to act immediately or be consumed by the heat of her sudden and overwhelming desire, the object of which was even now lying naked in her bed. The unforeseen, unexpected thrill of that image made her weak at the knees and she steadied herself against the table for a moment, before drawing her silk robe around her and returning upstairs, her body atremble, to her new lover, her new future, and this wonderful, wonderful state of revelatory bliss. She smiled to herself. Who would ever have thought . . . ? But that was the way of her psychic revelations. One minute a thought couldn't be further from her head, and the next she was left wondering how she could have been so blind.

The dark chocolate huskiness of her lover's voice reached her as she entered the room – the only sound she ever wanted to hear again.

'Va bene?'

'No,' said Evadne, slipping off her robe and sliding back into the warm embrace she had left so urgently a few minutes before. 'He's already left.'

'No problems,' came the whispered reply, erotically close to her ear. 'We just pretend we're not here when he rings on the bell. But then again, I don't know – *can* you keep quiet while I do this? . . . And this? . . . And – this?'

As strong hands and soft lips explored her body inch by inch Evadne sincerely doubted it, but boy – it sure was fun to try!

Minutes later when Christopher rang the front doorbell for the first time, she found that chewing the sheets had become an urgent necessity, but by the time that he and Beatrice had made a circuit of the house, banging on every ground floor window, rattling the back door and shouting her name, even a substantial corner of the pillow was barely sufficient to muffle her ecstactic cries. How could it be that she had deprived herself of this for so long?

Outside the back door, which Christopher's fists were now assailing with frenzy, Beatrice told him to stop. 'Listen!' she said, her head on one side. 'Did you hear something?'

Chris listened too, but heard nothing. 'What?'

'It's stopped now,' she said, 'but it sounded like an animal in pain.'

Chris shrugged, and as they gave up and walked back to the

Vespa, he felt that the egg on his face was dripping almost visibly from his chin. He just hoped that this wouldn't spoil everything. 'I'm so sorry,' he told Bea, utterly embarrassed, 'I just can't understand it. It was all arranged.'

'Are you sure she said this morning?'

Christopher felt a rush of anger. What was he – a moron? He never cocked up on appointments. 'Yes, *this* morning at *this* time and at *this* place,' he asserted tetchily. 'She must have forgotten, that's all.' Almost instantly he regretted getting cross. Seducing Beatrice now without the psychic bribe was going to be difficult enough, without making her feel guilty and losing his temper. But Bea had been trained from birth to respond well to anger. Hadn't she been put upon God's earth to mollify malevolent male moods? She put her hand lightly on his arm, and with the other ran her fingers through her hair, tossing it back from her face.

'I'm sorry,' she said. 'I'm just being silly.'

Chris relaxed and smiled, and turned to put his hands on her waist, planting a small kiss on her forehead. 'No *I'm* sorry,' he said, 'I so wanted to give you a lovely surprise.'

'Oh darling, you are sweet,' Bea smiled, and gave him a hug. 'And you have. You've got this lovely little scootery thing, and we've been having a super time so far.'

'Well *I* predict,' offered Christopher gamely, 'that this will continue. I see a wonderful journey, a fabulous lunch, and a deserted bay made for two by the sparkling blue waters of Lake Trasimeno. I see swimming and sunbathing and you being massaged with sweet-smelling oil.' 'Perfect!' said Bea happily, hugging him again. 'Just bliss. Oh Chris, I'm so glad you're here too. This holiday would have been murder without you.'

'Hold that thought!' cried Christopher, springing back on to the Vespa and starting it up. Bea slid on behind him and he could feel the warmth of her thighs around him, the smooth softness of her encircling arms, her sweet breath on the back of his neck. 'All aboard for Paradise,' he said, 'and hold on tight!' She giggled and squeezed him and kissed the tip of his ear as he eased the bike gently back on the road. God, she was lovely. He was almost grateful to Evadne for standing him up. What if her psychic vision hadn't coincided with his? Now he was free to make his own future, for better or worse. And now he was getting over his initial shock at the idea, he knew exactly what that was. He wanted to marry this beautiful young woman. He wanted her to have his baby. He wanted to hold his grandchildren on his knee and tell them the story of what he hoped and prayed would be this auspicious and wonderful day.

Chapter Twenty-Four

In the National Gallery of Perugia, Terence had all but given up on the auspiciousness of his day by the time his thigh finally started tingling with news via satellite from Fi. He had been trailing around after Marion for hours, learning more about the evolution of Italian painting techniques than he would ever need to know, even were he to compete for Brain of Britain. He grabbed the vibrating phone from his pocket and held it up for her to see.

'Phone call, sorry, I'll take it outside. Do you want to join me in a moment, or shall I come back and find you in here?'

Marion was glad to have a few moments alone with Saint Anthony, or rather, the angel that Piero had painted over his head. 'No, I'll come out in a while,' she said, her eyes barely moving from the picture, greedily drinking it in.

'Take your time,' said Terence generously, but hoping she wouldn't, and practically skipped out of the room to hear news of his lunch. His ardour for Marion was in no way diminished, so naturally he was also keen to reassure himself that Fiona had booked the hotel room, but first things first – he was starving.

This painting had been a favourite of Frank's, combining his great love of both art and architecture, for Piero had grappled not only with light and colour, but also with the mysteries of perspective and geometry. In the centre was the Madonna and child, enthroned and surrounded by saints, and beneath that were three representations of miracles, Marion's favourite being Saint Elizabeth of Hungary whose bread had turned to roses in her lap to avert her husband's wrath. But it took a great effort of will to gaze on this part of the polyptych, for the eye was drawn inescapably to the scene of Annunciation at its pinnacle. At the very top, in a flash of gold from the blue skies of heaven, flew the Holy Spirit in the form of a dove, bringing God the Father-to-be's potency on the wing to a tunnel of arched columns that receded in perfect perspective (which had so excited Frank), and which spoke to the viewer of the pink depths and mysteries of the womb. But it was the figures either side of this pictorial metaphor that held Marion's rapt attention now. Or rather, the figure on bended knees to the left. For here knelt the Archangel Gabriel, arms folded across his breast, gently come to bring the news to the virgin bride of her impending immaculate conception, and the way his dark blond hair curled on to his neck made him a dead ringer for Patrick Donleavy. But then again, perhaps she was just seeing him everywhere she looked. *God*, how her tunnel of arches ached to receive his dove! She trembled at the thought.

A discreet cough at her elbow made her aware that she had hogged the picture long enough, and smiling an apology to the couple waiting behind her, she braced her shoulders to return outside, to reality and to tedious Terence.

In the piazza it was hotter than ever and there was a heaviness in the air. Perhaps the waiter had been right, she thought — maybe they were going to be in for a storm. She only hoped it didn't happen until after she had ridden back to the shelter of the Palazzo. She found Terence at last lurking rather appositely, she now realised, under the Loggias of Fortebraccio, winding up his call on the phone and lying through his teeth.

'Thank *so* much, Fi — and by the way, I'm glad you called now . . . I'm just in a shop trying to choose you a present — Shall I get you the Chanel again, or shall I dare to try you on an Italian this time since I'm here?' He saw Marion and winked, drawing her in to his conspiracy. 'I was thinking Moschino. Yes? . . . All right, darling, my pleasure – Ciao.'

'Sorry about that,' he said, switching off his phone for the first time that day. 'My PA in London – have to keep her sweet.' Marion shrugged. What did she care who he lied to? 'She's been researching locations for me, for a movie I'll be making next year. She says there's a place here which might be perfect which she's arranged for me to see, so I'm afraid I really do need to go and recce it. Would that be all right? It shouldn't take long.'

'Okay,' said Marion without enthusiasm. If he expected her to be impressed by reminding her she was with a film director he had another think coming. 'By the way, do you know where you're standing?' she asked, returning to her role as guide.

'Er – just by the famous fountain?' suggested Terence, eyeing the work of Pisano and Son a few yards away and hoping to God they didn't have to give *that* a minute inspection before having lunch.

'Yes, but here, in this precise spot?' asked Marion in her Miss Hardcastle voice, and then continued, knowing he hadn't a clue, 'You're standing under the porch which your fifteenth-century namesake commissioned for the people of Perugia. Fortebraccio – translated it means Strongarm – or Armstrong, if you will.'

Terence rewarded her for her lesson with a smile. 'Forteb-raccio, eh? Yes, I like it. Terence Fortebraccio. Was he a good guy?'

'Depends if you were for him or against,' said Marion, 'but most of the Perugians thought so. All except the one who murdered him, of course, who didn't go a bundle on noblemen.'

'Heavens,' said Terence, who got the sense, correctly, that she was speaking for the murderer and herself. 'Anyway,' he continued, desperate to get going with his plan while trying to sound offhand, 'the good news, apparently, is that by coincidence it also happens to be a wonderful place for lunch, so she made a reservation. Shall we?' He offered her his arm and steered her firmly away from the Duomo and the fountain lest she should feel the need for any more lessons, and following Fi's instructions, guided her down the length of the Corso Vannucci towards the Piazza Italia and Perugia's top hotel, where to his horror, Marion ground to a halt.

'What is it?' he asked in alarm. 'Not a site of bad memories, I hope?'

'Not at all,' Marion replied. 'But it's a hotel.'

'Is it?' asked Terence disingenuously, taking her arm again and striving to move her steps forward. So near, and yet so far! 'Well yes, it would be I suppose, that's what I need for the movie. And Fi said the lunch is superb.'

'One rarely finds the best cooking in hotel restaurants,' said Marion doggedly. 'And I do remember the most fantastic trattoria I have ever been to, back there by the Duomo.'

'But you haven't been here for years,' protested Terence desperately, almost tugging her along. 'It's unlikely it's still going.' If he couldn't persuade her to lunch in the hotel, how the hell would he get her to the room Fi had booked on his behalf?

'Well let's go and see,' Marion insisted. 'If it's still there we'll eat at my place first, and then we'll go and see your hotel. There's plenty of time after all — the day is ours to do as we please.'

What was it about this woman, thought Terence impotently, as he found himself being turned around and guided back towards the piazza they had just left, that made her constantly subvert his best laid plans? He was used to being in charge, to his word being law. He had forgotten at this moment that it was this spirit of independence that had first drawn him to her, and he almost found himself missing the nice acquiescent Bea. His last hope, that the trattoria would have disappeared through the mists of time, were dashed at the second assay down a little street behind the Duomo, and petulantly he followed an ecstatic Marion inside.

'Are you sure this won't reopen old wounds?' he asked her as they settled themselves at a table in the family run restaurant. 'Bring back memories that were best laid to rest?' The last thing he wanted was for her to get all sentimental and depressed.

'No, all that's over,' said Marion confidently. 'The only memories here are happy. And I know exactly what I'm having if they still do it . . . falchetti verdi – it's a kind of casserole of ricotta gnocchi with spinach and tomato sauce and cheese – delicious!' She peered at the blackboard across the room. 'Ah – they do! Followed by . . . hmm – tough choice . . . The lamb or the veal? What about you – do you want me to translate?'

'No,' said Terence weakly, his spirits having sunk to somewhere around his knees. 'You order for both of us, whatever will be fine.'

In the event, when the food was delivered, even he had to admit that this had been the understatement of the century. 'Fine' didn't come near to it – it was simply superb. They ate happily in near silence, giving their full attention to the home-cooking as it deserved, only pausing to speak to draw the other's attention to the flavours and textures, and proffering guesses about mystery ingredients. With his stomach filled so pleasantly (and having made sure they both quaffed their fair share of wine) he felt a return of his old optimism by the time they paused to consider dessert, and he was about to reopen negotiations by flirting, when she floored him again.

'So what are you doing with Bea if you don't like her?' asked Marion, recklessly bold, and waited, pinning him with her gaze.

'I . . .' blustered Terence, completely knocked off his stride, 'I'm not sure what you mean.'

'She's obviously crazy about you,' pursued Marion, happy to see his discomfort. She knew very well that, in his mind at least, they were not sitting here just as friends. 'You can tell at a glance. She wants babies and marriage, and both of them with you.' Let him get out of that and then still try to flirt.

'Does she?' he parried. 'She's never mentioned it to me.'

'So how do you see your relationship?'

'Much more light-hearted than *that*,' he replied, laughing in what he hoped was a light-hearted way, and waving over at a waitress. 'And besides, I'm not the marrying kind. Do you want pudding, or shall we just have coffee and liqueurs?'

'Due espresso, due Sambuca,' said Marion to the girl who had arrived at their side. 'But Janice tells me you were married once – to Angela Thing?'

'Still am,' replied Terence, happy to be reminded of this protection of his bachelorhood. 'She won't think of divorce, even though we've been separated for years.'

'Surely you could override her if you wanted to after all this time?' Marion insisted. 'Are you still in love with her then?'

'With Angela?! Good Heavens, no!' he laughed. Where the hell was this supposed to be leading? Wherever it was, he feared it was far, far away from the room at the hotel.

'Perhaps it suits you to stay conveniently unavailable by being wedded to the past,' said Marion perspicaciously.

'Perhaps it does,' he agreed, fixing her with a meaningful look. 'And what about you – have you never remarried since the tragedy of your first love?'

'Touché,' said Marion, glancing down at the table as the coffee and liqueurs arrived. 'No I haven't. Like you, I've been wasting my life.'

'I wouldn't say that!' Terence protested, rather crossly. Who the hell did she think she was? 'At least, not as far as I'm concerned. I have a rich and fulfilling life as it happens, thank you so much.'

'But without love,' said Marion thoughtfully, 'and someone to share it.'

Terence knocked back his Sambuca in one and tried to divine what on earth she was really trying to say. Was this a put off, or a come on? Was she trying to kill any hopes of a conquest by reminding him of his other affairs, or was she saying, heaven forfend, that she wanted a serious relationship and commitment before she would give up the goods? 'And that's what you want is it?' he asked, testing the water. He watched her shrewdly as she tussled with something inside.

'I'm not sure,' she said finally, coming out of her dream. 'I thought not, but now I don't know.'

'Have you — anyone in mind?' he asked, trying to sound casual.

'Sort of,' she smiled, 'but I've been trying to resist.'

Terence felt his pulse quicken and a stirring in his loins. Good God, he thought, I can always *pretend* a commitment if that's all that stands in my way — heaven knows, it's worked countless times in the past. 'Well,' he said softly, his voice sounding thick in his throat. 'Thank you for overcoming my objections and bringing me here for this truly memorable meal. And now, if you're ready, shall we go and look over the hotel?'

Marion, in a world of her own, rose obediently and followed him out, her head still ringing with the unexpected thoughts she had just found herself expressing. What had started as a ruse to get Terence's mind on to another tack, had now backfired. Maybe she was at last ready to share her life with another, maybe she did long for love? And if so, then why was she still laying obstacles in her own path? Why was she here with Terence instead of in Orvieto pursuing Patrick? And why did that thought fill her with overwhelming, irrational fear? Was it simply a fear of rejection? No, that didn't seem to ring any bells. Then what the hell was wrong with her? It wasn't as if she had forever to make her mind up, for God's sake — in less than forty-eight hours, the chance would be gone.

Time, or the lack of it, was in Terence's thoughts too as they finally entered the hotel foyer at a quarter to three. He was all too aware that he had to succeed *now* in his seduction. He'd never be able to blag more time away from Bea tomorrow, and the next day he'd be returning to London.

On the sunny shores of Lake Trasimeno, albeit for different reasons, the imminent end of their holiday was what was occupying the thoughts of Janice and Tom too. They had gorged themselves on tuna chunks and fresh baked bread, and were now lying replete, bellies up.

'Shame it's nearly over,' offered Tom, his hands clasped under his head.

'Yeah,' Janice agreed, smiling. What had she said to herself only days before? Didn't he always come round to a place by the time they had to leave? 'Would you come here again?'

'Maybe,' he said. 'Expensive though.'

'We're not doing bad for cash though, are we?' said Janice 'What with economising on food, and you being clever and getting a good deal on the scooter.'

'Not bad, but we've still got to be careful,' Tom replied cautiously. He knew very well what she had in her mind, and he thought he had already made his feelings clear – water plus speed equals danger plus danger. He turned over to warm his back and to close the subject. 'Think I'll just have a snooze, then d'you fancy a swim?'

'Mm,' said Janice, looking around her at all the opportunities for much more fun in the water than that. The holiday was nearly over and here she was, just lying still. There were pedalos, water skis, boat trips, wind-surfing, and best of all, those fast water scooter things that looked absolutely bazzing. She was dying to have a go. She'd never seen one before she saw Tom being rescued at Viareggio by that hunky guy, but had she been able to interest him in it today? Had she chuff. Still, it wouldn't hurt to try again. 'I say though,' she said now, 'you know what I'd fancy more, Tom? Tommo? Tomboy?' She poked him with her toe, but elicited barely a grunt. Either he was already flat out or feigning it well. Bloody Nora! She sat for a moment watching others play and envying them their sports, and considered trying a sulk like Tom did when his wishes were thwarted, but it felt far too inactive and just didn't suit. Well, she thought, rallying herself, what his mind didn't know his heart wouldn't grieve over, and if she was quick, by the time he did know it'd be too late – she'd have a go on her own. After a while, when she was fairly sure he really was nodding off, she reassured herself of the contents of her purse and satisfied, bent to tousle his hair.

'I'm just going for a little walk,' she announced loudly. 'I'll bring us some ices back, shall I?' Tom grunted faintly again – he really was out for the count. 'You just lie there and have a little nap, my dove, and Janice'll be back in a sec,' she continued unnecessarily, and slipping on her sandals she flip-flopped softly away towards Life and Excitement.

For half an hour Tom was dead to the world, and when he did start to come round it was to find himself having dribbled, slack-jawed, on to his towel, and that he was now consumed by a terrible thirst. The tuna had been too salty, he'd said so at the time. 'We got any pop left?' he croaked, licking his parched lips. 'Jan?' Getting no answer he opened his eyes, squinting against the glare of the sun, and saw that he was alone. Now where had she gone? He sat up and searched through the beach bag and found the lemonade, and, after slaking his thirst, started to have a vague recollection of hearing her say she was going for ice cream. How long ago was that? He looked up and down the shoreline but didn't spot her, and hoped that even now she was hurrying back. He could murder a cornetto.

The sparkling waters of the lake looked temptingly cool, and if he could avoid the berks on the water bikes this time, who were even now carving up the water in a wantonly dangerous way spoiling everybody's innocent family fun, a paddle would be just the thing. He struggled to his feet, slipping his shirt on self-consciously over his burnt back and the dreaded pot that had affixed itself to his tummy, and pottered down to put his toes in the wavelets. Phew, what a relief! It was lovely. When his feet had thoroughly acclimatised to the change in temperature, he continued on up to his knees. Even out in the water it was almost unbearably hot, and he was starting to regret putting his shirt on now, thinking how nice it would be to be fully submerged, when he heard Janice *shrieking* his name. Where was she? What was up?! A quick glance back at the beach provided no answer, nor did inspecting the occupants of the nearby pedalos, but there it was again, loud and clear, sounding almost as if it came from thin air! It couldn't be that she was one of the pillocks racing on water bikes, could it? he thought in alarm. She'd been banging on about them ever since they'd arrived. He looked over at the speeding flotilla not a hundred yards away. It was hard to see their faces with the glare of the sun bouncing off the lake's surface, but squinting at them he realised that none of them had Janice's distinctive shape. So where the hell was she? Nowhere to be seen, that's where, but nevertheless here was her voice again.

'Tom! Tommo!'

By now he was panicked, she sounded so urgent. He didn't believe in spooky nonsense, but he had heard quite sensible-sounding people on telly speak of hearing loved ones in danger calling their name. Was she nearby and drowning? He started to run through the knee deep water with difficulty, thrashing about, his eyes glued beneath the surface, seeking her out. And now came her voice once again, only louder.

'To-o-m! Tom-meeee!! Up here!!!'

Utterly confused now he looked at last to the sky, his hand shielding his sun-dazzled eyes, and found to his total heart-stopping amazement that he (and the rest of the lake's occupants, come to that) had a worm's eye view of her bum. For there she was, hanging off a parafoil right over his head, being towed at high speed across the water, laughing and waving and playing the fool. So shocked was he to see her there, his body arching over backwards to follow her transit as she sailed through the air behind him, that before he knew which way was up, his earlier wish for total submersion was granted without further delay. He could hear her laughter receding into the distance as he surfaced, gasping, to shake the water out of his ears and eyes, his wet shirt clinging to him like a second, wrinkled skin.

Not even the chocolate covered ice cream on a stick that she finally brought back as a peace offering could raise a smile from him for quite some time as he sulked wetly on the shore, his shirt spread out in the sun like a flag of remembrance.

'Aah, sorry, Tommo,' she said, making short work of hers. 'But it was great! I just couldn't resist! Go on, eat your lolly – it's lovely.'

'And how much did that set us back?' he asked coldly.

'The lollies? Not much — and they're worth it. I told you I'd bring you one back.' She unwrapped his and handed it to him, shoving it into his unyielding hand. 'Come on quick, it's melting all over the shop.'

'*Not* the lollies,' he snapped crossly, his tongue now forced to deal with the wretched dripping mess. 'That go on the parachute thing.'

'Not as much as hiring the scooter,' she said, looking at him directly in a meaningful way. 'That was your treat, and this was mine.'

'The scooter isn't my treat!' he responded hotly, flushed with guilt, ice cream splattering everywhere. 'The scooter's for both of us, to get us from A to B. We wouldn't be here now if we hadn't got that.'

'Ah Tom, don't begrudge me some fun,' said his wife, and leant over to lick his face. 'Choccy,' she said, by way of explanation. 'Waste not want not. Look, I'll have the ride as my early birthday present if you like. And I'll give up eclairs on Wednesday at work for two months.'

'Early bastard birthday,' Tom concluded sulkily, who wasn't a swearer by nature. 'It isn't till next bleddy May.'

'Anyway, listen,' she said, 'I'm bursting to tell you. You'll never guess who I saw from the air!'

The grim set of her husband's pursed lips told her he wouldn't even consider a stab at it.

'Chris and Bea, in a little cove over there!' she said, pointing over the top of a promontory to their left. 'Just big enough for two. And a bloody good thing and all. They were at it like knives!'

'They weren't!' exclaimed Tom, drawn in despite himself, his imagination providing a technicolour picture of the event. Who would have thought that Beatrice Miller-Mander, who looked as if butter wouldn't melt . . .

'They were!' confirmed Janice gleefully. 'He was up her like a rabbit—'

'Ay, ay, ay!' warned Tom. 'There's no need for that sort of talk.'

'And I reckon he'd been at her for ages. Even from the air you could see that his bott was all pink from the sun!' As were Tom's cheeks from the thought. 'I wonder if Terry knows,' she continued irrepressibly. 'Can't wait to tell Maz.'

'Steady on!' said Tom. 'You don't want to get involved in other people's business like that! You could cause untold damage!'

'Well, I mean – if she's not getting stuck in there because of him being with Bea, she might change her mind when she knows. And there she is, gone off all on her own this morning, when she could be enjoying herself with Tel. And I wonder where *he* is?'

'Minding his own business,' suggested Tom shortly.

'That he's *not* doing,' said Janice undaunted. 'Cos if he was, his girlfriend wouldn't be doing rumpy-pumpy in that cove.' Tom shuddered at her choice of words. 'Poor old Tez,' she continued, 'probably gone off on his lonesome after Maz stood him up. He should be at it himself if his girlie is. After all's said and done, what's good for the goose is good for the gander.'

But of course, had she known it, the gander in question was even now striving for parity with all his might.

Chapter Twenty-Five

Terence's fears that Marion would overhear him talking to the hotel receptionist about his booking, rather than the bogus film location recce, proved to be unfounded, for she stayed sitting where he told her in the foyer while he went to sort things out, in some sort of daze. She didn't come back to her senses until he had returned to her side and, with a smile that would have alerted a toddler to remembered stories of spiders and their parlours, dangled the room key in front of her eyes. No, it wasn't until they were halfway up the huge swirling staircase that led from the grandiose foyer to their room that she started to be trouble, as if finally waking from sleep.

'But this is fantastic!' she exclaimed, stopping mid-stride and turning at last to survey her surroundings. 'Aren't you going to use this?'

'Use what?' asked Terence, his mind reeling, for now the business was done and they were on their way to the room, he had already forgotten the necessity for fabrication about the nonexistent film, and had in fact been wondering at that moment where Marion stood on the less glamorous subject of sheaths.

'This staircase. Wouldn't it make a fabulous entrance?'

'Oh, for the film, yes!' he said, dropping back down two stairs to take her by the arm. 'Don't worry, I've already made a mental note of that.'

'But haven't you brought a camera? Don't you want to take pictures as an aide-mémoire?' she persisted as they reached the top of the stairs and he steamed them down a corridor, ever closer to his goal.

'Well, I didn't know I'd be looking at locations until Fi phoned,' he replied, exasperated, 'so no, I didn't bring one with me.' At last they had arrived at a door whose number coincided with the key he had in his hand. 'But don't worry – most of the film is set in the hotel bedroom, so I shall spend more time in here, jotting down dimensions, looking at shots and so forth, if that's all right with you.' So saying, he flung the room door open, and with a wave of his hand invited her to precede him, which miraculously, she did.

'Oh wow,' she said on entering, standing in the middle of the large and gracious salon. 'It's *gorgeous*! Look at these windows! What great proportions! And the moulding on the ceiling! Don't suppose you'll be able to get a shot of that though, unless you shoot from beneath them, angled up. Just sit there a minute,' she ordered, pushing him on to a sofa and kneeling at his feet from a possible camera position, framing him between her hands. 'No, a bit forced unfortunately. Unless you had one of the characters lying on the floor, and you shot the person he was speaking to from his point of view. Would that be possible?'

'Perhaps,' conceded Terence, forcing himself to play along. Even though this recce was entirely fictitious, it annoyed him to have control wrested from his grasp. Normally it irritated him enough when his director of photography suggested shots, for heaven's sake, let alone a mere amateur getting enthusiastic on him and trying to run the show. Besides, what was really so special about this room? He'd stayed in hundreds like it, all over the world. It had a bed, and that, in this instance, was all that mattered. 'Actually,' he said now, jumping to his feet as if entering the spirit of the exercise, 'it's good that you're an artist. Could you just help me pull the covers off the bed and rumple it like so? That's it. And if you could just lie there for a moment while I . . .' The sound of a businesslike knocking of bare knuckles against wood halted his manoeuvres and, cursing softly, he strode over to the door to take delivery of the two bottles of champagne he had ordered moments ago at reception. Before Marion could see him presented with a bill, he shoved a wad of notes surreptitiously into the surprised waiter's hand, grabbed the bottles, and shut the door firmly in his face.

'How nice!' he exclaimed wildly to Marion, a bottle in each hand. 'The management have sent us some complimentary champagne!' If he was hoping for a gleeful response he was disappointed.

'Bloody typical!' said Marion frostily, a republican to her core. 'To them that have shall be given bucket loads . . . I'd like to see me getting this treatment if I could ever afford to stay here. I suppose you just get it everywhere you go.'

'Well, no, not really,' Terence protested, grappling with cork and wire. 'But I suppose they're thinking that, if we *did* make the movie here it would be worth it's weight in advertising to them.'

'Exactly,' declared Marion, rising now from the bed, 'you scratch their back and they'll scratch yours. It's like that old film *The Million Pound Note* — the more you've got, the less they'll let you spend.'

'Well anyway, it's here now,' said her would-be mutual back scratcher, proffering a glass with outstretched arm, 'And poured.' To his delight she took it and emptied it in one, wiping the dribbles with the back of her hand and holding out her glass for more. Bad behaviour! she was back on track!

'Okay,' she said, accepting her refill and taking it back to the bed to lie down. 'Where were we?'

'Well, you were lying there on the rumpled sheets, and I was looking for shots,' he supplied, following her, unable to believe his luck.

'I could do some sketches of the room if you like,' she offered, riffling through her bag and producing drawing block and pencils. She plumped up the pillows behind her, leaned back, and had started sketching before he could open his mouth to protest, sizing up the space and making rapid strokes on the page, interested in everything in the room except him. 'What's the film about anyway?'

'It's about passion,' said Terence, almost defeated, passing a hand wearily over his eyes. 'And how near bloody impossible its pursuit.'

'Really?' asked Marion, never lifting her eyes from her work. 'That's interesting. What's the story?'

'Well,' Terence started, playing for time and racking his brains. He felt suddenly exhausted. Could he be bothered with this? She clearly had no idea at all that she was here to be seduced, and if she had, she was playing a game even cleverer than his. But he'd come this far, he thought, rallying, and had flung millions of lire at this last ditch attempt. 'It's about a woman with a past – more than that actually – she lives in her past, emotionally. A tragedy happened – her lover was killed . . . in a war. They were to have been married, but now, still a young woman, she feels her life is over.' He felt Marion's eyes on him at last, and knew they were narrowed dangerously. Was the story so transparent? Better embellish. 'But all that comes out in flash-back. The film opens with the image of her wearing her wedding dress twenty years later, sitting alone in her room.'

'Like Miss Havisham,' offered Marion thoughtfully.

'That's right,' agreed Terence, warming to his theme. 'But in this case there is no Estella for her to use to break men's hearts. Instead, she breaks them herself.' He paused, waiting for her to ask how, but he could see from her glazed eyes that she was still picturing herself wearing an old and dusty wedding gown. Well, whatever it took. 'At the beginning of the film, she is just starting to ask herself if she has the heart for this any more. She's tired of defending herself so resolutely from love. She is like a fortress, cold and strong, her drawbridges tied up tight.'

'Love?' asked Marion, stretching over for the bottle to refill her glass. 'I thought you said it was about passion?'

'Love, passion, same thing,' said Terence airily, dismissing it with a wave of his hand. 'Anyway, there is this man . . .'

'It's not at all the same,' Marion countered pedantically. 'You can feel huge passion for somebody and not love them, and love somebody dearly and feel no passion at all, come to that.'

'Yes, well in this instance the love comes *because* of the passion,' said Terence irritably. Jesus, if she was going to be this pedantic she would kill his passion and leave no love lost between them. 'There is this *man*,' he began again with greater emphasis.

'Yeah, okay, what's his story? More champagne?' she asked, topping up her own glass again.

'Thank you,' said Terence, and used it as an excuse to stroll casually over to the bed, where he sat gingerly on the edge to take the bottle. No big reaction. So far so good. But then again, with the size of the bed and Marion's seeming obtuseness, there was still a distance the size of the Sahara desert between them.

'We're going to have to do some serious exercise to walk this off before we drive back,' warned Marion, suddenly practical, nodding towards the champagne. 'But then again, since it's free . . .'

Free?! thought Terence. At hotel prices every mouthful of this stuff could feed a family of four for a week. 'Don't worry, we'll take some exercise before we leave,' he reassured her, and hoped to God it was true. 'Anyway, they meet, this man and woman, and there's an overwhelming attraction . . .'

'Wait, wait,' protested Marion. 'What's the man's history? What's he been doing while she's been playing Fortress Havisham?'

'He's been playing at love,' said Terence. 'Only he didn't know it until now. When he sees her he is filled with an emotion he hasn't experienced before – he is consumed with passion and longing.'

'So what's the problem?' asked Marion, returning to her sketch. 'He fancies her, she fancies him . . .'

'More than fancy, Marion. This is big, this is huge, this is tidal. This is typhoon waves crashing over concrete defences, this is two people dragged along helplessly on the relentless, surging current of desire . . .'

'So?' said Marion again. 'What's to stop them? Where's the story? I thought drama was all about overcoming obstacles?'

'What stops them is themselves and their stupidity,' Terence asserted with feeling. 'The audience *longs* for her to give up her past and take what's on offer. We can see, even if she can't, that the man's feelings are genuine, that he wouldn't hurt her for the world.'

'And what does the audience long for him to give up?'

All hope probably, thought Terence, exhausted. 'I'm not sure. It's work in progress.'

'Maybe he's married,' Marion suggested, her eyes clouding, thinking about Patrick. She hadn't even considered that.

'Mm,' said Terence yawning, 'not married, but there is someone else who loves him, whose heart he would have to break.'

'And what does he feel towards her?'

'A certain fondness, nothing more.' Gosh he was tired. He slipped off his shoes and put his legs on the bed, lying beside Marion top to toe.

'Is it comedy, tragedy, a romance?'

'Certainly not a comedy,' said Terence, humourlessly. 'A romantic tragedy, I suspect.'

'So, we've got a man who's got to break a woman's heart to find the love he never felt before, and a woman who's lost love and is scared to try again . . .'

'Concisely put. You should try your hand at pitching films.'

'But what's she scared of, I wonder?' asked Marion genuinely. 'That's what puzzles me.'

'Can't be rejection,' yawned Terence. 'He couldn't have made his feelings more clear.'

'No, not fear of rejection, she's too experienced for that,' said Marion dismissively, squinting at her sketchbook.

'Obviously she's frightened of being hurt again,' Terence suggested, propping himself up against the footboard to look at her and wondering, despite himself, if this were true. And if it were? Should he be more circumspect about her feelings?

Watching her sketching the room on his behalf, her strong features framed by her new blonde hair, he could see the cost of her courage quite clearly, hidden somewhere behind her eyes and at the corners of her mouth. Uncanny, he thought, that this fictitious hero of his imaginary film was feeling emotions he had never felt before, for here was he, Terence Armstrong, ladykiller, lying in a hotel bedroom beside a desirable woman and finding to his immense surprise that the overwhelming feeling he had for her was that he *liked* her. 'Perhaps she thinks, however unconsciously,' he continued with a sudden burst of perspicacity, 'that if she falls in love again she will again make herself vulnerable to death.'

'What, that she'll die of it?' Marion laughed.

'No, no. That he will. Death took her last great love. Maybe it could happen again.'

Marion's laughter stopped and the half smile that was left froze before his eyes into a look of deadly earnestness. 'Yes, that sounds plausible,' she said slowly after quite some time. 'She couldn't risk that pain again. That's why she's only had affairs since then.'

'Exactly,' agreed Terence, fighting off his friendly feelings, 'And then again, there's absolutely nothing wrong with that. Affairs can be very nice. Some people are more than happy with affairs.'

'Oh *she's* been happy with affairs,' said Marion, speaking for the heroine, 'but now she's at an age where she's wanting something more mature. She doesn't want to be wedded to the past any more, she doesn't need the veil. She's looking at her life and finding she's outgrown it.'

'Is she?' asked Terence thoughtfully, his mind racing for cover. 'Then shouldn't we perhaps see just *one* affair tip her into this new mode of thinking? A raunchy, sweaty, no-strings attached sort of a do? A kind of last-ditch attempt at passion without commitment? Before the main hero enters the picture, as it were? Perhaps a holiday romance!' he concluded as if it had suddenly occurred to him, and wondering how much plainer he could be.

He'd been plain enough, as it emerged. Marion's look of introspection turned suddenly to a knowing smile. 'Terence, we couldn't be speaking of *us* here, could we?' she asked, pinning him with her forthright gaze. 'And if so, which role do you see for yourself? The real true love, or the zipless fuck?'

'Well – ha! – I mean, good heavens . . .' blustered Terence. Which one was he? A lot of what Marion had described as the heroine's feelings was almost familiar in a strange and spooky way. He was feeling jaded, nothing really touched him any more – witness his feelings for Bea, and after all, she was only at the head of a long queue stretching back. Maybe he was ready for the big C word that he had so successfully avoided for so many years? He felt giddy at the thought, and reckless. Why not take the plunge, the voice of the Devil was whispering, if that's all that's holding you back? 'I . . .' he started again, and found himself struggling forward on to his knees to perch in front of Marion and to take her hands in his. 'Actually, I'd like to be the real true love,' he said shyly, and then raised his eyes to look directly and smoulderingly into hers. 'If you'll have me?'

Marion's smile died on her lips as she checked his face anxiously for any welcome sign that he was joking. He was not. 'Now look here, Terence,' she said, her voice now serious and intense, 'you've got Beatrice . . .'

'I'll finish it. Should have done it ages ago like you said.'

'I never said that!'

'Don't worry,' Terence reassured her. 'There won't be any trouble. I won't implicate you. It's my own decision. It's just that you helped me to realise it.'

'Well I didn't mean to – not like this anyway . . .' said Marion desperately, trying to free her hands from his earnest grasp. He clung on tighter, bringing her hands to his chest and holding them against his heart. 'And what about your wife – Angela Whatsit? I mean, the fact that the two of you have never divorced surely means that you . . .'

'I'll divorce her immediately,' declared Terence. 'It's long overdue. Marion,' he continued, his voice soft, 'How would you feel if I . . . I mean, would you . . .' He cleared his throat and tried again. 'If I were to ask you to . . .'

Marion's eyes were wide with alarm. 'Now Terence, stop. It's the champagne, the wine, the Sambuca. Don't say anything that you'll later regret . . .'

'My life would be filled with regret only if I didn't say this,' he said resolutely, brushing aside her objections. Still holding her hands, he slithered to the floor and on to one knee, looking up tenderly at her handsome face, his heart pounding in his chest. 'Marion Hardcastle,' he began rather formally, 'I, Terence Armstrong, ask you on my bended knees. Please. Will you marry me? What do you say?'

Dear Reader, she was gobsmacked.

Chapter Twenty-Six

'*Marry* you?!' asked Beatrice Miller-Mander as she attempted to struggle out from under Christopher Bassett's post-coital embrace on the shores of Lake Trasimeno. She felt suddenly very naked and exposed as she grabbed for her sarong.

'Yes,' said Christopher fervently, his bottom burning just as Nurse Cowlishaw had diagnosed from her aerial inspection. 'Ow!' he cried, as he struggled with his underpants.

'What's the matter?'

'Too much sun on my behind. It's burnt to buggery!' They caught each other's eyes and burst out laughing, the tension easing between them.

'Oh darling,' sighed Beatrice when their laughter was exhausted, 'you are *so* sweet and *so* lovely . . .'

'And I love you *so* much.'

'And I love you, as a friend . . .'

'Friends don't do *this*,' said Christopher, alluding to their love-making.

'Of course they do!' protested Beatrice. 'All the time. At least in our business they do. It's not something I'd do with a stranger,' she added. She had her limits.

'All right,' Christopher conceded, 'Sometimes they do. But this time is different, Bea — at least for me. I was hoping that it was the same for you . . . ?' The vulnerability in his voice hung in the air between them.

'You know how I feel about Terence,' she replied, feeling dreadful. She hated not being able to give something when asked.

'But how does he feel about you?'

'The same, I think,' she said, faltering momentarily. 'It's just that he expresses it differently.'

'Has he asked you to marry him?'

'He more or less did a few days ago,' she answered defensively, 'when he was talking about babies and things . . .'

'So what date have you set? Where's the ring?' asked Christopher, feeling he had scored a point or two.

'Discussions never went further because he got upset and suspected we were having an affair.'

'Which we are.'

'No we're not, Chris,' she said firmly. 'We've just been having friendly jiggy-joggies while we've been on holiday, that's all.'

'Really?' asked Chris archly, but cut to the core. 'And how have jiggy-joggies been between you and him? Does he desire you with every fibre of his body? Does he think of you constantly like I do? Does he love you, and cherish you, forsaking all others?'

'In his fashion,' she said defensively.

'No he doesn't!' replied Christopher hotly. 'He's been drooling over that Miriam/Marianne/Marjorie – whatever her name is – ever since we got here!'

'Nonsense!' said Bea. 'He's just interested in her personality that's all. He's always collecting odd people – just like we do – it helps in our work!'

'So he just goes gaga when he sees her so he can file her away in his mind for future character study, does he?' challenged Christopher sarcastically. 'Is that what you really believe?'

Tears pricked behind Beatrice's eyes. She hated conversations like this, they were simply too hurtful. And now, when she was already feeling unsure and upset about Terence, it really was too much. 'I'm not sure,' she said honestly, and the tears escaped to roll plump and scalding down her cheeks.

Chris fought off his desire to hold her and kiss those tears away. Let her feel her pain. The quicker she admitted to herself that she was on a hiding to nothing with Terence, the better for him. 'Tissue?' he asked, unable to stop himself. It was heart-breaking to see her distress. Bea nodded, her face hidden in her hands. Her head felt all whirly and confused. All she wanted was what her mother had had before her, was it really too much to ask? Marriage to a dashing man, babies, a nice home with French windows and a big garden, roasts on Sundays, and a lovely comfy motherly nanny like Nanny Andrews to keep everything calm and in apple pie order. She was twenty-*eight*, for goodness sake, time was running out.

'Come on, sweetie,' Christopher cajoled, sitting painfully on his throbbing buttocks to enfold her in his arms and let her weep upon his chest. He gave up on his tough approach. A man would need a heart of stone to sit there watching her distress and not respond. 'There there, it's all right, just let it all out.'

'It's not that I don't love you,' said Beatrice, feeling comfy and secure in his embrace, the flow of tears abating. 'It's just . . .'

'You think you love Terence more.'

She nodded. 'I'm sorry,' she whispered.

'And if it weren't for him?' Christopher pursued. 'Would I have a chance?'

'Oh yes,' she reassured him gratefully, feeling better already. She could at least give him that. 'If it weren't for him you'd definitely be my number one.'

Chris nodded, feeling unusually wise and mature, and nestled her dear head into his neck, brushing her cheek with his lips. 'I'll wait then,' he said softly. 'See how things turn out with him.'

'You can't do that,' protested Beatrice, feeling guilt and alarm rise again. 'I don't deserve you—you must get on with your own life!'

'I wish I could,' declared Christopher sincerely, 'but Bea, you are my life.'

Never before had anybody ever said anything remotely similar to Beatrice. Except perhaps Daddy, but only when he was pissed; and then again, she always suspected it was just to upset Mummy. Certainly no boyfriend had said words of that kind, and as for Terence, he always made her feel as if exactly the opposite were true.

Lying now, safe and secure in Chris's strong arms, something inside her creaked and shifted like layers of groaning arctic ice. It was frightening, and at the same time exhilarating, as if a dam inside her were about to burst and all her feelings would be allowed to rush and flow where they chose. The effort of holding the dam intact was making her body vibrate.

'Don't worry, darling,' said Christopher, feeling her fear. 'It will all turn out best in the end. I honestly feel, and I don't believe I've ever felt like this before, that all I want is for you to be as happy as you deserve to be. Whether that means with Terence, or whether that means with me.'

The dam gave a final shudder, and was gone. It was as if a protective casing around her heart suddenly sprang apart and melted within her breast, the pent-up feelings now cascading out and rushing to find their own level. After all these years, and all this effort to control herself and settle for what she was given. And, to her astonishment, it wasn't so frightening after all. She felt safe. She was loved! Subsumed by these tumultuous feelings surging round her body, she found herself turning her face upwards, her eyes meeting Christopher's in a profound communion where time stood still, and with no more words spoken between them at all, their lips met in a kiss.

'There you are, what did I tell you?!' hissed Janice to Tom, huddled together in their hiding place behind bush and rocks some distance from the cove. After avidly discussing the ramifications of what she had seen from the air for something like an hour, it had been irresistible to go and show Tom for himself and to see how things had progressed.

'Sshh!' warned Tom, who, because of his name, had been sensitive since his school days to allegations of peeping. 'They'll hear you!'

'The only thing they can hear at the minute is violin strings,' said Janice mistily, her eyes never leaving their tender embrace. 'Least, that's all I can hear. They look beautiful together actually, don't they? It's like watching a film.'

Tom nodded. It was and it wasn't. In a film he was free to imagine himself in Christopher Bassett's place. This looked altogether too real. He knew he was daft to feel jealous, but he'd fancied Beatrice Miller-Whatsit for longer than he could remember.

'Looks like they've really fallen in love, doesn't it?' said Janice.

'You're not going to start crying are you?' hissed Tom in alarm. She was always the same watching romantic films, and when Janice cried, as with everything she did, she was loud. 'Come on, let's go.' He led her reluctantly away to start the mile-long trek back to their beach towels, her hand almost crushing his with the depth of her emotions.

'Are you glad you married me, Tombo?' she asked suddenly, with an unfamiliar seriousness in her tone.

'Of course I am,' he replied irritably. Where the hell was this leading to now? 'There was never any question, was there?'

'There was Audrey,' she said, making it sound as if there were inverted commas around the name, as if it were a disease. 'I took you away from her.'

'You did no such thing,' Tom replied hotly. Bleddy hell, they hadn't had this old record out since their courting days. 'That was over before it was begun, well before we met, if you remember. She went off with Steve Turner.'

'You were on the cusp. You still loved her. If I hadn't come along you'd have tried to get her back.'

'No I wouldn't! She had buck teeth and bow legs. She just happened to live next door but one, that's all, and our Mums went to bingo together. I knew nothing about anything – I'd got no experience of girls. I was hardly out of short pants, for God's sake! Audrey Bostock! I mean blimey O'Reilly, we're digging up ancient history here!'

'What if we weren't though?'

'Ay?'

'What if you had married her instead?'

'I wouldn't have, that's what I'm saying!'

'I know. But say if. *If* I'd never come along. *If* you'd married her . . . ?'

'There is no "if I'd married her", Janice — what have I just said?!'

'Shall I tell you what I think then?'

'No, don't bother, we're dealing with fantasy here. I'm married to you and that's that.'

'You're right, that *is* that, and that's my point,' said Janice, whose voice was now broken by tears. 'You're married to me, and that's all there is.'

'What is all this about, Jan?' said Tom anxiously, now worried for his wife's mental health. 'You're making no sense at all.'

'There's nobody else is there?' she replied, stopping to address him directly. 'There's just the two of us.'

'Of course there's nobody else. For better or worse, sickness or health, richer or poorer, it's you.'

'But if it *had* been Audrey . . . ?'

Tom's head was spinning. He felt as if he'd got stuck in a time loop, doomed to circle endlessly around a meaningless conversation designed to drive him mad. He felt stifled by the heat, and stifled now by his wife's obsessive questioning and her Big Emotions. It was as if he were being slowly suffocated by things beyond his ken. He looked over at the cool waters of the lake and felt an almost uncontrollable urge to run into them, to run and run and keep running until he was chest deep and floating out towards the blank horizon in a sea of quiet and calm. He couldn't think of a single thing to say in reply to Janice's insistent, questioning gaze, but was only aware of their conspicuousness on the beach among the normal happy families, standing together with Janice's hands making marks on his arms, her eyes burning holes into his. 'I don't know,' he said finally, defeated. 'What if I'd married Audrey? You tell me.'

Janice's eyes brimmed over with tears, her grip on his biceps loosening. 'You'd have two children,' she whispered. 'You'd be a proper family, like we meant to be. You wouldn't have a barren wife.'

Tom sighed and brought her head to seek refuge on his chest. Now he understood where this had been leading. He'd thought all this had been done with long ago. 'Now come on Jan,' he said softly, gazing over the top of her head to make sure they weren't being gawped at and gossiped about. 'We've been through this, we've settled it a thousand times. I'm happy with you. I'd sooner have you than any other woman and a dozen kids. You know that. Don't you? Ay?'

'I know it's what you say,' said Janice through her sobs. 'But how do I know it's not just you trying to be nice?'

'Cos I'm telling you, and it's the truth,' he declared. 'And I never lie, do I?'

'Not usually,' she sniffed.

'Have you got a hanky?'

'In my bag,' she said, obediently looking for her tissues.

'Come on then, let's dry your eyes.' He mopped her face, and then kissed it, his heart lurching in his breast. 'Silly sausage getting all upset. All right? Better now?'

'Mm,' said Janice, attempting to return his smile. 'If you really mean it.'

'I really really really mean it,' her husband vowed sincerely. 'And don't you ever go doubting it again. Come on, let's go back to our towels before they get nicked. We don't want any more palaver in one day, do we?'

'No,' agreed Janice, and consented to walk along hand in hand by his side.

'That's better then.'

'I really love you, Tommy,' she said suddenly, evidently reassured, and slipped her arm around him to lean two thirds of her weight on his hip.

'I really love you too, Janice,' Tom said gently, 'and I always will. Just watch your bag on me scalds.'

Chapter Twenty-Seven

Romance was in the air in Orvieto that day, so much so, that Patrick could barely breathe. It started even before the minibus disgorged him and his group of fellow students outside the world-famous Duomo to gaze in awe at the sun bouncing off the gold mosaics of its façade, making it seem as if it were ablaze with blinding light, like some rich temple where the Incas might have worshipped. Standing there, his head tilted back, trying to listen to his tutor telling the history of the miracle which led Pope Nicholas IV to commission the building of the Cathedral in 1290, Patrick could still only hear the soft murmurs of the couple who had sat entwined together in front of him on the bus, could see only the after-image of their first kiss burnt on to the inside of his skull. They were young, very young, and it was clear from the way they found enough wonder in each other's eyes to blot out anything else that might be of interest in the world, that they were tasting true love for the very first time. This he needed like a hole in the head.

He had spent most of the journey with his mind replaying images of Marion. Not only was she gorgeous, but she was also an inspiration. For here was he playing at changing himself, and there was she, actually transforming herself before his eyes, right down to the roots of her hair. And what about that bike! Why hadn't he thought of that as an image-changer, instead of this cultural whisk through the Italian Renaissance? Why? Because he was dull, that was why. But with a woman like Marion at his side, anything might be possible – he could become exciting, unpredictable, fun . . .

He suddenly saw where this was leading and firmly addressed himself once again to the view outside the minibus windows. It hadn't worked. It wasn't that the scenery wasn't beautiful – it was that it begged to be the backdrop to a couple in love, walking hand in hand. When he found himself superimposing pictures of himself and Marion on to the pastoral Tuscan landscape, in soft focus, looking into each other's love-filled eyes, running carefree through olive groves, he realised he needed a more compelling image to take his mind off what he was certain would be folly. He had come here to heal himself, *for* himself, not to make a fool of himself by falling in love with a woman who was obviously already spoken for. Did he need to remind himself continually that forbidden fruit looked sweet, but tasted sour? He felt the old familiar tug of depression as his guilty conscience kicked in, filling him with self-loathing, and he started to see his wife Kathryn in Marion's stead.

At first there were the emotionally loaded images of her when she had discovered him, in flagrante delicto, with Bernice – the look of shock and horror which had so quickly turned into disgust, the turning on her heel, the slamming of his office door. The shame of it was one hundred per cent effective in banishing images of Marion completely. But then had come the deep and terrible yearning to push back the clock, to still be happily married, to still be in love.

And that was when he had become aware that the friendship between the kids in front of him had started to blossom into love, their voices becoming at first low murmurs, and then, speech seeming suddenly to become too crude and unnecessary a form of communication, they were in a shared world of silent, blissful meaning. From that moment, Patrick was only a brief sentimental journey away from a hopeless, headlong falling in love again, never wanted to, with Kathryn, the love of his youth, the love of his life, the mother of his children. Beautiful, intelligent, cool Kate, in her crisp linen blouses, her chestnut hair swept up perfectly with that clever little twist and flick she did without even seeming to think about it, her lovely hands with their manicured nails, the tiny golden hairs on her arms which had so arrested his attention the first summer they had met — the way they had sparkled in the sunlight as if she had been dusted in glitter.

Kate, Kate! Nostalgia gripped him, squeezing his heart painfully in his chest, lodging itself like a sword in his throat, misting his eyes with tears. Gone were the memories of the rows they'd been having, with increasing frequency, for years. Erased were the images of her coolness sliding into contempt, of her growing disdain for his profession, of her over-spending, of her snobbishness, of her lack of feeling. For why dig about in the past for misery, when, in choosing to remember only the good, you can feel completely and utterly miserable *now*, as you realise how stupid you were to let those good times go? And now here he was in Orvieto, Italy, having travelled thousands of miles and spending thousands of hard earned dollars to get here, and wishing he was back home in a time gone by.

He reminded himself what his therapist had said about living in the present, and realised with a start that he had just missed a significant chunk of it, for he was now inside the Duomo, having eaten a lunch that he couldn't quite remember but which lay heavily and painfully against his heart, and he was standing in the Chapel of Saint Brizio, where his lecturer was waxing lyrical about Luca Signorelli and the painting of one of the greatest fresco cycles in the whole of the Renaissance period. How appropriate to his mood, therefore, that he now found himself regarding the first fresco, *The Preaching of the Antichrist*. Perfect. He could even see himself in one of the faces of the damned — he could have *been* that lewd and lascivious drunken peasant who must have stood before the artist in his studio five hundred years before, hauled out of a taverna and cajoled into taking his clothes off for a flagon of wine and a few lire, to be the model for sexual depravity, faithlessness, and an insatiable appetite for filth. And wasn't that whore in the foreground the spitting image of Bernice?

How could he have done what he did? He'd asked himself a thousand times, and still didn't have an answer. It wasn't as if he even liked Bernice, let alone lusted after her – he'd always had the sense that she was laughing at him in some strange sophisticated way, although what she found so amusing about him he was damned if he knew. She was one of Kathryn's closest friends (he had screwed his wife's best friend!), and she had come to visit him as a client (he had screwed a client!). And the happenstance sequence of events had been so flukey: the row with Kathryn the night before because he'd brought up once again the fact that they hadn't made love for months; the fact that Bernice had had the last appointment of the day, and on the one day of the week that Linda left early for her appointment with her shrink, leaving him to assist himself; and finally – oh God, sweet Jesus and all the sainted martyrs – that Kathryn had walked through the door, unexpected and out of the blue, having arranged for the kids to be at a friend's for a couple of hours, to apologise for the row and for her coldness, and to take him home to make love. For that was what she had told him afterwards, through tears of rage and heartache, in the long hours they had spent that night, sifting through the broken shards of what once had been their marriage.

Tortured by these memories, he had sleep-walked, unseeing, past *The Resurrection of the Flesh* through *The Crowning of the Chosen* – for where was the resonance for him in hope, and virtue rewarded? – and now, as a cold and sickly sweat crept over his skin, he was confronted by the terrifying fresco of *The Damned in Hell* and, bang slap in its centre, the bright blue demon carrying off the woman with the obvious implants (Bernice again), who gazed out at him like his own reflection, as sad and sickened by his behaviour as Patrick Donleavy was himself. He was damned, all right, for eternity. He needed air. He needed to call his therapist. He was going to upchuck. He ran from the Cathedral like a vampire from the sun.

*   *   *

Marion never dreamed that Patrick was suffering such torment over his failed marriage. On the contrary, she dreamt that he was happily married to a woman whose smile was like spring sunshine, whose form was full of grace, who was an international supermodel when she wasn't busy doing charitable work. For, long after Patrick had been rudely reminded of the contents of his forgotten lunch as it re-emerged, undigested, in the Via del Duomo; and shortly after he had sought refuge from his anguish and the oppressive, impossible heat by pacing through the small dark Orvietan backstreets willy-nilly, like a man pursued; and around the same time that he had come across signs for St Patrick's Well and followed them – for perhaps it was meant, and some small God-sent sign of comfort was waiting for him there? – to plunge down the two hundred and forty-eight steps built four hundred and fifty years before, to view the water at the bottom of his namesake's well (and for the dubious pleasure of walking back up again), Marion lay sleeping on the hotel bed in Perugia next to Terence, her head full of images of her own private angst, that Patrick was happy and spoken for.

Terence's proposal of marriage had come as such an unexpected shock (to both of them, in fact, although Terence, with his vast theatrical experience, had managed to retain a creditable degree of outward calm for appearances' sake, even in his astonished state) that they had drained the first bottle of champagne within minutes of his bended knee hitting the floor, and had proceeded with indecent haste to claw off the wire of the second bottle and sink its contents in huge and lusty gulps. After which, of course, the inevitable had happened. They had fallen asleep.

Naturally they had exchanged some words before indulging in the refuge of unconsciousness, but neither could remember many of them (except that 'No' had featured quite heavily in its various forms) when they awoke, swollen-eyed and dry-mouthed, to the clamour of the bedside phone, the insistent ringing of which had been incorporated into both of their private dreams for some time before they were forced from their bibulous stupour to deal with the here and now.

'Pronto?' Marion demanded of the receiver, her head aching dreadfully in the still spinning room.

'Signora, I am so sorry, but it is six o'clock,' the receiver replied. 'You have the room for afternoon only.'

'Right. Va bene. Momento. Scusi tanto.' Marion replaced the receiver and turned to Terence in time to see his eyelids trying to prise themselves apart. 'It's six o'clock and we're being chucked out,' she said, which helped to do the trick.

'Shit!'

'Exactly. They want the room back.'

'Yes. Of course. Better get up.'

Neither could find much to say in the way of polite niceties as they jockeyed for position in the bathroom to repair the damage to their ravaged faces and haystack hairstyles in embarrassed silence, although both had plenty to think about. For Terence it was pride and the loss of it which occupied his immediate thoughts, whereas for Marion it was unsureness about her choice. Had she been right to turn down his proposal of marriage out of hand, when thousands of women worldwide would have jumped at the chance of such a change of lifestyle? What about the galas, the press nights, the dinners, the frocks? How about the travel, the first-class treatment, the rubbing of shoulders with the stars? Would there come a time when she would regret her knee jerk reaction of not-on-your-Nelly-in-a-million-years? Would she find herself enduring another winter in front of the telly in Wigston Magna, huddled alone by her old gas fire, with only her marking for company, eating a takeaway pizza straight from the box? Would she stop then, and think 'You fool, Marion Hardcastle! You had it all for the taking, and instead you chose *this*?!' Glancing over at Terence to check out her feelings, she knew in her bones she had made the right choice. Even if he hadn't been hawking up some smoker's phlegm into the toilet bowl at that precise moment, he would have excited no flutters in her heart, no catch in her throat, and certainly no deep desire Down There.

'Ready?' he asked now, as he turned businesslike from flushing the loo.

'Sure.'

'I think coffee, don't you, before the drive back?' he asked, checking the room rapidly with a sweep of his eyes for things left behind.

'Yeah. About a gallon should do it.'

He held the door open politely for her departure from the scene of what might have been, and the two of them descended the grand staircase side by side, stiff with unspoken thoughts, as if they had been married for years.

Neither of them could bring themselves to break the awkward silence until two espresso grande had been sunk at a café in the piazza outside, and another two had been ordered and delivered, and even then it was only 'Sugar?' (Terence), and 'Thank you' (Marion). It wasn't, of course, that they had nothing to say – on the contrary – but it was choosing exactly what to say and finding a way of saying it that they both found so perplexing. Whatever was said now would have to be face-saving and tactful for both parties, and be a convenient and tidy way to conclude their finished business. Terence was perhaps even more aware of this than Marion at that moment, since unless they could settle on an agreed and amicable blurring of events, he would have to live with the memory of rejection until his dying day. He found himself thinking about a production he had done some years before of Tennessee Williams' *The Glass Menagerie*, and heard his ex-wife Angela in the role of Amanda Wingfield saying, 'the future becomes the present, and the present the past, and the past turns into everlasting regret if you don't plan for it!' How true those words. But what would be the plan? His mind was turning and twisting, looking for a bolt-hole dark enough to shade him from an unflattering version of the truth, when Marion finally cleared her throat to utter the most dreaded word of all.

'I'm sorry,' she said self-consciously.

'Sorry?' demanded Terence quickly. There was no way he could allow that. 'What on earth have you to be sorry about?'

'Turning you down,' came immediately into Marion's mind, but even she could see that, though truthful, this could only make matters worse. 'For – for – perhaps I sent out confusing messages?' she concluded delicately, willing to take the blame. She was, after all, no stranger to this scenario, and knew her part within it. She had despatched Colin Menseley with similar sentiments expressed, not to mention his predecessor's predecessors back through time, post-Frank. Screwing them had been one thing; marrying them quite another.

'Well . . .' said Terence. Hm. Not bad. For a start, at least. 'Perhaps there was some confusion, yes.'

'And for getting so drunk I fell asleep,' Marion laughed, now generously embracing her required role as flakey female.

'The worst crime of all,' agreed Terence, relaxing into a smile, 'not being able to hold your booze. Tsk tsk. I shall have to report you to the champagne police.' He wagged his finger playfully at her, appeased that she knew the meaning of grace. Over the past few hours he had gone from being in lust with her, completely besotted by her, wanting to spend the rest of his life with her, through anger, hatred, and never wanting to see the bitch again as long as he lived. It was comforting to know that there might be some middle ground.

'I do like you, you know,' offered Marion, pressing her case for a successful closure. 'It would be a shame if we couldn't be friends.'

'Oh, I do hope we can,' agreed Terence earnestly and truthfully. His mind was clearing nicely from alcoholic influence, and he was beginning to remember his sudden revelation earlier on in the hotel bedroom, that he liked her too. She was one of those rare and alluring creatures who managed to be sexy while remaining one of the boys. 'You remember that I told you I'd be filming in your area, later in the year? It would be lovely to meet up again then, if not on one of your trips to town before.' And you never knew – the glamour of filming, introducing Marion to a couple of the stars, whisking her off to a suitable venue for an intimate dinner – he might well be able to wangle falling into her bed by the end of the evening if he played his cards right. For old times' sake. Just between friends.

'It's a date,' said Marion. 'I shall look forward to it.' They shared a smile that strove to emulate lasting mutual affection, although the truth of it was that the thought of possible future success had cheered Terence enormously, and for Marion's part, she was relieved to have reached an amicable resolution to a potentially tricky situation. She called for the bill for the coffees and paid it. She felt it was the least that she could do.

Like genuine old friends they walked together companionably arm in arm back down the Corso Vannucci towards their separate modes of transport, relaxed and comfortable in each other's company at last.

'So it starts in Belper and moves on to Perugia, does it?' Marion prompted conversationally.

'What?' asked Terence, completely at sea.

'The film. Didn't you say the other day you'd be filming in Belper?'

'Oh I see. No. Well, close by. We've hired a house and grounds in Nottinghamshire.'

'Terence Armstrong! You'll start to sound like a southerner if you confuse your Midlands counties! You'll be having us all talk in Brummie accents next.'

Terence grinned at her teasing. It was nice, actually, this friendship thing. 'No I woon't, me duck,' he reassured her, in a creditable attempt at Leicestrian. 'Norrif I know woss good for meh.'

'Not bad,' said Marion, 'for a Belper boy. But anyway, same question – how come it moves from Nottingham to Perugia, this story?'

'It doesn't,' said Terence airily. 'We're doing *The Seagull* in Nottingham. Perugia's another story.'

'Is it?' asked Marion, a small seed of suspicion that this had all been a ruse starting to take root in her mind.

'Oh yes. One works on more than one film at once, you know, in their various stages.'

'Does one?' asked Marion, her class prejudice reawakening with a prickle at the back of her neck. 'How nice.' They swung left into the dark cobbled alley which led off the Corso towards the car park, and had started to trudge down the steep and winding steps away from the city when she felt Terence stiffen at her side. 'What is it?'

'Gypsies,' he hissed, nodding towards three men and a woman a hundred yards distant, loitering ahead of them at a crossroads in the hillside steps.

'And?' asked Marion, her class prejudice now fully awake, dressed, breakfasted, and ready for battle.

'They might rob us,' he said, his footsteps dragging. 'Isn't there another way down to the car?'

'Jesus, Terence, give them a break! They've got every right to hang about where they bloody well like! And these days, for your information, we call them Romanies or travellers, not gypsies.' What a plonker he was! Frightened of the peasants like any guilty member of the bourgeoisie.

'I know that!' said Terence, defending himself hotly. 'Slip of the tongue. I did a play about them once, as a matter of fact.' To his horror a harsh cackle came from Marion's mouth in a poor imitation of mirth as she walked relentlessly towards Trouble, dragging him along behind her.

'Just try to act normal,' she instructed him in a cold and quiet voice, 'although I know that must be hard.'

He felt his heart pumping in his chest, the adrenalin surging, his muscles quivering, ready for flight ('or fight' being quite out of the question, he adjudged, by the look of the biceps of the woman alone) as the distance shrank between them with his every reluctant step. He pushed his free hand deep into his pocket, covering his wallet protectively. If push came to shove he would give them the cash but beg nicely to keep his credit cards. The inconvenience! Why couldn't Marion just behave 'normally' herself? Did she have to prove her class credentials at every turn?

Sweat had broken out all over his body, and he knew he smelt of panic. Memories of the school yard came to him, and of the bully, Gavin Mantle, who had behaved as if he had owned it. No wonder Terence had elected to play with the girls. If only he were with one now, instead of this daughter of Madame Defarge.

Ahead of them, the chatter stopped, and eight dark black eyes turned to watch them in silence as they walked the last ten yards. And there was nobody else in sight who might save them. Terence's grip tightened on Marion's arm and his mind spun off into a hundred lurid versions of what might come next. Would they use force straight away, or ask them civilly first and at least give them a chance to comply? Would it be a straightforward beating, or did they have knives? He became uncomfortably aware of his clothes and how they signalled his wealth. They were in Italy, for heaven's sake, where probably even the gypsies could recognise a Gucci loafer at a hundred paces. What if they were kidnapped, and held in some dreadful hillside shack for ransom?

'Ha una cicca?' said one of the men stepping forward and looking them in the eyes.

Terence felt his bowels turn to water as Marion stopped in her stride and plunged her hand into her bag. 'Certo,' she replied, and smiling, produced a packet of fags. She took out four and handed them to the man, nodding in a friendly way to them all. 'Va bene?'

'Grazie.'

'Prego.' And with nothing more lost than Terence's tongue, they were back on their way down the steps.

'I was robbed once by gy–travellers,' said Terence stiffly, finding his voice again finally as the car park hove into view. 'On my first visit to Rome.'

'But not all of them steal,' Marion replied, irritatingly smug.

'I wasn't for one moment suggesting they did.' Not for the first time that day, Terence started to think fondly of sweet acquiescent Bea. Poor lamb, all alone all day. He would take her for dinner à deux tonight, to make up for it.

Marion swung her leg over the Harley as Terence unlocked his car door. 'See you later,' she said, starting the engine with a roar.

'I don't know that you will . . .' said Terence hurriedly, shouting over the noise. The last thing he needed was Beatrice knowing he'd spent the day with Marion, however innocent the outcome. 'Unfortunately I've got a previous engagement to-night.'

To his surprise Marion laughed. 'Oh, me too,' she said. 'Figure of speech. Ciao,' and with wheels spinning, she vanished from sight. Dust stung his eyes as he fumbled his way into his driving seat and fastened his belt. Damn the supercilious bitch. He must have been mad. Thank God she had proved to be frigid.

Back on the road again, just woman and machine, Marion heaved a sigh of relief and still chuckling, started to sing. What an escape! It wasn't until she was halfway through the second verse of the song that she realised it was the lyrics of 'California Dreaming' to which she was giving voice. The smile left her face. 'Dream on' indeed. She started to think about Patrick again and wondered what he had planned for the night, and if her dream had been true, that he was married. Thirty-six hours of the holiday left. Didn't she owe it to herself at least to find out? But then again, even if he were available, where would it lead? She already knew she had the hots for the man. Did she really want to make it worse by falling into bed with him and almost certainly falling in love (if her fantasies were anything to go by), only for him to disappear back to the States for the rest of his life, while she languished in Leicester? Hadn't she pined over an absentee lover for long enough? Wouldn't it be just more of the same that she had been trying so hard to rid herself of — sliding straight out of Frank's frying pan and into Patrick's fire — and where was the future in that? Wrestling with herself, her face now set into an anxious frown and her body rigid with tension, she drove through some of the most beautiful countryside in the world seeing nothing but the inside of her head.

Suddenly, ahead of her, a gaggle of village children ran out of a side street to watch her pass, waving excitedly and jumping up and down. What was the matter? Were they trying to tell her something? She glanced down at the bike, checking to see that she still had two wheels, and finding the bike was riding well and that everything seemed to be in order, she realised with a jolt that they were merely excited to see her, an unusual sight, woman on motorbike, Marion Hardcastle on a Harley. What the hell was wrong with her? Had she forgotten so soon the unalloyed joy of being single? How many times in her life had she flown down Tuscan roads on the back of a machine like this, her hair cropped short and blonde, driving away from a proposal of marriage from an internationally renowned film director in a posh hotel? Would this be possible if she was one half of a partnership? No way. Apart from anything else, if she was with a guy right now, *he'd* be the one driving the bike. Would she be able to come and go as she desired, on a whim, pleasing nobody but herself? Absolutely not. Laughing again now, this time at herself, she shook her head at her folly. From agonising about the past she had passed seamlessly into angst about the future, bypassing completely the here and now, and here it was in all its glory.

Well bugger that for a game of soldiers, she thought, as she leaned low over the bike and accelerated out of a bend. She'd just bloody well enjoy it!

Chapter Twenty-Eight

Freddie had had the most wonderful day ever and, since it was about to end, he was treasuring every precious moment of the drive back in Joe's car. Soon enough he would be back in London dotting the i's and crossing the t's of his clients' contracts, and all this would become a memory – but what a memory! He had met Joe that morning at his dig, expecting nothing more than the enjoyment of watching him sort and sift and catalogue his finds, but to Freddie's surprise Joe had been in a rebellious, holiday mood, and had suggested a field trip to see the second century BC Etruscan tomb, Ipogio dei Volumni, just south of Perugia. 'After all,' he had said, his blue eyes twinkling, when Freddie had expressed concern about taking him away from his work, 'what's the point of being the boss if you can't play hookey?'

The tomb itself had been fascinating, an underground cinerarium built like a house, filled with carved reliefs of totemistic animals and gods, and still with the ashes of the famiglia Volumni residing in their urns. But having Joe as his guide had been the biggest thrill of all – the way he became so animated about his subject, generous and without condescension, made it a joy to listen and learn. They had lunched together, just the two of them, in a tiny out-of-the-way trattoria that a tourist could never have found alone, and they had talked about everything under the sun, laughing and joking – even quipping with each other in Latin! – which had been pure unadulterated bliss. Joe had even wanted to know about Freddie's work, which made a change, and had asked interested questions about the warp and weft of his working day. Never had Freddie enjoyed anybody's company more, and as the day wore on he had felt himself slipping, rather than falling, into an intense and abiding secret love, as deep as the blue of Joe's eyes. After lunch, while Terence and Marion had slumbered unaware above their heads, Freddie and Joe had plunged down beneath the ruined Rocca Paolina, into the labyrinthine streets of Perugia's underground medieval city, stumbling upon forgotten fountains and churches buried for hundreds of years, by the romantic light of Joe's torch.

And now, here they were driving back past Lake Trasimeno, the party almost at an end, to Joe's dig near Cortona, where they would split up into their separate cars and go their several ways. Sneaking a surreptitious glance at Joe's strong hand on the gearstick as he shifted up into fourth, Freddie felt a rosy glow of contentment deep inside, and censured himself sharply. Joe was a married man. It didn't take a genius who could banter in Latin to work out that this meant a) he was already spoken for and b) that he was heterosexual. So where could this lead except doomward? As painful as it was, Freddie must harden his heart *now*, before it was too late. Wrenching his eyes away from the beloved hand, he forced himself to look steadfastly straight ahead through the fly smudged windscreen, in time to see a motorcyclist disappear in front of them, overtaking at a crazy speed.

'Wasn't that the lady who made such an entrance at your dinner party?' asked Joe, breaking what, for him at least, had been the comfortable silence between them.

Freddie peered ahead. 'Was it? Maureen, I think she's called.'

'Marion,' Joe corrected him. 'She's had her hair dyed. Looks good on her. She could be a modern day Valkyrie on that beautiful steed, sweeping the battlefields for Odin.'

Oh let her claim us, thought Freddie recklessly. Let us die now, at a stroke, to enter Valhalla for eternity together! For how could he part from this man, now he had found him, who was as educated as he was handsome, who was as conversant with Norse myth as he was with Etruscan cinerary urns – who could even name a fellow dinner guest, met only once, passing at eighty miles an hour on a motorbike in disguise?

'Thank you,' he said now, conscious of the fact that they were so close to their destination where they would part, 'for a wonderful day. You've been tremendously kind.'

'Kindness had nothing to do with it,' Joe asserted, twinkling a quick smile at him. 'It's been an absolute pleasure to – hullo! Wasn't that Beatrice and Chris?'

Freddie forced himself to tear his eyes from Joe's face and twist around in his seat to look through the rear window at the scooter they had just overtaken. 'So it was,' he said, thinking, Why now, when it was just getting interesting? What had Joe been about to say? It had been an absolute pleasure to what? To be with Freddie? Or to get away from work? Two sides of a spinning coin, and how different their meaning! He realised he was spinning out of control himself, and faced forward again, his hands loose in his lap, to calm himself.

'And if my eyes don't deceive me, here's Janice and Tom!' exclaimed Joe, as he took evasive action against a wobbling scooter which kangarooed out of a parking space and into his path.

'Heavens, yes,' said Freddie. How did he remember all these names? 'Quite a bike rally. What a coincidence.' The moment had been broken, and there was nothing more to say. Save that he wouldn't see Joe ever again. For no matter how politely Joe might ask if he'd care to join him tomorrow, he must wean himself away from Joe without further delay. And even that might be too late for heartache to be avoided. It was only unfailing politeness that fuelled Joe's interest, of that he was sure. How could it be otherwise, when he was married to Evadne?

'Well, here we are, back at base,' announced Joe, turning into the car park at the dig and pulling up next to Freddie's hired Lancia.

'Yes indeed,' he said briskly, unbuckling his seat belt and opening his door to make a final, wrenching exit from this beautiful man's life for ever. 'And thank you, most sincerely, once again, Joe. It's been a fascinating experience and you've been so generous with your time.' He forced himself out of the car then, to save himself the embarrassment of a long and awkward goodbye, and offered his hand back through the door to be shaken.

'Not a bit of it,' demurred Joe, taking his hand and turning that wonderful smile on him again. 'Actually, I have to visit the Museum in Chiusi tomorrow, which has some wonderful pieces. I don't know if you'd be interested in coming along – you've probably had enough of cinerary urns by now?'

Freddie opened his mouth with the best of intentions to fabricate a story about previous commitments, but heard himself say, 'Not at all, not at all!'

'Great,' said Joe. 'I'll pick you up from the Palazzo in the morning then, about eight, save you driving over here?'

'Lovely,' murmured Freddie, all thoughts of wrenching exits now fleeing from his mind, his senses reeling from his hand still held warmly in Joe's.

For a moment Joe faltered as if he were about to say something else, something difficult perhaps, but, 'Till tomorrow then,' he said, and finally released his hand.

'Till tomorrow,' Freddie agreed eagerly. He watched Joe drive out of the car park, his heart pounding in his chest, and then settled unsteadily into the Lancia for the drive back to the Palazzo, his face creased softly into the silliest of smiles.

By the time he finally arrived back – love did nothing for his already poor navigational skills, he noted with uncharacteristic giddy amusement, as he made a random tour of neighbouring villages – he found Beatrice and Terence already about to make their exit for a dinner à deux, Christopher in a strange dark unfathomable mood, and all of them complaining of having been presented with invoices from Pamela for their stay. Retreating to his room he found his own bill, itemising linen hire and laundering thereof, use of electricity for light and hot water, sugar, coffee, milk, bread, butter, jam, soap, wine, olives, paté, candles and toilet tissue. He sighed, landing back on Planet Earth – or that tiny corner of it called Palazzo Fratorelli – with a bump, and realised that he must seek Pamela out and offer to take her to dinner to mollify her – after all, she was his client, tricky or not. He tracked her down eventually, lying on her bed in her darkened room complaining through clenched teeth of a migraine, and using negotiating skills to which United Nations ambassadors could only dream of aspiring, he managed at last to get her to lift her eye mask for long enough to utter the name and telephone number of the most expensive restaurant within a fifty-mile radius, and to coldly consent to be taken there.

Searching next for Christopher, he found he had retreated alone to his room to drink brandy from a bottle, his hair standing on end and his eyes rolling dangerously. When pressed gently on the subject of what could be the matter, he only swore furiously, refused Freddie's invitation to join them point blank (even though Freddie had made it quite clear that *he* would be paying), and spoke of Pamela in an unnecessarily rude manner, calling her a string of slanderous names in a tactlessly loud voice. Astonished at his ferocity, Freddie sensibly retreated quickly out of his room, pulling the door shut on Christopher and his misery, and found himself safe outside in the corridor. What a curious and unpleasant homecoming after such a wonderful day.

His thoughts roved back to Joe as he dressed to take Pamela to dinner, recalling earlier precious moments with him, his beautiful smile, the warmth of his skin. Already in full headlong descent from his former euphoria to soul-crushing dolour, he supposed that Evadne was enjoying those pleasures now, sitting opposite his beloved over supper and looking into his heavenly blue eyes, her hand casually in his. Torment, torment – he couldn't bear the thought!

The last shred of happiness Freddie had gleaned from his day soured and dissolved into a miserable mire, which was entirely of his own making. For had he his rival's gift of clairvoyance at that moment instead of his own finely tuned talent for pessimism, he might have been whooping for joy.

Chapter Twenty-Nine

Marion was already showered and on her first martini when Janice and Tom finally puttered back on the scooter, and Janice lost no time in pouring one for herself, plonking down heavily into an armchair, and dishing the dirt about Beatrice and Chris.

'You're kidding!' exclaimed Marion with relish. 'And it wasn't just a bonk? You reckon they're really in love?'

'Looked that way to us, didn't it Tom?'

'I'm going to have a shower,' he said disapprovingly, and did so forthwith.

'Doesn't like his girlfriend being unfaithful to him,' quipped Janice in one of her stage whispers, rolling her eyes.

'No more will Terence,' said Marion, looking more than a little pleased.

'I know! That's what I said to Tommo! Poor Tel. It's not on, is it?'

'No,' Marion agreed, suppressing a smile. She was certainly not going to make Janice's day by giving her the details of her own.

'So what have you been up to? You seem quite chirpy. Did you go for a nice ride?'

'Oh yes,' said Marion lightly, sending herself up for Janice's benefit. 'I went over to the gallery in Perugia to look at the work of some of the old Renaissance masters, and consider the meaning of Art, Life, the Universe, that kind of thing.'

'Ah, what a shame!' cried Janice. 'You could have come paragliding with me!'

'Another time,' Marion said, striving to sound disappointed.

'Ah, it was brilliant, Mazzer, it was just like being a bird,' Janice exclaimed, with enough enthusiasm for both of them. 'Anyway, did you work it out?'

'Work what out?'

'The meaning of life.'

'Oh that. Yes, I did as a matter of fact,' Marion grinned.

'Yeah?'

'Enjoy it. That's what it's there for.'

'What, and you needed to go to a gallery to find that out? Bleddy hell, Maz, I've been doing that for years!'

'Some of us are slow learners,' said Marion. 'But I'm going to start making up for lost time. Got any plans for tonight?'

'We've got to stay in,' Janice confided ruefully, going through into the kitchenette. 'I broke the budget today – Tom's a bit miffed. But I'll rustle us all up something nice out the cupboard so you can still feel you're learning your lesson. How does tuna and baked bean casserole sound?' she called back, sifting through tins. Marion was too polite to say.

'Tell you what,' she said instead, joining her and stuffing the tins back where they belonged, 'Let's all go out to Claudio's for dinner, on me. My treat. The holiday's nearly over – we shouldn't waste it staying in.'

'Ah, fantastic, Maz, thanks!' exclaimed Janice, and banged on the shower door. 'Oy, Tomboy! Hurry up in there, it's my turn! Marion's taking us out for a feast!' She turned back to her friend and grabbed both her hands to dance her enthusiastically around the cramped space. 'Shall we walk there so we can get completely and utterly khalied? Tom won't even sniff a drink else.'

'Sure,' said Marion, twirling underneath Janice's arm with her new-found zest for enjoyment.

'And let's get dressed up. With make-up and everything,'

urged Janice, grasping her firmly round the waist to tango her through into the living-room.

'You're on,' said Marion after a moment, the gleam of challenge in her eyes. For who knew, she thought, as she danced into her room to make herself over into a walking man-trap? Patrick ate his breakfast at Claudio's. Maybe he'd have supper there too . . .

An hour or so later, looking fabulous, and ensconced at a table with a view of the road which led directly from Orvieto to the Palazzo (unless you were Tom or Freddie, of course, in which case it could lead practically anywhere, but nowhere directly), Marion was learning that there was more to this living in the moment and enjoying life business than she had thought. The problem, she now realised astutely, was that when she had received this Buddha-like enlightenment, the moment had been fantastic and impossible not to enjoy. What woman wouldn't feel pretty pleased with herself having downed a bottle of champagne, turned down a proposal of marriage, and then burned the rubber off a '73 Harley Davison on beautiful Tuscan roads? So it was no wonder that, by comparison, dinner with Tom and Janice Cowlishaw just didn't somehow cut the mustard in the living-in-the-moment stakes. It was when she caught herself constantly craning over Tom's head to get a good view of the road that she suddenly deduced glumly that she was living *for* the moment when she would see Patrick, and not *in* the moment at all. She decided then and there against being a philosopher or mystic leader, and settled back in her seat to give herself over entirely to enduring the evening.

The storm that the Perugian waiter had forecast had still not broken and the air was impossibly hot and sticky, making the alfresco meal with the Cowlishaws even more of a test of endurance. Tom was suspicious of everything on the menu (which Marion had laboriously and with many repetitions to translate) except steak and chips, and even then he wanted reassurance that it wouldn't come 'mucked about in a sauce', and Janice found more amusement than seemed humanly possible in the fact that the English for trippa Milanese was 'Milanese tripe'.

'What's this then?' she asked Marion, when Claudio brought the famous Tuscan speciality zuppa di fagioli to their table, which Marion had finally ordered on her behalf.

'Tuscan soup,' said Marion.

'Yeah? What's these?' Janice asked, poking the ingredients with her spoon.

'Fagioli. Beans. It's bean soup,' Marion said, walking right into it.

'I can see that, but what is it now?!' Janice guffawed, slapping the table till the cutlery rattled.

It doesn't have to be said that the rest of the conversation was less than scintillating to Marion, revolving as it did around the subject of the heat ('It's so muggy I'm going to melt in a pool of lard in a minute!'), what a shame it was that the holiday was nearly over ('Just think – this time in two days we'll be sitting in front of the telly back home') and little marital digs fuelled by the booze ('Tom always does that,' 'No I don't', 'Yes you do,' 'No I do not!' nudge nudge, wink wink, 'He does.'). And thus the evening, for which Marion was paying, seemed destined to continue. But around the pudding stage there was a small moment of false hope when Janice, who was sitting next to Marion and therefore also facing the road, suddenly grabbed her arm, screaming 'Blimey – Look who's here!!!', which made Marion's heart race around her rib cage as if pursued. When she had calmed herself sufficiently to recover her sight and see that it was Christopher who had just arrived and whom Janice was waving over enthusiastically to join them, she was almost glad it wasn't Patrick, for quite clearly, in her present state of living-for-the-moment-when-he-might-appear, she might have fainted dead away.

However, as far as ending Marion's boredom went, Christopher – who was quite clearly extremely drunk and therefore, with any luck at all, might prove to be deliciously indiscreet –

couldn't have been a better distraction. To Tom's horror and Marion's delight, within moments of dragging the film star bodily to their table and pouring him a huge glass of wine, Janice began digging out the details of his day.

'You went to Lake Trasimeno then,' was her loaded opening gambit, as she nudged Marion heavily in the side with her elbow.

'Yesh,' said Christopher, 'thanks for zhe tip. It wasss great.'

'Thought you'd say that,' said Janice, grinning broadly and winking at Tom, whose face and entire body appeared to be suffering from temporary paralysis. 'We saw you there, on the beach.'

'Did you?' Christopher replied, too drunk to be perturbed, and too distracted by trying to catch the attention of the busy Claudio.

'What was it you wanted, Christopher?' asked Marion helpfully, not wanting Janice to be knocked off her fascinating and dangerous course. 'Food? More wine? This evening's on me.'

'Oh, well,' said Christopher, attempting a rakish smile but achieving a drunkard's leer. 'Came here to eat, but . . . later maybe. Cognac?'

'Oooh yeah, me too,' said Janice with relish. 'I'll trade me pud.'

'Tom?' Marion asked. Turning to him and watching his frozen face struggling unsuccessfully to free itself, the words 'rigor mortified' came into her mind and, biting her lip to control her own features, she decided on his behalf that brandy would be the best – indeed, perhaps the *only* medicine that could help him in the current circumstances. With her uncanny knack of catching a waiter's eye, she smiled over at Claudio and called, 'Cognac – una bottiglia, per favore.'

'Doesn't she do Italian well, Chris?' said Janice chummily.

'Vair good. Bravo,' Christopher responded, already more cheerful. Just now, cognac was a word he could understand in any language. He watched its progress greedily all the way from the bar to their table and smiled his approval as Janice poured him a generous tumbler.

'So go on, tell us about your day,' she challenged him wickedly, holding his medicine temptingly before his bleary eyes.

'Nnngggughhhh!' Tom said suddenly, which was still the most his mouth could do, and his arm shot unexpectedly forward to take the glass.

'Scuse me,' Christopher insisted firmly, his hand managing to close round it too, 'Think thass mine, ackshally, ole spore!' They stared at each other, wild-eyed for their different reasons, as a brief ungainly tussle ensued.

'Ay ay ay!' Janice admonished them, slapping the boys' hands to gain back possession of the glass. 'I'll give you yours in a minute, Tom – I can only pour one at once!' She replaced the cognac securely in Christopher's hands and kicked Tom under the table. From his anguished response it appeared that some feeling was at least coming back to his shins. She dispensed a similarly generous dose of brandy for her husband with the admonition, 'Now drink that up and calm down,' before pouring slightly less for herself and Marion and turning her attention back to Christopher.

'So did Bea like It at the Lake?' she enquired of him with innocent eyes and an encouraging smile.

'Loved it,' Chris responded, holding out his already empty glass for more. Marion was forced to bury her smile in her glass.

'Yeah, she looked like she was having a good time,' said Janice with wicked enjoyment, showing off for Marion's benefit, who promptly choked on her first swallow of brandy. 'Bleddy hot though, wasn't it?' she continued. 'I hope you didn't get burned.' Marion, her eyes bright with tears and trying not to distract Christopher from her friend's interrogation, found it suddenly necessary to clamp her mouth with her hand as small 'murff-ing' noises came from somewhere deep inside her throat and chest.

'Did as a matter of fact,' admitted Christopher ruefully as, reminded of his discomfort, he shifted his weight on his chair.

'She's lovely, isn't she, Bea?' said Janice, her smile of mischief disguised as admiration. 'I was just saying to Marion earlier, wasn't I Maz? That she's even more beautiful – in the flesh.'

'Nnmmm,' said Marion, nodding vigourously, since her mouth had now become as unbiddable as Tom's.

'She is beautiful. She is,' agreed Christopher morosely.

'And the two of you make a gorgeous couple together,' said Janice daringly. 'It seems a shame that Terry got in there first.'

'No he didn't!' growled Christopher, helping himself to another tumbler of cognac. 'I saw her years before him!'

'Did you?' Janice enquired sympathetically. 'So why didn't you get in there quick?'

'Did,' said Christopher, smirking at the memory, 'When we worked together on *Man of Steel*.'

'Oh yeah, we saw that, didn't we Tom?' said Janice, flicking a look at her husband and deciding wisely to leave no time for his response. 'I thought at the time that those love scenes looked for real!'

'Not ass real ass when we were off camera,' Christopher bragged with a lascivious leer.

Janice was unable to resist. 'And not as real as this afternoon either,' she said, which left Christopher looking like a stunned mullet, or to put it another way, like Tom's twin. Even Marion thought that she might have gone too far.

'Wotcha mean by zhat?' he demanded belligerently, when he regained the use of his jaws. 'Could have you for shlander if you shtart shpreading rumours like that.'

'Ah, don't be like that, Chrissy, not to nice Janice,' chided Nice Janice, unperturbed. 'I'm hardly going to sell it to the *Sun*, am I, when the two of you looked so happy and in love. Call me a hopeless romantic if you must, but I just don't know what she's playing at, that's all, messing about with our Tezza when she could have a hunk like you!'

Christopher was somewhat mollified – or perhaps, by this time, he was just anaesthetised by the booze – and his look of outrage was replaced with a crumpled sentimentality, his shoulders sagging at his sides. 'I love her,' he said hoarsely, his eyes filling with tears, 'I love her like I've never loved anyone before.' In the silence left after this astonishing confession, Tom managed to regain the use of his arm enough to empty his brandy glass more or less roughly into his mouth, while Janice and Marion simultaneously adopted the posture of Girlfriends Who Listen, leaning forward with sympathetic eyes, their chins resting on their hands.

'Have you told her that?' prompted Marion softly, and Christopher nodded bleakly, the tears now rolling down his cheeks. Tom was shocked to his core. He had never seen a grown man cry before, except on a football pitch.

'And what did she say?' asked Janice, now sorry that she'd pushed him into this.

Christopher gave a shrug of hopeless despair. 'If it wasn't for Terensh she'd feel the shame way.'

'What's she see in him?' cried Janice. 'He's old and balding and flabby! And you – well, you're like a Greek god!' Still speechless, Tom had another go at using his hands, this time to refill his glass to the brim.

'Power, of course,' said Marion. 'One of the most potent aphrodisiacs known to woman.'

'Thass it,' agreed Christopher glumly. 'He's got the power to *employ*. Can't blame her. I'm an actor mesself.'

'Well I think that's terrible,' Janice announced unequivocally. 'I don't go sleeping with my Unit Manager, and Tom and Maz here don't go jumping into bed with their Headmaster! – Do you?' she asked Marion quickly, since with her one never knew.

'Wacky Wicks?! Oh yes, we usually have a quick fumble before assembly,' came the outraged reply, with a withering look. 'Do me a favour, Janice!'

Janice was not, of course, the withering type, and turned plumply back to Christopher. 'So what are you going to do about it?'

'Can't do anything. Can't force her to love me.'

'Chris,' said Janice slowly and clearly, as if to an elderly patient, 'she *does* love you. I saw the two of you this afternoon with my own eyes, and I know acting from genuine. Ask anybody

– ask Tom – I can spot the difference a mile off, and that girl is in love.'

'With me?' asked Christopher doubtfully.

'Yes, with you! What have I just said?!'

'Had a lovely day. Lovely. Soon as we get back, everything changes. Terence says jump, and she jumped. Leaves me, jumps off with him.'

'Well she shouldn't ought to, she should follow her heart and not his wallet. Anyroad, I bet she'd think different if she knew he's been trying to score with Ma-ah-ahhh!' Where withering looks had failed, Marion now discovered that pressing her weight down hard on Janice's foot worked a charm. Christopher was boggle eyed with astonishment.

'With you?!' he asked incredulously of Janice. 'Terensh tryin' t'bonk *you*?'

'NO!!' Tom barked, finding his voice at last. They all turned to him in surprise. Even with his sunburn it was easy to see the blush rise from his collar to his crown. They waited expectantly, but more words than this seemed to fail him.

'Well,' said Marion after enjoying his discomfort for some time. 'Nice evening, but I'm bushed. Mind if I call for the bill?'

Chapter Thirty

Hours later Marion still couldn't sleep. She had just managed to drift off, in spite of the stifling heat, only to be woken almost immediately by the sound of a motorbike on the gravel below. Or so she thought, but when she went to her window to check, her Harley was still safely outside in the drive, as were Tom's and Christopher's scooters. She could only assume she'd been dreaming. And now here she was, at three a.m., fully awake and feeling like she'd never know sleep again in her lifetime. She gazed at the sky, willing the low dark clouds to break. She loved storms, but hated the waiting — it made her restless and agitated. Stalking back broodily to her narrow bed she felt like a dangerous lioness ready to kill, and decided that getting back into its sheets, damp from her sweat, was not an option. Her body longed for Patrick.

Images came to her, as clearly as if it were happening, of running across the lawn outside towards his room, only to find him running towards her, of being in his arms, of making love in the rain, her head flung back in ecstasy, clawing off each others' clothes, licking the rain off his neck and tasting his sweat . . . And at that moment the sky cracked open with a great roar of thunder, and a massive fork of lightning illuminated her room into stark monochromatic contrasts.

Before she could regain her wits and counsel herself towards caution, she had pulled on her T-shirt and jeans and was out of the door, running down the stairs of the secret passage which led outside to the garden and to Patrick, the tumultuous sound of torrential rain surrounding her.

At the great oak door below she paused for a moment, panting for breath, her hand on the latch, willing herself to reconsider. She could not. There was only one more day to go, and that day was already upon her — there could be no more prevarication! With the single-mindedness of a female on heat, she tore open the door and ran blindly out into the driving rain, her bare feet sliding on the wet grass. She had to have him *now* or surely she would *die!* It occurred to her in the split second before the next explosive clap of thunder that she didn't know where his room was, but dismissed it as a mere detail. She would find the halls of residence in the college buildings opposite, and tear down every door with her bare hands until she found him . . .

She sat bolt upright, alone in her bed, drenched in sweat, stunned by the astonishing realism of the images of her passion and by the sound of the thunder crashing outside her room. Dreaming again, Marion Hardcastle? said her teacher voice sternly in her head. Of course it was a dream. She sat for a while, her head in her hands, trying to hold on to the pictures as they slithered away into the night. Too sad, too cruel, a middle-aged woman having adolescent fantasies of sex — too embarrassing by half. The reality of her life was as Janice had said at Claudio's — this time in two days she'd be sitting in front of the telly at home.

At least the storm was real, she told herself, with a bitter attempt at a laugh, and disentangling herself from the twisted sheets, she went over to the open window to see. It was beautiful, this sweet relief of rain that bent the trees, illuminated intermittently by the lightning that cracked the sky from mid-point to horizon. And so deliciously cool on her skin. Now that she was fully awake she found that she still longed to be out in it, but this time for the solo pursuit of the sensuous pleasure of rain upon her hot flesh. What the hell — this much at least she could do.

Again she crossed the room to go through into the secret passage, this time for real, and went down the rough stone steps to the garden, and again she found herself pausing, her hand on the latch of the great oak door, to reconsider. What on earth was she doing? Hadn't she at least better dress first in something other than her night-shirt? Even in her tempestuous dream she had stopped to put some clothes on. But this she rejected as a further sign of her drift towards a middle-aged suburban life. Live for the moment, enjoy life now! Was she never going to learn? Besides, surely it was still early enough for her to be completely alone out there, particularly on such a night? She wanted to be light and free for this enjoyment, unencumbered by water-logged clothes, to feel only the weight of the raindrops on her skin as they fell from the dark heavens, each one a single, special individual like herself. She gripped the iron handle with renewed resolve, and bracing herself for the deluge, turned it, as a deafening clap of thunder exploded in her ears. As she flung open the door and dashed outside, a dazzling flash of lightning blinded her, turning everything to burning white, bleaching everything out of existence.

Everything, that is, except the tall, dark, terrifying silhouette of the bulbous-headed alien towering above her in the driving rain. The last thing she heard as she collapsed to the ground was the sound of her own terrified scream . . .

Dazed, she opened her eyes to find herself once more in bed, and lay perfectly still for some time in the darkness, the sound of the storm still raging outside, trying to gather her wits. Her nightdress and hair were soaked and stuck to her skin with — what? Was it rain or perspiration? Was all this part of a dream within a dream within a dream, or was it possible perhaps that she had in reality gone out into the storm and been struck by lightning? But how then had she returned here? She turned her head to look around the room to get some clue, and saw the alien with its back to her, silhouetted against the window as another fork of lightning streaked the sky. Struck dumb, her pulse racing, she blinked and rubbed her eyes. Still there, with its strange swollen knees and elbows and bulbous head. She struggled to make sense of things — soaked to the skin in her bed as if she had just swum an ocean, an alien in her bedroom . . . Still dreaming, then, she decided — everything was fine.

Even so, she was dying for a fag. She supposed, since the rest of her dream images seemed so real, that she would enjoy a dream-cigarette as much, if not more, than the real thing — at least there wouldn't be the accompanying guilt about cancer. She sat up and reached for her handbag, and felt so comfortable now that she knew she was suffering from nothing worse than a serial dream, that she gave no more than a nonchalant nod to the alien when, turning towards her, it enquired in a spooky version of Patrick's voice, if she was feeling better. For why not? Whose voice would she expect it to use in a dream of her making — Mr Spock?

She took her time to light her dream-cigarette and inhaled its dream-smoke deep into her clean dream-lungs, and exhaling, chanced the quip, 'Actually, chance'd be a fine thing. 'Fraid I've been feeling nobody but myself for quite some time. Hence these dreams, I suppose.'

'Pardon me?' asked the alien.

'You're pardoned,' said Marion drily. 'Now go. I want to get back to the sexy dream, before I turned you into a thing from outer space.'

'I'm sorry?' asked the thing from outer space.

'Don't be,' said Marion. 'After all, it's all inside my head, not yours.'

'Actually, I'm not sure you are feeling quite yourself yet,' the alien said, now approaching her across the dark room. 'I'd sooner wait, if you don't mind, till you do.'

'Now wait just a minute,' said Marion, halting it in its tracks. 'Whose dream is this?'

'Nobody's? . . . Oh,' said the alien, who then put its hands to its head and pulled.

'No!' said Marion. 'That's not fair! I can't stand the sight of gore, not even in a dream!' But before she knew it, its bulbous head was off and in its hands, and where there should have been nothing but blood and gunge was Patrick's face, peering at her in concern. This dream was now way out of control. Jesus! she thought, Can't even have a straightforward fucking fantasy without things going weird. Don't tell me it's the frigging menopause, that's all I need. But of course, even as she thought of it, it made perfect sense. Weren't you supposed to wake, drenched in sweat, suffering from flushes and hallucinations?

'You're soaking wet,' said the alien, as if it could read her mind, for surely she hadn't spoken that out loud? 'Shall I find you a towel? Don't want to catch a chill. Where do you keep them? Mind if I turn on a light?' He had crossed the room to do so before she could demur, and as her startled eyes registered the real Patrick in the stark overhead light, dressed in motorbike leathers, his helmet tucked under his arm, she realised with sickening certainty that this was no dream at all.

'Oh my God,' she said, 'it's you!' She felt suddenly naked and exposed, and looking down in alarm, realised that she practically was — the rain-soaked nightdress had become transparent and was sticking to her skin. She drew the sheets around her, up to her chin.

'I know, don't tell me,' said Patrick, walking towards her with a towel extended before him and his eyes turned tactfully away. 'We have to stop meeting like this, with me unannounced in your bedroom, at night.'

'What happened?' asked Marion, her senses reeling, quickly covering herself with the towel.

'I'm not sure,' said Patrick, his back turned. 'Were you sleepwalking? You opened up the downstairs door and fainted, I think, at the sight of me. Guess it must have been a shock, me standing there in my leathers and helmet. Is it too bright for you now by the way? Shall I turn the light off?'

'Wait till I turn this one on,' said Marion, her voice shaking with the sudden rush of adrenalin, but mindful even in extremis that the soft bedside light would be more flattering by far. What the hell did she look like? How was her hair? And if she remembered correctly, hadn't she gone to bed too drunk and exhausted to take off her mascara – was it still on her eyes, or smudged all over her cheeks? 'Have a seat,' she said, trying to normalise things after the lighting change had been effected, gesturing towards the chair at Pamela's desk. 'Actually, if you don't mind waiting, I think I'll just go and change into something warmer. Can I bring you a drink?'

'If you're sure it's not an imposition?' said Patrick, politely studying his boots as she got out of bed to scoop up her clothes.

'Not at all.'

Creeping quietly into the kitchenette, she could hear Janice and Tom's brandy soaked snores the other side of the thin partition wall, and willed them not to wake. What on earth was she doing? Making coffee, she reminded herself practically. With trembling hands she filled the little macchinetta, then put it down again. Or gin? No, coffee – she'd had enough drunken bedroom scenes for one day. Tip-toeing through to the bathroom, she pulled on her jeans and T-shirt and examined herself in the mirror. Her mind raced as she surveyed her sleep-ravaged face with horror, and while her hands were busy removing and reapplying make-up, she scanned through a list of possibilities of what on earth Patrick could have been doing outside the secret passage door in the garden. Naturally her first and favoured version of events was that he, unable to sleep for the depth of his feelings for her, had risen from his bed on an impulse to seek her out and declare himself, much as she had done in her dream – but then, what would he have been doing wearing motorbike leathers in bed? Okay, so he had hired a motorbike and driven it wildly through the night, inflamed with passion for her. Returning to the Palazzo he couldn't persuade himself to go to bed – he had to come to her room to tell her he loved her, and beg her to be his. Or something. But then, with a sinking heart and a firmer grip on reality, she remembered the cause of his last nocturnal visit to her room. He had been on his way to Pamela. She paused in her make-over regime and met her own eyes in the mirror.

Fool, they said, idiot! And she flung down the pot of natural look lip gloss and stalked out of the room.

Next door, the macchinetta was letting off enough steam to wake the dead, but not, apparently, the Cowlishaws, which was at least a small mercy. Marion poured out two small cups of strong black coffee and then dithered over sugar. Did he take it, should she presume, or should she take some in separately in a bowl? Stuff him, came the sulky reply, he can have what he gets — if he has the bad taste to choose Pamela over me, he can have unsweetened coffee and lump it.

He was still sitting at Pamela's desk where she had left him when she returned to her room, and, as ungraciously as a hostess can be without actually showing her guest to the door, she thrust the hot cup into his hands.

'Thanks,' said Patrick, smiling, and lifted his cup to her. 'Cheerio!' Really, thought Marion crossly — what old English movies do Americans watch that give them the idea that we say that?

'That's rather old-fashioned in this day and age,' she corrected him with an icy smile, and lifted her cup in return. 'Up yours,' she said. 'That's what we English say nowadays.'

'Really?' said Patrick in surprise. 'That means something entirely different in the US.' Taking a sip of the scalding hot, bitter espresso, he wished he had mentioned he took sugar, but thanked his stars the cup was small.

'How was Orvieto?' asked Marion, still with a defensive chill to her tone.

'Orvieto?' echoed Patrick, playing for time. Terrible. Dreadful. When he had finally climbed back out of St Patrick's Well, he'd tried to call his therapist but got his machine, which had told him to 'Leave a message if you're wanting to make an appointment, or, if you're a client in crisis, try to work it through for yourself, using the techniques we've explored together. Above all, be happy and have a nice day.' As if. After that, in his mood of guilt-edged nostalgia, he had called Kathryn to beg her to forgive him and take him back, to get undivorced and try again, at least for the sake of the kids. When he heard Rick's sleepy voice on the telephone he had realised with shock that not only was there a time difference between Italy and America, but that it was also way too late in all respects. 'Terrific,' he now answered Marion without conviction. 'The Duomo – superb. Masterful.' He was more than aware that he sounded dumb.

'Take lots of nice snaps for the folks back home?' she enquired with a smile which didn't quite make it to her eyes. Was she being sarcastic? It was so hard to tell with the English, particularly since his only close-up experience of them to date was Pamela, who seemed to ooze sarcasm from every pore.

'I . . . No,' he said, and turned his attention back to the coffee. At least he could be certain of the bitterness of that.

'So how come the leathers?' asked Marion, curious, despite herself.

Now he was on more even ground. 'I bought a bike today,' he announced with the broad grin of a boy who has just made all his own Christmas wishes come true.

'*Bought?*' checked Marion enviously. 'Not hired? What kind?'

'Bought,' Patrick confirmed. 'A Ducati 996.' For how else could he have cheered himself up after hearing Rick's voice, and realising that Memory Lane was a dead end street? He had wandered disconsolate through the town for some time, and when his mind had exhausted itself with images of Kathryn, he had found himself thinking of Marion once more. There was a person who was really changing herself, not playing at it with therapists and dream analysis, whining her way through the rest of her life like him – she was out there doing it, grabbing life by the horns and giving it a good shake. He had pictured her as he had last seen her that morning at breakfast, in her clean white T-shirt and her cropped hair. Strong jaw line. Great figure. Nice eyes. Lovely lips . . . Move *on*, Patrick, he had told himself, what is wrong with you? You know you're attracted to her, go to it. Why not? Well, for two reasons, he had thought in his organised, logical way, as he'd scuffed along, eyes down, over cobble-stoned alleys. One, there was that guy with her, so she's obviously spoken for, and two, I'm still not ready for another commitment. Who's talking commitment? he had heard his analyst ask him in weary tones inside his head. You're on vacation, it's called a holiday romance, a fling! Patrick got angry and had kicked a can, dropped by a tourist in front of him. I've tried that! he had replied angrily to the spectre of his shrink, I already took your advice with Pamela, and it was horrible! I'm just not that kind of guy!

He had gone several blocks having this furious internal conversation (he was always much more assertive with his therapist during the sessions they had in his imagination than in real life) before he had caught sight of himself in the glass of a showroom window, and seen that his face was contorted with frustrated fury, and that moreover, he was talking aloud. The next thing he had seen, through the glass, open-jawed, had been the gleaming scarlet Ducati, and before he knew it, it was his.

'I just thought, what the hell,' he said to Marion now, 'I want it, so I'll have it. I'll have it shipped back home when I go back.'

Knowing little of current bike prices, Marion was still certain that he had just spent a fortune, and was curious again to know what Patrick did for a living. Perhaps she had been right in her second attempt at fantasy in the shower – perhaps he was a successful architect. A very very successful architect. 'New?' she asked, just to check.

'Zero mileage on the clock when I wheeled her out the showroom,' he confirmed proudly. 'But I've racked up a couple of hundred since then. That's how come I'm so late back. I just hit the road, and vrooom!'

'Heavens!' said Marion, and lit a cigarette. How to bring the conversation round to enquire how he earned his living, then, let alone, what would the missus say when he got back home? For his beautiful, charitable, supermodel wife had become fixed in her mind as fact. What was the casual conversational gambit that queried marital status? She wished now that she spent more time reading women's magazines.

'Actually,' said Patrick hesitantly in the silence, 'it was you who inspired me to buy it.'

'Me?' asked Marion, coughing as she exhaled, and crushed her cigarette out. He'd been thinking of her! She had been his inspiration!

'Seeing you this morning,' he continued falteringly, wishing the words had never escaped his lips. 'I don't know – the hair, the bike, the change of image . . . It struck me as an act of great courage, and I could sure use some of that! I'm sorry – is this getting too personal?' He made to get up. 'I should go.'

'No no, not at all,' said Marion quickly, waving him permission to reseat himself and remain. 'What . . . er, why . . . ? So, you feel the need for change?' she suggested, in what she hoped was a soft and encouraging tone.

'I sure do,' said Patrick ruefully. 'I've been – well, not wanting to sound melodramatic – I've been in a dark place for some time.'

'I'm sorry to hear that,' she sympathised, trying to keep the jubilation from her voice. 'Divorce?' she offered optimistically. When he nodded confirmation, it was all she could do not to throw herself across the room and on to his knee. 'Recent?' she enquired, practically shaking her head at him to discourage his agreement. It would be no good if he was still in mourning – others had tried that with *her* and gone grey in the process – she just didn't have the time at her disposal to wait for his full recovery.

'Not really,' said Patrick, feeling strangely as if he were at confession. 'Couple of years. But it's taken me a while to come to terms . . .' His voice trailed off, embarrassed. What the hell was he doing, spilling his guts to a woman he barely knew, at this time of night and in her room? It was all very well acting on impulse to buy a bike, all very well to ride that bike at close to a hundred miles an hour for several hours, a daydream taking shape in his mind as the countryside had flown by, about the attractive, strong-looking woman he had seen at a distance and with whom he had only exchanged a few words. But what on earth had possessed him, once he had returned to the college in the nick of time before the storm and parked his dream machine in the courtyard, to pursue the stuff of fantasy, to cross the lawn to that woman's room? Seeing her emerge through the door he had been about to enter had spooked him almost as much as it had spooked her, and for the first heart-stopping moment it had seemed an even bet as to which of them would faint first.

And now he was here, how could he ever get the conversation around to what he had come here to say, that with every exhilarating mile of his ride he had thought of her more, wanted her more strongly, that today had brought catharsis, freeing him not only from the past of his broken marriage, but also from the behaviour that had begun with self-loathing, and had ended up so recently with his going to bed with Pamela? That he might once, on one occasion, have been unfaithful to his wife, had a couple of times been stupid enough and lost enough in the last few weeks to have been seduced by an ageing Contessa, but that was not the picture of the whole man? That he stood before her – or sat, as it so transpired – reborn, optimistic, and wanting to try his life over again, clean, with somebody else, and that the somebody else of his choosing was none other than herself?

His mind struggled to shape the telling of his story to put himself in the most favourable light. Should he start at the beginning, or in the middle – the hopes he had entertained as a young man for his married life, or his terrible act of betrayal with his wife's best friend? Or, casting caution to the wind, should he lay his cards on the table, tell Marion how he couldn't get her out of his mind, had been attracted to her from the very first moment they had met, here in this room?

'What happened?' asked Marion, oblivious of what was inside his head, seeing only that he needed encouragement. 'Was there somebody else?'

Oh God, thought Patrick, straight for his Achilles' heel! So then, the worst first! Begin in the middle and work his way outwards . . . He nodded, his mouth dry, as he tried to find the words to describe the most shameful crime he had ever committed, the murder of his marriage, the killing of his children's innocent hopes of having a responsible father. 'Not . . . in the usual sense,' he said at last. 'Not a love affair, it was no grand passion, but I – suffered a moment of madness.'

'You were unfaithful?' Marion checked, just to be sure. It didn't surprise her – how many offers had she had from the married men she had known over the years? The marriage contract seemed less than binding to a husband, it appeared. But she registered a sense of disappointment when he nodded yet again. 'Weren't you happy with your wife? What's she like?'

'She's . . . She was . . .' What? Honestly now, without nostalgia tinted glasses? What had Kate been like before he had flung his fling? Loving? ha. Tender? as leather. Bitchy? you betcha. Cold? oh yes. Faithful? he had often wondered . . . 'No, actually, now you mention it, I don't think we were very happy at all, not for some time before – before . . .'

'Your moment of madness,' Marion supplied helpfully. He nodded again. 'How mad was this moment, exactly?' she asked, since evidently he was not about to be liberal with details.

'Completely crazy. Out of the blue. Nothing had been further from my mind.' Was that true? he asked himself now, striving for the courage to be ruthlessly honest with himself. No more innocent victim stuff now, not if he was changing his life and coming clean to start over. 'I knew things were badly wrong between us. And I did try to talk to Kathryn about it for a long time before – It – happened, but . . .'

'Kathryn's your wife?' asked Marion, jealousy colouring her tone. Kathryn. Katie? Kate? She of the long and lovely legs and the work with the limbless orphans.

'*Was* my wife,' he corrected her, 'Yes. I guess now that we started drifting further and further apart practically from day one of our marriage. I always felt – I don't know, I could be wrong – that she never really wanted what I wanted – kids, and camping out on weekends – just a regular family life.'

'Kids?' said Marion. Shit. So they'd sprogged. How now was she going to get him to emigrate to Wigston Magna?

'A boy and a girl,' he answered proudly, and then remembering, added sadly, 'Our lawyers are still fighting over the details of custody, and Kathryn makes it as hard for me to see them as she can.'

'Why, if she never wanted them in the first place?' asked Marion, brightening. If he could get custody, why then, he could bring the kids along.

Patrick shrugged. 'Still holding out for more money is what my attorney thinks.'

'God, she sounds awful!' said Marion. 'And is she with somebody else now?'

'She took a lover almost immediately.' Even after all this time, there was surprise still in his voice. 'Rick. I used to think he was my friend.'

Marion sat forward with interest. 'So do you think she'd been having an affair with him for a while before you had your — moment? That maybe she had your friend Rick waiting in the wings all along?'

'Oh no, I don't think so,' he said, shocked at the suggestion. But wasn't it tempting to think it were true? 'No, impossible,' he said after some consideration, and as if this clinched it, continued, 'We used to go to ball games together, right up until the end. He couldn't have deceived me like that.'

'But Kathryn could?'

'We-ell . . .' Of course she could. She'd done practically everything else short of poisoning his breakfast cereal to drive him away. 'It's possible.'

'And who was your Other Woman?' Marion probed, determined to get the whole picture. After all, if she were to take him on she'd need to know exactly what — and more to the point, who — was his weak point.

'Kate's best friend,' he whispered, examining his knees.

'Your wife's best friend?!'

'I know.' Patrick shifted uncomfortably in his seat. There it was then, out in the open, and he'd blown it.

'Your disaffected wife — she who didn't ever want your happy-ever-after-with-the-kids, who refused to discuss your marital problems, who took up with your mate practically before you'd moved out — *her* best friend?'

Patrick cleared his throat. 'It's kind of you to try to find mitigating circumstances, but it doesn't excuse my behaviour. I could have said no.'

Now this was interesting. 'What do you mean, could have said no? Did *she* seduce *you*, this what's-her-name?'

'Bernice.'

'Details, details, what happened exactly?!' Marion was on the edge of her seat.

'Bernice came to see me, the day after Kate and I had had a terrible row about . . .' What was he doing, telling the woman he was trying to attract all about the intimate details of his sexless married life? 'Something — I forget. And I was alone — it was Linda's day to go to her . . .' Shrink. Oh God, the agony of being a modern-day American. What seemed so everyday and normal back home in California sounded utterly decadent and dysfunctional in Europe. 'Her regular weekly appointment,' he concluded.

'Linda being your secretary?'

'No, pardon me — my nurse.'

'Your nurse?' A doctor, then, not an artist, nor even an architect. Fact clouded fantasy, and for a moment, her brow. But hey, she could handle that — after all, he had an interest in art, for here he was in Tuscany studying the Renaissance. Gorgeous, interested in art, and out saving lives! Was she mad?! 'Okay,' she smiled at him, recovering, 'had this been building for some time between you then? Was Bernice a regular patient?'

'Not at all. I was surprised when Linda told me she'd phoned to make an appointment, that she'd decided to come see me at all — I never got the impression she liked me.'

Marion sifted through the evidence laid before her, and a wild possibility came to mind. 'Did Kathryn know that Linda had a regular appointment on the same day every week, that she wouldn't be there that afternoon?'

'Ye-es, I guess so. Why do you ask?'

'Probably ridiculous – you'd know better than I if Kathryn was capable of being so devious, but ... Could she have persuaded her friend, do you think, to seduce you? So she could get a good divorce settlement and still have Rick?'

'Oh good heavens no! That's out of the question! I really don't think . . .' Patrick stopped. But why not? It not only made perfect sense seen in twenty-twenty hindsight, it also explained what he had never understood, namely why Bernice, who had until that afternoon spoken to him with nothing warmer than contemptuous irony in her voice, had suddenly expressed a hitherto completely unsuspected passion for him? 'You're not suggesting it was all a set-up?'

Marion shrugged. 'I dunno. You know her better than me. But how did Kathryn find out? Surely it wouldn't have been you who told her you'd been bonking her best friend?'

'That was the worst part of it,' he said, feeling the shame as intensely as he had at the moment she had walked unannounced through the door. 'Kate came by the surgery that afternoon – a thing she never usually did – and . . .'

'Found you at it with Bernice?!' He nodded glumly. 'Oh come on, Patrick, of course you were set up! Did Bernice ever call you again?'

'Well no, obviously.'

'And is she still a friend of Kate's?'

'Yes, she is.' Patrick's eyes widened. Could this be true? How he longed for the Sisyphean boulder of guilt to which he had been chained for so long, to slip from his grasp and to roll back down to the bottom of the hill where it belonged. Naturally he wanted to believe it, but wasn't it just wish fulfilment, to let himself off the hook? Freedom, freedom, he could be free to like himself again! No, it was too good to be true. 'It feels a mite too tempting, putting all the blame on them,' he said nobly. 'And I've never been much of a conspiracy theorist.'

'Worth checking out though?' urged Marion, who had at least convinced herself. 'Couldn't you hire a private detective to check, retrospectively? Maybe other people might have known if

Kathryn and Rick had been having a clandestine affair? And wouldn't it help your case for custody of your children if she'd lied?' Use any weapon at your disposal, Marion, she comforted herself, this is war.

'I might just do that,' Patrick said thoughtfully, and then rallied himself. 'But hey – enough about me. How about you?'

'Me?' asked Marion girlishly, her hand straying to her head to play with the long hair that had now been shorn. God, he looked hunky in leather!

'Married? . . . Divorced? . . .' *Dating?* he wanted to ask.

'Neither,' she replied, making an effort to pull herself together. 'But I think I know how you feel about taking time to come to terms with the past. I was bereaved. Long ago. A lifetime ago. Ages since. Completely over it now, though.' *And available.* 'Thing of the past. Dead and buried. Done with.' They smiled at each other a little too long for polite conversation, and then both started to speak at once.

'Pardon me,' said Patrick, still smiling, and gestured for her to continue. 'Please, go on.'

'No, sorry – what were you going to say?' Marion smiled back.

'Oh, nothing. Just that I'm happy that you're – happy now,' said Patrick, his vocabulary deserting him. 'And you?'

'Delirious,' declared Marion, and they laughed.

'Well,' said Patrick, still beaming, after they had milked the hilarity of the moment as thoroughly as a pair of teenaged kids. 'Thank you for listening, and for being so great. I'm sorry to take up so much of your time. I certainly will think about hiring that detective.' He glanced at the window. 'Guess I ought to get going. Class tomorrow, and it's almost dawn.'

'Right.' Marion's face fell with disappointment, for he was on his feet and walking back towards the door. She stood up too. 'Well, thank you for rescuing me.' It suddenly occurred to her that he must have carried her up the stairs in his arms, to lay her on her bed, and she felt weak at the knees all over again.

'My pleasure.' Patrick turned to face her in the doorway of

Chapter Thirty-One

Only a few short hours later, after a dreamless and peaceful sleep, Marion was in the grip of a nightmare. Lying on an operating table in an alien spaceship, she had been given an anaesthetic and was struggling against unconsciousness. She knew if she gave in and slept, that her body would be dissected for research and she would die. In vain she tried to open her eyes, to move her paralysed limbs, while some kind of argument raged over her head amongst the aliens. They were fighting over her, but why? Suddenly she felt herself being lifted roughly off the table and into the air – was it the handsome alien, trying to rescue her? But then there was a struggle, and she fell with a crash back onto the trolley. Again it happened, and again, up into the air, crash down on to the trolley, up, down, her head banging about on her paralysed neck like a rag doll . . . She would be killed in the struggle, she had to move, she must wake up, she had to open her eyes . . . !

'Bloody hell, Maz, I thought you were dead!' said Janice Cowlishaw who, she found, was kneeling astride her hips on the bed, and hauling her up and down by her T-shirt, shaking her awake.

'Ngah,' said Marion, her eyelids fluttering.

'Why have you still got your clothes on? Ay! No going back to sleep!'

This time Marion fought back as her head was banged on to the pillow again. 'No more!'

'Did you take a sleeping pill? I've been trying to wake you for ages! You'll never guess what's happened!'

'Tired, go 'way. Get off.'

'TOM!' screamed Janice, close to her ear, 'Can you figure out that coffee pot of Marion's? Don't put Nescaff in, she doesn't like it, you have to use that ground stuff!'

'Wass going on?' Marion demanded, attempting to sit up. 'Janice, get off me for God's sake, I can't breathe!'

'Look!' said Janice, obligingly getting off the bed, but dragging her with her to the window.

'I'm on holiday!' Marion snapped, protesting all the way but being taken nonetheless against her will. 'I don't have to get up, I'm having a lie in!'

At the window, Janice pointed excitedly to a long black car in the driveway, a chauffeur, smoking a cigarette, waiting patiently by its side. 'Look down there! It's for us!'

Marion blinked, trying to focus. 'Is it a hearse?'

'It's a limo! That bloke Mr Sonelli's sent it to fetch us! Oh, I wish I'd got a hat!'

'Sonelli? What – the guy whose baby you delivered?'

Janice nodded and threw her arms around her, jumping up and down in excitement. 'They're having her christened today and they wanted us to come, but they didn't have our phone number and they've only just tracked us down, so there wasn't time and he's sent this car! That's what Pam says, anyway – the driver doesn't speak English.'

Tom arrived in the bedroom doorway, the machinetta deconstructed into pieces in his hands. 'I think I've worked out where to put the water,' he said, 'but where'd you say the Nescaff goes?'

Upstairs, the Contessa was marshalling her forces and organising transport with an iron hand. Naturally she included herself in the back for her date with destiny, and what if this shindig were to go on into the night? 'And for your information,' she added, unusually in defence of Tom, '*Mr* Cowlishaw will be returning his scooter for a refund to Franco in the village – I'm sure you'll understand that, Mrs Fratorelli, with your enthusiasm for saving money.' Steely eyes met steely eyes. 'You can drive off if you want to, but just make sure you wait for him there.'

The chauffeur had finished his entire pack of cigarettes by now, and was impatient to be off. 'Per favore, Signora Carrlischiara, chi è?'

'Her,' said Marion, after a moment of mental translation, and pushed Janice forward.

'Ay?'

'"Who is Mrs Cowlishaw?" You are.'

'Oh yeah, that's me!' grinned Janice, extending her hand to the man in livery, which he took with some awe. 'How do.'

'Piacere, Signora! Lei è un'eroina! Lei è l'ospite d'onore! Prego, prego,' he insisted as he helped her respectfully into his car, forcing Pamela to take cover in the corner of the seat. Satisfied he had the most important of his passengers on board, he walked around to the driver's seat, waving the rest of them to hurry as best they may. 'Andiamo, andiamo!'

'What's going on?!' Janice wanted to know, and Pamela, realising now that she was sitting next to the hottest ticket to the ball, patted her hand reassuringly with her bony talons, saying, 'You are dear Luca's guest of honour, aren't you proud?'

'Proud?' asked Janice, settling back into the luxurious upholstery. 'I feel like I've won the bleddy lottery – I feel like Lady Muck! Come on then, Chris, get yourself in, park your arse!' she urged, as the engine purred into life, 'HURRY UP TOMMO – RACE YA TO FRANCO'S!!' she screamed back out of the window, as he and Marion scrambled for their bikes.

There was a further delay at the garage, since Franco was not best pleased to see his scooter returned, and claimed at first that he couldn't give a refund as he had no cash on the premises, which Tom refused to leave without his money. But Pamela, fearing they would be late, at last entered the fray, and forced the poor man to empty out his pockets. 'That will suffice,' she said, grabbing notes as they fell and bunging them into Tom's hand. 'Now get in the car, before he changes his mind!'

At last the convoy was on the road: the stately limousine leading the way with its ill-matched cargo of Pamela, Christopher, Janice and Tom, followed by Terence and Beatrice in the open-topped Merc sports, and both overtaken after less than a mile by Marion, gunning her '73 Harley for all it was worth, while daydreaming of a certain Ducati.

Chapter Thirty-Two

Never in all her life had Janice been to such a bash, and never ever, not even in her wildest dreams, had she been so fêted. If the Catholic pomp and ceremony in the beautiful church had not been enough (with a *Bishop* officiating, if you please, in full drag – she couldn't wait to tell Eliot Winterbottom at work), then try on 'this is the vessel through whom our gracious Lord was pleased to perform his miraculous works' for size, as a way of hearing yourself introduced at the reception.

'Are you sure that's what he said, Maz?' she asked, as they stood together with Tom, awestruck, in front of a multitude of well-heeled guests in the town hall's function room, paparazzi flashguns popping, television crews jostling each other for a better shot of her, said vessel, while Luca Sonelli made his oblation.

'Literally,' said Marion, who was providing a spontaneous translation at her side. 'It turns out,' she continued, 'that Paola didn't even know she was pregnant till her waters broke, a few minutes before we happened along. That's why Luca was rushing around like a flea in a fit and fell down the stairs. They've got those four grown-up kids already.' She nodded over to a group of young people in their twenties. 'So they thought all that was behind them.'

'Fancy him being so famous, Tommy! And if it hadn't have been for you messing up at baggage reclaim we'd have missed all

353

this,' said Janice, beaming back broadly at the crowd, and blowing them kisses as they applauded. Obeying shouted commands from members of the Press, Signor Sonelli's publicist swiftly rearranged their grouping into the shot that made it two days later into the women's pages of England's *Daily Mail* under the headline 'Thank Heaven for Little Girls – And British Nurses!', with Janice holding baby Giannissa (named in her honour as closely as Luca and Paola could transpose the spelling), and flanked by the proud parents.

'I'll tell you one thing, Mazza,' she called back as she was taken from her side. 'I'm never going on holiday without taking me wedding hat and frock again, just in case. Look at them all! I feel right dowdy.' But once Giannissa was in her arms, all other thoughts were gone, her eyes melting, like her heart.

'Look at her – she's in her element,' said Marion, smiling, to Tom as they both looked on. 'I'm surprised the two of you never thought of having babies?'

'Bit of a problem in that department,' said Tom gruffly, to hide his own emotion. 'We can't, and that's that.'

'Stupid of me, sorry,' Marion apologised, realising her gaffe. 'Never fancied adopting?' she ventured after an awkward pause.

'We've always thought that it's not the same if it's not your own . . .' Tom's voice trailed off. *He* had always thought it, anyway, and Janice had stopped mentioning it now. 'Besides, we're happy as we are.'

'Right,' said Marion, her thoughts turning to Patrick's children and of the possibility of step-motherhood. She had grieved long and hard over her own defeated pregnancy, and the desire for children had never left her, but it had always come down to the lack of a suitable father. She doubted that she would have Paola Sonelli's luck in late conception, so Patrick having kids already was just perfect, providing they liked her, of course . . . Dreaming again, Marion! she chided herself sternly, you haven't even had the first date!!

'What's he saying now?' asked Tom, as Luca Sonelli embraced Janice in his huge arms and wiped away his tears.

'He says he can never hope to repay the service she has given him and Paola, and he looks forward to a lifelong friendship between your families. And he hopes Giannissa will grow up to be a nurse,' Marion translated, as the crowd laughed and applauded.

Behind them, Terence, Beatrice and Christopher dropped their poses as the cameras disappeared, and similarly demanded a translation from Pamela. 'He is enormously in your debt,' she translated, very loosely, for Terence's benefit. 'He would do anything in his power now to help you. Even, perhaps, sing the part of David in Daddy's musical for a limited opening period in the West End? Unless you have a more "household name" in mind? I appreciate of course that Luca Sonelli, hugely popular as he is in Italy, might not be quite the same draw in London or New York?'

'Very kind of you to give up your valuable time to thoughts of casting, Pamela,' Terence said coldly. He had spent less than no time while on what was supposed to be this working holiday thinking about the musical, and the more time he had spent in Pamela's company the less inclined he was to do so. 'Lesser mortals than yourself might consider that to be part of *my* job.'

'Well naturally it is up to you, I wouldn't dream of interfering, I only want to help,' Pamela agreed testily. At dinner the night before, Frederick had been unusually assertive with her, and had spoken in no uncertain terms about the sending of the bills, which must be withdrawn immediately, he'd said, for fear of damaging relations with Terence. No Terence Armstrong, no musical, and no payola. She had put up a spirited defence, but she knew that she had acted rashly, in a moment of rage. 'By the by, Terence,' she offered, at pains to rearrange her features, 'I don't know if Frederick cleared up that silly misunderstanding about the bills you found in your rooms last night? He explained, I hope, that it was my stupid secretary who took it into her own ridiculous head to do that? She was supposed to prepare accounts only for the paying guests downstairs.'

'Your secretary?' asked Terence, doubting every word. 'I didn't know you had one?'

'But *of course* I have a secretary, *ma certo*, I don't know how I'd cope without one!' lied Pamela. 'She comes twice a week to help me with my writing – I'm surprised you haven't seen her – but then of course, perhaps you have been out, having fun, when she's come? But anyway, the main thing is to ignore the bills – tear them up!'

Terence had already done so, so there seemed nothing more to say, and he turned away to close the subject. In fact his thoughts were preoccupied with Beatrice, and whether to propose. Marion, annoying as she had been yesterday, had been right when she had pointed out that Bea was desperate for marriage and babies – one only had to look at her face during the christening ceremony to see that she was now at That Age where all women could hear was their hormones raging, and the ticking of their biological clocks. But did he want that, that's what exercised him now. Beatrice was very pretty, and it was very nice to have her at his side at first nights and press launches (her presence almost always ensuring his photo in the papers the next day), but did he really want to see her waistline ruined by his growing seed? Did he want to come home to dirty nappies, the smell of milk, the inevitable rows with au pairs, the loss of his freedom? After all, he had come this far, got to this age, without issue, and hadn't felt the lack – on the contrary – he still had no paternal feelings whatsoever. He liked having a regular partner, that was true, but he also needed to be free to roam, and to change his mind as soon as the regular partner became a bore. And if that partner were the mother of his child she would not be so easily got rid of.

He had been lucky with Angela in that respect – she had loathed the thought of children as much, if not more, than him. Faced with the unappetising thought of Beatrice enceinte and matronly, his mind now roved back to the excitement of his old relationship with Angie, of the blazing rows and the passionate making up afterwards, of the affairs, the three-in-a-beds, the sex, the drugs, the rock and roll! Now there was a woman after his own heart . . . He was brought back to the present by Beatrice tugging at his sleeve to have a close look at the baby, which she was now holding in her arms. 'Very nice,' he said, as discouragingly as he could, and then, catching sight of someone he knew in the crowd, 'Good heavens – is that Bernardo Rossa? Must have a word – he's been filming in Milan.'

Christopher watched her, left holding the baby and looking dismally after Terence's retreating back, and knew that now must be the moment of his greatest resolve. 'She's beautiful, isn't she?' he asked, manoeuvring himself with difficulty through the throng to take his place at Beatrice's side.

'She's just adorable,' Bea agreed, with misty eyes.

'I love babies and children,' he ventured. 'I'd like to have loads.'

'Really, Chris?' Beatrice looked up at him, seeing him with fresh eyes.

'Definitely,' he avowed, and then, since it had been troubling him ever since she had left his sight the evening before, added stiffly, 'By the way, did you enjoy your dinner last night?'

'Not really,' she admitted. 'I kept feeling guilty about – what had happened in the afternoon, and then afterwards, when we went to bed . . .'

'Yes?'

'I said I had a headache, and slept alone.'

Christopher beamed at her. 'I'm really glad to hear it. Bea – darling—' he began, deciding the time had come to be bold.

'Hush,' she chided. 'Don't, please. I'm still so confused.'

'No pressure,' he retreated, wounded. 'Shall I fetch us some food?'

It transpired later, as the champagne flowed and the waiters presented a never ending procession of dainty dishes before the guests, that, when not concussed or giving birth, both Luca and Paola could speak perfectly adequate – indeed, charming – English, thus freeing Marion from her role as translator, and leaving her disconcertingly prey to Pamela, who had been waiting to pounce.

'I do hope you have been enjoying your holidays with us at Palazzo Fratorelli,' Pamela offered, with what passed for her as a warm and sincere smile, as they both reached for drinks from the same proffered silver tray. 'And I am so glad that by giving up my private office, however much it delayed the work on my book, I was able to resolve your accommodation problems to your satisfaction. You have been comfortable, I hope?'

'It's been okay,' Marion responded, underwhelmed, her eyes scanning the crowd for someone better to talk to.

'I did so enjoy our chat about my father's work at dinner the other evening,' Pamela pressed, undeterred. 'But then, I have always, since childhood, preferred the company of Artists, like yourself.' At last she had Marion's attention, albeit puzzled. 'I don't know what I would have done if you hadn't been there – the others are so dull, aren't they? Theatre is all very well, but it is an interpretive art, is it not? Whereas Art, no matter if it is oil on canvas or merely a quick pencilled sketch, is created in the Artist's own soul.'

Marion wasn't sure if it was as a result of having to listen so acutely to the Italian language over the past two hours, or the effects of the champagne, that was responsible for her suddenly having difficulty grasping what on earth Pamela was on about. 'Sorry?' she asked.

'Depressingly few people, except of course the international community of art connoisseurs and collectors, have such a fine appreciation of the work of my father, Benjamin Fox. But of course, as you said yourself at supper, if he had only been more prolific, he would undoubtedly be as well-known known to the masses, if not more so, than the lesser talents of Augustus John and the wretched Duncan Grant.'

'I said that?' Marion queried. 'But I like Duncan Grant.'

'The adjective is mine,' Pamela conceded. 'He was rude to my father on countless occasions. But I believe the other sentiments were yours. Which instantly marked you out above the common herd to me, even had I not had the great privilege of seeing some of your own works.'

'Sorry,' said Marion finally. 'You've completely lost me. Marion Hardcastle, teacher. Used to have long brown hair, now had it cut and dyed blonde?'

'Delightful. So original.'

'You've not got the wrong person?'

'Of course, you couldn't know!' exclaimed Pamela, while at the same time confiscating a new bottle of champagne from a passing waiter and refilling Marion's glass. 'And I suppose I should apologise for what you might erroneously think of as trespass — although quite how one could be trespassing in one's own office . . .!' She laughed shrilly, throwing back her head. 'I had occasion to need some of my files while you were out yesterday — I don't know if you're aware that I am writing my father's biography to coincide with the opening of the musical which Terence is going to direct? — and I am afraid that on entering my office, I couldn't help noticing your sketch pad, open on my desk.' She ignored the part, in her reportage, that she had also been almost unable to help herself from tearing it to shreds, which had contributed to the rage that had produced the bills for Terence and party. How dare the bitch presume to draw Patrick — *her* Patrick?! — for the likeness was unmistakable. And presumably also, to turn him against her and steal him from under her nose! But curiosity had got the better of her, and she had flipped through the rest of the pages, unable to believe what she was seeing. 'And I saw that you had been experimenting with some sketches of the countryside after the style of my father.'

'Oh, that,' said Marion, outraged. 'That was just for my own amusement. I was just messing about after we'd talked about him — I didn't intend them to be seen . . .!'

'As I believe I already made clear,' countered Pamela, the usual frostiness now entering her tone, 'if, under the circumstances of *you* using *my* office for your bedroom, you feel that an apology is required, then it is given. And really, my dear, your secret could not possibly be safer than with me.'

'It's not a secret,' snapped Marion, equally frosty. 'It's private. That is my personal sketchbook, and not for public view.'

'Oh you temperamental artists!' exclaimed Pamela laughing again, and again refilling Marion's glass. 'Daddy was just the same! But I say to you now as I always said to him, when one has a talent such as yours, it must be shared with the world!'

'Yeah, right,' said Marion, catching sight of Terence and thinking any port in a storm. 'Excuse me.'

'My dear,' said Pamela intensely, catching her wrist in her hand to prevent her escape. Marion glared down at it, and then into Pamela's eyes. 'I'm sorry,' Pamela continued, smiling, and relaxing her grip. This really was not going the way she had rehearsed it, damn the woman. 'But I simply cannot let you go before you have heard my little proposition . . .'

'And what little proposition may that be, pray tell?'

'Perhaps this isn't the time or place, but I am concerned that you are leaving tomorrow. Why not come up to my apartment this evening – for cocktails, around seven?'

'Sorry,' smiled Marion, the cat who'd got the cream. 'Previously engaged. It's now or never, Pam.'

Pamela's features contorted through a range of emotions, and ended finally in another smile. 'One would suppose that a teacher's salary could not be described as – over generous?'

'You keep your finger on the pulse of world news then,' said Marion. 'What's your point?'

'You will already know, having studied the work of Benjamin Fox, that he died, alas, leaving behind a rather slimmer portfolio of work than an artist of his magnitude really should . . .'

'He was a dilettante,' Marion confirmed cruelly. 'What else would you expect?'

Pamela chose to ignore this. 'What you may not know is that there is currently a great demand among the cognoscenti for anything painted or drawn by his hand.'

'Oh dear, bad luck,' said Marion sarcastically. 'Not enough treasures left to you in the family vault?'

Again Pamela continued, inured, it seemed to antipathy.

'Only last year I sold a couple of sketches for a considerable sum . . .'

'Wait a minute,' said Marion, the light beginning to dawn. 'Are you suggesting that I forge your father's work for you to sell?'

'I was hard pressed to convince myself that your sketches were not by him,' Pamela flattered her, 'such is the nature of your extraordinary talent. Just think what you could do with the money! You could give up your teaching, and concentrate on your Art!' Marion opened her mouth to speak, but Pamela cut her off. 'Now I know what you are going to say,' she insisted. 'It isn't talent that is important, it is contacts. But my dear, I have friends who own galleries in London, Paris, Rome, friends whom I can influence to give you your own exhibition, once this small commission is complete . . .'

'No, actually, that wasn't what I was going to say,' Marion corrected her, savouring the moment. 'What I was going to say was that I had hitherto misjudged you – underestimated you perhaps.'

'There!' Pamela congratulated her. 'I knew you would see reason!'

'And you're right,' agreed Marion, for who could stop her now? Today was the beginning of the rest of her life, and what a fantastically happening life it was proving to be! Fawned over by a Countess, photographed by the Press, and all of that before tonight, her date with destiny, getting Patrick into bed. 'I had thought that you were just a disgustingly over-privileged upper-class git with fucking awful manners and a voice that could grind glass, but now I can see that you're a crook and a swindler as well. Though how I ever managed to think that the two weren't almost always mutually inclusive – that's the mystery all right.' Pamela's open mouth and bulging eyes gave her the appearance of a beached fish, gasping its last. 'And one more thing. I choose to teach because I'm good at it and I love it – not as second best.' And with that, she turned on her heel to go.

'If you dare ever mention a word of this . . .' the Contessa spat at her back, recovering as best as she could. 'The evidence of your planned duplicity is already there in your sketchbook, and I shall tell of course, how enraged you became when I refused to be involved . . .'

Walking away towards Terence, Marion decided that this did not need to be dignified with a response. Besides, she thought smugly, she was already about to deliver Pamela's punishment, by snaffling her ex-lover in only a few hours. 'Hi there Terence,' she said as she arrived at his side. 'Having fun?'

'Terrific,' he said, looking at his watch. 'Just bumped into an old director chum.'

'Have a nice time with your previous engagement last night?'

'What?' he asked, having momentarily forgotten his excuse for not spending the evening with her. 'Oh, yes,' he continued, 'very good. I took Beatrice to a very nice restaurant. Marvellous food.'

'As good as our lunch?' she asked, teasing. It suited her purpose to continue chatting to him for a while. If Pamela was still watching her, she wanted her to be very worried indeed as to what she was saying.

'No, not quite as good as that,' Terence smiled. As annoying as he had found her yesterday, there was no getting away from the fact that Marion was very attractive. Even here, among the glitterati, she stood out among the crowd. 'By the way, we're leaving tomorrow . . .'

'Yes, so are we,' said Marion wistfully. What was she going to do about that? Leave her bed, with Patrick in it, at eight o'clock in the morning, and say goodbye? Pack this evening to save time, so they could have an extra hour together? It just didn't bear thinking about.

'And I haven't taken your telephone number,' he continued, thinking ahead to the potential loneliness of his hotel room when he went up to Nottinghamshire on location.

'That's right,' agreed Marion, and gave it to him, making it up digit by digit. Who needed Terence Armstrong? Even if Patrick should prove to be a once in a lifetime fling, she'd sooner be celibate for the rest of her life than get involved with Terence.

'This is going to give Beatrice ideas, isn't it?' she asked wickedly, looking over at her now, still hovering within milking distance of the baby. 'Have you thought any more about what you're going to do about that?'

Terence, tucking Marion's false phone number into his pocket, crumpled it into a ball. How could he have forgotten what an irritating woman she was? Wild horses wouldn't make him call her now. 'Another drink?' he asked, pretending not to have heard, and promptly disappeared through the throng in pursuit of a cute little red-headed waitress.

Marion grinned to herself and glanced for the hundredth time at her watch. Only four more hours before the appointed time, and she still had the drive back and the agony of indecision over what she was to wear. Time to go. She just needed to tie up the couple of loose ends that were Janice and Tom, who were still chatting convivially to the Sonellis.

'I'm going to have to go,' she told them all. 'Thank you so much for inviting me.'

'You can't go yet, Maz!' Janice exclaimed, pink with champagne. 'Luca and Paola have invited us back to theirs after! We're having a sit-down do with lobster, and Luca's going to sing!'

'Really?' asked Marion, very relieved to hear that her two flatmates would be safely out of the way during the seduction. 'How wonderful! But I'm afraid I feel as if I'm coming down with something – it feels like flu – and I wouldn't want to risk giving it to Giannissa . . . I'm just going to go back to the Palazzo and go to bed. Have an early night. Sleep it off.'

'Let's feel your forehead,' said her internationally famous nurse friend. 'Blimey, yeah, you are hot! Will you be okay on the bike?'

'I'll be fine, I'll take it nice and steady. Have fun – don't worry about me.'

'I'll look in on you when we get back,' Janice promised, 'see if you need anything.'

'No no, don't do that! I'll be asleep long since by then. And this is your day, Janice — treasure it, enjoy it to the full! I'll see you both in the morning, in plenty of time for the plane.'

'We'll have to leave early,' Tom warned, 'What with not having the car any more. It'll be all that bus and coach business, and we'll need to check in a good two hours before — more probably, to be on the safe side, after all that palaver we had getting on a plane on the way here. I think we should be off around seven at the latest. I'll set me alarm clock for half past five.'

'Half past *five*!' exclaimed Marion. 'No way, Tom!'

'And don't forget, you've still got to take your bike back — *you* might need to get up earlier than that.'

But the Sonellis, radiant, their arms around each other's waists, wouldn't hear of it, to Marion's joy. 'We will send the car to take you to Pisa in the morning,' Luca insisted. 'And there will be no mix-up with the plane, I will make sure my secretary phones ahead to secure your seats for you. The only thing you will have to worry about, Tom,' he continued, releasing Paola for a moment to put his massive arm around Tom's shoulders, 'will be claiming the right suitcase when you arrive back in England!' They all laughed convivially, even Tom, and after a bear hug from Luca and a couple of kisses from Paola, Marion took her leave.

Her hour had come. Destiny was calling.

Chapter Thirty-Three

Destiny had not been so much calling him all day, as doing a clog dance while signalling with six-foot semaphore flags, but Freddie Mayer had been oblivious. For, to have known what was in store for him, he would have had to have paid far more attention than he knew how, having been single for so long, to the obvious signs that Something Was Up With Joe.

He might have asked himself, for instance, why his friend's mood seemed to swing between the extremes of warm familiarity and emotional distance on the drive over to Chiusi; why same said friend, so different from the day before, seemed so distracted when they took their tour through the Museo Archeologico Nazionale Etrusco, and only smiled weakly in response to his own astonished delight at the extraordinary display of cinerary urns therein. He might have been curious as to why his eminent archaeologist companion seemed so reluctant to plunge down into the narrow passages of the excavated Labyrinth of Porsena which had formed the vast plumbing system of the Etruscan city above; or indeed, why he had not been keen to use his professional contacts to visit even a single one of the dozens of important Etruscan tombs in the surrounding area, closed to the public for preservation but eminently visitable by one such as he. He might have asked himself why instead Joe seemed only to mope? Why he seemed so preoccupied, and with what? And what was at the end of so many unfinished sentences, so eagerly begun, left to hang in confusion in mid-air?

'Let's have lunch,' Joe had said finally, and instead of popping into any of the highly regarded restaurants in town, had puzzlingly chosen to drive him the three miles out to Lago di Chiusi, to dine on a vine-covered terrace with a view of the lake.

'Lovely,' said the incurious Frederick, glancing at the view and, pushing his glasses higher up his nose, buried it in the menu. 'What do you recommend?'

'Oh – everything's good, have whatever you please.'

'The veal, I think – yes, I think I'll have the veal,' Freddie said studiously, his eyes never leaving the page.

'The veal is good,' Joe nodded, looking for a waiter.

'Or then again, perhaps the rabbit.'

'Also very nice.'

'Oh, but I see they have wild boar. And suckling pig with apple.'

'Whatever you say.'

'Mm. I'm really rather hungry,' said Freddie, who for a lifetime had taken comfort in food. 'Are you having primo and secondo? I'm thinking affettati misti followed by the linguine al forno and then . . . the veal. No, the boar. But then again they do have fish fresh from the lake . . . No, suckling pig it is,' he concluded, as the waiter appeared at his side.

To his surprise, when Joe gave his large order in flawless Italian, it appeared he asked only for salad for himself, and toyed with it when it arrived.

'Not hungry?' Freddie asked self-consciously as he pigged down a plate of cold meats. 'Sorry about this. It's the last day of my holiday so I'm pushing out the boat.'

'Yes I know. I . . .' said Joe glumly, another unfinished sentence dangling between them. 'Would you care for more wine?' He smiled as he poured it, apparently bracing his shoulders, and cleared his throat to speak. 'I . . .' he said, and lapsed into silence.

It wasn't that Freddie was completely unaware that there was something occupying Joe's thoughts, nor indeed that he did not rightly suppose that that something was him. Where he got it so wrong was that he guiltily assumed that Joe was regretting having asked him along that day, when he probably had another million important things to do.

'No, no, I mustn't take up more of your time,' he responded to Joe's urging to partake of dessert, after he had munched his way through three courses.

'My time is yours,' Joe offered daringly, willing him to take up his cue.

'You are very kind,' said Freddie stiffly, crumpling his napkin, 'but I know you have business in Chiusi to which you need to attend and I mustn't detain you longer.'

'Not at all,' Joe insisted, as he lost the polite battle to settle the bill and watched helplessly as Freddie stood up to leave. 'I've taken the day off, I'm on holiday like you.'

They were silent on the drive back into Chiusi, each harbouring his own thoughts, and at best monosyllabic during their tour, at Joe's insistence, of the Museo della Cattedrale. The worst for Freddie were his feelings of utter foolishness, that he had so misinterpreted Joe's kindness for interest, had so looked forward to spending the day in his company. He trailed up the stairs of the museum disconsolately, barely remarking on the magnificent illuminated antiphonals from the fifteenth century, and hardly moved at all when later they arrived in the garden to view the remains of the Etruscan city walls and the tower built in the third century BC. Indeed, it wasn't until Joe brought his car to a halt on the gravelled drive of Palazzo Fratorelli at around half past six, that any kind of conversation really got going between them at all.

'I'm sorry, you must think me very rude,' Joe ventured as he pulled on the handbrake and turned at last to look at Freddie.

'Not at all,' Freddie replied, trying to be formal, while feeling himself melt against his will into the two blue pools that were Joe's eyes. 'You've been more than kind, and thank you for another pleasant day.'

'But it hasn't been, has it? And it's all my fault . . . I've had . . . There's been . . . There's something I've been trying to . . . And really not succeeding . . .' Joe said cryptically, wishing there were an easy way to explain the extraordinary tale he so needed to tell.

'Joe, I'm sorry, are you all right?' Freddie asked, aware at last that something was seriously amiss. 'But you should have said something! How stupid of me! What on earth is the matter?'

'Evadne . . .' Joe started. 'When I got home last night . . .' he started again.

'Not ill, I hope?' said Freddie, his heart sinking at the mention of her name.

Joe shook his head. 'She's had – another of her revelations,' he managed finally to say with an embarrassed laugh. 'Concerning herself, and also concerning me.'

'Heavens,' said Freddie flatly. How on earth this intelligent man could be so taken in by the ravings of a woman who could only be described, even if one strived for politeness, as deeply eccentric, was an unfathomable mystery to him.

'To tell you the truth,' Joe now volunteered, 'I've never truly believed in her – gift.'

'No?' said Freddie, mightily relieved.

'But I don't doubt that *she* does,' her husband added loyally.

'Oh, quite.'

Joe turned away to gaze, unseeing, straight ahead through the windscreen. 'It's a question of knowing quite where to start . . . My life was in flux when I met her a few years ago. I'd just gotten divorced again, and I was finally coming around to starting to deal with – an issue I'd been avoiding most of my life . . .'

'I see,' said the blind man, unhelpfully.

'The issue of my . . . That it was possible that I could be . . . That emotionally, and even perhaps physically, I might be drawn more towards . . . And ironically, of course, Evadne, who has never even considered the issue for herself, has just merrily gone off and done it, without a second thought!' Joe turned back to him to laugh in astonishment, as if this now made everything clear.

'Joe,' said Freddie, completely lost, and speaking slowly, 'you must forgive me – I am not the kind of person in whom people usually confide, and I find myself having a little difficulty following your train of thought.'

Joe took a deep breath. It was now or never, then. 'My wife claims to have had a vision in which everything became clear to her about herself, and about me. Evadne is having an affair with a woman from her Goddess worshipping circle of friends,' he said, finally finding the words, or at least some of them. 'She's found herself at last, she says, and we must all follow our own desires.'

'I see,' said Freddie uncomfortably. 'That must have come as a terrible shock to you. Last night you say. Good heavens. I'm so sorry. And she'd never previously hinted that she might in fact be . . .'

'Gay,' said Joe bravely. 'No. And nor indeed had I.'

'Well, why should you?' demanded Freddie, rising to his friend's defence. 'She married you, after all, you would have no reason whatsoever to suspect such a thing!'

Joe, turning to look again into Frederick's eyes, gave a small self-conscious laugh and found that words failed him. 'I don't think I'm really making myself very clear,' he said with difficulty after a silent impasse, and, in the hope that actions might speak louder, he proceeded to elucidate in a language that even Freddie could not fail to understand.

While comprehension of a kind he never knew existed suffused Frederick's entire body in Joe's car in the driveway downstairs, upstairs in her bedroom, Marion grappled with the apprehension that coursed through her own. Naturally she had arrived back with hours to spare, had tried on every combination of costume from her limited holiday wardrobe and settled (five times so far) on the jeans and T-shirt; had showered twice, used the other bathroom facilities at ten-minute intervals, had shaved everything except her head within a millimetre of its life, and done and redone her make-up. She had packed everything that would no longer be needed into her tote bag to leave herself an extra few minutes in the morning, and had made the room as pretty as possible, placing a candle over by the mirror and one close to the bed. On the drive back she had stopped in Cortona to purchase some delicacies — roasted artichokes, spiced olives, sun-dried tomatoes, mozzarella di bufala, salami, a loaf of fresh bread — which she had arranged artistically on a platter in the kitchenette. A bottle of good red wine was uncorked and chambré, a bottle of white was cooling in the fridge. As the clock crept closer to the magic hour of seven she calculated that at most, even with the Sonellis' generous offer of transport to Pisa, she had only fourteen hours before her holiday romance was over and she would be gone. No way was she going out tonight. Patrick could have his date, but here, in her lair.

At seven on the dot his knock came at the secret passage door, echoing the pounding of her heart. No time now for anything more than a quick glance in the mirror to wish herself luck, before opening the door as casually as she could muster, framing herself with a backdrop of candlelight.

'Hi there,' he greeted her, wearing a shy grin and his leathers, 'I've booked us a table. Shall we take my bike or yours?'

Terence Armstrong would have marvelled, had he seen it, how this most intractable of women lost her will to resist.

'Yours?' she answered, as she blew out the candles, and obediently followed Patrick down the stairs to the college courtyard at the back, to stand beside the Ducati and admire.

'Would you like to drive it?' he asked her politely.

'No no!' she cried, more than willing to swap her usual assertiveness for the pleasure of holding him in her arms from behind. She watched as he mounted and turned on the engine, and swung herself on to the pillion as close as could be. Ah, the smell of his leathers, his shoulders so broad, her arms so full, her head so dizzy! Patrick drove slowly and carefully over the gravel and through the college gateway into the Palazzo's front drive, where Marion just had time to clock, through steamy car windows, the psychic woman's husband still engaged in explaining his feelings to the bloke called Freddie by way of a passionate clinch, and before she could share her astonishment with him, Patrick had opened up the throttle and they were out on the road, speeding together through the cool evening air.

Patrick had been worrying all day about the evening, but he had turned his anxiety into action, for in everything except emotional cleansing he was meticulously thorough. It was of the utmost importance to him that, if called upon to do so, he should ride the Ducati brilliantly, thereby communicating some attractive components of his personality right at the start of the date, such as manliness, competence, and daring. To this end he had cut lectures that morning after only a couple of hours of a half-hearted attempt at concentrating on the drone of his teacher's voice, and had spent the rest of the day practising his riding skills over hill and down dale, so that by the time it came to shower and shave he could manage the machine efficiently, safely, and with brio. He had even made reservations at three separate restaurants that he'd happened upon during his drive: one nearby, one in the middle distance, and one over the hills and far away, in order that he be covered in the event of his nerve failing him, but could show off if he found he was driving at his best. Even so, his heart had sunk when Marion had elected to go on his bike and ride pillion, for there had always been the cheering possibility that she would want to be in the driving seat herself.

But now she was behind him, her body pressed against his back, her arms around his waist, their thighs glued together in perfect chevrons, man and woman merged with the machine, he found that not only had he worried quite unnecessarily, he found that he could fly. Long behind them was the first restaurant, conveniently close to Cortona in case of his courage deserting him, gone was the middle-distance pit stop, passed by in an exhilarating blur of lights, and here, after what seemed too short an hour of breathtakingly skilful driving, they were climbing up the winding tree-lined hillside roads to the magnificent ancient monastery that had been converted into restaurant number three.

The only eventuality he hadn't prepared for, as he and Marion sat opposite each other in the dauntingly formal surroundings, deferring the moment when conversation became unavoidable by studying the huge leather-bound menus at their candle-lit table, gleaming with silver and crystal, the white cloth stiff with starch, was the sudden and unexpected loss of appetite he experienced and the complete aversion to the thought of food. For how could he begin to swallow anything when his throat was choked with unsaid words? How could he force a single morsel into his body, when it was already so full of anticipation and fear?

'Wine,' he ventured tremulously, hoping to tease his appetite awake, or at least to sedate his nerves.

'Yes,' agreed Marion gratefully, since her feelings were mirroring his precisely. 'Wine. Indeed.'

The waiter was duly summoned and dispatched, and returning with wine, was stood down again.

'Up yours,' said Patrick solemnly, in the English way she had taught him, as he offered Marion his glass to clink against hers in a toast.

'To that,' she rejoined as solemnly, in a supreme display of self-control. While Patrick savoured a small sip of the one glass he would allow himself before the long drive back to the Palazzo, Marion drained hers completely in one parched and greedy draught. 'Well,' she said with a nervous smile, as their eyes met and their mouths went all funny, 'Here we are at last.' So charged was the moment that neither one of them could sustain their gaze for fear of abandoning the preliminaries and grappling with the fastenings on each other's clothes, and both turned their attentions once more to the menus.

'There's so much to choose from,' complained Patrick after what seemed to him an age of indecision over 'Carne'.

'Mm,' said Marion. 'I missed you today.' Now where the hell had that come from, she asked herself in shock?! She had meant only to say, 'Perhaps I'll just have antipasto.'

'Did you?' asked Patrick, raising his eyes to meet hers again, his face positively shining with pleasure. 'I missed you too.' Again they gazed at each other, this time wreathed in ridiculous grins. 'You're so beautiful,' he said.

'So are you,' she returned. Their hands travelled of their own accord across the arctic wastes of the tablecloth, where they met in the middle to snuggle companionably together, her smaller hand nestling in the warmth of his.

'I feel so comfortable with you,' Patrick ventured, 'though I hardly know you at all.'

'Me too,' said Marion, despairing of having a single original thought of her own. Where was her usual wit when she wanted it? By this time on a normal date she'd have them rolling in the aisles.

Across the room their waiter had retired to his station to polish silver and to try to wait patiently until called. 'Look's like we've got another couple like the honeymooners last week,' he said to his Captain, nodding over to Marion and Patrick in concern.

'Try again to take their order,' said the Captain, hurrying by, 'or just tell them what you suggest, Marco.'

'But if they don't eat it . . . ?' said Marco anxiously.

'As long as they pay . . .'

Marco shrugged and took up his pad to cross the room once more.

'So tell me about yourself,' Patrick was saying, while his eyes communed effortlessly with the mysterious depths of Marion's own, sharing all kinds of knowledge which needed no verbal expression at all.

'Well – my name's Marion Hardcastle,' Marion began, grinning self-consciously, 'and I'm an art teacher. And I live in Leicester, and er . . . and . . .' What to tell him? Her mind was a blank. '. . . And you?'

'I'm Patrick Donleavy,' he giggled back, 'and I'm a d—'

'Signora, Signore,' said Marco at their side. 'Prego?'

Like naughty schoolchildren caught talking in class, they sobered immediately and returned to the Herculean task in hand of deciding what on earth to eat.

'What you like — meat, fish?' prompted Marco after enduring another yawning pause.

'Uh huh,' said Patrick.

Marco pursed his lips, willing himself to have patience. 'The fish is good today,' he offered, unashamedly leading the witness.

'Is it?' said Patrick.

'Baked with tomato and olive. Very nice, very good.'

'Right,' said Patrick, which Marco decided to take as an order and duly wrote down.

'Then before, the penne with the ragu of . . .'

'Mm hm.'

Again Marco was happy to take that as a yes. 'And to start, some bruschetta mista.'

'Bruschetta, hey?' replied Patrick, having heard not a word. 'Signora?'

Marion had glazed over, gazing at Patrick's hands, the hands of a healer. For, though he'd been cut short by the intrusive waiter, she'd been reminded of his calling. 'I'm Patrick and I'm a doctor,' he'd been going to say. It couldn't *be* more Mills and Boon, she marvelled — she had hit the jackpot in the romantic stakes. Her mother would faint if this lasted. 'My son-in-law the doctor . . .' Respectable at last.

'Signora?' Marco prompted again.

'Uh? Oh! What he said. For two.' What did she care what she ate? She just wanted this distraction to be over.

'Where were we? Ah yes,' said Patrick when they were alone again, and took her hand again in his. Oh yes, a woman could certainly be healed here in this warmth. 'You were telling me all about yourself.' Again their eyes spoke volumes to each other, while their lips were utterly silent.

'What are we doing here?' asked Marion, as if waking from unconsciousness, looking round at other couples who had passed well beyond their stage of courtship, and were more than happy to be fed.

'Getting to know each other?' offered Patrick.

'I can think of better ways to do that,' said Marion, as bold as brass.

'You can?' said Patrick, with the air of a bashful virgin learning to flirt.

'And besides, to be honest I'm not hungry. Are you?'

'Only for you,' said Patrick, shocked to hear his own response.

'Let's go,' urged Marion, and stood up.

Out of automatic politeness Patrick stood too, but balked at following her. 'But – haven't we just ordered the food?!'

'We'll cancel it. Can you see our waiter?' asked Marion, looking around the restaurant.

'No.'

'Okay. So run!' she said, and grabbing him by the hand, she pulled him after her at great speed, giggling all the way through the vast entrance hall and outside to the Ducati.

'You're outrageous!' Patrick, who had never so much as nicked a penny candy from the corner store when he was a kid laughed with reluctant admiration.

'You think so?' said Marion, urging him on to the bike and swinging on behind him to clasp his body tightly to hers. 'Honey, you ain't seen nothing yet!'

Again the countryside passed by them in a whizz of sensation; again Marion witnessed the steamed up windows and dark silhouettes inside Joe's car; again she let Patrick into her room through the secret passage door. Her eyes flicked to her watch. Eleven hours left. Nothing could stop her now.

'Well, here we are again,' Patrick murmured, turning to her with open arms.

'Here we are,' agreed Marion, as she popped the fastenings on his leather jacket and, sliding into his embrace, they kissed.

And kissed.

And kissed.

making love. Years of Kathryn lying coldly at his side had eroded his self-confidence in his powers to arouse a woman's passion. She had complained about every move he had made — too hard, too soft, too rough, not rough enough, too clumsy . . . Forget it, he told himself with a shudder, them were the bad old days. Here, in your arms now, is the woman of your dreams. 'My angel. You're so tender, so loving, so — enthusiastic!'

'You took *that* for enthusiasm, did you?' asked Marion, a wicked gleam in her eye. 'But I was just warming up . . .' She couldn't get enough of him, she had been starved of this for so long. How could she leave him in the morning, after this? And she had yet to tell him she was leaving. 'I love you, Patrick Donleavy,' she said to her horror before she could stop.

'I love you too, Marion — Hard castle? Not true. You're soft as a . . .' As similies went, the loud growl that Patrick's stomach supplied was so off the wall it cracked them up. They laughed and laughed as if they would never stop. Nothing had ever been funnier.

'You've worked up an appetite then at last, I take it?' asked Marion, as their laughter subsided. 'Shall I feed you?'

'To be honest, I'm starving,' Patrick admitted. 'Do you have anything in?'

'It just so happens,' his new lover replied, dragging herself away from him, 'that there is a little something in the kitchen that I prepared earlier . . .' He watched her, smiling, naked and beautiful in the candlelight, cross the room to pull on her gown. Such grace. So lovely. He ached at her beauty. When she disappeared through the door, it was as if he'd been bereaved.

'Hey, can I come too?' he demanded as he bounded out of bed to follow her into the kitchenette. He couldn't bear to be apart from her for a single second now.

'And you call that being dressed for dinner, do you?' she asked in mock disapproval as she turned, holding plates of antipasto, to view him in all his glory.

'Pardon me,' he said gravely, draping a tea towel over his loins, 'I thought it said dress casual on the invitation.'

'Well, that's about as casual as it gets,' remarked Marion, relinquishing all thought of food again to further inspect his costume of naked man in tea towel. 'And what's this you're hiding behind here? I'm afraid I'll have to frisk you for weapons . . .'

'Could you frisk me while I'm eating?' asked Patrick mischievously. 'I've just come from another party where the hostess didn't feed me at all.'

'Really? How remiss of her,' said Marion coquettishly, and, backing away from him in the tiny space to jump up and perch on the counter, she waved a piece of salami enticingly before him. 'Come and get it.' In one step he had melted into her embrace, one hand feeding him, one arm around him, her legs clasped around his hips, her lips hungrily kissing his neck.

'Oh Marion!' groaned Patrick.

'Oh Patrick!' moaned Marion.

'Aarghhh Maz!!' screamed Janice, arriving in the doorway. 'What the bleddy hell . . . ? I thought you was in bed with the flu!'

'No – with Patrick, as it happens,' Marion grinned over his shoulder, barely batting an eyelid, too drunk on love to care. She grabbed hold of the tea towel and covered his bottom. 'Patrick, this is Janice. And Tom.'

'How do you do,' Patrick enquired, with as much politeness as he could muster, not daring to turn more than his head out of cover of her embrace.

'Charmed, I'm sure,' said Janice irrepressibly, getting an eyeful. 'This calls for a drink! Tom! Tommy? Don't run away – he's got nothing you haven't seen before!'

It took some persuasion ('Don't mind me, I'm a nurse!') before she agreed to join Tom in her bedroom for a moment so that Patrick could retreat in modesty to Marion's to dress, but finally she was gone and Marion found she could not resist picking up where she had left off.

'No, no!' Patrick weakly protested. 'Later! Marion! Oh!'

'Coming, ready or not!' screamed Janice, who had been

counting down loudly from ten, and freeing himself from Marion's teasing embrace, Patrick bounded out of the kitchen and was gone.

'Where've you been hiding him?' Janice demanded admiringly as she dashed back in, too late to catch another glimpse. 'He is bleddy gorgeous!'

Marion grinned smugly, pulling her robe around her. 'I haven't been hiding him. This is our first date.'

'You don't let the grass grow, do you, you mucky pup?!' said Janice happily, never one to miss out on pleasure, vicarious or otherwise. 'Is he as fabulous as he looks?'

'Janice!'

'Go on!'

'More. Utterly fabulous in every way,' grinned Marion. There was something different about her, some new look to her eyes, that Janice couldn't quite put her finger on. She looked – defenceless.

'You're in love!' screamed Janice, pointing at her friend and pogoing on the spot. 'You are! You've gone all mushy! Marion Hardcastle's drawbridge is down!'

'Shut up!' said Marion, but even then it wasn't the old fierce Marion who could freeze your piss at a thousand paces, it was a happy, giggling, teenage girl. It warmed Janice's heart to see it.

'You know what you need, don't you?' she asked rhetorically, and then suddenly grabbing hold of her, hauled her down from the counter, and began administering a hectic, gambolling, over-excited gavotte, first in the kitchen and through to the bathroom, into Tom's bedroom ('Oy! If you *don't* mind I'm getting ready for bed!'), and out into the living-room, both of them laughing, as mad as could be.

Passing through the room en route to the kitchen, now respectably clothed, Patrick paused briefly, unseen, to admire his lover and her girlfriend and hoped that the dance was for him. 'And I thought the English were supposed to be undemonstrative?' he queried, returning with wine. 'Did I hear somebody order a drink?'

'Ooh! Pretty *and* useful!' Janice exclaimed, relinquishing her dancing partner for a glass. 'Tommy! Drinks up! Sit yourself down, Patrick, tell us all about yourself.'

'Janice!' Marion admonished her, but smiling still, and now back in Patrick's embrace.

'Just calm yourself down,' said Janice, still high from the party and taking control, 'I'm your mother and I know best. Now then, young man . . .'

'Oh, thanks for that,' Patrick grinned, enjoying her affectionate gaiety, and sat himself down as ordered, pulling Marion on to his knee.

'Now then, Dad, what do you think about this?' Janice challenged Tom, who had arrived in the doorway wearing dressing-gown and slippers.

'I think you ought to keep the noise down,' he said flatly, pointing to the ceiling. 'The others said they were going to bed.'

'This young man has come courting our Marion,' Janice continued at full volume as if his opinion had never been sought. 'Ask him about himself. Make him show his credentials. Aaahhhh!' she screamed, getting her own joke. 'No, not them, Paddy, we've seen them, thank you!'

'Good party then?' asked Marion, unnecessarily.

'Oh Maz, it was the best! Luca sings like a thrush, doesn't he Tom? I said, didn't I? – you can keep your Pavarotti. Luca's lungs are like bellows! And he brings tears to your eyes with it, he's that sincere. And what a laugh! And Paola's the same. She used to be a ballet dancer. We had a dance, it was hysterical!' Janice cackled hysterically, wiping away her tears. 'We did *Swan Lake* after nearly everybody had gone. I tried to lift her, but we both fell over! It was hilarious!'

'Sorry I missed it,' said Marion, with some of her old irony.

'God's honest truth, Mazza, this has been the best holiday I have ever had.' Janice toured the assembled company, filling up their glasses. 'Here's to next year! Shall we do it again?'

'We'll have to see,' said Marion, her thoughts going suddenly to the practical details of her new affair. How would she next see him, and when would that be? Christmas in California, Leicester for Lent? Patrick, too, had sobered at her side.

'Do I take it it's nearly over?' he asked anxiously. 'Your holiday this year?'

'First thing in the morning,' Janice confirmed, so oblivious to the horror she brought that she burst spontaneously into a fortissimo rendering of 'Leaving on a Jet Plane', which this time Tom was not the only one to 'shush'.

'You too?' asked Patrick of Marion. 'You're leaving tomorrow?' She could only nod dumbly. 'Out of the question,' he said firmly. 'No way. You can't go back now.'

'Come with us Patrick!' announced Janice. 'Come to Leicester!'

'No!' exclaimed Marion, who never wanted to see Leicester again as long as she lived, and besides, she had only recently made the decision to tidy up her house — she hadn't implemented it yet. It was unthinkable that Patrick should witness the sloth to which she had sunk in her depression — she had a sudden, horrific flashback to the half-eaten pizza she'd shoved under the bed, still in its box, the night she had packed. 'I shall stay here!' The words were out of her mouth before she knew they were in her head.

'You couldn't afford it,' said Tom, ever practical. 'I don't know about you, but the prices here have completely cleaned us out.'

'*I* can afford it,' Patrick rejoined assertively, now unwittingly returning to the role of their daughter's suitor that Janice had given to him in jest. 'When do you have to be back in school?'

'Three weeks,' said Marion. No man had ever offered to look after her before, and nor had she let him. She didn't know how she felt about this. 'But I've got plenty of money of my own, thank you.'

'That isn't how it works between husband and wife, honey,' Patrick murmured in a voice thick with love, nuzzling her cheek.

'Aaarggghhhh!!!!' screamed Janice. 'He's proposed! And on the first date! You can go to Vegas and get married there, by a preacher in an Elvis costume! We could *all* get dressed up — bags

I be Tammy Wynette! Tommy, can you believe it?! We can come, can't we?' she pleaded. 'If we start saving now?' Needless to say there was no answer from Marion or Patrick, who were gazing dumbfounded into each other's eyes. Could it really be as simple as that? And wasn't it a little early in their relationship to commit to anything so drastic so soon?

'Well,' said Tom, taking this opportunity to rise unsteadily to his feet. 'It's gone one, and I'm for my bed. Up early in the morning.'

'Some of us'll be up before that!' screeched Janice crudely, staggering after him, and Tom's back twinged horribly in anticipation of another full-blooded assault. He'd been wrestling with some big issues for most of the day, which he'd decided he was going to discuss in the quiet of their room. Now he'd be lucky to get a word in edgeways, judging by her present state of over-excitement. 'Don't do anything I won't be doing,' she bragged, winking lewdly at Marion, and mercifully disappeared to do it.

'Too fast too soon,' said Marion, once she had found her tongue. 'You said yourself earlier that we hardly know each other.'

'I've learnt to know you better since I said that,' Patrick answered mischievously.

'In one area,' said Marion firmly, trying to keep his mind on other areas of herself and smacking away his wandering hands. 'And besides, where would we live?'

'Details, details,' Patrick murmured, and with what Tom would see as a reckless disregard for his lumbar region, picked her up to carry her back through into her room. 'I want you. I love you. The rest we can work out. Do you really mean it about staying here for another three weeks?'

'Well, not here . . .' said Marion, gesturing around Pamela's office where they had arrived.

'No, not here,' agreed Patrick, almost shuddering at un-wanted remembered images of his own previous activities in this room. 'But we could take off on the bike. Go touring. I could even drive you back home to – Leicester, was it?'

'Don't you have to get back to work yourself?' asked Marion. 'And what about your course here at the college?'

'I'll drop out!' said Patrick gleefully. 'It always sounded so glamorous when I was a student – never too late to fulfil a dream. And who needs to study the old Masters when they have a new Mistress to explore?' And so saying, he laid her gently on the bed to begin explorations immediately.

'I love you,' he whispered, deaf to Janice's screams.

'I love you,' Marion returned, as Janice bounced in again.

'Whoops, sorry both, don't mind me,' she said unapologetically, in great excitement, 'But you'll never guess what now!'

'That's right,' sighed Marion, raising herself on to an elbow.

'Tom says we can put in to adopt when we get back home!'

Despite the intrusion, Marion was genuinely pleased. 'That's brilliant, Janice, I'm really happy for you.'

'I'm so excited!'

'I can see that.'

'I'm going to have one of each!'

'Lovely.'

Standing there, beaming in the doorway, even Janice could see that she was losing her audience. 'Anyway, sorry – as you were, carry on,' she said, turning to go. 'Just thought you'd be wanting to know.'

'Yeah, thanks.'

The door closed behind her as she returned to the new adoptive father-to-be.

'Looks like things are turning out happily for everyone tonight,' said Patrick, returning to his role of expeditionary leader.

Marion gasped. 'Keep on with that, and some of us will be ecstatic,' was the last whole sentence she could manage before they woke again the next morning, still wrapped in each other's arms, and even more in love.

Indeed, on that last night, the Palazzo guarded several happy couples within its ancient, unsurprised, embrace. Next door,

Janice and Tom, having made love Tom's way (big on affection, low on vertebral risk), lay dreaming of their family life to come. Upstairs, Freddie was wrapped around Joe like ivy, their limbs entwined, like their dreams. And Christopher, having decided on recklessness as the only way to pursue *his* dreams, had slipped a sleeper into Terence's bedtime brandy, and was now curled up fast asleep with Beatrice in her bed, waiting to be discovered the next morning.

Only Pamela and Terence dreamed alone.

Chapter Thirty-Five

In the brief no-man's land between sleeping and waking, Beatrice found herself to be suffused with an ineffable joy. She saw herself from behind, at the altar, dressed in white, and when she turned to take her husband's arm to process back down the aisle, she could see that she was radiantly pregnant. By the time she was in her going-away outfit of peach pink silk, her hair swept up under a pill-box hat, she bore the frou-froued infant in her arms. She looked up into the blue sky, pink with fluffy clouds, and heard the songbirds trill. Snow-capped mountains sparkled in the distance beyond lush green meadows and a dancing, rippling brook. She was riding in an open-topped vintage car, the camera behind her, baby in arms, looking ahead to the road that came up to meet them. She turned to the driver, her new husband, her face full of excitement and love. She knew that by some heroic act he had saved her life. How she loved him! The camera lingered on her sideways look of adoration and optimism, before panning right to see the object of her dreams. She woke, panicked and screaming. It was Chris.

'What are you doing?' he asked, sitting up himself, as he watched her flinging on her gown.

'It isn't too late!' she declared, struggling with the wrong armhole. 'He won't be awake yet!'

Chris was out of bed and had headed her off at the door. 'Don't go, please. Stay here with me. We'll face him together!'

'I can't, I can't!'

'Marry me!'

'I'm marrying Terence! We should never have done this. Let me go!'

Christopher's arms dropped to his sides. 'You love me,' he said simply, as a matter of fact. For a moment she hesitated, then seemed to recover.

'I'm going in to him now. Please leave my room. Please Chris.' She put her finger to his lips, 'And say nothing. I'm sorry. I made a mistake.'

The door closed behind her, and in despair Christopher sat down heavily on the bed, his face in his hands. What could he do? If he stayed there, let Terence find him — or followed her in now, faced him man to man — Bea would hate him. Like a condemned man he rose at last, and grabbing his clothes made the silent journey back to his room. Time to pack. The holiday was over. So were his dreams.

Freddie and Joe had woken early, and after hundreds of cuddles and murmured endearments, Freddie had stolen to the kitchen and brought back a picnic to bed. Poor Joe was starving, having eaten practically nothing the day before. They breakfasted on egg bread fried in butter and dripping with honey, fresh peaches, Parma ham, and coffee, while grappling with the exciting notions of living together in London with Joe commuting, or living in Cambridge with Freddie doing the travelling by train.

'I'm so happy,' said Freddie, mopping honey from Joe's mouth with the corner of his napkin.

'Me too,' agreed Joe, and kissed him.

'The next two months are going to be dreadful without you.'

'I could try to come earlier,' said Joe.

Terence woke from a sexy dream of Angela to find Beatrice draped round him, and felt suffocated to the point of claustrophobia. He couldn't remember her coming to his bed. Couldn't remember anything much after drinking with Christopher, but then these days that wasn't so remarkable. Probably needed to cut back on the juice. He never used to drink that much. Never needed to before Bea. God, she was tedious. He flung back the covers and got up.

'Darling?' she asked anxiously, seeing his white and hairy paunch disappearing behind his gown.

'Got to check my e-mail,' he said gruffly without a backward glance. 'Hadn't you better go and pack?'

Beatrice sighed and lay very still on her own for a few moments, before rising gracefully from his bed to obey. This life she was choosing may be hard, she reminded herself, but she owed it to her mother, and to herself, to try to do her best. Hadn't she given her sacred vow to her betrayed and weeping Mummy as a child that she would never, ever, make the same mistake as her? However sweet and handsome and sexy he might seem, marrying an actor was out of the question.

Rising earlier than usual and even more unusually, making breakfast for her guests with her own patrician hands, Pamela was in an apoplectic rage to discover that there was a thief among them, working in her home, emptying her larder. Yesterday she had gone to the trouble and expense out of the *goodness of her heart!* (and one last-ditch attempt to get a positive response from Terence before his return to London), to buy the best and plumpest peaches, the most sought-after honey made by the busiest bees, the thinnest, sweetest slices of prosciutto crudo, to lay before these *ingrates!* as a parting gift and final reminder of her *beneficence!* and the munificence of her table. Now everything was *ruined!* There weren't *even* enough *eggs!* Instead there was a trail of breadcrumbs over *every surface!* and a dirty *frying pan* in the *sink!!* Well, let them eat panettone. Let them starve, for all she cared. The whole enterprise had been a *waste of time!* As usual her better nature had been taken advantage of and *thrown back in her face!!!* She squared her shoulders and scraped together a plate of peaches, ham, bread and honey and retired back to her bed. She couldn't *wait* for them to be *gone*.

Solicitously she fed herself her breakfast, taking comfort where she could. The proletariat would be leaving today, which was something — the dreadful tart with the bottle blonde hair would be flying back to her semi-detached life in the Midlands, thank God. Swallowing the last of the peaches, she ruminated over raw ham whether to forgive Patrick his lapse in good taste, and decided, if he begged her, that she might.

For the last time that summer, Janice bounced into Marion's room. 'Rise and shine!' she carolled, opening the curtains. 'Ah, don't you look sweet together? Breakfast's ready, come and get it — you're not having it in bed — we'll never see you else.' She steamed out again, calling to Tom, 'You'll wear that bleddy carpet out, waiting for that car. It's not due for another hour — Come and have your brekkie!'

Waking for the first time in each other's arms, Marion and Patrick opened their eyes to see their contentment mirrored in each other's sleepy smile. 'Hello there,' said Marion happily.

'Hello there,' said Patrick, with joy in his heart, and holding her close, covered her face in sweet kisses.

'No starting any hanky-panky!' cried Janice from the living-room. 'Upski, now! I haven't wrestled with this ruddy coffee pot of yours to have it go cold!'

'Oh God,' groaned Marion, burying her face in Patrick's chest. 'Janice's coffee. I hope you're feeling strong.'

'As an ox. Like a lion. You've made a beast of me.' They looked at each other and giggled with pleasure. Nothing could harm them now.

'If you don't make haste Pam'll be down in a minute to kick us all out,' shouted Janice through a mouth full of food. 'You know what she's like!' Of all the threats she could pick, that one worked like a charm.

Breakfast proved to be an odd collation of left-overs from the fridge and cupboards — baked beans with tuna, the remains of Marion's antipasto, slices of tinned corned beef and garibaldi biscuits — but miraculously, the coffee was good.

'You finally got to grips with the macchinetta then,' said Marion approvingly, waving away offerings on plates.

'Daddy figured it out,' beamed Janice, looking with pride at Tom.

'Steady on,' he said gruffly, but quite clearly, despite himself, he was a happier man. 'There'll be a blizzard of paperwork before we can say that.'

Marion stole a smiling glance at Patrick and squeezed his hand under the table. Good coffee, good friends, beautiful man — could life get more perfect than this?

'Look at you two!' said Janice admiringly. 'Don't they make a lovely couple, Tom?'

Tom grunted, swallowing down a slab of corned beef. He was a brave bloke, this Patrick. He wouldn't have liked to have been the one to get Marion looking like this. It was like seeing another woman. She seemed to have shed a ton of armour plating overnight. 'Have you decided what you're doing?' he asked, worried about the time, since it was alien to his nature to worry about nothing. 'Will you be coming in Luca's car with us? Cos you've still got the Harley to return.'

'I think we've decided to tour on the Ducati,' said Marion, looking to Patrick for confirmation.

'Sounds perfect to me,' he smiled. 'Then I'll drive her back in time for school, Pop, so don't worry on that score.'

'Don't you have to be back at work?' asked Janice.

'I've taken a sabbatical,' Patrick informed her. 'Due back end of September.' Marion felt panic seize her heart. 'But we'll figure something out. We've got three weeks to do it.' He smiled happily, as if nothing were simpler.

'Would you move to the States, Maz?' asked her friend blithely, crashing straight through to the core of her fear.

'I — we'll see,' Marion parried, avoiding Patrick's eyes. 'It's early days yet, Tom,' she continued, changing the subject to practical matters which could easily be solved, 'would you mind taking back some of my things with your luggage? There won't really be room on the bike.'

'I'll cram it in my suitcase, there's plenty of room now we've eaten the food,' Janice offered gaily, 'and you don't know whose stuff you'll get back if you put it in Tom's!'

'I'm never going to be allowed to forget that, am I?' Tom said testily. 'But who'd have a famous opera singer for a friend if I hadn't made a mistake?'

'Who's a gorgeous likkle cutie pie then?' asked Janice irreverently, chubbing his cheeks with both hands and planting a baked bean stained kiss on his lips. 'Who's Janice's best boy?'

'Better get on with the pots,' said Tom, wiping his mouth with his sleeve. 'And you've got your packing to finish.'

Janice watched him with pride as he walked to the kitchen. 'Hasn't he just got the cutest little bum in all the world?' she asked, before following him out.

'One of them, certainly,' Marion agreed smugly, stroking the other.

Having been unable to face eating anything at Janice's breakfast table, and both of them secretly worried now about discovery by Pamela, it was agreed that while Marion packed and returned the Harley, Patrick would arrange with the college bursar to have most of his stuff shipped back home, and officially drop out of his course. They would meet again at Claudio's, where they would feast before starting out on their adventure. But first they had to kiss and hold each other and reassure each other of their love. Parting was such sweet sorrow, particularly when it was only for an hour.

Returning to her room to decide what to send home with Janice, Marion surveyed her hippie wardrobe and decided it could stay. She knew she couldn't just wear jeans and T-shirts for the rest of her life, but she knew also that she had finally grown out of her past. And if she didn't have time to shop before term started, she thought, as she shoved crushed velvet flares and

afloat. Her heart leapt as she entered her room and saw that a sketch had been left behind, propped on a bag on the bed. Could it be that the tart had relented? Dizzying sums of money entered her head, along with a hit list of possible buyers, as she snatched it up and put on her glasses to examine it by the light from the window.

Her scream could be heard clear to Cortona.

Chapter Thirty-Six

Marion and Patrick were silently sipping Claudio's freshly squeezed orange juice, sitting in the sunshine at a roadside table, lost for words again in the bliss of each other's gaze, when Janice forced the chauffeur, against Tom's protestations, to halt the car. She sprang out at them again for one last time.

'Ay up, Claudio!' she bellowed, gesturing at the limousine as he came out to greet her. 'Cop a load of this! Couldn't resist a swank,' she explained to her friends, the startled couple in love, slapping them both heartily on their backs. 'Soon be over, and back to real life and the bus! Nearly ready for the off yourselves?'

'Guess so,' said Patrick, mopping his shirt with a napkin.

'Where're you going? Anywhere nice?'

Marion and Patrick looked at each other and shrugged. Details, details. 'Everywhere nice,' beamed Marion. 'Where the wind blows us.'

'Well send us a postcard in sunny Leicester, and come and see us when you get back.'

'That's a promise,' Patrick said graciously. 'It's been a pleasure to meet you.'

'Janice!!' screamed Tom, banging on the car window and pointing at his watch.

'Whoops, best be off,' said Janice, reluctant to go. 'You just make sure you take care of her, and go careful on that bike. She's a very special lady — I want her back in one piece.'

Looking at her blond-haired beloved, his blue eyes shining, his perfect teeth sparkling in a genial grin, Marion couldn't resist a bit of a swank herself. 'Don't worry, he's a doctor,' she boasted smugly, 'I'm in safe hands.'

Patrick's brow creased into a puzzled frown. 'No, I . . .' he started, but was cut short by Janice's whoop of approval. 'You're kidding! I'm a nurse! What's your specialty? We could start our own clinic!'

'Dentistry,' Patrick corrected her. 'I'm not a doctor, I'm a dentist.'

Marion's smile disappeared to hide her confusion and her teeth. 'Oh, yeah,' she said, tight-lipped, trying to recover. 'Sorry, that's what I meant.'

'You lucky dog!' Janice congratulated her, blind to the romantic fantasy she trampled underfoot. 'Handsome, rich, and civilised working hours! Bleddy hell, I wish I'd known, Pat — I'd have got you to look at Tom's bridge.'

'Jan!!' Tom bellowed through the car window, exposing all his fillings. 'We'll miss the blithering plane!'

'I'll take a look when we reach Leicester,' Patrick promised her, 'though without my instruments I'll only be able to offer an opinion.'

'Bazzing,' said Janice, content with the deal, and hugging them hugely she returned to the car to hang out of the window as it drove her away. 'Take care then, both!' she called back, her voice still with them after she was long out of sight. 'See you Claudio! T'ra Maria! Arrivederci Roma!! Hasta la vista!! Bye Maz! Bye Pat!'

At last all was quiet, save for the banging of Marion's heart. She looked anew at Patrick, who, oblivious, smiled back at her and sighed with the pleasure of once again being alone with her. What else was there about him that she didn't know, besides everything? The gilt was off her gingerbread. A *dentist* for a lover. Out saving teeth then, not lives. Where the hell was the romance in that?! And of course, she should have known – hadn't he asked her last night if she had any floss? Of *course* she had floss, yards of it, in Leicester – bought out of guilt, banished to the back of the bathroom cabinet out of boredom. The bathroom cabinet! More evidence of her slovenliness. She could picture the mould and the grunge on its chaotic shelves now. But why stop at the cabinet? The whole bathroom was a disgrace. She felt panic rise in her. This couldn't go on. If he didn't go off her in the next three weeks because of her less than perfect English teeth, he'd reel from her in horror when he got past the front door in Wigston Magna . . . She must finish it now. There might even be time to get on the plane if she hurried . . .

Patrick was looking at her, and took her hand between his. 'Alone at last,' he smiled. 'Having second thoughts?'

'No no,' she replied, flustered that he should find her so transparent. That was another downside of being half of a couple – your every mood observed and monitored. She'd been single for so long, did she really want to lose that freedom? Is that what I am afraid of, she asked herself, is it just that I'm as afraid of the C word as Terence Stupid Armstrong? She heard a voice in her head, clear as a bell, Terence's voice: *Perhaps she thinks that if she falls in love again she will make herself vulnerable to death?*

'Marion,' Patrick was now saying carefully, looking at her intently, 'it would be perfectly natural for us both to be nervous. Both of us are taking a risk.'

'Risk? Ha! I thrive on it,' she answered flippantly, her stomach churned into knots. And still Terence was whispering in her ear: *Death took her last great love. Maybe it could happen again.*

'Well then, that's where we're different,' said Patrick. 'Personally, I'm terrified.' He had her whole attention now – could it be that *he* was going to finish it himself? She watched him, her mind racing, as he searched for the right words: his lovely blue eyes with the laughter lines at the edges, his tanned skin that smelt of lemon and spices, his beautiful, kissable mouth . . . Was she mad? What was she thinking of, entertaining any doubts at all? He was like a Greek god. Okay, so a Greek god of dentistry, not quite the soap opera hero she'd imagined — but at her age, wasn't that a plus? Hadn't she had her first root canal surgery only last year? A woman could bankrupt herself with the price of porcelain crowns, let alone when it came time for implants . . . Stop *thinking*, Marion, she told herself sharply. Just concentrate on how you're *feeling* — do you want him or not?

'I want you,' she said quickly, before he could tell her it was over, grabbing his hand so it hurt. 'So don't die.'

His face relaxed, his eyes melting into hers. 'And I want you,' he said. 'So don't you go dying either.'

It was on the tip of her tongue to reply in all honesty that, though of course she would try, she couldn't guarantee it, when she realised that was the answer to the question which had terrified her for most of her adult life. It was that simple. Loving another was an act of courage and of faith, a leap into the darkness — there could be no lifetime guarantees. All she could know for sure this time, was that she was going to ride across Europe on a Ducati, to make love to the most beautiful man that was ever born of woman, to wake in the mornings in the warmth of his arms . . . All this, *and* free dentistry? She should have it so rough!

'So where shall we dine tonight?' Patrick was asking, stroking her hand. 'Florence, Sicily, Rome?'

'Decisions, decisions,' complained Marion, smiling. She leaned across to kiss him and felt the warmth of his cheek against hers, smelt the lemon spice of his skin, saw in his eyes only honesty and love. 'Somewhere not too far on our first day, I think,' she murmured. 'I might need to kiss you some more.'

While Marion and Patrick reviewed nearby cities, Janice and Tom arrived at the check-in desk at Pisa airport, where they were shown with great reverence to the VIP lounge. True to his word, not only had Luca had his secretary phone ahead to confirm their seats, he had also got her to schmooze the airline into a First Class upgrade for his new best friends.

'Bleddy hell fire,' Janice announced as they left behind them the impossibly hot shopping concourse where tourist class passengers could wander at will with their screaming children, and entered the privileged portals of the hushed air-conditioned lounge. 'How the other half, ay? I was sweltering out there. Look Tommy! Real leather sofas! Isn't it lush?!'

'Bet the drinks cost an arm and a leg,' said Tom disparagingly, glancing at the unctuous waiters fiddling with fancy bits behind the bar, while he tried to assume an unimpressed air.

'Oo-oo!' screeched Janice, waving across the room. 'Coo-ee! Come on Tommo, look, there's Bea and Chris! Where's Tel?' she demanded as she joined them, plonking herself down at their side.

Beatrice nodded glumly over to a bank of courtesy computers. 'E-mailing again, I think.'

'Can I get you a drink?' Christopher offered, not as gallantly as it seemed, since he knew they were complimentary.

'Ooh yeah – can I have champagne?' asked Janice. 'I could get into this five-star life!'

'What would you like, Tom?' enquired Christopher, getting his name right for once.

'What I want is a pint of bitter,' said Tom bitterly. 'But that's beside the point. They won't have it here – it'll be some poncey German muck in a bottle.'

'A pint of bitter,' Christopher repeated, as if trying a foreign language. 'I'll see what I can do. More fizzy water, Bea?' Beatrice nodded her assent, unable still to meet his eyes, unable to stop watching Terence. Sadly, Chris turned towards the bar.

'Actually I'll give you a hand if you like,' Tom ventured hastily, wanting to put distance between himself and his wife as she stretched out her legs luxuriously (and conspicuously) to rest them on the glass topped coffee table in front of her, the better to take her ease. 'See what they've got,' he said by way of explanation, as he scurried after Chris. Janice and Beatrice watched them all the way to the bar.

'He's gorgeous, isn't he, Chris?' Janice prompted her, deciding to play Cupid. With her present new status of VIP miracle worker, she wasn't far off sharing Evadne's delusions of goddesshood.

'Yes, he's very sweet,' agreed Beatrice mournfully.

'No comparison between him and Tel, is there?' said Janice, nodding over towards Terence and cutting to the chase as per. 'In the gorgeousness stakes.'

Beatrice shifted uncomfortably in her seat. 'I'm sorry?'

'I bet you are. I would be, in your shoes.'

'No, I'm sorry, I don't quite . . .'

'Well, it's obvious, isn't it? It is to me. Chris loves you, you love Chris, but you've given your promise to Tez and you're too nice to break your word. Mind, if it was me, I wouldn't think twice.'

'You wouldn't?' asked Beatrice, dazed by her directness.

'Nah,' said Janice. 'It'd be Chris for me every time. But then I'm a sucker for a nice bum.'

Beatrice was, to say the least of it, taken aback. 'It isn't quite as simple as that,' she said rather primly.

'Isn't it?' queried Janice disingenuously. 'Aah, that's a shame. I was watching the two of you with baby Giannissa yesterday — you'd have beautiful babies, the two of you, and Chris couldn't take his eyes off her could he? Rare in a man, that. Still,' she continued, 'Tel was probably quite nice-looking once. I'm just surprised you're not worried about his wandering eyes. He was all over my friend Maz. She had to tell him where to get off in the end.'

'Did she?' asked Beatrice, her eyes narrowing as she watched Terence, his mood completely changed now he was no longer with her, laughing and talking animatedly into his mobile phone. He didn't love her — he couldn't care less if she lived or died. And really, this Janet woman was telling her nothing she didn't already know — he was a womaniser, the last of the great bachelors — why, he wasn't even divorced from the woman he'd left weeping ten years ago. So what was her self-sacrifice for?

Janice watched her from the corner of her eye as she stuck out her little chin in an approximation of determined defiance. Mummy's best girl, it appeared, was about to rebel. 'Here comes Chris with your drink,' she said, bruising Beatrice's tiny bicep with one of her nudges. 'And would you believe it — here comes Tel as well.' She swung her legs off the table. Another miracle cure effected, she hoped. 'I'll leave you to it. Better help Tommy.'

Approaching Beatrice after sending e-mail after e-mail and finally managing to speak to Angela by phone, Terence already felt more kindly disposed towards her. She might be irritating, but she was, indisputably, beautiful. He would let her down gently, he thought, nothing final — just tell her that the office needed him to go to New York. Immediately. For a short while. He'd be back before she knew it. Which, with Angela, was always a distinct possibility anyway, he reminded himself. She had sounded enthusiastic about him arriving today, had told him he was welcome to stay in her apartment, but with Angie one never knew. She could just as easily be in bed with a lover when he turned up, or out at a party, rather than, as she had teasingly promised, waiting for him in a hot scented bath . . . The thrilling frisson of uncertainty made his blood tingle. He was alive again, praise God!

'Bad news, I'm afraid,' he announced, beating Christopher to it and claiming the seat by Beatrice's side.

'Yes, I have some too,' replied Bea, her face unusually serious. She took the water Chris offered her with an over-solicitous smile. 'Thank you, darling. I'm sorry, Terence appears to have taken your seat. But don't worry, it won't be for long.' Both men were startled. Beatrice was never anything less than full of grace, particularly with the object of her amour. She turned now to face him, raising her hand to silence whatever he had been going to say. 'My bad news first, I think,' she said assertively, brooking no argument. 'Since I have already had to put up with your bad mood for most of the holiday.' Terence's eyes widened. No woman had ever spoken to him in that tone before, except Angela of course. He felt a sudden new interest in this young woman now. Too late, alas, to avert what came next. 'It is over,

Terence. I am in love with Christopher and we are going to be married.' She stretched out her hand across the table to Chris, who took it, unable to believe his luck or his ears.

Looking from one happy face to the other, Terence was filled with a furious rage. 'That's fine then,' he spat acidly, before he could stop himself. 'Because Angela and I have decided to renew our vows and I am on my way to New York as soon as I change my ticket.'

'Perfect,' snapped Beatrice, feeling just as much fury, and for the first time in her life, venting it spitefully. 'So you won't feel rejected. I just hope you will be as happy as Christopher and I.'

From across the room at the bar, Janice watched Terence leap to his feet and storm over to the airline clerk at the desk, while Christopher took his place on the couch and Beatrice into his arms. 'That's sorted that out then,' she said, turning in triumph to Tom. 'Janice Cowlishaw strikes again! See anyone else who needs saving?'

'What have you done now?' asked her husband, lifting his head from his pint of Belgian beer. He smacked his lips distastefully. 'This stuff tastes like birdseed. Can't wait to get back home, five-star life or no five-star life.'

Janice laughed. 'And you've drunk a lot of birdseed in your time, have you?' she asked, looking at him with affection. 'Well I'll tell you why I can't wait to get home, my lad . . .'

'Will you give over!' said Tom hotly, fending her hands off his bottom. 'People are looking!'

'Let them,' Janice invited equably. 'They're only jealous. Ooh look,' she exclaimed suddenly, 'there's Freddie and that feller Joe talking to Terry. Don't they look happy? They look like they're in love . . .'

Tom regarded her with utter amazement. 'I don't know what's wrong with you sometimes,' he said, shaking his head. 'You just see sex everywhere! That Joe bloke is married! Give it a rest.'

'Still love me?' asked Janice coquettishly, putting her arms round his waist.

'Course I do,' sighed Tom.

'Tell me properly then.'

'I love you.'

'So . . .'

'So what?'

'Give us a kiss,' said Janice, presenting her upturned face.

Tom hesitated. There was no refusing her when she was in loving mode, and it wasn't as if he didn't love her to bits, but terms must be negotiated for the sake of propriety. 'No tongues then,' he managed to hiss before his lips were sealed. 'And no grabbing me whatsit.' She obeyed him, fifty per cent.

Over at the desk, Freddie and Joe were indeed blissfully happy. It had been agreed between them after an agonising moment when they had arrived at the airport and were about to go their own ways that it would be silly, really, for Joe not to fly to London too. For one thing, how could he judge where to live if he didn't research it in advance of taking up his Cambridge post? And for another, how on earth could they be expected to part now, even for a few weeks? The only fly in their ointment had been that the flight was, as usual, packed, but there was just one seat in Tourist owing to a woman having phoned to cancel her return. They had grabbed it gratefully, but a little disappointed that they couldn't travel together.

'It's only for a couple of hours,' Joe comforted Freddie as they made their way to the VIP lounge, where they bumped into Terence and all ended happily. Money had changed hands, reservations had been switched, a new booking for Terence had been made.

And so it came to pass that, when the ten-thirty flight to London was announced, Christopher Bassett and Beatrice Miller-Mander, Frederick Mayer and Joe McCorquodale, and Tom and Janice Cowlishaw – happy couples all – were shown graciously to their First Class seats; Terence Armstrong settled back in his seat in the VIP lounge to wait for his plane to New York and an

405

uncertain reception from Angela; and Marion Hardcastle exchanged a loving look with her travelling companion Patrick Donleavy as they mounted their bike, and wondered how she could bear the short journey to Siena before she could kiss him again.